ALEX'S ESCAPE

L. Andrew Cooper

Horrific Scribblings, LLC, North Hollywood, CA, USA

To all the writers of transgressive fiction who have been kind enough to talk to me about your art--thank you for the inspiration.

CONTENTS

WARNING

This novel features graphic violence, graphic sexuality and sexual violence including rape, physical and psychological torture, animal cruelty, and probably too many other triggers to list, and most of the horrors involve minors. The book is intended only for mature readers who are not sensitive to extreme, taboo-breaking horror.

PART ONE: ESCAPE TO L.A.

1: FIRST ESCAPE

Alex

Alex was getting out, but first he had to get in bed, or at least on the bed, wearing the boxer shorts and t-shirt he'd sleep in later, but for now he sat up, spine rigid, eyes wide. The lamp on the nightstand lit the room, but everything blurred because he'd learned to relax his focus, to make his surroundings secondary to what went on in his head, where he had a *mantra*. His inner voice repeated:

I will go to my house.

I will go to my house.

I will go to my house.

After he lost track of how many times he'd repeated the sentence, after the repetition had taken on its own life, an old-fashioned record skipping, his blurred bedroom grew blue electric bolts that forked from his body and branched toward the walls. Silver sparkles crackled in the air, pinpricks from the edge of unconsciousness.

Thinking about going into a trance could make getting there impossible, but once he was there, his mind could acknowledge his arrival without making any difference. He had arrived. He had traveled from his house to *his house*. The house within the house. And tonight, things would be different.

He scooted to the edge of his full-sized bed and got to his feet. Tonight, his bedroom didn't matter. The closed door waited for him, and on the other side, the hallway led to his father's office and his parents' bedroom. He was the only kid. Brothers and sisters would have gotten in his way.

That was why he had almost killed his mother once before.

Mom made strong coffee, and she guzzled it, even after she was supposed to give it up.

The hallway walls, usually what Mom called a "Tuscan Yellow" that looked "elegant" in the sun from the foyer's high windows, were red now, and the outside wall had Alex's animals nailed to it. The first had been a rabbit, one he caught on his own in the yard by sneaking up behind it, and just when it saw him, just when it was about to jump away faster than he would have ever been able to catch it, he smashed its head with the long branch he was carrying. He saw blood on brown mottled fur, but the creature was still breathing, so he picked it up and watched it twitch for a while before he sat on the grass with it and took out his pocketknife, which was the best he had at the time. Poking out an eye made the twitching wilder. When he cut from its chin to its tummy, the twitching stopped. Rabbit insides looked like what he imagined people insides looked like.

Next to the rabbit husk, dried out now, the stringy insides hung on the wall, strung out guts, and a little rabbit heart. After that, he downgraded to a couple of squirrels, their bushy tails like ribbons on the wall, but then—THEN—he caught the neighbor's cat in the yard.

Snuffles the Cat.

Snuffles... snuffed it. He cracked himself up with that one over and over.

Snuffles was on the wall, facing outward, cat eyes stretched wide but cat lips stretched wider, a horrible grin, like the kitty's cheeks had tried to escape into its pointed ears. Dried blood matted the orange fur. Alex had eviscerated Snuffles, too. Hiding insides on the inside seemed like an injustice, didn't it?

In addition to putting Snuffles on display in *his house*, he buried the body in somebody else's yard two blocks away. He wasn't stupid, and when the neighbor—a lesbian cop—called his parents with her suspicions, she didn't have any evidence, and his parents, Dave and Letta Packard, well-educated about their rights and many other subjects, refused to let their son face unsubstantiated accusations.

Nevertheless, Alex heard his father ask his mother behind their closed bedroom door, "What's wrong with Alex?" Dad didn't confront him, though, and neither did Mom. Unsubstantiated.

The first dog he killed must have been a stray because no one ever came looking or asking. It was a mutt that might have been part collie. Alex duct taped its muzzle shut and cut off all four legs and the bushy tail and rolled it around in its own blood while it whined, and he giggled. What was wrong with him? What was wrong with him? Nothing *felt* wrong.

That collie mutt took up the breadth of the decorated hallway wall, all along the baseboard, parts sorted by type, head, legs, quadrisected body, tail.

Alex, you don't know what made Mom sick, do you?

No, Dad. Do you?

Vitamin C, cinnamon, castor oil, a few other things he'd had to search for, and to top it all off a splash of bleach that he was sure Mom would smell, no matter how powerful the coffee stink and how stuffed up her allergies made her nose, that acrid reek couldn't hide—

"We've got some very exciting news for you, Alex. You're going to have a little sister!"

Like Hell.

He dumped it all into her oversized mug as she read news on her Kindle at the table in the breakfast nook. He went into the living room and listened for what would happen next. She would smell it, and she would know he did it—

But she guzzled down the whole damned cup before she started coughing and wheezing. Dad had already left for work. Alex was dressed for school, and he had his earbuds in without any music playing. The sound of a chair falling over meant Mom standing up, lurching away from the table. He heard her stumble through the kitchen, bumping into things, making strange noises but not screaming. She got through the dining room, into the living room, and into Alex's line of sight. The blood on her lips and chin made him stand up, rip out the earbuds, and shout, "Mom!"

Like a good son, he called an ambulance. She lost consciousness before it arrived.

The total of the tragedy included damage to her throat—her voice gained a permanent rasp—as well as to her stomach, and, during the rescue attempts, internal hemorrhaging triggered a miscarriage. Alex would *not* have a little sister.

He didn't know what happened to the fetus in the world beyond his trances, but in *his house*, it was nailed to the wall at the top of the stairs. Alex smiled at it after passing his parents' room and turning toward the stairwell. He descended to the main floor.

On the bottom step he lingered by a doll, a plastic baby with corn silk hair. He'd been following a girl named Christina, maybe eight years old. He tracked her to a playground, and she left the doll on a bench while she went to play on the slide. Her caretaker, an older sister called Frankie, was watching her, not the doll. Alex took the doll and hid behind a tree. When Christina returned to the bench and found the doll missing, she cried and cried and cried. Alex felt happy.

In the kitchen, a butcher knife sat by the sink, gleaming as if a spotlight shone down on it from the ceiling. *They* obviously wanted him to take it, so he did. In the downstairs hall, which connected the breakfast nook to the foyer and stairwell, passing doors to a bathroom, the laundry room, and a walk-in closet, the red walls got darker as the quality of light became... grey.

At the end of the hall, at the broad entryway to the living room, a bicycle with a bent front wheel leaned against the doorless doorframe, a big kid's bike. Sumit, the bike's owner, had been twelve, plus or minus, and Alex had followed him for two weeks before taking his bike. The kid liked to ride to the convenient store close to his suburban neighborhood bubble and look at the candy bars, buying one if he could, and he left his bike outside without locking it. Alex didn't want a bike. He wanted to take Sumit's bike. There was a difference. The thing was, Sumit was actually scared to have to walk all that way home. He kept looking back over his shoulder. Alex was there, but Sumit never knew.

Alex delivered the bike to another kid's back yard. Sumit never got it back.

In the greylight where the walls and doors became redder and redder, the floor trembled. He watched doorframes vibrate, shiver, and shift until they leaned, right angles becoming acute and obtuse. Slanted. The house slanted. He listened to their whispers.

Wispy fog seeped upward from between the close blonde slats of the hardwood floor. It brought distortion. It brought change.

"Show me," Alex said.

His house showed him what they could do.

Letta

The thin layer of fog on the carpet had to mean she was dreaming, but she wasn't the kind of dreamer who thought about dreaming while she was doing it, and she remembered everything from dinner right up to the moment when she'd come out of the bathroom after her right-before-bed pee.

"Dave!"

He was already asleep. Lying on his side, bare back to her, sheet and blanket bunched near the elastic of his tighty-whities... the nice word would be "statuesque," the apter description "like a rock." "DAVE!"

With three staccato snorts he flipped onto his back and rose to his elbows. "Wh-wha?"

"Either we have a serious HVAC problem, or something very weird is going on." Letta bent forward and spread her arms to indicate the foggy floor.

Dave shook his head, sat up all the way, and gazed in the direction indicated. "What the fuck?"

"I was hoping you could tell me."

"Did you check on Alex?" He got out of bed.

"When would I have checked on Alex?"

"I don't know." He walked toward the door to the hall.

She wanted him to stop. They needed an idea of what was happening. "Do you think we should—"

"What?"

"I don't know," she said. Nothing felt right.

They went into the hall. Everything was wrong.

The wall that should have been Tuscan Yellow was red, and it was like some kind of sick... Satanic... museum. Guts, and parts, all animal, she hoped. She thought she recognized Snuffles, the kitty that went missing a while ago... and whose mommy suspected Alex. But not even Alex could have done... *this*. Transformed the hallway she'd walked down fifteen minutes ago? Assuming she wasn't dreaming. She had to be dreaming. "Pinch me, Dave."

"What?"

"This has to be a dream." She sounded so stupid. "A nightmare." More accurate, at least.

"We've got to check on Alex," Dave said. He moved into the hall, passing a series of severed dog's legs.

He kept moving. He didn't reach Alex's door. The hall stretched, and the dead animals multiplied. They also became more impressive. Letta didn't even realize she was walking behind her husband until the mutilated deer came into view. The wall had plenty more domestic cats and dogs, but one she could have sworn was a wolf, another a coyote, and the big cat—a mountain lion? The animals' conditions didn't make recognizing what they were any easier. Most had been dismembered, flayed, cut open, or some combination. She saw little method beyond cruelty. The museum, if that's what it was, served only to disgust.

Not too far in front of her, Dave stopped. In an instant, her mind suggested that the small length of hallway between them would expand, and she would walk and walk forever, never reaching him, and it *would* be a nightmare, but it would be real, and she would be trapped and alone, so her legs pumped her feet through the fog against carpet across the short distance that was still long enough for her to bound against Dave and almost knock him over.

"Jesus!" He grabbed her shoulders, securing them both.

"That hurt," she said. To herself, at least, she didn't sound plaintive.

Dave nodded. "I don't remember a dream ever feeling...."

"No, me neither."

Together, they looked in the direction where they'd been walking. Alex's door was practically within reach.

As they looked at it, it opened.

"If at first you don't succeed?" Dave's voice did not supply the motivational force required by his word choices. Nevertheless, they tried again.

And succeeded. After a few steps, they stood in Alex's doorway.

The boy's bedroom was empty. Part of it looked like a dungeon.

"Do you think he?" Letta asked.

"Do I think *what*?" Dave failed to sound incredulous. He thought what Letta thought.

She reiterated: "Do you think *this* is *him*?"

"Let's go downstairs," Dave said. "Look for our son."

On the way to the stairs, Letta noticed that the red walls not decorated with dead animal parts had bumps in them, almost like big ripples in the wallpaper, except they had paint, not wallpaper. What they were more like—and Letta didn't like to think about it—were veins showing beneath skin. After the comparison occurred to her, she thought she could detect a pulse. Going down the stairs, she was sure the walls had a pulse.

Letta and Dave turned into the downstairs hallway and met the same problem they'd had upstairs, only it was a *fait accompli*. The hall had lengthened by a factor of four or five, and though it should have had one door on the right, two on the left, it had four or five times as many, and Letta had a feeling she didn't want to know what was behind any of them. Cobwebs drooped from the high crooked corners of the vaulted ceiling. She thought she saw movement in all the small places.

She'd been so distracted that her brain only then registered that the lights, which she'd switched on everywhere possible, had always worked, but they'd been wrong. They were wrong because they weren't the vibrant whites and yellows of typical bulbs but grey lights. What made greylight?

Greylight made what used to be her house into a monstrous shadow.

"Mom, Dad." Alex's voice, coming from the living room. Letta and Dave hadn't entered the hall, so they stood next to the living room's broad entrance. They turned toward their son.

He sat on the sofa. The butcher knife she used making dinner almost every night was in his right hand.

The sofa sat in a circle of trees. The living room was a circle of trees. Her son and her knife waited for her in a circle of trees. Outside was inside, and she wished she were dreaming but knew that she wasn't.

Alex

Mom and Dad really had been going to bed when he'd gone off to his room: Dad stood there looking ridiculous in white briefs, belly dangling, and Mom wore silky pajamas that were lacy across her chest. Alex could see her nipples. He didn't want to see that. His parents looked like they'd forgotten how old they were.

Not that Alex was the picture of sexy in his t-shirt and boxers, both a little big on him, but he didn't look *ridiculous*.

The sofa and loveseat had stayed in about the same positions, as had the reclining chair and the rocker, but the coffee table had disappeared, leaving a big gap in the center of the... living room, a center now covered in patches of grass and patches of dirt. The TV seemed a little farther away from the sofa, but it was here, in the area surrounded by trees like the ones in the yard, but unlike in the yard, you couldn't look through the trees and see the next house. There were only trees.

Alex got off the sofa and wandered into the center of the living room gap. "Mom, Dad, am I glad to see you!"

"Alex, what's going on?" Dad asked. "Are you okay?"

"A little shook up," he said. "Are you guys okay?"

"What's going on?" From Mom, it sounded like an accusation.

"I got up because I thought I heard something... and then the hall was... different... and I came downstairs. You have to come over here. It feels so real, but it can't be, can it?" He studied his parents' faces.

They hesitated.

He added, "I'm so glad you're here. I was scared."

Dad took the lead. They joined him in the living room gap. Alex noticed all three of them had bare feet. He felt the dirt between his toes. Soon they'd all have dirt between their toes.

Alex thought Dad would go in for a hug, but he and Mom halted a few feet shy of contact. "What's with the knife, Alex?"

They were surrounded by *trees in the living room*, and Dad had to ask about the fucking knife? "I told you," Alex said. "I was scared."

"Put down the knife," Mom said.

Alex started walking, not toward his parents, but in an arc around them. They adjusted, keeping distance; Alex maneuvered them more exactly into the gap's center. "The knife makes me feel safe."

"We're here now," Dad said. "You don't need it."

"I'm not a little kid, *Dad*." He sighed and made his arc into a circle. He was about Dad's height, taller than Mom. "I know parents aren't superheroes. Do you think you can stop whatever weird shit is happening?"

"I—"

"PUT IT DOWN!" Mom commanded.

Alex circled, holding the knife at chest level, looking from it to his parents. "It's only a kitchen knife," he said.

"Give it to me," Dad said, and he reached for Alex's hand that held the knife.

Alex slashed his father's knuckles. Dad withdrew his hand with a howl. Alex circled, dirt between his toes.

"Alexander Packard, you put down that knife right this instant!" his mother barked.

"The full name treatment. That works." Alex circled. When he came back around to Dad, who held his bleeding right hand in his left hand, Alex dove into the circle and sliced the man's left shoulder. The cut was deep. Alex had gotten Mom a knife sharpener for Christmas.

"Dave, do something!"

"WHAT?!"

Alex circled. On the next round, he dodged Dad's grabbing, wobbly arms and slashed his back. Alex thought about Dad's thinning hair. He wondered how hard scalping someone with a butcher knife might be.

"Why, Alex? Why?" Dad sounded pathetic.

Alex circled. As he passed Mom, he faked a lunge at her, and she yelped. He laughed and kept circling.

When he got to Dad, the man finally had his wits. He hunched over, reddened arms out, and went for the tackle, screaming, "RUN, LETTA!"

A glimpse of Mom dashing toward the trees—why would she do that?—was all Alex got before he needed to crouch, stab, and sidestep. The knife plunged into his father's big belly, and Alex dragged it with him as he moved aside, splitting deep flesh. Dad's attempted tackle ended with a bellyflop in the dirt. Alex thought he might take at least a little time, so he straddled his dad's backside (gross) and brought the tip of the knife into his backflesh, over and over. A few times he got around muscle, grooves between ribs, maybe into a kidney, but too much of the back was solid. Alex dismounted and turned the old man over. He was conscious, eyes open, but his body was limp, pumping out blood in a lot of places. Alex stabbed him in the chest and heard the wound make a delightful wheeze. He went at the belly—rapidly—turning it into mash. His breathing was heavy. He was getting tired. Dad wasn't moving anymore, and he didn't have much more to offer, anyway.

But Alex had to go after Mom.

He summoned the energy to run in the direction he'd seen her take into the woods. Before long he heard her footfalls in the brush. She couldn't seem to control her wailing, sobs of panic, desperation, maybe even mourning because she was smart enough to know she'd left her husband to die. And she kept bumping into trees that appeared in her path as if from nowhere. Alex heard her cry out in surprise and pain, imagined the collisions. How could such a thing happen? *Alex, what's going on?*

Running to catch her made noise, too, and Alex huffed and puffed as he fought exhaustion. He wasn't a fucking jock. He wanted to kill his parents, not do aerobics. The distance between them shrunk, and when Mom came into view, she was looking behind her as often as in front of her, knocking against bushes and trees, each step a near fall. She saw Alex and screamed a raspy scream.

He stopped and called to her: "But Mom, I'm your son!"

She stopped and faced him with an expression so twisted he couldn't have matched words with it. Limited by the chemical burns that never healed, her voice sounded a guttural, primal sound. It wasn't terror, not quite. It was closer to revulsion.

His turn to tackle. Alex brought his mother down into the uneven, rocky forest soil so she lay beneath him on her back. He pressed his left forearm against her neck, and as her face swelled and colored, he asked, "Aren't you glad you're a mother?"

With his right hand, he moved the knife to the crotch of her silky pajama pants. He poked, searching.

Her eyes bulged.

He cut through the fabric. The thin blade found a groove and slipped between her lips. The knife's tip searched for the deeper opening.

"Aren't you glad, mother?"

Her face, changing from red to purple, shook with her head. Side to side? *Was that a "No," Mom?*

He rammed the knife into her vagina.

"Is this what makes you a mother?" he whispered into her ear, pressing his forearm harder into her neck. "Is this where I came from? Is this why I'm here?"

He pushed the knife farther, making circles with the hand gripping the handle, visualizing himself hollowing her out. His fist slipped inside her and drove the knife even farther. To keep pushing, he had to release her neck, but she wasn't fighting back anymore. Knife forward, he drove his arm into her womb, and once he got in past his elbow, he didn't know where the knife and his hand were anymore, anatomically speaking. He kept going, though, taking the time to get as much of his arm in as possible.

Then he had to cut his way out.

2. PICK UP

Bruce

The drive to LAX took more than an hour, which was too much time to think.

Would Alex ask why he hadn't come to the funeral? His sister and her husband had shared a single memorial service and interment ceremony. Bruce assumed they went into the same expanded plot of dirt, but nobody ever told him if they had a double coffin or a single tombstone, and he didn't dare ask. However it had happened—in Georgia, the opposite side of the country, a lifetime away—he felt sure it had followed detailed specifications from Letta and Dave's voluminous will. Bruce could imagine his sister sending late-night, emergency emails to her lawyer with codicils about minutiae. She had kept the document updated, but she had left one fourteen-year-old detail in place. It was inexplicable, but it wasn't an accident. Why had she done it?

"I don't know how you can drive and look so far away at the same time," Aaron said. He wore one of the long-sleeved collared shirts he reserved for meetings with potential investors. He was nervous. They both were. Today, their lives changed forever. The idea of it was so fucking weird. Having a child?

Having a *teenager*?

When Alex was born, Bruce and Letta had a good relationship. They were both in their twenties and full of how wonderful life unburdened by their parents' religious absurdities was. New agnosticism and liberal politics provided sufficient areas for friendly bonding. During a moment in the hospital room early in labor—Letta had an epidural—after Dave stepped out for a smoke, Letta got serious and said she knew that when Bruce was ready, he'd find someone, and when he did, she wanted him and that someone to be the baby's godparents.

Teary-eyed, Bruce agreed by saying, "Thank you."

His someone was Aaron, married five years ago, but for a little more than the last two of those years, Bruce hadn't seen or talked to his sister at all. The trouble started when Letta told him she was stopping her antidepressants and other psych meds during her new pregnancy because they were bad for the baby, which he could understand even though Letta off her meds worried him, but when she said she'd be microdosing psilocybin instead, he had... the audacity... to suggest magic mushrooms might not be so good for the baby, either. He imagined the fetus mutating like a hallucination, head changing into impossible shapes, body curling in de-skeletonized loops. After the fight, she told him she didn't want to speak to him anymore. Her clarity was unmistakable. Cruel. He heard about her miscarriage and its "very strange" circumstances from a distant cousin on social media. Calling her occurred to him, but he remembered her clarity.

Therefore, her email excoriating him for not checking on her after her "tragedy" came with some surprise. She accused him of trying to "murder" her by ignoring her. Imagining her high on shrooms—as she probably was when she put the Drano or whatever had caused the miscarriage in her coffee—he tried very hard to dismiss her outrageous behavior, but being accused of trying to kill a family member inspired fairly negative feelings about the accuser, whose status in his life had long been in decline.

No further communication ever passed between them.

Bruce now felt guilty for never really thinking of Alex, but he and the boy had never been close. Letta being out of his life meant Alex was out of his life, too, so until the lawyer called, that long-ago promise to be his sister's child's godparent never entered his mind. He'd even committed Aaron to godparental status long before he'd dreamed of Aaron's existence. Aaron was fourteen years old himself when Alex was born.

Your sister calls on you to keep a promise. A promise to the dead.

The melodrama made Bruce wonder if the will had included a script for the lawyer.

At first, Bruce thought he would say no. Decency required that he pretend to consider it, but damned if he didn't do more than pretend. Alex was staying with Dave's mother, who lived alone and could barely take care of herself, not a long-term option. Bruce's parents had disowned Letta and Bruce long ago, and the cancellation extended to offspring. There really wasn't anybody, so Alex would end up in "the system," which connotated only horror to Bruce and Aaron alike.

Aaron had been almost as surprising as the lawyer. "I'm too young to have a teenager call me 'Dad.' But if we had another young man in the house? Meh." From Aaron, "meh" meant "okay."

During a longer conversation they warmed to the idea. Next, they flew out to meet Alex, see if they got along. Next, they had a conversation with a different lawyer, and they coordinated with Child Services in both Georgia and California so their place in the San Fernando Valley could be inspected. They explained that they'd convert Aaron's office into Alex's bedroom. Aaron would carve a little workspace out in the corner of the living room using this partition he had kept since college. It featured a campy airbrushed picture of Elvis's profile with a microphone. Bruce had tried to throw it away a hundred times, but Aaron had insisted on storing it in the back of the big closet. Seemed like fate.

Their house wasn't huge—real estate in Los Angeles

wasn't like what it was in Decatur, Georgia—but it was big enough. And Bruce made enough money.

Bruce had still worried. Gay adoption was technically legal in all fifty states, but Bruce had grown up in Georgia and understood how authorities could navigate the difference between technically legal and doing what they thought best with regards to the faggots and other undesirables.

Before Bruce and Aaron even grasped what they were taking on, they signed documents. Alex said he wanted to come live with them in California. Bruce and Aaron said they wanted that, too.

Aaron

Alex woke up one morning, went downstairs to get a bowl of cereal for breakfast, and found his parents dead in the living room. More than dead. Hacked up. Mutilated. The psychologist they talked to during one of their visits to Georgia before they made the adoption official told them Alex didn't like to talk about it at all. A thing like that had to fuck a kid up. Luckily, Los Angeles had no shortage of therapists for people who had no shortage of insurance.

As they pulled up to the terminal at LAX, Aaron managed a shot through the car window with the handheld Sony video camera he'd brought along. He felt more natural seeing through camera lenses, and documenting—he was a documentarian—this upheaval in all their lives seemed natural. Alex and his two suitcases got bigger and bigger in the viewfinder as Bruce piloted the BMW through the dense chaos of bad drivers to get to where the kid waited. Before they reached him, Aaron lowered the camera. He didn't want to make the kid feel paranoid on his first day in his new city.

That night, Alex said he'd be happy to be in one of Aaron's movies. Bruce rolled his eyes, but Aaron didn't think Alex noticed.

Alex had also said he didn't want any of the furniture or much of the other stuff from his old house, just his clothes and his books. Before Alex's arrival, Bruce and Aaron, as a couple, had gone furniture shopping, coordinating a full-sized bed, a nightstand, a dresser, and shelves. They got a fairly big TV to mount on the wall and a PS5 to go with it. They changed their Amazon Music subscription to the family plan (which sounded strange) and an Echo Show for the nightstand. The kid would have distractions from his post-traumatic flashbacks as soon as he got back... home... from the airport. Home. *Their* home, where "their" now meant belonging to Bruce, Aaron, and a third. Alex, legally, *their* son.

Bruce hired somebody to pack up Alex's clothes and books—lots of books, the kid was a reader—and ship them to LA.

After a few days involving quiet conversations during which Alex revealed very little about himself, over dinner Alex said, "Why did you guys want me?"

Bruce put his fork down next to his pasta, waited a cool moment, and said, "We thought we'd like having you around."

"Yeah?" Alex looked at Aaron.

"Yeah," Aaron said.

That night, as Bruce and Aaron got into bed, Bruce commented on how vulnerable Alex seemed. Aaron agreed.

The next day, while Bruce was downtown at West Coast Global Integrated Wealth Solutions providing business and investment consulting for the rich, Alex's boxes arrived. Aaron insisted on helping to carry boxes down the short hall to the back of the house, Alex's bedroom, but Alex said he would unpack alone. Aaron hesitated but left him to it.

A half hour later, Aaron sat at his miniature desk behind the Elvis partition, frustrated with attempts to edit his footage about how much of gay public life *didn't* come back after the worst of COVID. He grabbed his handheld—the same video camera he'd used at the airport, the Sony, not his top-of-the-line equipment but his favorite—and tracked down the hall.

"And now we see how the newest addition to our household, Alex Packard, is settling into his new home." He figured he'd redo the audio with something more intelligent later.

Absorbed in the shot of Alex's open doorway, Aaron almost tripped over Herb, the cat he and Bruce had gotten after their honeymoon. Herb bolted into the master bedroom.

Aaron knocked on the open door while he stepped into the room that had been his office. The camera eye scanned the space until it located Alex. The kid sat on the floor between the new bookcase and a big open box, sorting and shelving. *My God, he's alphabetizing*—but Aaron wasn't sure. He could zoom in to be sure, but he didn't because the image of Alex himself was even more unsettling.

The kid still wore the jeans he'd had on when they'd lugged the boxes from the front door to the back room, but he'd taken off his shirt. He had a narrow waist, teen appropriate, but shoulders broad enough for a boy much older, a match for the well-defined pecs and biceps. His pale torso showed no traces of the dirty blond hair cut short on his head. His skin was smooth, the sort of smooth that people spent the rest of their lives using moisturizer to get back. He looked like a star from one of the billion twink porn videos you could find for free online. *Legal* porn. Not that Aaron watched that shit. Very often.

Not that Alex was legal. But he *was* a good-looking kid. Aaron framed him in a shot and said, "So, how's settling in?"

Alex didn't look up. "I think I'm going to need more shelves."

"I think we can squeeze another bookcase back here," Aaron said. "Ever hear of e-books?"

"Got a couple hundred in the cloud." Alex looked up, saw the camera, and smiled. "Aaron, can I talk to you about something?"

"Off camera?"

"You can keep it on." He stood, crossed to the bed, and sat on the edge, leaving ample room for Aaron.

Aaron positioned the camera on top of the dresser for a two-shot of the bedside and took his place. "What's up? Everything going okay?"

"It's... I wanted to tell you something. Something I've never said out loud."

"Okay," Aaron said. They weren't close enough yet for deep, dark secrets, but okay.

"It's kind of a miracle that you and Bruce were the ones. To take me in, I mean. I guess anybody would have been a miracle, but...."

Aaron looked at the kid's smooth white skin. Would he get a California tan? At that age, *half the age Aaron was now*, Aaron had still been struggling with baby fat. Alex was lean. "Bruce and I have a pretty good life, and we're happy to share it with you."

"Thank you, but... what I mean is... the two of you... a couple... I feel... I never told my parents...."

The kid was struggling. "It's okay." Aaron didn't know what else to say.

Alex took a deep breath. "I'm lucky to end up with a gay couple because I... I... I'm gay, too."

Aaron finally became conscious of the hand Alex had placed on his thigh. Aaron slid out beneath it and retrieved his camera. "Happy coming out, then. We're here for you. Any questions, anything. I'm proud of you for being brave enough to say it."

He'd said the right thing. He'd done the right thing.

He left Alex alone in his room.

Alex

His two new dads waited a week before putting him in school. Bruce said they should work on a "sense of normalcy" even though he'd already signed Alex up for a fucking therapist. How normal was that? Maybe Bruce didn't have a choice. The adoption people were probably watching him and Aaron to make sure they were good enough parents. Some kind of probation period. And everybody had to think that poor little Alex was screwed up by what happened to his parents. So yeah, he'd talk to a therapist. School, though. He hated school in general, but Rose Park High would have a whole new culture. If anybody heard he was from Georgia, they'd probably assume he was some right-wing country bumpkin, even though Decatur was bright blue and adjacent to Atlanta.

He could have convinced Bruce and Aaron to let him take off the rest of the semester and repeat the ninth grade because he was too distracted by what had happened to his parents, but then he would have had to put on a grief act, feigning distraction when he felt *invested*, alive with Bruce and Aaron and what he'd learned killing his parents, alive in a way he'd never been before. He wanted to live more. He wanted to learn more.

He wanted to fuck.

So, school wasn't a total waste, and before the first day was half over, he spotted Ollie. Oliver Pollock, according to roll call in English class, *Honors* English, which Alex's transcripts placed him into, but after roll Alex heard someone call him Ollie. Ollie wore a light jacket, mostly white except for the red-and-yellow school colors on the trim, collar, and cuffs, and a soccer ball stood out on the front. Not a letterman's jacket, but a team jacket. Best guess, he played JV soccer. He had the body for it, build of a jock but not bulky like football or lanky like basketball. Alex wondered if Ollie's hair was what people called "strawberry blond," too reddish to be comparable to the haystack on his own head. Ollie didn't have a dumb jock face. He looked smart and probably was because he was in the honors class. Alex wondered what Ollie liked to read.

He wanted to get close enough to be sure about what color Ollie's eyes were.

The locker-lined hallways were crowded enough between classes to make following Ollie after English class easy. Alex saw where Ollie went next, made a note, then rushed to his own next class, figuring he had "first day at a new school" as the ultimate excuse for being late if he needed it. When that class let out, he rushed to Ollie's class, managed to catch sight of him leaving, and followed him to the next, made a note, and so on for the rest of the day. Ollie talked to a lot of other kids as he moved from class to class. He was popular. Girls made googly eyes at him.

If he had a girlfriend, she didn't show up.

By the end of the day, Alex felt like he and Ollie had a connection. He kept noticing Ollie's skin. Maybe it was a racist, or just a *racial*, thing. Atlanta, Decatur, that whole area was pretty diverse, but Alex's neighborhood and school had been majority white. This school didn't have a majority, so all types of skin colors appeared in every class. Ollie's fair skin, probably like Alex's own, stood out. Alex thought of sheets of Ollie's fair skin, downed with strawberry blond, flapping on a clothesline.

Ollie had soccer practice after school, and Alex hid under the bleachers to watch. He didn't like sports. He, Bruce, and Aaron had that in common, and they laughed about it. He didn't like sports, but he liked watching the integrated movements of limbs and torsos as boys kicked and ran. Ollie appeared to be quite good. If Alex had had one of Aaron's cameras, he could have captured those movements, zoomed in on the flexing calves and thighs. He could have taken Ollie in by pieces.

Ollie looked strong, but Alex thought he could take him once he got him inside his house. *They* made the rules different in his house, and the rules tipped in his favor. He would pull Ollie in, and he would be careful. He would be careful, and he would get what he wanted.

3. THE BRANCHES

Alex

Bruce wasn't around, but Aaron noticed that Alex was late coming home after his first day of school. He didn't doubt the explanation: school was only a little more than a mile away, so Alex had decided to walk, and on the way, he'd stopped by the park to read. When Bruce got home a couple of hours later, he and Aaron agreed that Alex was free to do that kind of thing, but he needed at least to let Aaron know what was going on. Their part of the Valley was relatively safe and cozy, but it was still Los Angeles. To the end of everybody keeping everybody else informed, the three of them went and bought Alex a new iPhone ("*Don't* take it out in class," Bruce said, and Aaron said, "*Do* sneak pictures of cute boys").

On day two, Alex took pictures of Ollie, but when he texted Aaron that he was going to the park to read, he wasn't lying, not completely. He *was* going to the park. He didn't plan to read, but he might. His Kindle was in his bookbag. He'd been trying to read *The World as Will and Representation* by Arthur Schopenhauer. School wasted so much time on assignments that had nothing to do with his life. Why would he read Sandra Cisneros when he could be reading Schopenhauer? They weren't in the same league. Not even the same sport, not that Schopenhauer deserved to be included in sports metaphors.

As he wandered around the park, he didn't look for a good place to read, even though most of the benches were empty. He went to the park's edge, by the fence in the corner farthest from the entrance, where the impressionable dirt had the fewest prints. His gut guided him. Maybe *they* guided him because he found what he wanted in no time at all.

Two trees, not the palms omnipresent in the neighborhood but trees with light grey bark and low branches, stood close to each other, sturdy trunks of about average girth. Leafy branches drooped over the fence on one side, over an arrangement of agaves on the other, and in between the pair, branches intertwined, forming a canopy. The space it roofed wasn't picturesque—it was hardly noticeable—and the dirty ground would smudge clothes, and Alex couldn't identify all the bugs any better than he could identify the trees—but it was exactly what he wanted.

He sat beneath branches, shade cool, light strained by densely knit foliage.

Folding his legs into a half-lotus position, he looked at the others in the park, a giggling middle-aged couple on one bench, an old lady on another, an ambiguous man with a headband who appeared to be doing tai-chi, and Alex noted that no one his age or younger seemed to be around. Maybe parents didn't play catch in the park with their kids on weekdays, or maybe they didn't do it at all. Did young people come to parks? Alex didn't feel connected to "youth" or to much of anyone. People were inscrutable and hard to like.

But he felt reasonably confident no one would bother him in his new place in the dirt beneath the branches. Staring at nothing, he let his eyes unfocus.

The blurry park was the perfect place for his trances. His new, cramped home less than half a mile away usually had someone else in it. Unless Alex wanted to start locking his bedroom door and raising suspicions, Bruce or Aaron could always walk in... and then Alex would have to explain his meditative practice.

Partial truth: he had read books on meditation. He had taught himself.

Bruce and Aaron didn't need to know about astral

projection. His new dads certainly didn't need to know about *them*. They taught Alex new ways to link astral bodies to physical bodies. Because of them, Alex could make soft space, ethereal space, *hard*. Naturally, they wanted Alex to do things with his gifts to repay them. Luckily, their incentives aligned.

As spots sparked silver at the edges of his blurred vision, he felt more certain that they had led him to this spot. If they hadn't, they could interrupt, lead him elsewhere. They wouldn't *appear* to him. He could sense them, talk with them, but almost never see them. When he glimpsed them, they were like heat rising from asphalt on a scorching summer day. He didn't know if they had physical bodies. Maybe they hated physical bodies. They liked physical... damage.

However they felt, they worked for him as much or more than he worked for them. The work he did for them was stuff he wanted to do anyway. If the situation had a winner, he was it.

Who were they? Alex didn't believe in Satan or demons or ghosts, but at first, he'd wondered if they were angels. "Astral beings" was probably a better term. He believed in them because he'd had contact with them. Who or what they were beyond their shared encounters was anybody's guess, and Alex had more on his mind than looking in gift horses' mouths. He began the mantra:

I will go to my house.

Somehow, he managed the distance.

Bruce

Bruce didn't want Aaron to know about his morbid curiosity, and he definitely didn't want Alex to know, so he used his private office's desktop computer instead of his laptop to perform a few searches.

Although they never made the front page, the murders of his sister and her husband stayed in the news for weeks.

The crimes' brutality combined with the lack of burglary suggested that the attack was personal, perhaps someone seeking revenge for one of Dave's less advantageous used car deals or Letta's less attractive cookie-cutter web designs. If it wasn't personal, then imaginations turned darker. What if it was the work of a serial killer? The deaths were gruesome enough.

How gruesome were they?

Legitimate news sources said police had almost nothing to go on.

More searches, going into the blogosphere. Links led to more links that led to increasingly obscure sites. Socially acceptable true crime speculation gave way to pondering closer to what was in Bruce's own head, even though he felt self-conscious for harboring such thoughts. *What did Letta look like when she died?* Morbid. Horrid.

Unhealthy.

Click.

A site offered leaked crime scene photos. Bruce used "private" browsing.

Click.

The poorly designed page was slow to load, but when it did, the title "The Murders on Oak Lane" appeared in red against a black background, and beneath it, photos scrolled into view. Dave appeared on the right, Letta on the left. They both lay on their backs, limbs splayed, but the pictures didn't reveal how close they were to one another. Dave wore only underwear. Letta wore pajamas, partly shredded. Blood coated and soaked their skin and clothes, but wounds peeked through.

Dave looked like someone had used a knife to try digging inside him. Bruce saw gashes on his shoulder and a hole in his chest, but most of the attacks had landed in his round belly. Bruce knew Dave and Letta were stabbed to death with a kitchen knife, but the mess of Dave's abdomen hardly looked like the result of blade punctures. Where the belly's boundary was supposed to be, some plateaus of skin still stood, but canyons of blood and yellowish fatty tissue separated them, ripped, spread, and pooled, and torn viscera peeked out of the deepest dips. Letta didn't look better.

A helpful caption: "The killer or killers tunneled from her vagina up to her stomach and then cut from the inside out."

Sick, sick shit. And he was sick for looking at it. He felt sick. He could vomit it in his chic trash bin. His *sister*, the bloody corpse on the screen. His *sister*, ripped apart from the inside. So what if they were estranged? She was—

—*a psychotic bitch.*

But still…

He needed to stop looking at the pictures. He navigated to a link at the bottom of the page.

An Unreported Theory of the Crime

Although all police statements and official reporting have claimed that there are no leads or suspects in the Oak Lane Murders, our anonymous source told us that initially police did have one suspect, the victims' teenage son. Some considered him suspicious simply because he survived what seemed like a massacre targeting his house; others heeded reports of the boy being a "loner" whom one neighbor described as "antisocial." One investigator was skeptical of the boy's claim that he slept through the murders, as the investigator found no signs of the victims having been gagged and speculated that the events would have been very noisy. Nevertheless, no physical evidence contradicts the boy's claim that he found the bodies in the morning, hours after the estimated times of death, at which point he called immediately for police assistance. No physical evidence of any kind ties the boy to the attacks, and a broken window supports a hypothesis involving a break-in by someone outside the family. The boy was never charged, and since he is a minor, his name, whereabouts, and involvement in the investigation have been kept from the media.

One investigator did remark on the boy's "apparent lack of

emotion."

Apparent lack of emotion! Bruce shut down his desktop. That's what he got for following link after link until he satisfied his own morbid streak—asshole comments from an ignoramus. Alex had to be in shock after what he experienced. At least part of Alex was probably still in shock. How does a mind process *anything* like that, and your own *parents*? Alex was probably dissociative. And being surrounded by adults whose priority was putting down tape and picking up samples and finding out if maybe the child, also a victim, could be a killer? Being accused, if not directly, then indirectly? Bruce couldn't fathom what Alex had been through, was still going through. They'd probably spend the rest of Alex's teen years, hell, the rest of Alex's life, working through the trauma.

On the other hand, Bruce hadn't cared much for Letta and Dave. Maybe they'd also alienated their son.

Letta's miscarriage had occurred under "very strange" circumstances.

How alienated did Alex feel?

Bruce felt like such a jerk.

Ollie

No practice on Tuesdays, not this early in the Spring season. Ollie took the school bus, got home by four, sprinted up the stairs to his apartment, which would be his alone for about two hours, and let himself in. A normal kid would probably be in a hurry to take the parental lock off his computer and spend the private time looking at off-the-hook internet porn, but his addiction was far more embarrassing. He wanted the time to binge watch a little anime, probably as many episodes of *Demon Slayer* as he could get in. Once his older brother got home from the auto shop or his mom got home from the ad agency, they'd dictate living room TV use, and they were a united front against all things cartoonish. He could get Netflix on his computer, but it wasn't as good as the big screen.

Tossing his jacket in front of the coat closet and kicking his shoes off under the coffee table, he settled onto the sofa and set down his Diet Coke. He didn't like diet soda very much, but he counted carbs and didn't want to feel guilty later if Mom brought home some kind of dessert. Besides, Coach paid attention to how his players looked in relation to how they performed, and Ollie intended to make Varsity. Beyond that, he had girls to consider. At a party last weekend, he had made third base with Halle Dunstan, and he suspected he might be able to cash in his V-card by the end of the semester.

The TV was on for ten minutes, and he was just getting relaxed when the light overhead flickered out, and with a pop and a flash, the screen went dark. He tried the remote. No response.

"What?" Even with closed blinds, the room wasn't dark, but it seemed… grey.

He pushed the "on" button repeatedly. No response.

"My luck." He stood to check out the TV, but he halted between the coffee table and the sofa when he heard the faint noises.

Sizzles. Zaps.

Hair stood up on his forearms.

Ollie looked behind him, to the walkway that connected the hall to the kitchen and dining room. Sparks of electricity, branching like horizontal lightning, blinked on and off along the sides of the path. He didn't know what to think. An electrical problem, but he'd never seen or even heard of one like this. Wires? Static? He bent over and put his shoes back on. Rubber bottoms, grounding. He needed to call somebody; his phone was in his bookbag in the hall. He wasn't scared, but not being cautious would be stupid.

Slowly, he circled the sofa and approached the entrance to the hall.

One step beyond the sofa, he felt one of the electric

branches zap the side of his face. He slapped the contact point like a mosquito, then smiled. Not even as bad as a mosquito bite! Still, he needed to call someone. Could be a fire hazard. Worth a call to Mom at work, anyway, even if he got her voicemail like always. He stepped through the entryway toward the hall.

His feet took the rest of him to the wrong hall. In front of him, the wall was deep red, not the aquamarine of the hall in his apartment that linked the front door, living room, three bedrooms, and main bathroom. Beyond the red, the wall was... wrong. It had... dead things on it. A cat. A rabbit. Squirrels. A dog. They were all cut up. It was disgusting.

Ollie looked over his shoulder and saw a bedroom he didn't recognize. Questions overlapped in his mind. Where was he? How did he get here?

Most pressing: Which way was out?

4. SECOND ESCAPE

Ollie

He was too old to be so scared, but he was scared.

The sofa—the TV—he'd probably nodded off, and he was dreaming. The hallway didn't feel like a dream. His crawling flesh didn't feel like a dream. He didn't dream about animals with their skins torn off, bodies cut up, guts nailed to a wall... he'd dreamt of pissing on his math teacher's enormous tits, but that was about as perverted as he got... this place wasn't him. He was misplaced—

—no, *dis*placed. He'd moved in a blink, something to do with the static, something to do with the greylight, which was here, too. On the right, the hall dead-ended in a room. The open door showed shapes, human shapes, utterly still, posed. Mannequins? Some of them. Some were small, more like dolls on perches for display. The greylight revealed few details. He'd have to enter the room if he wanted to see more. What he saw in the hall made him afraid to see more.

The hall was longer to the left, where it continued to a room with double doors, Ollie guessed the master suite, and also branched to the left, most likely the path to the exit. Gathering resolve, he stepped into the hall, angling left, and the softness of the floor surprised him. His foot sunk into gentle bounce, like walking on a firm cushion.

Buoyant steps took him toward the double doors, but halfway to the leftward branch, the building shook. He reached for the wall without the mounted animal parts to keep his balance, but the wall jumped away from him, and he fell into it, smashing his shoulder after his arm missed the mark. The wall continued to recede as he used it to get back to his feet. On the other side of the hallway, the decorated wall receded as well. The hallway widened. Ollie decided not to hang around to find out why. Pushing off the wall, he stumbled forward.

The sounds of shuffling feet reached him over the house's rumbling, but he hesitated and didn't look behind him until after he felt the sting in his lower back. As the sting turned into a ball of fire, fire and lightning that shot up and down his entire body, he turned his neck and saw the boy behind him, tall, in decent shape but not an athlete, blond, white, a little familiar, like maybe Ollie had seen him at school, but not someone he knew. The boy pulled a knife out of Ollie's back. Ollie's chest, arms, and face throbbed with panic.

He tried to turn around. His neck strained. The knife with his blood on it didn't look like one he'd seen before. Sharp on one side, the metal blade curved to a point. The other side was almost flat, rising in a slight wave to where metal met the matte black handle in a niche where the boy rested his thumb. The blade was maybe five or six inches, only a little longer than the handle.

"Don't tell me I missed," the boy said. He flattened his free hand against Ollie's upper back and pushed.

Such a weak push shouldn't have done anything, but Ollie tipped over, face-first onto the buoyant floor. He turned to keep from crunching his nose, and the impact didn't hurt. In fact—

beneath the fiery sting of the knife wound, he felt nothing at all.

Oh God.

Ollie said, "I... I... I...."

The boy knelt within his line of sight. "You can't feel your legs? Did I get it right after all?"

The effort to form a word came out as a twisted cry that

dissolved into a sob. Ollie thought *paralyzed, paralyzed,* but at the same time he felt terrified by what would happen as he lay on his stomach, unsure if he could even turn himself over.

The light was brighter now. Paler grey.

The boy wiped the very sharp-looking knife on his lime green polo shirt and said, "You won't die right away? We can have fun first?"

Ollie sobbed again. What shame! He was supposed to be brave!

Did being brave matter if he was dying alone with this fucked-up kid?

The fucked-up kid took off the lime green shirt.

Ollie managed a crackling voice. "Who—what—why—"

"I'm Alex," the boy said. "You're Ollie. We have a connection."

Ollie tried to shake his head in defiance, *no connection,* but he only turned far enough to sink his eyes into the floor, its puffed silver diamond pattern that told him what he was lying on.

A mattress. The floor was a mattress, and the hallway had widened to accommodate a king.

What the—

The cold, unsharpened side of Alex's knife touched Ollie's upper back before the blade started ripping through fabric. Ollie felt and heard the knife splitting the t-shirt's rear and sleeves. As Alex peeled it away from his skin, he felt the blood in the fabric cling.

Pain might distract from the terror. He wanted more pain. Numbness horrified. His body below his waist didn't exist in his mind.

"Use those weight-lifting arms of yours," Alex said, "to push up off the floor as far as you can."

Alex knelt beside him again, so Ollie turned his head for defiance: "No!"

"If your arms won't be useful, I'll shut them off."

Thoughts clashed in Ollie's brain. Cooperating could get

him killed, or worse. Not cooperating could get him killed, or worse. If the goal was to stay alive, and that *had to be* the goal, playing along might buy time for, for, for—

what, someone to rescue him?

He had to hope for *something*. As soon as his trembling arms would obey, he did his best approximation of a push-up.

"Thank you." Alex pulled the shirt away and threw it further up the hall, toward the double doors. Ollie lowered himself, and Alex shouted, "Not yet!"

Ollie tried to suspend himself on his arms, aware of blood dripping around his bare sides.

Alex pulled at Ollie's lower body. His upper body registered the tugs. He looked down at the space his arms created between his bare torso and the mattress and saw Alex removing his jeans and underwear. Ollie didn't feel friction between the sliding clothes and denuded skin. When Alex lifted Ollie's knees to pull the clothes past them, Ollie collapsed. Alex didn't seem to mind. He took off the rest of Ollie's clothes.

Eyes on the mattress, Ollie willed himself to wake up, but he knew he wasn't dreaming. He willed himself *displaced*, to reappear anywhere but here.

The sound of Alex's zipper made him realize that the house no longer shook.

The heat of Alex's body hovering over his made him think of fighting, of using what was left of his ebbing strength to twist, grab, and throttle this kid, grab a hold of his neck and squeeze, not letting go until his eyes popped out of his skull, but as if he could read Ollie's mind, Alex traced around Ollie's shoulder blades with the knife's sharp point and said, "Shh. You'll hardly feel a thing."

Again, Ollie felt a flat, empty hand pressed against his back. It moved up and down, side to side, spreading pain with pins and needles and wetness, his blood, and an image from maybe first grade, fingerpainting, or whole-hand painting, giggling with wet color all over his palm, spreading it all over white paper, giggling, and now Alex was fingerpainting on his back and arms with his blood. Ollie giggled and felt insane and hoped Alex didn't hear.

The spreading wet sensation stopped—all sensation stopped except for breathing and the throb of terror—and Ollie could only lift his head and twist his neck enough to know that Alex, probably naked, straddled his backside. "So tight," Alex said. "And me without lube."

Oh God. He wanted to say "don't." He didn't say anything. He wasn't sobbing, but he was crying, and he lacked the capacity for anything else.

Alex

Improvisation! He'd decided to wait for Ollie in his house's version of the home office, where instead of Mom and Dad's work shit he kept various artificial bodies, from little kids' plastic dolls to mannequins he'd rescued from dumpsters, but he hadn't known whether Ollie would come into the room or walk down the hall the other way. When he'd chosen the latter, giving Alex a clear run at his back, Alex had thought—stab a guy in the back? In my own house? Why the cowardice?

But then he'd thought of going right for the spine, and the idea had become overwhelmingly attractive. He crouched, he crept, and he calculated. The knife penetrated right where he'd aimed, in the center, and Ollie fell.

He had this good-looking, athletic kid at his feet. At his mercy. And the floor was a mattress! What did they have in mind?

His cock was stiff as a rail.

Improvisation! He hadn't *planned* to use Ollie like a sex doll, but... why not?

Limited foreplay. Alex didn't want Ollie bleeding out before they got to what Alex had originally planned. Before long, they were both naked, and Alex straddled Ollie's upper thighs, fingering his tight asshole. He didn't know if the paraplegia would make Ollie's bowels release, not something he wanted but something he braced for. No shitstorm came, however, and Alex worked a second finger into Ollie's ass, then a third. Ollie cried and whimpered, but his reactions didn't seem linked to Alex's actions.

Alex would use Ollie's blood as lube, rubbing it all over his cock and massaging it into Ollie's relaxing, widening hole.

When he stuck in his cock, he slid into the warm, wet constriction slowly, not wanting to come too soon and not wanting to trigger too quick a reaction from Ollie. When he felt his groin press against soft ass cheeks, he lowered his mouth to Ollie's right ear. "If you fight me, I'll kill you." With his chest against Ollie's back and arms partially covering Ollie's arms, he pulled partway out and thrusted in, all the way again, rocking Ollie from head to toe. Involuntary twitches in Ollie's strained muscles made keeping control a challenge. Ollie groaned.

Alex said, "You know what's happening?" He thrusted again, sliding along Ollie's blood, in and out of his ass. Ollie's ass was probably bleeding, too. If he could feel anything, Ollie would probably feel new, excruciating pain.

Ollie turned his head to the right, eyes meeting Alex's eyes. "Don't," he croaked.

Alex thrusted again, again shifting Ollie's entire body, and Ollie winced. "Please," Ollie said. "Stop."

Keeping eye contact, Alex said, "No." He thrusted again and again, finding a rhythm that Ollie matched with little cries. As he sped up, he gained energy and added volume: "Let it out!"

"Please!" Ollie had more oomph in his beggary.

"Do better!" Alex slammed into the unfeeling backside.

"Please stop!"

"BETTER!"

"STOP! OH GOD, STOP, STOP, STOP!"

Alex came inside the warm bloody sleeve, which stretched his wilting penis as he pulled it out. "Good," he said. "Good."

Ollie cried.

Tightening his grip on his knife, Alex pulled away from the boy beneath him. "We're only getting started," he said, and he crawled toward Ollie's ankles.

Ollie snorted, probably trying to suck in snot from all the bawling he was doing. "W-what?"

"You're a jock, right? It's all about muscles, right?" Alex looked at his knife. He loved this knife.

For his thirteenth birthday his grandmother had sent him an Amazon gift card, probably figuring he'd use it to buy books, but instead he'd bought this "Deerslayer" hunting knife, good for, among other things, skinning your kills. His grandmother never asked what he did with the gift card, and his parents never noticed anything, so he'd kept the knife in a safe place and awaited the right moments.

Alex knew to avoid cutting too deeply above the ankles; a person could bleed out fast there. Above the Achilles tendon, though, would be a fine place to start having a look at what running around after a black and white ball could do for a young man. Alex chuckled as he aligned the blade with the curve of Ollie's lower leg. The rest was whittling. Ollie's skin, downed with strawberry blond, came off in strips, wider and longer the better Alex got a handle on the knife.

"Something's wrong! I know it! What are you doing? I feel...."

"Describe it to me, Ollie."

"I feel woozy. You're doing something to my legs."

After giving strands of red calf muscle a hearty squeeze, Alex went for a hamstring. "You're imagining things," he said. "Next thing you'll say I raped you."

"You did," Ollie whispered.

"How would you know? Tell me how it felt."

Ollie fell quiet, and Alex kept taking strips of skin from

his legs. He realized he wouldn't be happy unless he got the thighs' fronts, those glorious quads, so he would have to roll Ollie over.

"Remember what happens if you fight me," Alex said.

Alex knelt on Ollie's right and rolled the boy toward him. He straddled Ollie's waist and looked at his widening eyes for a second, registering their horror as they took in the image Alex's bare white skin coated with Ollie's lost red. Then Alex dove for Ollie's left and right shoulders, severing the pectoral tendons and enough muscle so that Ollie's arms, if they moved at all, would only flop. Naturally, Ollie felt these cuts, and he screamed.

"Don't want you to get all grabby," Alex said.

As Alex removed skin from Ollie's thighs, very wide strips, not very many of them, Ollie's screams diminished to blubbering. The strands of quadricep, stretchy and slick, might have been guitar strings in his fingers, but he had to move on. Ollie was barely coherent. He would soon be an insensate puddle on the mattress.

So, Alex flayed his chest, bringing out the screams one last time. The skin removal was careful and slow, starting on the left, digging all along the side, and working under a little at a time so that the skin came off all together. Alex got both nipples and a huge rectangle of skin in one great swath.

Ollie checked out. Shock, blood loss... Alex wasn't a fucking doctor and he didn't fucking know. The fun was over.

Almost.

Alex came out of his trance in his spot under the branch canopy in the park, jeans a little dirty but, like his lime green polo shirt, unblemished by bloodstains. The splotches of semen in his underwear—his body had gotten excited without him—didn't matter. He took a deep breath of the air turning to evening and knew he needed to hurry, so he uncrossed his legs, stiff from the long meditation, and jogged. He knew the way to Ollie's apartment building. Ollie didn't, hadn't, lived too far away.

Winded by the time he reached the apartments, Alex still jogged up the stairs, not wanting anyone to find Ollie before he got a look. He reached Ollie's front door, saw nobody spying, and peered through a window, straining to see the doorway between Ollie's living room and the front hall. He got what he wanted.

The electric lights in the apartment were working again, and enough daylight came from behind Alex to help make the body visible. For extra help, the hallway floor had whitish tiles against which the blood expanding around Ollie contrasted marvelously. His body was face down and naked. Alex didn't have a great line of sight, but he had a partial view of the backs of Ollie's legs, skin missing, muscles exposed and pulled away from their proper places. The temptation to break in and turn the body over, to see the peeled-away chest and thighs, niggled at Alex's brain, but he resisted, and furthermore, he knew he had to leave soon, or someone would see him and people would ask why he'd been there. People needed to focus on other questions.

Where had the clothes gone?

Where had the *skin* gone?

What kind of monster would do such a thing?

This time, no one would question that a maniac was on the loose.

5. BUILDING

Letta

(about thirteen years ago)

The baby sat in his highchair at the kitchen table. He didn't do anything.

"Smile! Smile for the camera!" Dave loved his new digital camera. It made Letta long for the days when rolls of film limited the number of pictures a person could take. The flash went off over and over. Sometimes Alex looked toward the blinding light, and sometimes he didn't. No smile, though.

"For God's sake, Dave, blow out the candle. It'll get wax all over the cake." The cake's yellow coating and pink puffy border matched Alex's conical party hat, affixed to his head by elastic under his fat chin. He looked absurd. He was supposed to be a boy. At least his jumper was blue. Letta had picked it out. She'd picked out the cake and party hats, too, but they were just what the grocery store had handy after she'd fetched her Starbucks this morning.

Dave flashed the camera, and Alex stared into space. The cake didn't spark his curiosity one bit. Neither did the stack of presents beside it on the table. She stepped forward, body between the camera and the boy, and blew out the candle. Alex looked at her. Expectant? Sad? Mothers were supposed to know these things. Giving birth was supposed to switch on so many magical abilities. *Don't give me those eyes. I don't deserve those eyes.*

She shifted back to her place beside Dave, leaving him closer to the highchair. Remembering she'd only poured twice, she took a gulp from her wine glass.

"We should have invited people," Dave said. He switched into baby voice: "Not much of a party, is it big guy?"

"I wonder if he's even aware of us. Us as us, I mean. Or are we negligible objects, like the cake or the wrapped boxes?"

Dave set the camera on the table and fetched the decorative paper plates—they matched the party hats—from the kitchen counter. He returned and set the plates and a pie server on the table. He kept his glass of Jameson in his hand. "Should I cut the cake?"

"Who would we invite?" Letta asked. Dave's comment, "not much of a party," sounded like an accusation. "Which of our friends would be a good fit for a one-year-old's birthday party?"

"He must have friends his age."

"He's a little young for networking." Letta would need a third pour soon. "We'd have to make friends his age for him. Have you done that?"

"Letta, be reasona—"

"Me neither."

They both drank.

"I watched a video online," Letta said. "You don't cut the cake for them. You let them pound it with their fists and stick their faces in it."

"Should we put the whole cake on his tray?" Dave moved as if to do it.

"You're cleaning it up."

Dave stopped. "You seem icy today."

"That's right." Letta drained her glass and turned toward the counter. "I'm an icy bitch because I expect you to clean up a mess now and then."

"I'd be glad to know there was a reason," Dave said.

As she refilled her glass, she said, "You shouldn't say such things. You aren't that clever." Back at her tableside place, facing Alex, she said, "That makes me think—I mean, I do wonder sometimes—do you think he's a retard?"

"You've never bonded with him. And it's officially been a year."

She bent her knees so that her head was on his level, and she could try to catch his dopey eyes with her own. They didn't connect. "I keep... waiting. Thinking, maybe when he's a little older."

"He's hit all the right milestones on time, even early. He's just quiet. Introverted. He'll probably be an artist." Ice clattered in Dave's glass as he tipped it over his bottom lip.

"Just what we need. He'll live in the garage and never move out."

"We don't have a garage."

"You plan to stay in this house forever?"

"We just bought it, and you're thinking of moving out?"

"Everything's better the second time around." Sex. The first time was awful. Second time—much better. They'd climb up in the world and get a better house. And—"Maybe I'd be a better mother if he'd turned out to be a girl."

"Why do you say that?" Dave asked.

"I don't know," Letta said, and she honestly didn't. "Idle party chatter. Ignore me. Don't read into it. It doesn't mean anything."

Alex

(about six years ago)

"You've got to build a house," Grandpa told him. He was Dad's dad and a funny old man who didn't talk about his job or stare into his phone like other grown-ups. The baldness and the way his bones poked out and his skin got splotchy were from all the chemo and radiation, Dad said, and Dad warned that the Big C was going to take Grandpa away. Alex knew about cancer and death, and Mom and Dad didn't talk shit about heaven because their family didn't believe in heaven. What was happening was too bad, though, because Alex didn't mind talking to Grandpa, and Grandma was going to fall apart once he was gone. Mom and Dad agreed.

"Your grandmother will fall apart," Mom said.

Alex imagined her arms falling off, stumpy shoulders spraying blood like in some of the movies and cartoons he watched that his parents didn't know about. Then her droopy boobs slid out under her blouse and her wrinkled cheeks dropped from her skull right before her nose did and her legs crumbled like logs stacked end to end and—

He liked being around Grandpa more than most people. "What do you mean, build a house?"

"Did you ever hear the saying, 'A man's house is his castle?'"

Alex thought maybe he had.

"A castle is a place where you defend yourself. You've got to have a castle—" Grandpa tapped Alex's forehead with two fingers—"in here."

"A castle in my head?" Alex asked.

Grandpa's voice got softer, and he looked away like he wasn't talking to Alex anymore. "I've got to go somewhere when they pump that shit into me." His hand rubbed the place on his chest where he had his "port." Grandpa had explained about chemo and how doctors used his port to take blood and give him drugs. It made Grandpa feel less like a person.

Alex imagined Grandpa wearing a black cape and a hood so he'd look like the Grim Reaper. He smiled and asked, "What's it like?"

The dying old man looked even farther away. "It's the house I grew up in. In actuality, I guess it was smaller than where we live now, but to me it seemed big, and when I go back, it seems big. It sat on a huge plot of land, and while in... actuality... you could see neighbors a ways off, when I visit *my* house, I don't have neighbors. I can look out windows and see the small grass-covered hills rolling on and on."

Grandpa turned back toward Alex, but Alex still wasn't sure the old man, the Reaper man, saw him. "It's the house I grew up in, but it isn't, too, because I built it, and it's all mine, not my parents'. I made the rooms and fit them together using my memory and a little imagination. Some of the furniture, like the coffee table with the corner I'd chewed on while I was teething, I kept. Other stuff I changed. I made different colors. The most important thing is I put in a lot of guns. I like to sit at a window with a rifle and watch. Stay safe. Nobody bothers me." Breath whistled in his modified chest. "It's safe. Nobody bothers me."

"*My house is full of secrets nobody should know.*"

Alex would do as Grandpa told him and build his own house. He wouldn't let anyone in.

(about three years ago)

Hours after school each weekday, then hours after dinner, and pretty much full days on weekends—Alex's parents left him to himself. Dad was Manager now, and Mom was starting her own business… again. He got decent grades and didn't have any health problems, so they didn't worry. In his room with the door closed, he practiced meditation. He was never sure if he was doing it right because what he experienced didn't feel like what most of the books said, but he didn't care too much. Whatever he did, sitting on his bed, repeating his mantra, distanced him from what Grandpa had called "actuality." It made going to *his* house feel more real. He wished he could talk to Grandpa again and find out whether what Alex felt going to his house was like what Grandpa felt, but Grandpa had died while Alex was still putting *his* rooms inside the rooms where he lived, learning how to make a house in his mind out of the house where his parents kept him.

In his coffin, Grandpa looked like a skeleton in a loose skin wrapper. He wore a black suit, Reaper-ish.

Mom complained about his grandmother insisting on an open casket ceremony. Alex liked the way Grandpa looked. Grandpa's open coffin went into the big downstairs closet of Alex's house, an image made into an object in his mind's solidifying structure. That image he could store. The image that stayed with him in a deeper way, the image of Grandpa with a rifle keeping watch at a window in a house Alex never got to see, he couldn't capture. It was free.

Wanting to know what Grandpa felt made Alex curious about Charity Laughton, a middle school girl that kids talked about at the bus stop. The buses for the older kids came earlier in the morning, so the kids Alex waited with mostly didn't know Charity, but the Laughtons were neighborhood gossip because they had some sort of New Age religion that was like not believing in God at all only worse. If Alex ever wanted to talk to the other kids, he might have asked them to explain exactly what they believed in, but he didn't want to talk to them, so he listened and got the impression that Charity might know something about meditation and might understand about houses within houses.

One morning he left for the bus stop early. Nobody noticed.

He didn't mingle with the middle school kids, but he watched from a short distance, not afraid for them to see him. Charity wasn't hard to spot: she was the only Black girl. She also stood apart from the group, but she didn't look dejected. Maybe, like him, she had no use for such company.

School that day seemed pointless. Alex wandered around the neighborhood, looking in windows, until the middle school bus dropped off Charity. Still unconcerned about being seen, he followed her solitary walk home from a short distance.

The distance collapsed when she spun and said, "You want something, little boy?"

"Kind of." Alex was relieved. He'd had no idea how to start talking to her.

"Okay. What?" When she folded her arms across her chest, the straps of her bookbag shifted her bra, which was too big for her but nevertheless accentuated her budding breasts.

Alex had to answer her question. "Um... Christians say a lot of stupid shit."

She laughed but said, "Buzz off, little creep." She turned her back and walked.

"Wait!" He scurried to her side. "I like to meditate."

"Okay. Does that make us best friends?"

"I bet you could teach me something," Alex said.

Charity stopped and gave him a slow smile. "Why would I do that?"

A real conversation followed, and another, and another. Charity said Alex was smart, and Alex supposed Charity was smart because she wasn't stupid like everyone else. They spent time at Alex's because Charity's parents wouldn't allow her to spend time alone with a boy, even if he was only eleven. Charity thought they'd be better off if her parents didn't know about him at all. Alex's parents, on the other hand, didn't monitor Alex's infrequent associations or what went on in his bedroom. He and Charity sat side by side on his bed, legs folded half-lotus, and practiced meditation. They figured out right away that their practices differed. Charity talked about peace, calm, stillness, and blankness, and Alex talked about how he escaped to another place. He eventually described his house within the house.

"Your escape, a place you go without going anywhere," Charity said.

"Yeah." Alex liked that. His Escape.

"Sounds more like astral projection than meditation," she said.

"What's that?"

"Come on," she said. "Let's talk about getting you out of that body of yours." She laughed.

Before, he'd moved through his house like a ghost, unaffected by gravity, floating from room to hall to room, making objects materialize from memories and ideas, and he thought maybe *that* was out of body experience, but when he tried what Charity described, not going inside his head to find his house, his castle, but disconnecting from himself, going inside only to get out, and by getting out step into his own domain...

And he stood, feet planted, in the bedroom he'd created, *his* room inside his room, where chains with cuffs hung from the walls because he imagined one day—

"Holy shit!" The voice startled him. "You not only did it, but you brought me with you!"

He didn't. He couldn't. He wouldn't.

"This is the room where we... but it's different... *your* house, right?" Charity put a hand on his shoulder. He felt her hand. Physical hand, physical shoulder. The house had long been like a solid object in his mind, filled with solid objects from his mind, but now he was solid within it, and so was *she*.

She wasn't supposed to be here. Whatever she'd been, she'd become an *intruder*.

He grabbed her wrist.

A man's house is his castle.

She was older, but he was stronger. He twisted her arm. She cried out. In the other house, his parents' house, Mom might have heard. Not in *his* house.

A castle is a place where you defend yourself.

Grandpa sat at windows, well-armed, making sure nobody else got in.

My house is full of secrets nobody should know.

"Ow-ow-ow-ow-ow what are you doing?"

Chains hung from the walls because he thought if Grandpa kept watch that meant maybe someday people could come, and he'd have to be ready, and he imagined maybe the intruders would be his parents, and he could leave them in his bedroom, chained to the walls, for hours and hours, and he'd also built the closet not to hold clothes but to hold...

someone.

Alex twisted harder, and Charity yelled louder until he pushed her back into a wall with a hard thud. While she looked stunned, he took a giant step to the closet door and opened it. Inside the walls were metal. A bucket sat in one corner. He didn't remember putting it there, but he didn't think about it again. Buttons popped on Charity's shirt when he grabbed the front of it, pulled, and shoved her into the metal chamber. He closed the door and slid the metal bar in place to keep it shut.

On the other side, she pounded and screamed. Alex listened for a while before returning to the bed where he'd started trying to leave his body with Charity, who no longer sat in the half-lotus position but sprawled beside him, eyes open. He called her name. He shook her. She didn't respond.

She breathed.

He waited with her for a long time. She breathed, but she didn't do anything else. Mom called him for dinner. He closed the bedroom door behind him.

After his parents were asleep, he rolled her off the bed. Her body crashed on the floor, so he ran to his parents' doorway, the open double doors, to see if they were alert. Dad snored. Mom was motionless. Alex returned to Charity's limp, breathing body and dragged it into the hall.

The stairs were carpeted, but her shoes still banged on them as he held her middle and took each backward step with care. After that, the front door and porch steps were easy, though he wished he could have done something about the automatic flood light over the driveway. Having a garage would have made this part easier, but he had to leave Charity out in the open while he ran to the shed in the backyard, pulled out the rope and the wheelbarrow, and used the former to rig the latter to the back of his bicycle. He wasn't strong enough to pick her up all at once; getting her into the wheelbarrow required fumbling her body by halves.

The bike ride to her house was slow. Three cars passed him, but none reacted to his cargo. His heart pounded. His muscles buzzed. He felt alive.

In actuality, he left her posed upright on the swing that decorated her parents' back deck. Alex later learned that her parents had already been frantically searching for her, but they didn't check the back deck until morning, when they found her and called an ambulance. Charity was in a coma. Her body was covered in strange bruises, but examination revealed no signs of sexual assault or wounds identifiable as defensive. Police found some evidence in the Laughtons' yard, but it led them nowhere.

Alex returned to his house as often as he could to see what Charity was doing from *his* perspective. She was in the closet cell, quite mobile, banging on the door and begging him to set her free.

At first.

The banging got softer. The cell stank. Alex knew what the bucket was for. He looked in at her and saw wells forming around her eyes, true blackness in her brown skin, marks of anguish and deprivation that made her look older. She reminded him of Grandpa, but she was a thirteen-year-old girl. The comparison was funny. "Please," she said, and Alex snickered. He didn't think of hurting her, but he didn't want to let her go, either. "Please."

She asked for something to eat.

He left her alone.

When he came back, she asked for something to drink.

More visits provoked more begging, more and more for water.

Her voice became hoarse. The banging stopped.

She went limp. She stopped breathing.

In *his* house, Alex stopped opening the closet door.

In actuality, despite the constant infusion of fluids at the hospital, Charity died from dehydration.

Aaron

(now)

Stretched out and leaning on one cushioned arm, Alex covered the length of the sofa. Taller than Aaron, almost as tall as Bruce, the kid was hard to think of as a kid. He would put a shirt on when Bruce came home, which usually meant dinnertime, but he seemed to like hanging around the house shirtless in the afternoons when Aaron was the only one around. Random encounters had also informed Aaron that the kid had taken to wearing only boxers to bed. He slept by an open window and said he liked the cool California night air. They'd be using the air conditioning soon, but Aaron didn't see anything unnatural about Alex's choices.

One morning Aaron was prowling around the house, camera in hand, and he glimpsed Alex in boxers on his bedroom floor, doing sit-ups. He kept filming until Alex flipped over for push-ups and saw him. Holding himself up with one arm, the boy waved. Aaron waved back and retreated, thinking he could invite Alex to join him for his own morning workout routine. Something felt weird about that, though, so he only invited Alex for a jog. They started jogging together every other day or so.

And on afternoons, like this one, when Alex didn't stay out at the park too late, they talked. On video. Aaron set his handheld on a tripod, framing Alex's long body sprawled on the sofa, and positioned himself off-camera. "So, what do you *do* in the park after school? Do you really spend all that time reading?"

Alex turned his head away from Aaron and camera, rested a hand on his taut stomach, and sighed. "I could tell you, but you'll think I'm a weirdo."

"I hope you already think *I'm* a weirdo," Aaron said. Behind the camera, he reframed the shot, from Alex's blond head to the waistline of his white shorts. His lounging looked elegant. "Weirdos are the best kinds of people."

Alex laughed and tipped his head back, eyes on the ceiling. "Okay. Okay, I'll tell you." He looked at the camera. "I spend a lot of time in my head. A teacher in eighth grade called me a 'daydreamer' like it was the worst thing in the world."

A kid alone, staring off into space, lost in his own mind might not be the *best* thing, but Aaron planned shots and sequences in his head, imagining details within details, losing all track of time, so why should he worry if Alex liked to sit in the park and think? "What do you daydream about?"

Blushing, Alex turned from the camera to him. "Bad things, sometimes. Good things. Things that are good because they're bad."

"I guess I *am* talking to a teenager," Aaron said. "When I was fourteen, I liked more privacy for my daydreams."

The hand on Alex's belly migrated to his chest. "There's a place I go. It's private."

"Oh?" Aaron zoomed in on the hand rising and falling between Alex's nipples.

"Maybe you'll see it someday."

"I…." Aaron almost said, "I want to," but he had no idea what he would have meant.

6. BEAUTIFUL PEOPLE

Warren

"Who's the new guy?" Warren pointed to the back of the theatre.

"Fuck if I know," Anna said. "Do you think Mr. Chun will mind if I undo the top couple of buttons? I want to show cleavage."

Warren kept one eye on the guy in the back row while the other went to the front of Anna's PJs. "You know *I* won't mind. Not a guy in here's going to mind. Even Kerry won't *mind.*"

"He won't care, though."

"No." Warren didn't care that Kerry was gay and had been out pretty much since he was born even though he was straight-acting. Kerry actually didn't care if anyone in the cast showed skin because Kerry was, objectively speaking, remarkably good-looking, and his best friend Angie who came around rehearsals sometimes said he was dating a guy who went to UCLA.

If Angie could come around to rehearsals, then rehearsals weren't *closed* to visitors, so Warren couldn't have this guy in the back row thrown out... but he wanted to. For no good reason. It was just that—

"Do you want to run lines until Mr. Chun gets back? We're doing the first half of Act Two today, and I'm barely off book." Anna gave him a pleading grin and fluttered her lashes. Anna fucking Cortez. A lot of guys would have killed to get close to her, and because he'd decided to audition for the school play this semester, he got to kiss her again and again without even dating her.

Not that he wouldn't date her. And a lot more, but the kissing was great. Smack dab in the middle of Act Two.

The play was pretty weird. Mr. Chun wrote it himself, and it was about Hollywood teens at a fancy drug rehab place talking about issues with their famous parents and general life bullshit while they fooled around in closets and snuck into each other's rooms at night. Mr. Chun seemed really interested in putting students on stage in sexual situations, so Warren felt pretty sure he wouldn't mind Anna undoing some buttons. At the very least, her tits could sell tickets. Boys would come to look at them.

Like that guy in the back row was looking at *him*. Except....

Mr. Chun convinced Principal Herrick to let him stage his own play because he was hungry for exposure. Everybody was, right? Auditions for a high school production in the Los Angeles Unified School District, parts of it, anyway, were much more intense than mere "extracurriculars." Getting a part meant a line on a résumé. No, it wasn't pro or even semi-pro, but it could open doors where colleges were concerned, and managers and agents *did* come to the school's shows, and a couple of people in the Theatre program had landed commercials. Nobody with a part in A Cure for Secrets failed to think "what if?" They all wanted exposure.

So what if some kid sat in the back row looking at him? If he wanted to fuck him, so what? If he simply liked looking at him, so what?

Warren knew he looked good, objectively speaking. Mr. Chun didn't cast anyone who didn't look good. His play was about beautiful people with beautiful problems. Hundreds of beautiful students had competed to play the beautiful patients with beautiful angst. Students who lacked physical appeal, wherever they were, knew better than to apply.

The house lights were up, but the back row was too distant from where Warren and Anna perched on the stage's edge, running lines, for Warren to get a good look at the kid who was looking at him. The kid had a phone and might have been recording him. That was weird, wasn't it? Teenage paparazzi... Warren wasn't even doing anything interesting. His flesh crawled.

"Hello? Warren Dell? Are you still among the living?" Anna's impatience charmed.

"Sorry," he said, knowing he'd dropped a line as his multi-tasking mind had dropped its multi. "Can we take it from, 'They're all fakes and liars?'"

Gladys walked by. "*All* fakes and liars," she repeated. "That dialogue is definitely headed for a Tony." She was a senior and played a nurse, one of only two adult roles in the show and uncontestably, Gladys said, "a magical negro."

"Hey," Warren said. She stopped and turned around. "You know who that kid is? In the back?" He pointed.

"I asked Kip that same question yesterday," Gladys said, squinting one eye toward the guy in the back who still might have been using his phone in video mode. "Kip said he's seen him around. Thinks he's a freshman transfer. His name is Luke or something."

"If he's... recording us...." Warren felt a little foolish. "Should we make him stop?"

"It's against school rules." Gladys shrugged. "People do whatever they want with their phones between classes and after hours, but still, technically, it is against school rules."

Warren slid off the stage's edge and stood next to Gladys. "Come with me and tell him to fuck off?"

"Warren!" Anna protested.

"You need me to come with you?" Gladys combined incredulity with a clear implication of refusal.

"No, I... I'll go."

Warren walked up the slight incline to the back of the theatre. As he approached, the guy in the back row lowered and pocketed his phone. He stood when Warren reached the end of the aisle. He angled away in the opposite direction.

"Um, excuse me," Warren called.

The kid, who looked like he was probably a freshman but big for his age, turned back and smiled. "Hey. What's up?"

"You were, um." Warren didn't know what to say without seeming presumptuous. He and the others didn't *own* the theatre. And he couldn't be sure, but, well, what the hell. "Were you recording us just now?"

"Who?" the guy said. He looked toward the stage. "You and those two girls who are staring?"

Warren felt embarrassed. They were the ones asking to be looked at, not this guy, who might have come in out of mere curiosity, which was allowed, after all—"Yeah."

"No, how would—oh, you mean my phone. I was texting. Came in here to sit for a while before I walk home. Sorry if I fucked up—"

"No, no. You didn't...." Warren exhaled sharp frustration with himself. This guy was perfectly ordinary, good-looking enough to pass an audition himself, not some paparazzi creep, just someone who wanted to sit—

"You're Warren, right?" From zero right back to creepy.

"Yeah. How'd you know?"

"I've seen you around." He extended his hand. "My name's Alex."

Warren and Alex shook. "Good to meet you," Warren said. He smiled and looked into Alex's eyes, which he'd thought were blue. Instead, they were grey, and they seemed to emit light that cancelled other light.

When he got his hand back, the skin of his palm felt cold. Alex said he'd be getting on home, and Warren could barely say, "Yeah." The kid was bad news. Very beautiful, very bad news.

Alex

Alex hadn't thought much about where he'd end up after his parents died, but when Los Angeles got mentioned, he got interested, and now he was an LA devotee. The trade of humidity for dry air was almost as good as trading the barbarism that lurked around Greater Atlanta's borders for what seemed like an endless sprawl of wealth and humanitarianism, of which Alex approved not because he gave a shit about humanity but because, like the blue skies and palm trees, it completed the attractive surface, the "They're all fakes and liars" motif that made everything beautiful and everything worthy of a scalpel or some other implement that could split it open and expose the underneath.

"They're all fakes and liars" was a line from the awful play Warren Dell was in. Alex's iPhone had picked it up while he was recording Warren running lines with Anna Cortez. Alex didn't care that the play was awful because Warren was gorgeous, and Warren was a star. He was much better looking than Ollie. Short, wavy brown hair, brown eyes, tanned skin, solid build—a junior—Warren was what the girls called *dreamy*, and Alex had dreams for him, too. He had an experiment in mind. If he could bring in both of his parents at once, why couldn't he bring in two others?

First, though, he had different pleasures to pursue. The skin he'd taken from Ollie had stayed in his house where he'd left it, along with the body's remains, but it had dried, becoming leatherier. With hammer and nails, Alex decorated the smaller stretch of wall across from the display of animals he'd killed and taken apart. With strips of skin whittled from Ollie's calves, he made a large, thin, rectangular frame. With the larger swaths he'd cut from Ollie's thighs, he made shapes like pillars inside the frame, on the sides. In the center, he placed the skin from Ollie's chest, the biggest continuous piece he'd managed to cut. It was the featured portion, the injury most noticeable to those who found the body.

What Alex did now, after death, after the body's

discovery, wouldn't register outside of his house, out there in actuality. What he did still mattered to him, though, so he took his Deerslayer hunting knife and began his cuts behind Ollie's ears. He cut behind the jawbone, under the chin. To avoid tattered edges, he moved the blade slowly between bone and flesh. Celebrities had doctors cut off their faces all the time. Cutting off your face was how the beautiful stayed beautiful. Ollie became more and more beautiful. Alex would have to leave the eyelids and nose behind, but he got the lips when he lifted the face from the skull.

The face went above the rectangle of calf skin, centered, its crown.

Alex thought of Leatherface from *The Texas Chain Saw Massacre* and chuckled. Like he would ever wear such a thing! But where it was, it was beautiful. A testament to his accomplishment.

Ollie felt—and this didn't make much sense—like Alex's first human kill. The first kill he deserved a trophy for, anyway. His parents had been a necessity. Ollie was... an expansion of experience. A pursuit suited to his proclivities. Adventure.

What would he do with the rest of the body?

He still didn't open the closet in his bedroom. Charity wasn't a kill. She was a circumstance.

Grandpa was in the big closet downstairs. Occupado.

Alex supposed he could put Ollie where he'd put Mom and Dad, a place that belonged as much to *their* imagination as it belonged to his. He dragged the body, trailing blood on the grungy grey carpet that had been taupe, downstairs and into the circle of trees that was the living room. With rope he found draped over the back of the sofa—whatever tools he wanted had a way of showing up—he made a loop around Ollie's neck and hoisted him into a tree beside the ones where his parents dangled, not at the border of the room but ten or twenty paces deeper into the forest. Gravity had been at work on Mom and Dad. Viscera protruded from the wider wounds. They weren't rotting, exactly. They only got softer, spongier. Now Ollie could, too.

Alex felt a little breeze. The three bodies swayed. Maybe wind chimes should go with them.

Though hanging the skin might have been the best, he had another task in mind for his house today, and he didn't want to let time get away with him here with the bodies and the trees. Back upstairs, he paused for only a few seconds to admire the four pillars of skin inside the rectangle with the face on top before going into the office, his fake people room, the mannequins and dolls spread out, posed, where a desk remained, and on that desk he had a pile of 8x10s, glossy printouts of photos he'd taken with the iPhone gifted by Bruce and Aaron, the latter of whom might have given him a better camera if he'd asked—but the less they knew about his activities, the better.

The photos weren't perfect headshots because they'd all been candid, mostly taken without the subjects' knowledge, but he'd already learned a thing or two from Aaron about putting bodies in frames. He took the stack into the hall, past the displays of animals on the right and now a human on the left, and he turned to the part of the hall undecorated except for the fetus nailed at the top of the stairway. On the bare part of the red wall, he tacked pictures of beautiful people he'd started to connect with at Rose Park High.

Parts of the wall throbbed. Alex imagined they approved.

In one row he put boys, Rory and Mike and Tosh and Ken. Rory hadn't seen Alex taking the picture. He was a nerd and not well-liked but pretty under his glasses and long brown bangs, small, maybe five-three and skinny, but cute. Mike hung around with Rory—they were both sophomores—and was also an outcast for being smart but bigger with luscious brown skin and black hair and braces. Some girl hung around him, probably his girlfriend, but Alex didn't get a name or other details. Tosh, probably short for Toshio, saw Alex pointing his phone at him, smiled, and posed for the camera. A lot of kids hung around him; he was very outgoing and also stunning, the kind of androgynous that would make him pretty as a boy *or* a girl, though the pronouns Alex heard were he/him. Ken lifted weights and wrestled and got included with the others because he would have *so* much body to play with once Alex immobilized him.

In another row, he put girls. He saw no reason to discriminate. The girls he'd framed in digital rectangles were Kayla, Esme, Vicky, and a spectacular looking person whose name he hadn't learned yet. Like his first pair of boys, Kayla and Esme were friends, both goth girls; Alex thought Esme was a grade ahead of Kayla but wasn't sure. Esme was clearly Latina but wore pounds of white face makeup just like Kayla, and they accessorized their black outfits with flair, accentuating that they wallowed in doom, gloom, and *money*. Vicky appeared to be more of a loner, though boys often approached her. She didn't dress up but looked gorgeous with her long, thick, sandy blonde hair and oversized sapphire eyes. People said she was a model. Her body suggested she kept a strict diet. The girl without a name yet... she giggled in the halls with other girls. Her hips rocked back and forth as she walked from class to class, but not too much. Her posture was perfect. It conspired with the cross around her neck to tell the world she was a virgin.

Above those two rows, Alex put the stills from the video, close-ups of Warren, Anna, and Gladys. Gladys had called him "Luke." That was funny. All the theatre people were funny. But they were pretty, too. So much prettiness to play with.

He had an experiment to try. He'd start with two of them.

7. ESCAPE INTERRUPTED

Warren

He didn't smoke cigarettes because they had an aging effect, and they'd ruin his voice, too, and he'd had some private voice lessons in case he ever had to audition for a musical. Weed, on the other hand—legal in California for adults, really easy to get for minors, easier than alcohol, which wasn't as fun anyway—weed seemed acceptable and even downright necessary considering the pressure today's kids were under. Freed from rehearsal for the afternoon, Warren met up with Theo, and they rushed to Melinda's house, where bong hits with Janie were already underway.

The music was some old-style mariachi band, somber, lovelorn, and it got better with every hit. Warren didn't count the number of times the purple bong covered with heart stickers went around their small circle, but it went around fast. Failing the pop quiz in History no longer seemed to matter, and that meant the weed was doing its job. He smiled and sat back into his beanbag chair.

Crunchy cushion didn't stop his backward tilt. He flopped, and the surface that caught him made him expect a splash that didn't come. It was water, but... a mattress? Wait. A waterbed? He'd seen one when he was little at some old relative's house in Santa Monica. He couldn't remember the relative, but he remembered the house's view of the beach.

What would Melinda be doing with a—

Except the room was quiet, and the walls were closer, different walls, strange paintings, chains dangling, a place he'd never been, and no one else was here. Had he blacked out? Had he gotten so stoned that he'd gone somewhere else with his friends and then... forgot?

"Hey!" he yelled. "Where is everybody?"

The room had two doors, one closed, one open. The open one looked like it led to a hallway. A voice came from that direction, a guy's voice. Warren couldn't tell what he said, but he might have been Theo, and anyway the voice seemed like a good sign, so he fought the bed's waves to get to the edge and then walked toward the open door, not liking the chains on the wall, cuffs on their ends, people-sized, not liking the paintings, abstract, jagged lines and broken circles, soaked in reds and purples, and from behind you, when you weren't paying full attention, they looked like faces, spiraling faces sewn together and watching.

Warren stepped into the hall and controlled the attempted inversion of his stomach. In front of him, on the solid red wall... he had to be seeing things, hallucinating from something extra added to the pot, or dreaming, but why the hell would he dream something so fucked up? Animals torn to pieces.

From the opposite end of the hall, where double doors hung open, he heard laughter.

He turned toward the sound and saw the wall on his left, the skin. It had to be human. At the top—

It had to be the skin from a face, a *real* face.

This was what he got for letting Theo talk him into watching horror movies. "Do you know how many major Hollywood actors got their start in horror movies? Like, all of them," Theo said. Good to know the genre. Fuck that.

From the end of the hall, moaning. Warren walked toward it, trying to ignore the walls. The hallway seemed to grow as he traversed it. Haunted house shit. Special effects. At his feet, a thin fog covered what felt like carpet.

A moan turned into a shriek.

Warren hurried toward the open double doors and stopped where the hallway branched, a way toward stairs to—he could see in the greylight, darkness with mitigated intensity—what looked like a foyer, a foyer and a house's front door. *Exit.*

But someone through those double doors might need his help.

But he *did* know the genre, so—*fuck that.* This was his dream, or whatever it was, and he was headed for the stairs.

A part of his brain registered the pictures on the wall as he passed them, but he didn't stop to look. Later, he would remember the fetus at the top of the stairs, but he didn't register it at first. By the time he reached the stairs, he was running. His body slammed into the front door, and his right hand fumbled for the sliding chain, the bolt, and the lock on the knob.

The bolt wouldn't turn. Warren's hand loosened around it. "Please! Get me out of here!"

Near his fingers but not touching them, the bolt spun, and so did the knob. The door opened, and Warren stepped through.

He sat in a circle with Theo, Melinda, and Janie. "Waaa-rrreeenn," Melinda said. "Don't tell me this shit gave you brain damage. Cute with brain damage gets you nowhere."

Warren blinked, readjusting to his surroundings. He took the bong from Theo. "Dude, what is *in* this shit?" He forced a laugh. "I was having the weirdest... I guess you could call it a daydream."

"Your eyes were wide open," Melinda said.

"Trust me," Warren said. "That wasn't the weirdest thing."

Alex

Theatre rehearsal got cancelled because Mr. Chun had a last-minute "conflict"—Warren joked that it was probably a pitch meeting with somebody in Burbank—which meant Warren and Anna were free after school, which prompted Alex to go straight to the park to start his trance.

His experiment.

Something was wrong. When he went to his house, he always, at least as far back as he could remember, entered through his room, where chains that would never hold his parents still hung from the walls, and a waterbed was a recent addition because he'd seen one in an old movie and thought having one would be cool.

This time he entered through his parents' room, a room he'd never even decorated because he didn't like to go in, before or after. Its walls should have been that tan color that went with the actual house's Tuscan Yellow hallway, and the king-sized, four-poster bed should have had a duvet with a floral pattern.

The walls were black. Chains, thinner than the ones in his room, more like dog chains, hung from the bed's four posters. The bed cover had a mouth on it, open full human lips pulled back from spread spiny teeth, tongue inset but, like the rest of the orifice, hungry.

He could figure out this room and get the plan moving in another at the same time. His connection to Warren would make pulling him in easy, probably easier than Ollie because now Alex had a better handle on how to do it. What he didn't know was if he could pull in someone else from somewhere else. That part—

—that part would wait. Warren would be here in a moment if he wasn't here already, but now, from the corner of his eye, Alex saw something else, a higher priority, a distortion highlighted by the luminous grey that came from the faux chandelier in the vaulted ceiling. Another distortion wavered nearby. Alex understood: *they* had brought him to this room.

They were changing his plans. They wanted something.

"What?" Alex tried to catch a distortion with a direct look but couldn't. "What should I do?"

The house had a heartbeat, and Alex's ears filled with whispers. Walls pulsed.

Alex laughed. "Okay. If you want me to."

His blue button-up shirt had a pattern of black figures on it. You couldn't see what the figures were unless you got up close, but they were palm trees. It was Alex's first official California Shirt. He took it off, then kicked off his shoes and lowered his shorts and undershorts. After a pause, he slipped off his socks. "Okay," he said.

He listened. Trusting... beings... he knew and understood so little about seemed impossible, but at the same time, what he knew about them was that they helped him, and even if he didn't understand *them*, they seemed to understand *him*, and that was...

valuable.

He knew they made his house special. They always had, even before they'd announced themselves. They'd never asked him to do anything but what he wanted, but if they wanted him to do something now, why wouldn't he?

Why wouldn't he lie naked on his back on his house's version of his parents' bed? The idea of any version of his parents' bed grossed him out a little. The mouth on the bed, with its prickly teeth and needy tongue, grossed him out a little. He lay down anyway, and the chains attached to the posters were gentle as they knotted around his wrists and ankles, turning him into an X atop the broad bed.

He laughed. Lifting his head to look down the length of his exposed body and splayed legs, on both sides, two peripheries, boggling, almost headache-inducing, he saw the air ripple with distortions reminiscent of heat even though the room's air was cold, giving Alex tiny, perky nipples. He closed his eyes and relished a sensation that began at his toes and ran across his skin, from legs and thighs through his groin to his belly and chest and arms and along his neck and over his chin and across his cheeks and forehead, the dragging of soft velvet strips, tickling and teasing his nerve endings. He moaned.

"A reward?" he asked. The chains tugged at his wrists and ankles.

The invisible velvet kept up its work, finding its way beneath him as he found his way into the air, hovering, levitating above the bed. Soft, delectable texture rubbed his shoulders, the small of his back, his ass, and it focused on his cock, too, making him hard, making him eager for the roving texture to apply pressure, to grip and knead, to stroke with more purpose.

The chains pulled harder at his limbs. "What am I getting rewarded for?"

He moaned. He couldn't tell whether he stopped moaning.

"My parents? And Ollie? What? Oh!" The chains pulled harder. The muscles and skin around his shoulders and hips stretched as ball joints jiggled in their sockets. Alex clenched his teeth. "I deserve a reward for them?" The pain was delicious like the texture, or textures now, rubbing his skin, stroking his cock. Beneath him, the open mouth waited.

Half-moaning, half-speaking, Alex said, "Transform me?"

The pain became blinding. *Ready. Make me ready. Make me better.*

"Transform me," he whispered.

His skin and muscles, ligaments and tendons gave up. Arms detached from shoulders and legs from hips in bursts of blood. The chains, still knotted at the wrists and ankles, slackened, and Alex's limbs fell away from his floating body. He felt the rest of him falling, too, until a chain from nowhere wrapped around his neck and tightened, tightened, not sharp but tight enough to pierce flesh anyway, squeezing until his head detached. His head spun until he faced the bed, the open mouth, into which his limbs and torso plummeted, down into fleshy pink. His head fell. He saw pink, he saw grey, and he felt all his dismembered parts shivering in the delight of textures gliding over every cell, and his cock erupted. He came into the pink, falling, ecstatic, disarranged, rearranged, refit—

Bruce

"Um, Alex?" Bruce stood over the boy, who lay in the dirt beneath some branches at the edge of the park, too far away for anyone else to notice that his hand was firmly planted inside the front of his shorts. His eyes were open, but he looked like he was someplace else.

Alex didn't respond.

Bruce ducked so he could angle partway beneath the branches and give Alex's shoulder a shake. "Alex?" At least the boy didn't seem to be actively masturbating.

He blinked, sat up straight, and turned his head slowly. "Bruce? What are you doing here?"

Wearing tailored pants, Bruce didn't want to sit in the dirt, but doing so seemed strategic. He sat next to Alex. "Slow day at the office, so I thought I'd come home early and see how you're doing. I know you spend a lot of time here."

"I guess I do." Alex looked at his extended legs. He seemed disoriented but like he was trying to fight it.

Bruce gestured toward his bookbag. "I thought I'd find you reading."

"I am. Sometimes."

Bruce needed to be parental, but he didn't want to be presumptuous or intrusive, and finding the right tightrope to walk, much less walking it, was proving to be a challenge. "I... worry about you sitting here, alone. Not just alone, but... alone with your thoughts. I've always said I work long hours because when I slow down and think too much is when I get into trouble."

Alex stood and offered Bruce a hand up. "Wouldn't one

of the benches be more comfortable?" Bruce took the hand, and they moved to one of several available benches. Alex sat very close to him, but he supposed that was appropriate. "What kind of trouble are you worried I'll get into?" he asked.

reports of the boy being a "loner" whom one neighbor described as "antisocial"

"I don't mean *that* kind of trouble," Bruce said. "I mean I get myself screwed up. Psychologically."

"I talk to Dr. Schumer," Alex said.

"And those are your private conversations," Bruce said. He didn't want to devalue therapy, but he felt like he had to say: "But you can talk to me, too. And Aaron."

"What do you want me to talk about?"

"Anything. How you're adjusting to life here. Anything." Bruce looked back toward the spot where he'd found him. "What were you doing just now?" He dared a short laugh. "It was like you were having an out of body experience or something."

"You'll make fun of me," Alex said.

"I promise I won't." Bruce regretted his short laugh.

"I was having an out of body experience or something," Alex said, straight-faced, eyes earnest.

"Really? That's cool. Tell me about it." Bruce was serious. Open-minded. Understanding.

"You'll think I'm nuts!" Alex smiled.

"This is California, the land of fruits and nuts. We've all got fruity covered. Aaron and I are plenty nutty, too, as you'll see. So, you've got nothing to be afraid of."

"Okay, so, I taught myself meditation when I was still a little kid. I moved up to astral projection a few years ago. I… can leave my body and… go places. It's fun. It takes getting used to, but it's fun." Alex scanned Bruce, probably for disbelief, so Bruce did his best to show none.

"I've never known anyone who could do that," Bruce said. "It sounds awesome." He had to be careful. He wanted to connect with Alex, but he also wanted to take care of him, and the different goals meant different questions. Adult impulses prevailed. "Why do you come here to do it? Why not do it at the house?"

"I... my parents... never would have understood. The main reason I started doing it was... I was... never... I spent a lot of time alone, and I wasn't very happy. I think I got in the habit of keeping things from my parents." Alex looked away.

"Aaron and I aren't your parents." Did that sound wrong? "Not only are you allowed to date boys, but you can meditate, or astral project, or do any other, well, safe and reasonable thing under our roof that you want."

Alex laughed. "I'll do my best not to be *unsafe* or *unreasonable*." A more serious look washed over his face. "But you wanted to ask me about something else. Not about adjusting to life here, not exactly."

For a second, Bruce was stumped.

"You wanted to ask me about how I'm dealing with my parents. What happened."

Alex was right.

"I've thought about asking you," Bruce said, "but I don't want to push you if you're not ready."

"Dr. Schumer says there's no wrong way to feel," Alex said, "but I feel wrong."

"What do you mean?"

"It's like... what happened, and what I saw, are right behind me, following me, but I don't want to look back, because then I'd... have to feel."

One investigator did remark on the boy's "apparent lack of emotion."

Bruce stayed focused. "Sounds kind of like staying busy so you don't have to think."

"Maybe. But shouldn't I feel... more? I mean, there's sad, and angry, and scared, and a whole bunch of other stuff." Alex's list sounded perfunctory. "But it doesn't seem like enough."

"In a situation like this one," Bruce said, putting an arm around the boy, "I don't imagine anything ever seems like enough. Give yourself a break." He gave Alex a sideways hug and hoped he managed to exude paternal reassurance.

8. DEFINING BOUNDARIES

Bruce

Bruce's anxieties transformed into suspicions, and now his suspicions about Alex clouded his sympathy, and where Aaron was concerned, he let himself consider....

Aaron would have been the first to say that his obsession with capturing everything on camera reflected his voyeurism, but he believed contemporary culture turned everyone into a voyeur, and his filmmaking only made him more upfront about it than most. Still, Aaron's eyes were admittedly greedier than most, and lately, they couldn't get enough of Alex. Bruce's husband couldn't stop filming the kid, which meant he couldn't stop looking at him, and Bruce had tagged along to enough film festivals and parties populated by artists and academics to know he wasn't alone in finding something... lurid... in the camera's gaze.

At least there was when it lingered on the fourteen-year-old who was supposed to be *their son*. No one would deny that Alex was a good-looking boy, but "boy" was the key word, boy for whom Aaron shared responsibility, boy whom Aaron ought not to ogle.

But kids Alex's age broadcasted their entire lives on TikTok and YouTube, didn't they? Wasn't Bruce being paranoid? Perhaps bonding through video was the perfect way for Aaron to connect with Alex.

Yet... Bruce couldn't stop thinking about last night, and since it had been stuck in his head all day, he needed to talk to Aaron about it. They'd been on the sofa together, arms around each other's shoulders, streaming one of Bo Burnham's shows when Alex had passed through the living room on his way to the kitchen. Alex had gone to bed an hour before. Shuffling back among the living without a pause for greeting, on his way to fetch some milk from the fridge, not having put on anything other than the boxers he slept in—what Alex was doing seemed normal enough. Aaron, however, did not seem normal. As if switched on, he pulled away from Bruce, grabbed his handheld camera from the coffee table, and recorded the nearly naked, barely conscious boy's activity.

No, not normal.

"Aaron, would you join me in the bedroom?" Bruce spoke from the other side of the Elvis partition, behind which Aaron futzed with unknown footage.

From his seat at the kitchen table, where he sat with his Geometry book open, chewing on a pen, Alex said, "If you want some privacy, I can go to my room. Unless it's sex. You should go to your own room for that."

Aaron appeared from behind the partition. "What's up?"

Bruce turned to Alex. "It's not... don't worry about it. We'll be back in a few."

"Am I in trouble?" Aaron asked.

Bruce led to the bedroom without answering and closed the door behind them.

"Wow, the look on your face. I really am in trouble." Aaron sat next to him on the bedside.

"No," Bruce said. This whole thing was stupid. Overblown. *Unless it's sex.* "I've been... paranoid about something, being new dads, and with Child Services." He gave himself no points for being articulate. Why had Alex made the crack about sex? It made everything more difficult.

"Okay," Aaron said. "Since you're having trouble saying

it, it either has something to do with me, or you're afraid it will offend me, or both. Chill. It's okay. Say it."

Aaron was comforting him, and he was about to accuse him of—what was he accusing him of? "It's all the recording," Bruce said. "Of Alex. I worry that it might be inappropriate."

Aaron's facial expression drifted between sourness and sympathy. "Okay. Why?"

"Like last night," Bruce said. "He was mostly undressed. What if somebody... without the right context—"

Aaron laughed. "Jesus, you *are* paranoid. First of all, no context necessary. There's nothing wrong with a video of a teenager in his shorts. Otherwise, they'd have to ban smart phones at beaches, which would cause riots up and down the California coast."

Bruce faked a laugh.

"Second, the context—and it's weird, because I never thought about it this way until just now—is being a new parent. My mom and dad are practically Luddites, but they filmed an ungodly number of hours of me doing baby things while they oohed and aahed on the soundtrack as if they had Oscar bait. I know Alex isn't a baby... but don't you feel the urge? To chronicle... everything... now that it's all so fucking *new*?"

Bruce felt like a complete idiot.

Aaron

He kept up appearances of good cheer until Bruce was ready for bed, at which point he announced he felt restless and wanted to spend more time on his footage. With Bruce and Alex tucked away, he felt more comfortable getting the bottle of Redbreast Twelve-Year out of the cabinet and giving himself a generous pour.

Bruce had been careful with his words, but his questions about the "appropriateness" of filming Alex had implied a question that he hadn't been willing to admit. Aaron had heard it nonetheless.

Was Aaron getting off on filming a teenager in his underwear?

Bruce had a lot of nerve asking a question like that, echoing every piece of right-wing "they're coming for your children" propaganda that had once made adoption an impossibility for couples like them. To suggest that Aaron's documentarian interest in Alex was somehow... pedophilic... was absurd and offensive. Not that Bruce meant it that way. He was worried about appearances. Hence the blathering about Child Services. He was worried about the *appearance* of pedophilic interests. Playing into the bigots' hands. Right? He wasn't actually considering Aaron capable of... right?

Except, damn it, Aaron knew his husband, and he knew exactly what Bruce was considering.

But what did Bruce know, exactly?

Was Aaron getting off on filming a teenager in his underwear?

Things that were absurd and offensive could sometimes also be—

Alex came down the hall wearing boxers with a pattern of oranges on a white background. His skin, so much of it exposed, looked pale. They needed to spend more time at the beach. "Do you mind if I sit up with you, for a little?" the boy asked.

"Of course not," Aaron said. Why would he say no?

Alex sat in the reclining chair, facing Aaron on the sofa, and leaned back in the lamplight, smooth, bare chest and stomach visible above the waistline, thighs, knees, and calves visible beneath where the shorts cut off. His body called for the camera, but Aaron didn't know if taking video now would be... appropriate. He resented the second-guessing.

"Is that whiskey?" Alex gestured to the tumbler.

"Yeah," Aaron said. "I like what I like."

"Jameson?"

Aaron smiled. "No, but also Irish. Better. More expensive."

"I should have figured."

"How do you know Jameson?"

"My father liked it," the boy said.

Aaron could hardly fathom the implied comparison. "I'm not your dad. I don't think anyone should ever really call me 'Dad.'"

When Alex sat up in alarm, the visible muscles in his stomach tightened. "I didn't mean to say anything—"

"Relax." Aaron watched the boy's body sit back, softening. "I want to look after you. I care about you. But I'm too young to be anybody's dad."

"Well, *yeah*. Just because I noticed you drink whiskey like… better than… doesn't mean I think you're Dad the Sequel. Lots of people drink whiskey. If you poured me some, I'd drink whiskey."

"That's a definite negative from the non-dad who has parental responsibility," Aaron said, hoping he'd charm.

Alex grinned. "I didn't think so." After a pause, he shifted in his seat and said, "May I come sit next to you?"

Aaron thought of saying *no*. "Of course."

The boy sat next to him, bare right leg touching his left leg, bare upper body almost close enough for Aaron to feel Alex's heartbeat in his own chest. "You *are* too young to be my dad," Alex said.

Aaron cleared his throat. His head spun as his muscles rushed toward his spine. So much anger rose in response to Bruce's suggestion that he… but, on the other hand, he could…

"I've seen more of life than you." He tried to deliver his awkward reply with a smile, but he felt keenly aware that Alex was taller than he, and though his waist was narrower, his shoulders might have been broader than his, too.

"Did you know," Alex said, "that less than two hundred years ago, men your age married girls my age? And it was normal!"

go to bed," Aaron said. "You should, too."

Alex

Aaron didn't turn him on. *Fucking* with Aaron turned him on, and he was hard as a rock—Aaron had seen his hard-on almost breaking through the front of his boxers, and he'd come so close to touching it, Alex had twitched—not ready to say goodnight. Flustered, Aaron stood from the sofa, grabbed his glass of Irish whiskey, and stepped toward the hall.

He stopped, maybe realizing the hall led to his own bedroom, where all he could do was go to sleep by Bruce, and to Alex's bedroom, where his mind's current boogeyman awaited. He about-faced. "Alex, that wasn't okay."

Alex stood. He stared at the handheld camera on the coffee table until he saw Aaron glance at it. Then he made Aaron look into his eyes. "I want you to film me." His cock strained against his underwear's elastic waistline.

"I'm sorry... if I sent the wrong signals." Aaron was a bad liar.

"It's okay." Alex stepped closer to the idle camera. "Nothing happened." He picked up the camera, found the right grip, and pressed the right buttons. Aaron appeared on the viewfinder. Alex recorded.

"Alex, don't." Aaron gulped his whiskey. "We should talk about this. Off-camera."

"Nothing happens if it isn't on video." Alex found the zoom and got closer to Aaron's face, the quivering creases that were temporary now but would turn into worry lines when he was older. "Document everything."

"Do you believe that?" Aaron asked. He finished his whiskey, fetched the bottle, poured, and gulped.

"I believe—" Alex flipped the camera on himself, holding the lens at maximum distance from his face, at an angle as if Aaron were shooting—"I need a shower."

"You need to quit playing and go back to bed." Aaron stepped forward, gulped, and gestured with his free hand for Alex to give him the camera.

The camera began a slow descent over Alex's lips, chin, neck, torso...

"Stop it," Aaron said, free hand close to grabbing the camera—but stopping short. His eyes danced between the camera and what the camera was recording.

The lens captured Alex's flat stomach, and as it moved down, he secured the grip in one hand, and he used the other hand to stretch his underwear's elastic waistband. Aaron didn't stop him from pulling the camera close so the lens could capture what his boxers barely hid.

"I'll delete that," Aaron said.

"Yeah, and you'll delete the movie you'll make for me, after you give me a copy." Alex pulled the camera back out, stretching his arm to where he thought the lens might capture Aaron and him together.

"What movie is that?"

Alex offered him the camera. With an unsteady hand, he took it. When he looked in the viewfinder and, instead of shutting it, framed a shot, Alex felt the rare delight of an uncontrollable smile. "The movie you'll make of me taking a shower," Alex said.

"Why would I make a movie of you—"

"Because I want one. I need to know... if I look okay." Alex gained control, and the smile dissolved. "Around here, you need to look good. I need to believe in myself. I need you to believe in me."

"But... recording...." Aaron grunted and finished his drink. "There's a name for that, you know? Kiddie porn. I'm not making a porno of you taking a shower."

Certain the camera would get the naughty bits, Alex slid his underwear to his ankles. He counted: one, two, three, four, five, six, seven—Aaron finally ended the shot.

"Jesus, Alex, put your clothes back on!" Aaron tried to

avert his eyes with mixed success.

On his way to the hall, Alex dragged his naked body along Aaron's stunned, still, clothed figure, which held the camera at his side and followed Alex's movement with a head swivel. "Follow me to the shower," Alex said. "Help me set up the camera so there's a shot framed that'll get the whole shower. Then go. You won't be making kiddie porn. *I* will."

A long moment passed, but Alex was patient. Finally, Aaron raised the camera, filming, and followed him to the bathroom. As requested, the man helped set up the camera and frame the shot. He turned to go.

"Wait," Alex said. "A kiss goodnight?"

Aaron turned back. He looked... defeated. Alex had an intuition, one he considered quite precocious, that he hadn't been the one to defeat the man. He had merely helped the man to defeat himself. He let that insight warm his lips as he pressed them against Aaron's. No part, no wetness, no tongue. Innocent press and pucker, if you ignored that Alex was naked, his body a hand's width from his guardian's. At least he'd lost his erection before the kiss.

"Goodnight." Then Aaron was gone.

Alex adjusted the showerhead so that it wouldn't flood the bathroom floor when he used it while the curtain was pulled back to keep the camera's view clear. He shampooed his head quickly, then saturated the loofah with body wash and lathered his body. Conscious of where he estimated the center of the frame to be, he moved the sponge slowly around his curves, exaggerating each movement, not washing but performing. What would the Theatre kids think of such a performance? How many of them would end up doing porn?

The thought of Warren in a gangbang made his penis perk up, so he stroked it with the loofah. He hadn't been sure he would masturbate for the camera, but he decided he would. Aaron would probably come to his senses and not hand over the footage. But the real question was... would he watch it before he deleted it? Imagining Aaron watching the video made him harder. He stroked himself faster.

Would Aaron jerk off watching the video?

Alex came, thinking about Aaron watching him come.

Fucking with Aaron made him so happy. So many things about his new life made him so happy. He'd never dreamed he could have so many good things.

9. THIRD ESCAPE

Warren

He stood at the bathroom sink, watching his reflection as he brushed his teeth, when he saw the flash from the corner of his eye. In the mirror it was a glare, but his brain registered static electricity, a blue bolt from nowhere, to nowhere, maybe a trick of the light—

except it happened again, a fork of lightning, near his bare side, and he had a funny feeling.

It reminded him of smoking that tainted weed with Melinda, Janie, and Theo, of that awful daydream or hallucination or whatever it had been. Sensations in his stomach. Queasiness. Tension. Tickling along his skin.

Warren looked in the mirror—he was ready for bed, wearing only pajama pants—and set his toothbrush beside the sink. Blinking, he looked into his reflection's eyes. His stomach told him someone else saw.

Behind him, the bathroom door was closed. Nobody else was in the room, but collecting atop the tiled floor, mist, or fog, had appeared without cause, and Warren recognized it. He looked back to the mirror. His reflection stood in that hallway with the red walls and the dead things. In the mirror, the hallway stretched behind him, grisly displays on both sides.

He'd been brushing his teeth, hadn't he? Or had he already been in bed, which meant he could be dreaming?

He didn't want to turn around, but he did, and he wasn't surprised to see the red hall, and when he did a quick spin, naturally, the mirror was gone. The house he'd escaped, fog along the grungy carpet that pushed up between his bare toes, dead things on the walls, had enveloped him.

The hall was looooooooooonger than he remembered. It seemed to lengthen as he watched, blurring, a drunken feeling, and the house groaned as it stretched. Warren's careful steps followed the direction of expansion, and the growth slowed. The slaughtered animals, hacked to pieces, partially skinned, muscles displayed, organs displayed, became more diverse, wilder. What might have been a hyena had its brain exposed. Where would such a beast...?

In a dream, dipshit.

The hall ended with a closed door, and it didn't seem to be fleeing. Light came through the cracks around the doorframe. He didn't want to look behind him again, where the hall only got darker and darker. Dream or not, this place was scary.

He looked anyway when he heard a girl scream.

The dimmer greylight where she stood with bent knees and hunched shoulders made her features difficult to make out, but she had long black hair, brown skin, and impressive tits that she covered with folded arms.

"W-where—" She looked at him looking at her. "Warren? Is that you?"

Recognition clicked. Anna *fucking* Cortez, in panties, no bra, just as gorgeous as—

Her posture straightened, but she didn't stop covering her tits. "Warren? What the fuck! Did you bring me here? Did you roofie me or something? WHAT THE FUCKING FUCK?"

Stepping toward her, reaching toward her, intending to comfort her, he said, "No, I—"

"Don't you fucking touch me!" She backed away, stirring the fog with bare feet. "I'll bite off your fucking hand if you touch me!"

"No, I...." Warren kept a respectful distance and tried to look at her face. "I just showed up here. I guess you did, too?"

Anna looked down at her nearly naked body. Anna fucking Cortez. In a hallway surrounded by dead things. They weren't far from the place on the wall with the human face torn from its skull and nailed above other strips of skin. "I was going to bed," she said. "Maybe you, too?"

"I thought I was dreaming."

She looked at the walls. "You dream some fucked up shit."

"It's not like I—" He sighed. He'd dreamt about Anna before, but she hadn't been such a bitch. Seeing her naked, or almost, lived up to every fantasy, though. He'd heard of erotic nightmares, but this, whatever *this* was, went beyond everything. "I was going to that door." He gestured to the door with the light behind it.

"You think it's the way out?"

He knew it wasn't, so he wasn't sure why he was going, except the light made going seem sensible. "Maybe," he said.

"Okay," Anna said, nodding, not letting her arms budge from protective duty. "Lead the way."

He could sense her behind him but didn't know if she'd lowered her arms. A sneak peek back wouldn't be *too* awful. He'd kill to see what she'd been covering. Goosebumps stood out on his arms. *His* nipples were hard, which meant *hers* were probably hard, and he wanted to see that. The idea of it registered in his loose flannel pajama pants. Getting hard when surrounded by animal guts, people guts. *Fucked up shit.* She got that right.

"You opening the door or what?" The question struck him as bitchy.

If the hallway hadn't changed too much, they could turn around and run the other way. Eventually, there'd be a turn to the left and stairs and a way out. If things were the same, but he knew they weren't the same, and he was turning the doorknob to open the way he hadn't gone before.

The door opened, and he let it swing wide on its own. Anna appeared at his side, her arms folded over her tits. For the moment, the room he'd opened deserved more attention.

Dingy, foggy carpet continued into the room, but the walls were black, at distances difficult to discern in the greylight that still seemed to come from nowhere. Rows—aisles—of human shapes, some in clothes, some without, filled the room. At first Warren thought they'd found a room of corpses, but in a split second he recognized mannequins and dolls, the former missing arms, legs, and many other features, the latter a mix of porcelain and plastic, chubby cheeks, glass eyes. Most of the dolls were doll-sized, held up on stands like his great-grandmother used for the prizes in the collection she'd amassed since she'd been a little girl a million years ago, but some of them were... too big... like children on thick spikes.

At least the dolls looked like dolls. The mannequins had human proportions. Most of their blank faces, male as well as female, had make-up without eyes, noses, and mouths to make up. Warren wandered into the aisles before he knew what he was doing.

The mannequins without clothes—or maybe all of them—had genitals. No hair, but the males had penises, scrotums, the females, mons, labia, openings. Most of their skin looked fake and unyielding, but the areas between their legs looked soft, supple, real, or real enough.

Fucked up shit.

"Who the hell is that?" Anna asked. She stood close enough to his side to cling to him, but her hands and arms were too busy covering her tits. Warren's eyes moved from a mannequin's pussy to Anna's panties to the corner of the room she indicated, where a desk with its own light, a yellow light, sat, and someone sat at it, a laptop computer open in front of him.

As the guy at the desk turned, Warren recognized him: Alex, from that day at the theatre. The guy he'd thought was his stalker. The guy he'd thought was bad news.

The door where they'd entered slammed shut. Anna

yelped and jumped. Her body jiggled, but her arms didn't budge from protective duty. She and Warren focused on Alex.

"Warren," Alex said. "Glad you made it."

"You *know* this guy?" Anna sounded like she was accusing him.

"What are you—" Warren began, "what are *we* doing here?"

"Beats me," Alex said. "It's your dream, man. We should be doing whatever you want to do." He got up from the desk chair and took a silver roll out of a drawer. Duct tape.

"What's he talking about?" Anna said. Her attention shifted between him and Alex with nervous bounces.

"The question to ask," Alex said, "is what's *she* doing here?"

Anna looked at Warren imploringly. If they were all in Warren's dream, then Warren was in charge. That's why she looked at him that way. He was in charge. "No," Warren said. "I know why I'd dream about *her*. Why the fuck would I dream about you and all this... other shit?"

"I'm a figment of your imagination," Alex said, "and so is she, and so is... all this other shit. But I know I'm not wrong to say she's the main attraction, am I? The shit and I must be here to help you with her." Alex came closer.

Anna stepped back. "I'm not a figment of anybody's fucking imagination!" She was still imploring. "I can't explain it, Warren, but you're not dreaming! This is... happening...."

Staring at a mannequin in disbelief, she didn't see Alex coming. He lunged at her, pulled her arms away from her tits and twisted them around her back. Warren heard the screech of duct tape unrolling as Anna screamed. Her tits were magnificent as she struggled, the areolas browner than her skin, the nipples as perky as he'd imagined. As Alex secured her arms behind her back, taping her wrists together, her tits stuck out even more, and nothing he'd seen on the internet, no girl he'd ever gotten to take her bra off for him, equaled the sight. She kicked into the air; Alex must have had a hold of her because she flew instead of falling, smooth legs swimming in space as, undaunted by gravity. Alex dropped to his knees and with effort grabbed her ankles. This time she did fall. Warren hopped back as her front collapsed into the fog with a thud that shook the house. She was screaming. All this time she had been screaming. More tape screeched as Alex bound her ankles.

"What...?" Warren said as Alex got Anna back to her feet. She cried more, screamed less, and couldn't stand without Alex's help. Sweat on Alex's brow, glistening in the greylight, attested to his efforts.

"Help me with her," Alex said.

"Help me," she echoed, sobbing.

"Help me help you," Alex said.

"Help me what?" Warren said.

"Have a perfect day in dreamland," Alex answered.

Warren stepped toward Anna.

"Don't you dare." Anna locked her dark eyes on his.

Alex duct taped her mouth shut. Her eyes kept the lock. Alex held one of her shoulders and proffered the other.

Warren took the other shoulder, and gripping her by the shaved armpits, they half-walked, half-dragged her around the aisles of mannequins and dolls until they reached an unoccupied, human-sized doll stand. With Alex directing, they pushed her back against the stand.

"Keep her steady," Alex said, and circled to the stand's rear, leaving Warren at the front to hold her up and look at her imploring eyes.

My dream, he thought. *I must like this.*

Alex taped Anna's neck and midsection to the stand. Producing a knife from nowhere, a scary-looking blade, probably for hunting, he cut the tape around her ankles and resecured her legs to the stand so that they spread.

All the violent, crazy shit in the house. Primal. Some side of his manhood Warren was only just getting to know... primal and ugly, but okay in a dream. Purged in a dream.

Alex came to Anna's front and cut off her panties,

yanking them from the squeezed gap between her ass and the giant doll stand. "She's ready," Alex said. "Judging from the bulge in your flannel, you are, too. You can fuck her, fuck a mannequin, I don't know. I did my job. The goes however you want to dream it."

Warren understood. This was a *rape* fantasy. Common enough. Maybe not "woke" to talk about, but when you're dreaming, you don't have to be woke. Dreams didn't hurt anybody. But this dream, Anna's tits out, Anna's pussy out, Anna's mouth taped shut—this dream could feel really, really good.

Alex

When most people got pulled into his house, they thought they were dreaming, which got Alex thinking. What could he get someone to do if he thought he was dreaming and therefore acting without consequences? The experiment required him to pull in two people from different places, which *they* made sure he was ready to do. They also turned on the fog and hallway effects and did things with the mannequins Alex found admirably unquestionable. His house became dreamier, and Warren didn't take much more convincing. The outcome of the experiment began to unfold.

"Are you… going to watch?" Warren asked.

"You must want me to be here," Alex said. "You're an actor. An exhibitionist."

"Huh." Warren untied the drawstring on the waist of his flannel pajama pants and, after glances at Alex and Anna, pushed the pants to the foggy floor. His erection, not huge but not bad, bobbed up and down from contact with the pants, and he aimed it at Anna, who squealed under the tape. "Shh," he said. "Shh."

Alex felt Aaron's influence as he wished for a camera, the ability to zoom in and out as well as to keep the moment and share it.

The volume of the squeals was impressive, but it didn't make Warren go limp. With one hand he spread Anna's lips, and with the other, he guided himself inside. Alex had to bend his knees and contort his upper body to observe the penetration, and Warren continued as if unaware, sliding in as far as he could, making his midsection an arc into her restricted body, making the squeals become deeper, more like groans, and sliding out.

As he slid in and out again, he moved his hands to her breasts, squeezing them. His thumbs teased her nipples. She squirmed. Alex hoped Warren confused the movement with pleasure. Confused or not, Warren got lost in fucking the girl he kissed during the school play. His thrusts became faster, and despite the uncomfortable angle to her entry point on the doll stand, he pushed himself deeper. "Harder," Alex whispered.

Anna's sounds beneath the duct tape became rhythmic, pumped out of her as he pumped into her, muted coughs and gasps, grunts, snorts to get air past the tears and snot covering her face and into her nostrils. She wound down as Warren wound up. Alex didn't need to say "harder" again. Warren pounded so hard that each thrust had to hurt. Blood dripped down Anna's thigh. It was a dream, right? Who cares, right?

Warren's barbaric shout as he pushed into her, slamming his pelvis into hers, ejaculating what Alex imagined as a river, was a beautiful sound, like the climax of a symphony for people who liked that kind of shit. Every muscle in the boy's body tensed. Alex had time to consider that Warren might very well get sucked inside Anna's vagina, but then Warren's muscles loosened, and he staggered away from the doll stand, cock slipping out of the used, bleeding cunt, feet struggling for balance.

"Bravo," Alex said. "Bravo." He didn't clap because the knife and duct tape were still in his hands. He dropped the duct tape. "Tell me that wasn't the best orgasm of your whole young life."

"I...." Warren looked dizzy.

Anna's head lolled. She sniffled. The bleeding between her legs wasn't light. "I think you tore something," Alex said. He approached the doll stand.

"What did I do?" Warren wasn't as attractive naked, dick covered with blood, as Alex might have guessed. Complexion draining, Warren gripped his stomach. "Why didn't I wake up?"

"Answer to question one. What you did was..." he ripped the tape from Anna's lips, taking skin, "you raped your co-star, Anna Cortez."

The girl held up her head and shook some of the hair away from her eyes. She glared at Warren.

"No," Warren whimpered. "This is a dream, and I always wake up when I come."

Her voice was weak but fully audible: "It's not a dream, asshole."

"I didn't take off the tape for you to get sassy, young lady," Alex said. With the Deerslayer, he sliced the breadth of her chest, above the breasts.

"Don't hurt her!" Warren cowered as he said it.

"A little late on that one." Alex smiled.

Warren dropped to the carpet ass-first and went close to fetal. "I want to wake up." He had tears in his voice.

"Here," Alex said, and he cut into Anna's left breast. He figured the cut would be easy since the breast was mostly fat, but it took a lot of strength and a little bit of sawing with the blade, as well as some maneuvering to avoid bone, to cut the breast off. The tape had come off so that Anna could scream, and she did. She screamed and fought against the tape that held her to the doll stand, and she bled like he'd cut something important. The severed breast fell into his left hand, and he tossed it to Warren, who caught it, probably by instinct. When he saw what he held, he dropped it and screamed.

Anna babbled about being sorry she was bad and begged

someone not to let her die. She might have been talking to God. Alex couldn't tell and didn't care. He decided he wanted to cut off her right tit.

"Stop!" Warren yelled, blubbering almost as much as his new girlfriend.

Alex carved.

"Stop!" Warren got up, hands and some of his chest splashed with tit blood, cock coated in cunt blood. The dirty boy came at Alex, making fists.

Alex yanked the knife from Anna and stabbed Warren in the stomach, twisting the blade. "That hurts, doesn't it?"

Warren backed off the blade, clutched his wound, doubled over, and puked a viscous mixture of red and brown. For the moment, he was handled.

Alex finished his double mastectomy. What was Anna, sixteen? Such a tragedy. Her mouth kept up the litany of sorries and don't-let-me-dies. She didn't respond to the latest mutilation, probably shock. He slipped the blade between her legs, between her labia. He thought of his mother. Instead of going inside, he merely pulled the blade upward, expanding the slit toward her navel, such tender skin, so little fat in her belly, a wide sideways smile.

After a quick survey of all the mannequins, whose number *they* had multiplied and whose naughty parts *they* had supplied, Alex turned to Warren, who was still on his feet, clutching his stabbed stomach, weeping over the possibility that he wasn't dreaming and was therefore a rapist. "Poor, pathetic idiot," Alex said, approaching.

Warren held a hand, palm out, in his direction. "Don't," he said.

Alex rammed the knife through Warren's palm, winning a scream. He pulled the knife out and grabbed the hand before it fell. Pulling Warren closer, he slit Warren's wrist horizontally once, twice, again, and then let him go. Warren stumbled back and fell to the carpet on his side.

Alex knelt beside him. "I had higher expectations for

you." He pressed his lips to Warren's ear. "Rapist. Killer."

"I never," Warren said.

Alex made deep slices from the side of Warren's knee up to his hip, pushing deep into muscle. Each time, Warren cried out, but he barely moved. Striping him red, Alex continued with cuts along the ribs, to the shoulder, finally reaching the neck. "Should I put you out of your misery?"

"I never," Warren said.

Alex cut what he thought was the carotid, stood, and stepped back to watch the happy couple bleed to death.

10. SET UP

Rory

He and Mike sat at the corner of one of the big high tables with sinks in them, in Ms. Pendergast's Chemistry classroom, chessboard between them, Rory black, Mike white, an irony they both appreciated, even though Mike didn't identify as Black in the strictest sense. Mike had Rory on the run and would declare checkmate in three moves. Rory usually won, but today he felt distracted. He stared at the board, hoping to find a way to avert disaster that he had missed.

"It's got to be a trick," Mike said. "Nobody passes notes in real life anyway. Seems like she would, like, message you or something. Social media?"

Ms. Pendergast sponsored the Chess Club. The club didn't meet on Fridays, but she didn't mind if Rory and Mike hung out for a while after school and played a game or two as long as they got out of the way when the janitors came. Mike had a car and could drive them home whenever they wanted. He was seeing Sheri tonight, so he and Rory needed this time to talk about the present conundrum, which they would resolve, through action or inaction, at noon tomorrow. Planning seemed prerequisite for an optimal outcome. "We're not connected on social media, and she might not want to advertise," Rory said. "There's probably no way she could get my phone number to text." Rory moved his remaining knight.

Mike took the knight with a bishop. "Check." He leaned back, not really looking at the board. He knew he had already won. "The situation is fishy, my friend. A girl who wears black fishnet stockings and black miniskirts that barely cover her ass doesn't reach out to guys like us."

Esme Alvarez, with her retro-90s, perfectly accessorized goth look and perfectly shaped ass, had never shown an interest in Rory before, even though he'd been drooling over her since the sixth grade. She had this nihilistic attitude and pretended not to care about school, but he knew she could be in the Honors Society if she wanted. One of her disaffected accessories was a copy of *Thus Spoke Zarathustra*, which Rory had actually seen her reading, and if her brain could digest Nietzsche, her brain was sexy, too. "Maybe she's not so predictable." Rory took Mike's bishop with his remaining rook.

Mike took Rory's rook with his own remaining rook. "Why is it so important for me to show up? Check."

"Because she'll bring Kayla," Rory said, searching for any move on the board other than the one that appeared to be his last. Kayla Mason was pretty, too, but not as pretty as Esme. Kayla dyed her hair to make it as black as Esme's, and she didn't have to pile on as much white face paint to give her skin that corpse glow. Kayla's boobs were bigger, accentuated by the tight black bodice thingy she laced tightly up from her navel to her cleavage, but Esme's curves were more... svelte. Rory couldn't say why exactly she gave him such a boner. He gave up his search and took Mike's rook with his queen.

Mike's queen swept Rory's from the board. "Checkmate." Mike sighed. "So, if it's a date, it's a double date, you and Esme, me and Kayla."

The hard part, the part that might make Mike say no. "I guess." Rory shrugged.

"Do you think they know I have a girlfriend?"

"Anyone who knows you exist knows you have a girlfriend," Rory said. "It's not like you'd be cheating. We'll just talk, I'm sure. But it's my chance to... convince Esme to see me, just the two of us."

"Why the Pit, you think?" Mike sounded more serious. The Pit was a place behind the school, pretty much what it sounded like, a hole in the ground filled with rocks. After a kid cracked his skull open back there, getting high and horsing around with some other kids, it became off limits, grounds for suspension or worse for anyone who trespassed. Kids stopped going because cops supposedly patrolled it, but Rory didn't think so. The Pit was—

"It's private," Rory said.

"Too private," Mike said.

"Why do you say that?"

"The note is typed," Mike said. "Untraceable."

Rory snickered. "You want to do handwriting analysis?"

"Did it occur to you that it might not be from Esme at all?"

Yes, it had. "Then why was Esme staring at me in Algebra 2 today, right after I got the note?"

"Coincidence?"

"Big coincidence," Rory said.

"Some guys might want to beat the shit out of us, leave us there where nobody will find us...."

"You're paranoid," Rory said.

"You're willing to show up someplace dangerous because an anonymous piece of paper told you to." Mike had the same look on his face as when he said "checkmate."

Rory had *not* been outplayed. "It *isn't* anonymous. It's signed by—"

"Yeah, yeah, yeah."

"Will you do it? Pick me up a little before noon, come with me to—"

"Call me in the morning. I'll decide then." Mike started picking up the chess pieces.

"You're going to make me wait until *morning* to find out if I get to spend real time with the girl of my dreams?" Rory intended to sound super-whiny.

"That's right, bugeyes. Now help me put this away, and

let's get going."

Bruce

It sat in the center of the king-sized bed, which was odd.

Saturday morning. Aaron had left early to go out to West Hollywood for interviews with some business owners and other locals to add to his growing archive related to his untitled documentary on queer culture post-COVID, and as far as Bruce knew, Alex hadn't yet stepped out of his room. Juggling equipment while he got his *better* camera kit out of the closet, Aaron might have tossed the handheld, the very *expensive* handheld that was supposed to be broadcast quality, on the bed, and forgotten about it, so there it sat, centered, conspicuous.

Bruce didn't mess with Aaron's movie stuff. It was an unspoken understanding.

Aaron eventually shared his work. Not all his footage— the ratio of what he shot to what he used was hours to minutes —but the important stuff.

But Bruce was curious. Not suspicious, curious.

Bruce was lying to himself.

The camera—on the bed, unguarded—had a monitor for playback. Anything still on the memory cards he could watch by picking the thing up and pressing a few buttons, and he was reasonably confident he could figure out which buttons to push. Rewind. Funny how the language of film, tape, dominated the digital. Alex had probably never even seen a VCR.

Bruce sat on the bed's edge. A scoot back brought him within a stretched arm's reach of the camera. If Aaron had nothing to hide, why would he mind? Bruce didn't have anything he considered to be off limits for Aaron. Unspoken understanding? Probably all in Bruce's head.

He picked up the camera and opened its folded parts.

The monitor, the buttons, the mode for reviewing what was on the memory cards: they were all self-explanatory. Rewind.

You shouldn't be doing this.

But he *was* doing it.

His chest imploded as he immediately found justification.

Pausing the high-definition image, Bruce looked away. Seeing it made *him* feel guilty. Most parents, and he was a parent, see their kids naked at some point, but not at fourteen, unless by accident, and this wasn't an accident. What Bruce was doing wasn't an accident. Maybe Alex had taken the camera by himself, used it by himself, recorded himself by himself? But that had to be wishful thinking. Bruce had to work up the nerve even to touch Aaron's expensive camera, so Alex wouldn't... would he?

Alex was in the shower. Naked. Of course he was naked; the water was running. The water was running, but the curtain was open. Which was why the camera could see him, why Bruce could see him, why Aaron.... Alex had to know, though. Otherwise, the curtain would be closed. The boy knew he was being watched. Recorded. He was *in on it.*

Colluding. Alex and Aaron were in on it... *together.*

But if Aaron asked Alex, or told him, to let him record him in the shower, could the boy say no? Aaron was his guardian. Even *asking* a CHILD a thing like that would be coercion.

Bruce looked back at the paused, clear, perfectly framed image. Alex couldn't have done that on his own. Aaron was filming. Aaron was filming, digitally videoing, an underage boy, *their* underage boy, taking a shower. If Bruce pressed play, he'd be watching kiddie porn his husband had made with their adopted son.

How bad would it get?

Bruce pressed play. He tried to keep the image in his periphery as Alex soaped himself, but as the boy started to masturbate, the image captured both eyes. It got bad. The boy's expression seemed blissful.

The camera didn't move, didn't track, didn't zoom in or out. Static images might work for an interview, but for anything other than a talking head, Bruce would expect Aaron to add style. Maybe Aaron wasn't behind the camera.

When Alex finished, he got out of the shower, dried off slowly, walked to the camera, held the lens close to his face, and said, "I hope you enjoyed that." He kissed the lens, and the image went dark.

Aaron *hadn't* been behind the camera. Had Aaron instigated... or had Alex, on his own...?

One investigator did remark on the boy's "apparent lack of emotion."

How much trouble were they in?

What *kind* of trouble were they in?

Bruce's shaky fingers turned off the camera and fumbled until he managed to return it to its closed, compact form. His heart raced. His palms sweat. Trying to remember the exact position, he placed the camera back on the center of the bed. But he'd have to confront Aaron. Have to find out if he'd seen the video. Or had a part in making it. But could he trust Aaron? What if Aaron was—

What if Aaron was fucking Alex?

When he kissed the camera lens, Alex didn't look like a victim. But statutory rape was statutory rape for a reason. Bruce didn't know the age of consent in California, but in a situation tantamount to incest, kiss or no kiss, Alex would look like a victim in the eyes of the law.

One investigator....

Tears welled, preparing to fall. Bruce didn't think he could feel more upset until an older question reappeared in his mind.

Why had his psycho-bitch sister left Alex to him and Aaron in her will?

Alex

Being in the park under his branches would have been better, but this time he planned a long game, and he might have to go in and out to placate Aaron and Bruce—especially Bruce, who must have seen by now—so he would stay home, in a half-lotus on the bed. When and if he worked up the courage for a confrontation, Bruce might interrupt him, shake him out of his trance. Fine. Expected.

It wasn't like the people he brought to his house could escape.

Well, Warren had escaped. The first time. But only because *they* had had other priorities. Alex grasped now that they had an undeniably sexual essence, that some of his own power when he visited his house came from sex. Their ideas about sex were a bit... contorted... but hot nonetheless. Sex and violence, violence and sex. In middle school he'd had a gender-segregated sex ed class, and the teacher, Mr. Skillern, had started a "frank discussion" with the boys about "sex and violence in the media." About how the media make sex and violence *seem* to go together, but in reality, they don't, because sex in reality is gentle and kind. It was more of a lecture than a discussion because the boys snorted and squirmed and looked at each other but didn't want to say anything.

Alex wondered what "reality" Mr. Skillern lived "in." Alex had seen nature shows. Lionfucking. You couldn't tell him it wasn't violent. You couldn't tell him they didn't like it on both sides. Gender irrelevant.

They liked raw sexual energy of the young and inexperienced. Maybe they were like Aaron that way. Kayla and Esme were skanks. Probably gave it up before they got their periods. But Rory and Mike were probably virgins. Technically, depending on how you thought about it, Alex was a virgin. In actuality, his dick had entered no holes, and no dicks had entered him. In his house, he'd had Ollie... there'd been the thing with the dog... but kind of like Warren with Anna, it had felt like a dream.

Not that it had been a dream with Warren and Anna. He laughed.

They liked the energy of sex and violence, so Alex sat on his bed in only his shorts, would go to his house in only his shorts, would feel the blood splash his skin in only his shorts.

Concentrate!

Shifting Warren and Anna from different places to the same hall in his house had worked beautifully, but getting it done had felt like having a vacuum cleaner break through his ribcage and switch on maximum suck. A time difference had resulted, too. Alex had wanted them to appear together, but Warren had gotten there first. A bigger time difference might have led to them getting lost in different parts of the house, a delay that could have thrown off that whole game.

Therefore, Kayla, Esme, Rory, and Mike all had to come from the same place. Shifting them as a group would make them arrive as a group. It would dampen the chest-sucking effect so that he'd have the energy for playing a long time. In theory, at least.

Rory

The first time he called Mike, the call went to voicemail. "Mike, it's Rory. Call me back. You know why." He immediately texted: "You coming?"

No reply. Five minutes. Ten. If Mike left his house now, they wouldn't be there by noon. Shit!

Rory called again. No answer. He texted again. "CALL ME!"

A reply came: "I'm in your driveway, bugeyes."

"Bugeyes" was more a mark of friendship than a tease, had been for years, but Rory groaned anyway as he shoved his phone in his pocket, pushed his glasses up his nose, and ran for the front door.

On the short drive to the school, Mike asked, "What do you think's going to happen? You and Esme will see each other across a field of rocks, then run into each other's arms...."

"I said yesterday, we'll all... talk or something."

"This is some weird shit," Mike said.

Rory didn't have a good response. Mike was right. But he didn't feel like they could *not* show up.

They showed up, and a little after twelve, the girls did, too, Esme in her signature fishnets and Kayla bursting out of her bodice. They'd probably make fun of Rory and Mike for doing cosplay at Comic-Con, but what they did was pretty much the same thing.

"You *must* be joking," Kayla said. "These guys?"

"I don't know anyone *else* who says they're holding," Esme said.

The girls stood fairly close, balancing their pointy heeled shoes on the Pit's sizeable rocks. They had little purses. Rory meant to say hello but fidgeted with his glasses and smiled with half his mouth instead.

"Hi, ladies," Mike said with a grin that, even with braces, had more suavity than his by a factor of infinity. He offered a handshake. "You're Esme," he said with a nod, "so you must be Kayla?"

"Get real," Kayla said. "Handshakes are pre-pandemic."

"Pardon me," Mike said, lowering his hand.

Awkward one, awkward two, awkward three—Esme was *so* beautiful.

"Look," she said with her beautiful mouth, lips painted black, "we're not here to make friends, okay?" She unzipped her purse and grabbed a wad of bills. "How many does this get us?" The bills were twenties. She was offering them to Rory.

"W-w-w—" Rory said.

"You *did* bring our friend with you, right?" Esme said.

Kayla cocked her head to one side and smirked at Mike.

"Esme is very business minded."

"Who are you talking about? What friend?" Mike asked.

From the corner of his eye, Rory thought he saw a spark.

Esme got closer to him. A spark, a blue spark, turned into a bolt behind her. "You're the one who wrote to me, remember?" Again, she addressed him, money still in hand. "Our *mutual* friend, Molly?"

A blue bolt zapped beside Kayla, who flinched and said, "What the fuck?"

"Molly is MDMA," Mike said. "They think we're here to sell them drugs."

"Duh?" Esme's glance might have cut a foot from Mike's height.

"Somebody's fucking with us," Mike said.

"Did you guys see—oh!" Kayla tried to jump back from the spark that flared at the center of the loose circle they made, but her heel caught on a rock, and she landed hard on her ass. "OW!"

Little bolts of lightning surrounded them. "What the hell is going on? I don't like this," Esme said as if it were Rory's fault.

"I don't know." *Now* Rory could speak.

The light around them got dimmer as the bolts got brighter. "Esme." Kayla worked a lot of whine into the name's two syllables.

Esme looked at her friend on the ground but didn't offer a hand. Her gaze bounced among the sparks, the zaps making her twitch, the zaps making them all twitch. The Pit got darker, fading. For a moment, the lightning was the only light. Rory didn't know what was going on, but he forgot about Esme, forgot about everything but *trouble* and *wrong*, trouble and wrong and where the hell—

a sofa, but dirt on the ground, grass on the ground, a recliner, a rocker, a TV, all surrounded by trees. The four of them were in a living room where trees grew. Kayla got to her feet but stood further from the rest of them.

"What the FUCK DID YOU DO?" Esme demanded.

Rory looked at the ground. "I didn't...."

"Oh, wow," Kayla said.

"Seriously fucking with us," Mike said.

"This is probably some, like, experiment, right?" Esme looked from Rory to Mike to Rory again. "You drugged us?"

"You were the one talking about drugs," Mike said.

"Seriously goddamn wow," Kayla said. She drifted from the rest of them.

"You think *I* did this?" Esme sounded outraged.

"You seriously think *we* did this?" Mike sounded like he'd be amused if he weren't trying hard not to freak out.

"No." Esme looked surprised at herself for saying it. "Rory, you're the smartest kid in class. Do you have *any* idea—"

"You guys?" Kayla said.

"I have no idea," Rory said, and he looked in Kayla's direction.

And he puked up his frozen waffle breakfast.

He didn't recognize the woman hanging from the tree branch wearing the tatters of pajamas. Details of what drooped from her middle, large intestine, small intestine, stomach, he could recognize, but the colors looked wrong, too bluish, too whitish, not the pure pinks and reds of textbook diagrams. Something—no, someone—had hollowed her out but not disconnected the insides when they came outside. The entrails dragged along the ground as the hanging body swayed in a breeze he hadn't noticed before now. He thought of wind chimes and wished he heard them.

"Gross, genius, brilliant perfor—" but then Esme saw what he saw and screamed.

"I'm not dreaming, and this is real? A real live dead woman?" Kayla swallowed and added, "Gutted?"

"I don't think that's all that happened to her," Mike said. He was right. Too much of the damage was focused between her legs.

The gutted woman wasn't at the edge of the room. She

was set back in the trees. Kayla wandered into the... woods... that began where the room transitioned into trees.

"Kayla, wait!" As she called, Esme moved toward her friend.

Rory lurched as if to follow Esme, but Mike held him back. "What do you think this is?" the bigger boy said.

"I don't know." Rory wasn't sure if he would be able to say anything else, but then a surprise: "We should stay together." He followed Esme, who followed Kayla. Mike followed him.

A man hung not far from the woman, his gut also open, but cut in different ways. The trees led to more hanging bodies, one mostly skinned, unrecognizable, one a girl, open-gutted—Esme said she recognized her from a school play—and one a boy, throat slashed, one side sliced like portions of meat in a butcher shop. Rory understood what he didn't want to understand.

He and Mike and Esme and Kayla had been *lured*. Through some means, someone had brought them here. Someone planned to capture them, like the people hanging in the trees. Someone planned to kill them.

Beyond that, someone planned to do terrible, terrible things.

PART TWO: ALEX'S ENTERTAINMENT

11. HIS THEM

Letta

(about a year ago)

Dave didn't like her smoking, but she had a right to smoke if she wanted. She had a smoker's voice anyway. For some reason he was still worried about bad influences and raised a fuss about smoking around Alex, so she didn't smoke when Dave and Alex were both around, but she smoked around each of them separately because Alex would find a way to smoke if Alex wanted to smoke because Alex, she was convinced, found ways to do what he wanted even when what he wanted might be deplorable.

At four o'clock in the afternoon, Letta smoked a cigarette and sipped her second glass of a red blend she and Dave had bought wine tasting last Christmas. Alex, long home from school and allegedly done with his homework, sat across from her at the table in the breakfast nook. She had told him to sit down. He fidgeted.

"Sociopathy," she said.

His expression remained blank.

"A complete failure to empathize... an *inability* to empathize... with other people. With other living creatures. There's no proof about Snuffles. I wonder about you and animals, though. Pull any wings off flies lately?" She couldn't make eye contact, so she looked at the bottom of her glass as she sipped.

"No, Mom. Flies don't interest me."

Letta pulled the sculpted glass ashtray closer and stubbed out her cigarette. "Equivocal. Anyway, I suppose they don't call you sociopaths anymore. You are 'people suffering with antisocial personality disorder.' Tell me, Alex, are you suffering?"

"When did you stop beating your wife?" Alex said.

"Excuse me?" Letta drew another cigarette from her pack. Marlboro Reds. Her smoking was intermittent, but during an on phase, she saw no point in going halfway.

"You asked me a question that's impossible to answer," Alex said.

She lit up, took the first drag, exhaled, and said, "You're not that clever."

"Apparently, I'm suffering from a mental disorder."

"I didn't say just one," she corrected. "Oh no. Sociopathy, psychopathy. Some say ASPD can't be diagnosed in someone your age, but the signs are all there. The Dark Tetrad. I think you're kind of dissociative, too. Not DID, multiple personality dissociative, but on that spectrum. Maybe bipolar. Or schizophrenic. Would explain the psychotic episodes."

"*What* psychotic episodes?"

She stared at him, this time waiting, and bracing, for eye contact. He finally made it, and she held it. Had his eyes always been grey? She felt like she stood in grey headlights, not rushing but inching toward her, but she couldn't move. "I'd hate to think you *weren't* psychotic and still did the things you do."

"What do I do, Mom?" The eyes held.

"I... you...." Ash fell from the tip of her cigarette, and she broke away from him. She took a quick drag and followed it with a gulp of wine without exhaling and almost coughed and spat. Managing composure, she swallowed and exhaled. "You probably have a *them*," Letta said.

"Huh?" Alex sounded far too innocent.

"Projected antagonists. Maybe your father and I are

your *them*."

He laughed.

"No?" She studied his face. He was still a kid. When he wasn't blank, she could read him. "Maybe I'm off target. Maybe your *them*... isn't antagonistic. Maybe you've got... imaginary friends?"

"What the hell are you talking about?" His voice was weak.

Her turn to laugh. "Oh, brilliant! Like Davey Berkowitz and his dog! Are they animals? Like the ones you kill? *Are* they the ones you kill?" She laughed again and thought there wasn't enough wine in the world.

"Shut up!"

"Voices in your head, or do you see them?" She smoked, drank, and laughed.

"Shut up!"

"Are you following orders from a h-h-higher power, Alex?" Guffaws, uncontrollable.

"SHUT YOUR FUCKING CUNT MOUTH OR I'LL RAM THAT GLASS INTO YOUR THROAT!"

Sudden sobriety. "You're not that clever."

His quick breathing slowed into control.

"Go to your room, Alex."

"With pleasure," he said. He stormed out, which was comforting, as it made him seem more like a normal teenager.

Letta finished her wine, poured another glass, and took a long drag from her cigarette.

Alex

(now)

His *them*.

Mom had come close, so close she had scared him, but nobody ever really knew about them. He didn't know if he'd dreamed them into existence—imaginary playmates who took on lives of their own—or if they'd come from outside, filling in the spaces Alex had made for imaginary playmates when he was seven or eight years old. They'd been there when he'd started working on *his* house, so, in a way, *his* house had always been *their* house, too, but Alex didn't mind sharing. Not with them. Though he talked to them, and they had strange voices, choppy like sound filtered through whirling fan blades, making impressions like needles on the back of your neck, over time, they needed words less and less. They knew how to transform his house before Alex knew how he wanted it transformed. They might have hated every body but Alex's, but they loved when he touched himself, and when, at age twelve, he started ejaculating, their excitement joined his own. They liked when he took the animals apart, pulling their insides to the outside and rubbing his fingers through their guts, rubbing their guts against his private places. As Alex explored human animals, they got further away from him and closer at the same time. They seemed more distinct, more separate from him, as they encouraged, rewarded, and remade him, but they became more intimate, too, more often a tingle behind his eyes looking out, more often an appetite, like an extra stomach, expanding his own.

To sate their appetite for sex and violence, *theirs* as well as his, they'd changed the way his body worked while he was in his house. As Rory, Mike, Esme, and Kayla tried to orient themselves to the living room, he could watch.

He could watch because he crawled on the ceiling without making a sound.

Where the room transitioned into trees, he could crawl or even walk in high branches, and his unwilling visitors wouldn't notice shaking in the heights or falling leaves or nettle because they were too distracted by what hung from the low branches, Mom and Dad and Ollie and Warren and Anna. The bodies swayed in a breeze that shouldn't have been; it might have been *their* breath. Rory puked, and Esme screamed.

Mike, who was bigger than Alex and the guy Alex expected to take the lead, looked like he'd been hit with a stun gun. Only his mouth moved, forming shapes almost like words. Rory said, "We should stay together," but at first, all they did was tour the corpses.

Mike's mouth found success: "What kind of place is this?"

Rory turned around and walked back toward the part of the living room that looked less like a forest. "The kind of place we don't want to be."

"Wait!" Kayla shouted. "How do you know...."

Rory looked back at her, the impatience in his eyebrows not masking the fear in his eyes.

"Maybe the trees are safer than the house," Kayla said.

"Do the trees look safe?" Rory said. Rory, skinny, short Rory with the thick-rimmed glasses, asserted authority.

"I just want to go home," Esme said.

In unison, a chorus of needles on his neck, *they* said, "Now."

He jumped to the ground, a distance that would have shattered the legs of any visitor. Not *his* legs. Not in his house. Not anymore.

The boys and girls were suitably startled. They formed a bundle and faced him, Rory and Esme in front, Mike and Kayla behind, rows arranged by height. "Relax," Alex said. "I had to be sure."

"You... huh?" Mike backed up a step.

"You're a guy in his underwear who fell out of the damned sky," Rory said.

"I was—"

"You what?" Mike said.

"I had to—"

"Sure of what?" Rory said.

"Sure that you were—"

Rory grunted. "HA! Sure that *we*—"

"Would you let him fucking talk already?" Esme flipped

from sounding like a lost little girl to sounding like a bored, exasperated bitch, but she was bitching in Alex's favor, so he felt amused, especially at the astonishment that shut Rory up like a hammer to the jaw.

"I was hiding," Alex said. "I had to make sure you weren't the ones who did... this."

"How do we know you weren't the one who did this?" Rory reasserted his authority with a keen edge.

Alex looked at the ground, hoping to seem hurt.

"Maybe you know," Kayla said. "Which is better, deeper into the trees, or back to the place that looked like somebody's living room?"

Alex raised his head and tried to look haunted. Without overdoing the campfire effect, he went for a spooky voice. "The trees aren't trees," he said. "I think the only thing real out here is... the bodies."

"Do you know who they are?" Kayla asked.

"No," Alex said. He didn't look much like either of his parents even before death reworked their colors and shapes. "Do you?"

"I recognize the girl from school," Esme said.

"Okay, okay," Rory said. "If the trees aren't trees, what are they?"

"Walk into the trees, and you keep walking. Trees appear in front of you that weren't there a second before. One minute it's like you're walking in a grid, the next in a spiral, the next, in chaos. The trees are a trap. The trees are madness."

Esme got quiet. "How long have you been here?"

"Not long, not yet," Alex said. "Not this time."

"You've been here before," Kayla said.

Mike left the bundle and picked up a dead branch, one that looked heavy. Mindlessly, the four people forced to act as a group had assumed roles along gender lines, the girls in gothic black playing good cops, the boys in glasses and braces playing bad cops. Esme and Kayla tried to learn about Alex, maybe even establish trust. Rory asked skeptical questions. Mike prepared to fight.

This part of the game wouldn't last long.

"*They* have brought me here before. Each time I thought I'd end up hanging from a tree. Do you think?" Alex looked at each of them, widening his eyes as much as possible. "Do you think you'll end up swaying in that breeze, *their* breath, or do you think the door will let you out?"

"Door?" Rory said.

"We're going back toward the house," Kayla said.

"It's the only way," Alex said. "*If* it's a way."

Checking over his shoulder as much as he looked forward, Alex led. The girls stayed close to him, but the boys, unpossessed by chivalry, hung back, Mike with his natural bludgeon that now doubled as a fat walking stick. As if he had absorbed Warren and Anna's talents, Alex pretended to look disturbed as they passed the corpses, enhancing his charade as one of the Prey.

As they walked by the sofa, Rory said, "So who is this *they* you're talking about?"

"They brought you here, too," Alex said over his shoulder.

The group left the living room through the wide opening onto the downstairs hall's transition into the foyer. As Rory, the last through doorway, crossed, the house rocked like a train car coming to a sudden halt. Everyone but Alex cried out. Esme fell; Rory, on unsteady feet, rushed to help. Kayla grabbed Mike's arm and kept them both steady. Around them and beneath them, boards popped and crackled. The walls' veins pulsed, lifting the chipped red paint in branching pathways, darker, redder, dripping, stretching—the consistency of dense taffy—the walls widened, the hallway lengthened, and doors multiplied.

The foyer didn't grow as quickly as the hall, but it grew, and the front door got farther away. "Hurry!" Alex yelled, grinning a grin no one could see, and he dashed for the door. He tried the bolt, which wouldn't turn, not that he wanted it to. He made a show of struggling with the knob. The Prey gathered around. "It's not working!" Alex infused his voice with anguish.

Esme flipped back the juvenile. "We've got to get out of here! What do we do?"

"I know!" Alex exclaimed, and he stepped back from the door, which made the others back up in a wave. The mat in front of the door, grimy grey like so much of his house's floor covering, was clear now, so he tossed it aside and picked up what he knew—they didn't tell him with words, but they let him know—would be there. A sickle. It had a thick, sharp hook, maybe fifteen inches, with a sturdy wooden handle, which he had in his grip after he swooped down to retrieve it and spun to reveal that he was the Predator after all. "Maybe you'd better run," he said, and through a laugh he added, "because maybe you should know *they* are my *them*." He brandished the blade and bared his teeth.

Alex would have preferred for the kids all to turn and run screaming, which the girls started to do, but they stopped when they saw Mike swing his tree branch with skull-crushing force into the side of Alex's head. Alex flew backward. His body slammed into the impassable front door. He emitted an "OOF!" He held on to the sickle, but the Prey did not see that. Another phenomenon held their attention.

Mike's bludgeon, after contact with Alex's head, turned to dust. It did not break on impact; it crumbled, shattered to particles. Mike's weapon was a useless strip of powder on the hardwood floor—which was spitting out fog—and Alex still stood, blood dripping from the corner of his mouth near where the branch had hit but basically unharmed. Everyone was very, very quiet.

Alex straightened his posture. He squinted at Mike, who stood closer than the rest, too close for a reliable uppercut to catch his belly with the hook, but a swing from the side—

"RUN!" Rory commanded.

All four of the kids scurried toward the downstairs hall,

which grew around them as they ran.

But Alex had to—

Bruce

The first two knocks didn't get an answer, and though Bruce considered walking in on a teenager uninvited to be bad policy, he resolved to try the doorknob on the third knock. Alex had a lock and knew how to use it. If he really needed privacy—

Bruce would be even more worried—

but he could have it. Bruce had grown up in a zero-privacy household. He didn't know whether Letta had duplicated that aspect of their parents' child rearing philosophy, but Bruce considered almost all his parents' decisions anathema. Nevertheless, he tried the knob on the third knock.

The door opened.

"Hey, um, sorry to walk in, but I thought with your earbuds—"

Alex sat on the bed with his legs folded, wearing only boxers, which made Bruce feel awkward as hell given what he'd seen this morning. It was one p.m. now. He'd taken hours to work up the nerve to come talk to the boy. Should he ask him to put some clothes on?

The way he sat with his eyes open, looking... vacant... was unsettling. Bruce tried to understand the meditation, astral projection stuff Alex was into. He read articles about it online. "Alex?" He didn't know whether waking up an astral projectionist was dangerous like waking up a somnambulist.

Alex blinked, smiled, and turned his head to look at Bruce directly. "Sorry, Bruce. Guess I was checked out. Didn't hear you knock."

What if this "astral projection" was unhealthy, a way for Alex to dissociate and avoid dealing with the realities of his life? Bruce thought about asking Dr. Shumer. Distraction!

He was here to talk to the boy who had filmed himself masturbating in the shower and had done so with his husband's camera, presumably for his husband to see, possibly with his husband's knowledge. Even after the hours spent trying to wrap his mind around the situation, he wasn't sure what to say. "Sorry to interrupt."

"No problem." Alex unfolded and stretched his legs, letting his bare calves and feet hang over the edge of the bed. "What's up?"

The kid who asked "what's up" could have been a completely different person from the kid in the video. The Alex who asked "what's up" might have been the most introverted person Bruce had met, but that only increased his aura of... innocence... which was nowhere to be seen when he kissed the lens in that video. But if Aaron put him up to it.... "I was going to make a sandwich, and since I hadn't seen you all day, I thought I'd check to see if you wanted anything." Dipshit, dipshit, dipshit.

"No, but thanks," Alex said.

The boy smiled at him, the next move clearly Bruce's, the move itself clearly to leave, but long seconds passed with Bruce standing a few paces from the bed, looking like an idiot. "Um," he said. "Um," he repeated, and he laughed at himself. "Look, I *am* happy to make you a sandwich or something, but what I said just now was a total lie."

Alex raised an eyebrow. He was awfully cute. Not in a sexual way, but charming. Though if he came out of his shell and turned into a party boy, parenting would become a lot more difficult. At what age do you buy a boy condoms?

A boy who films himself masturbating with your husband as the intended audience.

"O... kay," Alex said. "What's on your mind?"

"Okay if I sit down?" The question popped out of Bruce's mouth before he considered that the bed provided the only place to sit.

"Okay," Alex said, looking at the bed's corner, the logical

spot. Every spot was close to where he sat in his underwear.

Bruce perched. "You know you can talk to me about anything."

"Yeah." Alex looked earnest. Too many seconds of silence passed. "You think there's something I should talk about?"

"I...." *Tell him you saw the video.* "I wonder how you're getting along with Aaron."

"Aaron's great," the boy said. "I really get into the movie stuff." No hint of *double entendre.*

"You don't feel like he's... pressuring you to be on camera?"

"No. Not at all." Alex cleared his throat. "Bruce, I've got a question for you."

"Anything." His nerves caught fire.

"What do you know about psychomachia?"

Psychomachia? He knew what the word meant. He just couldn't remember right now. "Um...."

"Nowadays they're in cartoons, a devil on one shoulder and an angel on another, but they go back to medieval times, morality plays where people would act out spiritual influences at work in different aspects of the mind, you know, personified." Alex sounded so erudite!

"I knew that," Bruce said. "At some point." He'd lost control of the conversation.

"What do you think of that idea?"

The question didn't link to any train of thought Bruce was following. "The idea being...."

"Angels and devils, or maybe bad angels and better angels, influencing what you do."

"As... figures, like in a play, that stand for what goes on in your head, sure." Bruce had a thread to follow! "But literal angels? I'm not a believer."

"It seems kind of silly, doesn't it? It's hard to believe... in them. It's hard to be a believer."

After that, the conversation went nowhere.

12. GOTH GIRLS AND NERD BOYS RENDEZVOUS IN HELL

Rory

"Hold up!" Rory took his own advice, slowing to a halt, his breath in heaves, his eyes uncertain.

The others stopped running and looked back at him like he was crazy.

Getting control of his breathing, Rory looked behind him—the direction everyone else faced—and said, "Nobody's chasing us."

"That guy," Kayla said. "He had to be about our age. It was like that hook just… appeared… and he turned dark." As she spoke, she struggled for breath, too. The struggle made her bodice-squeezed chest move up and down. *Heaving bosom.* Rory almost smiled at *heaving bosom.* "Do you think he did… what we saw?"

"It was a sickle," Mike said.

"He fell from the sky," Esme said. "I wonder where he'll show up next. I don't want to be here. This place is bad."

"She's right," Kayla said. "We're into some next level haunted house shit."

Rory didn't suppress the smile, but he hoped it looked kind. "You're referring to the fog-covered floor, or all the cobwebs along the slanted ceiling, or the uncomfortable... redness, or the fact that the hallway has gotten at least twice as wide, as if it wants us all to run side by side, or the fact that the hall has been kind of stubborn, refusing to end, or—"

"I wonder if things change if we try one of the doors," Mike said. The doors were black. They made all the red seem redder, more profound.

"Maybe we all died," Esme said. "Maybe we were all murdered at the Pit, and this is Hell, and we're stuck together because that's the sort of thing that happens in Hell."

"Do you believe in Hell?" Rory asked, thinking about her Nietzsche reading.

"No," she said. "But it's a place I wouldn't want to be, like I don't want to be here."

Fair enough.

"Whatever it is, this place is on *his* side," Kayla said. "He said they were 'his *them*.' Maybe... maybe he's not chasing us anymore because he's behind one of those doors." She looked at Mike. "Like Esme said, he fell from the sky." Actually, Rory had said it first, but who cared, right? "He could be behind all these doors."

"When I hit him, the branch... *dissolved*," Mike said.

"The trees aren't trees," Rory said. "This hallway isn't a hallway. But he couldn't be behind all the doors, could he?"

Kayla shrugged. "I'm not looking for things to start making sense any time soon."

Where had this idea even originated? With Kayla, but —why had it entered her head? Why would the guy in his underwear with a sickle and a homicidal attitude be *behind every door*? If he could manifest himself in so many copies, he could overwhelm and kill them at any time, so survival would be a moot point.

Thinking about the probability of surviving in relation to their outré circumstances didn't seem like a good idea.

Perhaps the teenage boogeyman in boxer shorts wasn't *already* waiting behind every door. Maybe their choice of what door to open determined which door he'd be behind. A tad like science fiction.

Or maybe all the doors led to the same place.

But probably—probably—he wasn't behind any of the doors at all.

They couldn't go down this hall forever.

Rory decided. "I'm opening a door."

"I'm scared of the doors," Esme said.

"Yeah," Kayla said. "Me, too. But I'm at least a little bit scared of everything right now."

"I'm right beside you," Mike said. He was. He was also looking at the same door as Rory. So were Esme and Kayla. Somehow, they'd all agreed on which door to open, even though the black doors, in their uneven frames that made them as screwy as everything else in this unreasonably wide, unreasonably long hallway, all looked very similar to one another.

Rory reached for the doorknob, shiny black in the hall's greylight. The light flickered. The light itself, from unknown sources, almost like a substance, a glowing shadow haze, might have dimmed. He half-expected the knob not to turn. Locked. But it did turn, no resistance from a lock, and he started to pull the door toward him—

and it burst in his direction, pushing back both him and Mike. The movement was confusion, the hand at his throat under the jaw, the strength that pulled him. Screams, Esme and Kayla. Mike tried to grab his hand, but the boy with the sickle yanked him away, through the open doorway, and the door slammed shut behind them.

Kayla

Nobody was doing anything, so Kayla figured she had

to and sprung for the door, wrapping her hand around the knob while the other two dildos still had their heads spinning from how fast demon boy had popped out and taken Rory. The knob didn't budge when she twisted. She shook the door in its frame. It didn't give.

"Stand back, I'm going to kick it!" Mike yelled.

Seeing Mike get all macho with the door reminded her that neither he nor Rory had been unknown to Esme and Kayla. Rory drooled over Esme, and he and Mike were like straight boyfriends, inseparable, so Kayla had once entertained the notion of admitting Mike for some level of dalliance.

Mike kicked. The door didn't give more within its frame than when Kayla had tried to shake it.

Mike kicked again. Again. Kayla looked over her shoulder, feeling a little embarrassed, and noticed. "Esme?" She pointed.

Esme looked where Kayla pointed, toward the direction in which, long ago, they'd been running.

The hallway ended in a brighter room.

"Holy shit," Esme said, concisely indicating that she saw what Kayla saw.

Kayla interrupted a kick. "Mike. We're not getting through that door. But there might be another way."

"What are you talking about?" He didn't take his eyes from the door.

Kayla waved her hands in the air to draw his attention, then pointed two-handed, like a man directing planes on the tarmac, toward the newly available end to the hall. "I think we're as likely to find Rory that way as if we go through that door." She pretended to whisper. "And I don't think *they* are going to let us through that door."

Mike looked doubtful, but he got over it, and they all went to the end of the hall and entered what looked like a conjoined breakfast area and spacious kitchen separated by a broad counter/bar, all of which would have been lovely if the red walls didn't have shit smeared all over them. The smell was bad. It wasn't just the shit, as if that weren't enough, but the table in the breakfast area was covered with bowls of cereal in sour curdled milk, little bits of rotten eggs and meat and what might once have been, before the mold, starchy. The kitchen, though. The kitchen was all about the rotten meat, the maggoty ground beef, the maggoty steaks, pretty much everything maggoty. Chicken breasts and thighs. A whole turkey. Rack of lamb. Ribs, attached and separated. The fish added a distinctive yet indescribable (far beyond "fishy") layer to the odor. Rotten vegetation garnished the rotten meats, seething with life, in places, but mostly, the kitchen had rotten meat and shit themes, and the breakfast area was themed with shit and that monstrous milk.

Alex

After the door slammed, Alex had to decide what to do with the featherweight kid who struggled hard in his grip, kicking and punching and making a few good sickle-lashes hard to resist, but Alex had a... script to follow... and he didn't want to get ahead of himself. So, he threw Rory on the floor next to Grandpa's open coffin.

Rory, in a button-up short-sleeved shirt and khaki shorts with new high-end tennis shoes, scrambled to sit up against the closet's off-white back wall, bracing himself in the corner. His glasses were askew. He righted them.

Using the sickle as a pointer, Alex gestured from Rory to the coffin. "Rory, meet Grandpa."

After a long stare at the sickle, Rory glanced into the coffin, at the skeleton draped in skin some undertakers' arts had failed to render with humanity. His wider eyes returned to Alex and his blade. "What do you want?"

"I have a suggestion," Alex said.

"I'm in a position to be suggestable."

"You are smart," Alex said. "Be smart and take off your belt."

"What?"

"Cutting through it could get messy. Take it off, before I change my mind."

"Why—"

"No questions. Follow orders."

The satisfying clink of metal signaled the belt's unbuckling. Then came the friction of fabric as leather traveled through loops, and Rory had the free belt in his hand.

"It's not a whip, so don't try," Alex said. "Toss it in with Grandpa. He won't mind."

Rory obeyed. "Now what?"

"Hold still," Alex said. He decided to start near the neck —the blade at the neck would make him freeze—and work downward. A giant step closed the distance, a quick reach brought the sickle's tip to the collar of Rory's button-up shirt, and a lean in brought Alex's sneer close enough to Rory's face for a kiss, which wasn't on Alex's mind. "I really mean hold still." He lowered the sickle's tip, surfing along the shirt's fabric as well as Rory's skin. The breath froze in Rory's chest as, before it got to the first button, the blade slid over skin, splitting it, drawing blood. Then it cut open a button, slit some fabric, and surfed downward. It split skin a few more times as it cut the shirt open until it took a break at the beginning of the shorts, into which the shirt was tucked. Alex retracted the sickle and pondered his next angle of attack.

"Y-you don't have to cut," Rory said. He sounded less confident, but his voice asserted soft authority, persuasiveness buttressed by a tone of knowing. "You want the shirt? I'll give you the shirt."

The shirt, bright stripes of medium width that went well with the khaki shorts, was soaking up blood from the scratches the sickle had made while cutting buttons and otherwise opening the front, exposing Rory's puny chest and stomach with a line of hair leading downward from his bellybutton. His chest had hair, too, surprising given how little he was, but if Alex had started getting hairy already, he might have shaved anyway, so he wasn't jealous. The shirt, though, was already getting ruined by the blots from the scratches. Why would Alex want the shirt? "I want to cut the shirt *off*, and I want you to be still so you're not all bloody by the time I'm through. Nod if you're with me."

Rory nodded, setting his glasses askew. He righted them.

Beginning at the collar again, Alex sliced through fabric, moving over the rounds of the shoulders and down the arms until the short sleeves ended, leaving scratches—they probably felt worse than scratches—on both sides. With the blade at the kid's neck, he told Rory to scoot forward. Rory did, and Alex cut at the cloth on his sides and the skin covering ribs underneath. With his free hand at Rory's throat, Alex reached around and slid the sickle flatly between the back of the shirt and Rory's spine until it emerged at the collar and back of his head. The kid trembled, fought hard to be still but trembled, but Alex felt sure that when he cut the shirt's back in two, he didn't leave a nick.

The shirt peeled down in sections, leaving Rory's upper half exposed like an unwrapped candy.

Next, the shorts. This part would tougher, bloodier. More scratching, more scraping. But only a hint of what was coming.

They said that after the clothes were off, he could shift himself along with Rory to another part, a new part, of his ever-expanding house. The wonders never ceased!

Mike

The drawers and cabinets might have been where the smell of rotting meat was thickest because so many butchered slices and parts were piled together on countertops, mounds, almost pyramids of animal pieces, proper to a kitchen if they weren't rotten, to a freezer, at any rate. Also proper to a kitchen were knives. Mike would let the stench fill his nose and lungs on the chance that in the drawers or on a countertop hiding behind a mound or even in the dishwasher he could find—

Clatter, clatter. A drawer full of sharp kitchen options, including a bloodstained chef's knife. He picked it up. Whose blood?

Why did he assume the blood belonged to a *who* and not a—

This place. He wasn't going to waste time on stupid questions. They had to find Rory.

He swiveled to escape the kitchen's depth and return to Kayla and Esme, who lingered near the stools at the bar that set off the kitchen from the breakfast nook, holding their hands over their mouths and noses. A change in the wall, the long, shit stained wall that connected the doorway from the hall to a doorway that led into what seemed like a dining room, stopped him. Before, the wall had been uninterrupted.

Now, near its middle, it had a door.

"What the hell." He crossed to the door, feeling the girls' eyes on him. "When did this get here?"

Kayla lowered her hand from her mouth. "Sometime between the last time I looked at that wall and when you said, 'what the hell.'" Pause. "Nice knife."

"There are more," Mike said, looking at the door. It differed from the black doors in the hallway that grew until one of the doors—before that guy with the sickle—took Rory. It was brown, not shit brown like the smears on the walls but regular wood with a medium stain, and it had a dull brass knob.

His head turned as Kayla brushed by, going into the deep kitchen funk to fetch weapons from the drawer where he'd found the bloody chef's knife. She came back, showing that she'd chosen a long carving knife for herself and a meat cleaver for Esme, an item Esme accepted with—not a smile exactly—but approval. They stood back a short distance from Mike and faced the door. All three of them knew where they were going.

Mike opened the door that hadn't been there a few minutes ago.

The door's other side was darker, but in the greylight they could see wooden stairs and cinderblock walls. Basement.

"Basements creep me out," Esme said.

"Kitchens full of maggots with shit on the walls creep me out, too," Kayla said.

"Fair."

Mike took a deep breath. "So," he said. "Who's going down first?"

"You're the guy," Esme said.

"I believe in equal opportunities." Mike didn't want to sound chickenshit, but he didn't feel responsible for these girls, either. They were supposed to like dark and creepy shit, weren't they?

"I'll go," Kayla said. "Get out of my way."

Surprised, Mike stepped aside, and Kayla began her descent. Mike went second, and Esme came last. The stairs creaked. The smell from the kitchen faded quickly; something he couldn't identify replaced it. The further they descended, the warmer the air became. Part of the smell was dirt, like they weren't going to a basement but were going underground. Kayla got to the bottom of the stairs, turned a corner, and said, "Sweet fucking Jesus."

Esme

Maybe they should be headed back to what had looked like the house's front door, or maybe they should be continuing, like they were, assuming where they were headed would lead to Rory, whose annoying affections she minded less than she'd ever admitted, even to herself before now, but every step further down into the smells of damp earth and the sounds of crackling fire brought back a ruling emotion with compelling simplicity: she did not want to be here.

At the bottom of the stairs, around the corner, she imagined a graveyard with a bonfire where the dead, newly risen from their moist, wormy graves, danced. The thought was comforting.

Sweet fucking Jesuses aside, Kayla moved toward whatever she saw at the bottom of the stairs. Mike followed. Esme let indecision conquer reluctance. They were doing something stupid, but they might not be able to do anything that wasn't stupid. She joined Kayla and Mike, who had a girlfriend and was just as scared as Esme and Kayla were. Maybe more scared. He and Rory were close friends. What were the chances that the next time they saw Rory, he'd be dangling from a tree?

Except the answer was in the room at the bottom of the stairs, where Esme stood on Kayla's left side, Mike on her right. The hallway opened onto a peninsula, concrete floor that extended outward, solid, a comfortable width, surrounded by gaps. In the gaps, pits, fires roared, devouring an unknown fuel at an unknown depth, licking up at the air above the gaps, giving the room bright orange to go with its greylight. Across from the gaps, earthen walls bordered the room, dripping, insects and worms moving within them. All walls but the one with the entrance included open, barred rectangles more brightly lit. Cells. A dungeon.

The cells, nine, three left, three right, and three forward, had doors connecting to adjacent cells and doors connected to... whatever lay beyond the room. The cells didn't have beds. They had hammers. Spikes. Blades with shapes she didn't recognize that looked designed to inflict various forms of pain. Her position on Hell wavered.

She'd been trying to avoid what the others stared at, but it slipped into her consciousness.

Rory didn't look bad naked. He was skinny as fuck, but

Esme didn't mind that, and he was... cute. Spikes secured him to the wall, piercing his wrists and lower calves—he was close enough for them to see the blood—his body hung like an X. He still wore his shoes, dangling off the ground, soaking up blood. He didn't have his glasses. The distance was a little much to make out his facial expression, but from what Esme could see, and from what she could sense, there was fear, agony, and... *shame*. He knew they were there, looking at him on display.

It was a torture chamber and a zoo. Rory was an *attraction*. Rory was a show in Hell.

"I don't want to be here," Esme said.

"Rory, we're coming for you!" Mike shouted.

No, Rory, we're not. Rory was about to become a star. They tucked away their knives as best they could.

They were here to watch.

13. INNOCENCE

Aaron

Too tired to bring in everything, Aaron left the boom mic, tripod, wires and other accessories in the trunk of the car, lugging only the Arri Alexa, which was worth more than the car. He got the camera case through the front door and exaggerated his struggle, thinking Bruce would come help, but Bruce stayed at the kitchen table, a hardcover mystery novel opened in front of him. Aaron hauled the case to the closet and stowed it. After a big breath, he turned toward Bruce. "Well, the gay geezer at the antiques shop was a bust, but the lesbians at the bookstore were fantastic."

Bruce turned a page. He was stewing about something.

Crossing halfway to the table—keeping a safe distance —Aaron said, "Looks like you're having a relaxing afternoon?"

Without looking up from his book, Bruce reached into the chair next to him, pulled up Aaron's favorite handheld camera, and put it at the table's center.

Oh shit.

Bruce didn't snoop. He wouldn't go looking for the camera, search through the footage.... "What are you doing with that?"

Aaron hadn't cleared the memory. He'd meant to, but he'd been distracted.

"Have a seat." Bruce indicated the chair across from him, which would suspend the camera between them on an invisible tightrope. "Let's try to keep our voices down. Alex is in his room. Been there all day."

Aaron thought of objecting that it was barely three o'clock, but he couldn't make sense of the objection and kept it to himself. Nervous, he took the chair Bruce indicated, not his usual spot. "You've got something on your mind."

Bruce nodded, then scowled at the camera. "What do you think I've got on my mind?"

"You've got my camera."

"It was just out there, in the bedroom, so yes, I picked it up." Bruce inhaled deeply and exhaled slowly. "What do you think I've got on my mind?"

What Aaron said now would determine what he could say later. If he was too evasive, if he denied all knowledge, he might lose all credibility, but he'd have to stick with the oversized lie. Bruce would be able to detect a big lie. Aaron needed to stay close to the truth.

Alternately, he could go with the whole truth. Tell Bruce everything. Stop this thing, whatever it was, before it got out of control. Further out of control. Aaron didn't want anything further, and Alex—who the fuck knew about Alex? The shower video was weird, and Aaron shouldn't have let it happen, and from the look on Bruce's face, he had seen it and agreed ten times over.

The whole truth was too complicated. Maybe if Aaron understood it himself, but as it was, not an option. "Assuming you've seen what I think you've seen, I've been trying to figure out how to bring it up with you." Good. Aaron liked where this was going. "Otherwise, I would have deleted it."

"Somehow a film of our adopted son masturbating ended up on your camera," Bruce said. "Consider it brought up."

With a gulp that seemed too dramatic, Aaron said, "I didn't know how to bring it up because I thought you'd react badly. You're proving me right. You think I had something to do with it, right?"

"Did you?"

Aaron pointed to the table's center. "I obviously don't keep my cameras under lock and key."

"He kisses the camera at the end and says he hopes you enjoyed it. Did you?"

Aaron scoffed. "You saw it, too. Did *you*?" How much had Bruce seen? The shower scene only, or the conversation beforehand? The conversation might be more damning.

"No, I didn't." Bruce closed his book with a snap and glared. "I can't say I'm a fan of kiddie porn, especially not the homemade kind, especially not the kind made in my home. You didn't have *anything* to do with it?"

"You shouldn't have to ask."

"I want an answer."

"No!"

Bruce's face and shoulders relaxed—partially. "Did you say anything suggestive? That could be taken as coercion? People will say we're exploiting his innocence."

"I don't think I said...." Aaron thought of Alex kissing him, Alex undressing, Alex demanding to be filmed. Being fourteen didn't stop Alex from being aggressive. "What innocence," Aaron mumbled.

"What?" Bruce said.

Aaron decided to pursue the angle. "I said, 'What innocence?'"

"Keep your voice down."

"I am keeping my voice down."

"What do you mean?"

"He talks like an adult," Aaron said. "And some of the things he says when I've got him on camera... he flirts with me. A lot. At first, I thought it was 'innocent.' But this video...." His eyes went from Bruce to the centered camera. "Where did you say you found it again?"

"Found—"

"The camera."

"It was on our bed."

"I didn't put it there," Aaron said. "It wasn't there when

I left this morning."

"You're saying Alex left it there."

Aaron understood what he was saying as he said it. "If I'd had some part in what you saw, would I leave it like that for you to find?"

Bruce sunk back into his chair. "You're saying Alex wanted me to find it."

"What else makes sense?"

"You think he's trying to drive a wedge between us?"

"Maybe," Aaron said. Probably. Yes, yes, yes.

"Maybe it's a reflection of his feelings of loss and abandonment, an attempt to, a misguided attempt to bond with us by doing something he actually thinks, he actually thinks might please us?"

"Maybe." Aaron took the camera from the table's center and removed the memory cards. He wouldn't forget to delete questionable footage this time. He'd already transferred everything to a password-protected hard drive anyway. After the transfer, he'd meant to delete the memory, but he'd gotten caught up in watching Alex on the camera a second time, and his mind had become... lost. "All the maybes aside, we have to be careful. We have to be on our guard. Something isn't right."

Alex

They had outdone themselves. The house where he grew up didn't have a basement, but he'd long wondered whether he could add one, and he'd imagined it as a theatre of sorts, a showcase, and they'd understood and combined earth and fire with steel bars and enough weapons for hours and hours of playtime fun. He pinned Rory to a cell's wall like an entomologist's specimen—though insects still held no interest for him—and left him there until the others arrived. His script, a little scenario he'd scribbled in his head, called for an audience.

"Rory, we're coming for you!" Mike's voice. Very butch.

The blood from the wounds he'd already made was drying on his bare skin, sticky, crusty. There'd be more of it soon. The idea of taking a shower in *his* house amused him. The easiest thing to do would be to pop out and pop back in, resetting himself, giving the surviving kids time to wander before he came for another.

But that was getting ahead, wasn't it?

The wait was over. Leaving his nest in the tunnel, one of many tunnels, he entered Rory's cell and took a giant step toward the bars. Kayla gave him an audible gasp. He thanked her with a nod. The blood on his face, chest, stomach, arms, thighs—it all probably made him look older, less like *one of the kids*. All their eyes fastened to him. He drifted to the cell's center, imagining a spotlight. A glance over his shoulder showed Rory, obviously woozy, holding up his head and looking his way. How bad was his vision without his glasses? Alex regretted leaving them behind. Their absence could blunt the experience. At least he'd left the shoes and socks on. Pure porn star. Porn Star Rory. Getting ready to get close up.

First, Alex walked all the way to the bars, as close to his audience as he could get. Mike, Kayla, and Esme, all in a line, all cringed, but they didn't stop looking. He held up the sickle with his left hand. It would shift to the right in due course. They were close enough to see the blood on the sickle as clearly as they saw the blood on his skin. The quality of light, the firelight and the greylight, made the dried blood look black. Mike held up and studied a knife—Mom's butcher knife!—and Alex considered whether Mike could throw it across the short distance that separated them, throw it hard enough to lodge into Alex's chest, pierce his heart, and, and would it matter?

They hadn't chosen to tell him whether he was invincible.

Kayla held a long knife, and Esme had the cleaver Mom used when she thought meat could help with her frustrations. Only Mike's knife had dried blood on it. Alex knew why.

Dragging the sickle so it bounced from one vertical rod of steel to another, landing on each with a clang, Alex paced in front of the bars.

CLANG, CLANG, CLANG, CLANG!

Alex mesmerized them.

Behind him, Rory moaned, which snapped him to attention. He had work to do that required turning his back to the audience. What would Warren and Anna say?

First, though, he could walk backward to Rory's side, never turning away from the others so he could always tell if they were watching. They didn't have to think, but they had to *feel* that something terrible would happen if they didn't watch. Rory's life depended on them watching. Their own lives depended on them watching. Esme, crying, buried her head in Kayla's shoulder, but she rolled her forehead to an angle so one eye could still align with Rory's cell.

With his right hand, Alex rubbed Rory's chest. He applied little pressure, teasing the boy, making little circles around his nipples, pinching his nipples, rubbing the joining breastbone where hair sprouted. Playfully, he plucked a chest hair. Rory's whole body twitched. He made a "NNN" sound.

"So, this is some kind of sex thing," Kayla said. "Naturally, the guy who fell from the sky in his underwear and then chased us with a hook—excuse me, a sickle—wants to nail us to a wall and rape us before he kills us."

"Shut UP," Mike said, staring eyes widening.

Alex had to turn away some to reach around with his left hand, with the sickle, with which he rubbed, and made nicks on, Rory's stomach while his right hand kept rubbing at his chest. Every nick made Rory say, "Ow," maybe not loud enough for his friends to hear. After "Ow," he said, "Please."

"This is getting weirder," Esme said. "I don't like it getting weirder."

Some goth girl she turned out to be!

Alex's right hand skipped from Rory's chest to his groin, his flaccid penis. He took the shaft in his palm, teased at the glans with his fingers, squeezed and tugged, making it longer. When it was long enough, when he could feel the hairs on Rory's scrotum stand up and tickle his hand as if lifted by static electricity, he stroked. Rory bled from his arms and legs, but he could still get an erection. His cock got hard in Alex's hand. Alex spread his fingers, holding the firm member—impressive, especially in proportion to Rory's height—for the audience to see.

Esme gawked.

Alex stroked more, and Rory moaned again. The moan was the same as before, so if it conveyed pleasure. Pleasure and pain sounded the same.

Careful not to let the kid climax, Alex let go. The penis bobbed up toward Rory's concave belly and down toward the vacancy beneath his clenched testicles.

Alex moved into place in front of him, back to the audience. Sickle at left, right hand empty, he traced down the sides of Rory's body, to his hips. Alex had pinned Rory at the exact height where their eyes would meet when Alex stood in front of him. Porn Star Rory in his socks and tennis shoes.

Alex put his right hand between Rory's legs, reached through, and felt along the muscle of one cheek until the index finger could trace down the cliff to his anus. A quick trace around the circle, and then the finger's tip pushed inward, making Rory's body convulse with an "uh." The index finger went in as far as the second knuckle, then pulled back out, dry skin fighting him. As the hand pulled back, the fingertip followed, zig-zagging along a line as it mapped the perineum. The right hand groped the shriveled scrotum, squeezed the tumescent shaft, then dropped down by the left hand, which dangled, fingers wrapped around the sickle, by Rory's right thigh.

The right hand accepted the sickle, which it took almost as low as Rory's knees, far enough down for Mike, Kayla, and Esme to see its ascent begin. "Oh, God!" one of them yelled.

Up, up, up went the sickle.

member off. He took off the balls, too, leaving some of the sac skin to stay with the other skin and broken tissue between Rory's legs. Rory's screaming had diminished to howls upon exhales of desperate breath. He didn't sound very human.

Alex pushed the sickle into the void where the penis had been. He pushed it farther in than it had gone before and twisted it like a key in the back of a wind-up doll. He pulled it out and let it clatter on the floor.

"What is he doing?" Mike said.

Alex stood aside and made sure all could see the bloody gash between Rory's legs. Rory's head drooped, but he still made the howling noises, a little softer each time. They helped Alex get a hard-on.

Rory

In the eighth grade Rory got blindsided walking home from the bus stop by a kid in his class who'd been held back at least twice, had to be like sixteen, big kid, and the kid said he was going to kick Rory's ass because he failed the test Rory wouldn't let him copy from his paper for. Rory didn't think the test was the issue. The kid was mean, and he had it out for Rory for being smart and little and the kind of kid bullies picked on but who himself seemed, for some reason, to be without bullying. So, the kid supplied. Knocked him down, broke his glasses, kicked him in the stomach until he puked.

CONCENTRATE. CONCENTRATE ON WHAT THE KICKING FELT LIKE.

This is so much worse.

Alex's eyes looked into his, and Alex's breath was hot on his cheeks. The guy almost *marveled* at him. Like he felt something for him. Even though he was a piece of meat, like all that meat piled up in the kitchen.

And he was going to die.

He had been drunk before, twice, and the feeling was

similar, except it was the

(blood loss)

place where the guy who was taking off his boxer shorts

(he fell from the sky!)

"Stop it! STOP IT!"

That was a girl's voice.

IT HURTS IT HURTS OH GOD IT HURTS SOMEBODY HELP ME!

He heard, in a voice like his, "HI, OH, HI, OH, HI, OH!" His mind completed, *It's off to work we go!* He was a fucking dwarf. One of the seven fucking dwarfs. Dasher and Dancer and Donner and—

CONCENTRATE ON THE FUCKING DWARVES.

But it hurts and OH MY GOD WHAT IS HE DOING?

Drunk on blood loss, drunk on pain, not too drunk to know the kid whose grey eyes looked into his was *sticking his cock inside him—*

sticking his cock where there was nowhere to go—

sticking his cock where his own cock had been—

and pushing deeper, deeper, and deeper. His nerves cried out like a thousand nails dragged across chalkboards, and his vision became strange distortions of red and purple. He could no longer discern whether he was screaming. Every fiber screamed, and he seemed wrapped in plastic, unable to breath, unable to move, unable to make a sound. Pain filled every orifice, ears nose eyes the hole in his center through which all his insides might flood as soon as they let go because the one orifice that cried loudest was the one filled with another boy where he thrusted where he had cut where he thrusted where there was blood where he slid along blood inside and outside and inside and outside and he wasn't too drunk to know

this was fucking

his genitals were a gash and

Alex was fucking his gash

and "STOP IT!" had been Esme's voice, Esme was watching.

Esme would watch him get fucked before his insides flooded out through his gash, and he died not a man not even human but a hole.

The face in front of his smiled, tension around the eyes increasing. Rory heard a grunt.

Rory didn't bother wanting to die. He knew he would. The pain was too much.

The other boy tore into him until he stopped, shuddered, and pushed their foreheads together. Rory assumed he had come inside him. Was he still a virgin?

"You... goddamn... HOLD ON RORY!" Mike's voice. Calming.

The cock pulled out of him. His vision blurred, but he could make out the shape of the one who killed him approaching the bars of his cell.

"You son of a bitch." Mike again. "I'll get you."

"No," the one who killed him said. "I'm going to get you."

After that, he didn't see or hear, but he felt breeze on his broken skin, breeze from nowhere that soothed.

14. LEAVE HIM

Kayla

At a party some gnarly BD/SM porn was on the TV in the background, which was where she preferred to be at most parties, when the host announced he had a snuff film and was going to play it for anybody who wanted to watch. The idea of seeing somebody killed for real didn't flip her switch, but the screen was right there, so she paid attention as the girl on screen got dismantled by masked men with beer bellies, and her mind said *fake*, just like when she watched *Guinea Pig: Flower of Flesh and Blood* and thought *fake*. Those movies didn't look like what she saw with demon boy's back to her, to all three of them, his ass muscles tensing and releasing as he shoved his cock inside Rory where there should be no way in. Those movies didn't capture the diminishment of the sounds Rory made with each deep violation. They didn't include smells. They didn't make her want to cry and throw up at the same time.

When demon boy stepped back, leaned over, and pulled up his blood-soaked boxers, Rory was quiet, probably dead. The pool of blood, which spread from the wall where his legs were nailed toward the cell's bars, looked too enormous. She'd never seen anyone die.

Demon boy said he was going to get them. He was probably right.

But he left the cell without another taunt. They were alone.

Kayla looked at Mike, who stared slack-jawed at his mutilated friend, and she looked—

Esme! No longer beside her. "Esme!"

"Over here!"

Esme had managed to turn away from Rory dying or dead. She stood to the side of the room's entryway, in front of the portion of dirt wall where narrow, concrete floor between entrance and firepit allowed her to stand. She pushed on the wall.

"What are you *doing*?" Kayla resisted the tremendous gravity that held her. She went to her friend.

"Light's coming through this part of the wall." With one hand, Esme pointed near her knees. With the other, she pushed against dirt.

Yes. Light through a crack, but—"So?"

"The wall is hiding something."

Kayla looked back at Mike, who stared at Rory's body, limp on the nails that held it up but still trickling between the legs. *It.* Rory was an *it* now. It looked paler than before.

A crumbling sound brought her back to Esme, who had pushed through the wall. Light shone through the hole through which she retracted her muddy fingers. "It's another way," Esme said. "A secret way. A way out."

Esme didn't want to be here, and neither did she. "We could go back upstairs," Kayla said, noting a worm and a beetle working their ways through wall mud.

"He'll be at the top," Esme said. "He'll be waiting."

Demon boy could be anywhere, but Esme had found another way to go, and Kayla reasoned—or maybe sensed— they were supposed to go the way Esme had found, or Esme wouldn't have found it. What determined what they were *supposed to* do? Would doing the *supposed to* get them killed? Or was it the only way out of the trap?

Esme cleared more dirt, widening the opening. Kayla said, "Mike! Mike, come help!"

Her voice hit Mike like a brick. He teetered, bent over, and retched. It was a dry heave, mostly, some spittle and bile. He looked at Kayla with no comprehension.

"Esme found the way out," Kayla said. "We need you."

"We can't," the boy, who towered over Esme and had to look down to talk to Kayla, said. He was broader than them both, and a lot of it looked like muscle, natural brawn, not gym meat. "We can't leave him."

"We can," Kayla said. Fuck waiting for him. She helped Esme with the wormy mud, pulling out clumps, then loose sections. Together, they needed only a minute to clear enough away to make an opening big enough to use as a passage.

On the other side they could see a small, yellow-lit room.

Esme looked at her. "The way out?"

Kayla nodded. "Mike, get your ass over here."

"What?" the big boy said.

"You're going first."

"I... no!" A spark of comprehension lit up his dull, slack features.

"This isn't about equal goddamned opportunities," Kayla said. "And it's not about what's between anybody's legs." Without thought, she glanced over at Rory. Then everybody looked. "I mean it's not a girls guys thing. Mike, you're the biggest."

"Huh." Mike nodded. "Like that makes a difference." His round, dour expression bombarded her with disapproval.

He clearly didn't know how many dour looks of disapproval she got on the average day. She stared back at him, all her instincts telling her that she needed to win this conflict.

Staring. Staring so long that, meekly, Esme said, "You guys, we don't want to be here, remember?" In her periphery, Kayla detected Esme by the new passage, waiting for one of them to go in. Esme wouldn't go first. Nobody questioned.

More staring.

Finally, Mike exhaled, like a quick cough that expelled exasperation, rolled his eyes, turned his head and said, "Yes!

I'm the biggest! I'm the guy! Whatever! I'll go... fucking—" the word sounded forced—"first!"

For a split-second Kayla thought she might have to respond, but Mike stormed by her and made more dirt crumble as he pushed through into yellow light with a grey tint. Kayla thought about demon boy saying *my them* and she thought about *greylight*. Despite the warmth from the firepits, she shivered.

Mike

What waited beyond the "way out" Esme had discovered was like a node where slightly rounded dirt walls joined at odd angles. The node connected the big, grandiose room with fire pits and cells to an unrefined tunnel where the yellow light faded, and the concrete floor yielded to dirt. The tunnel was the only way for them to go.

The bugs liked the dirt more here than they did near the firepits. Worms dripped from the walls as if they'd tumble to the concrete, but they reentered the dirt through passages previously invisible. Beetles and other crawling things with many legs had equal disregard for gravity. Mike didn't want to imagine, much less hear, the *crunch* of his shoes crushing them as he stepped off the concrete, onto the tunnel's dirt. But he said he would go first. Part of him—

part of him *wanted* to come face to face with that... inhuman... *thing* that had hurt Rory. Maybe the branch he'd swung at him had been rotten. Maybe Mike *could* hurt him. He wanted to try.

But he also wanted to live. He wasn't stupid. If he found a way out, he wouldn't stick around for some vendetta. If he found—

He cut off Rory's dick and fucked the wound.

Mike took a deep breath, tried to shake the thought from his head, and stepped into the tunnel.

140

Crunch.

Who would do that why would anybody how could anybody

—

At first, the tunnel was wide enough for Esme and Kayla, behind him, to walk side by side. It wasn't wide enough for them to walk three abreast, but Mike imagined the girls would want him out in front anyway. The biggest. The best human shield.

Crunch. In his head? Or creeping, crawling lives coming to flattened ends underfoot? The walls, so dense with life... underfoot would hardly be different. Mike felt nauseated. Mike felt—

He turned Rory's manhood into a bloody gash and stuck his hard—

dizzy, almost. The movement that surrounded them sounded like crumpling tissue paper. At least the girls—goth girls, maybe that was why they weren't squealing about the bugs—Mike didn't care if he was stereotyping because they made him go first—but it was a compliment anyway.

Crunch.

The yellow light got dimmer, almost like it dissolved in the thickening greylight. The passage narrowed. Soon they had to walk single-file, Mike in front, Esme behind him, Kayla in the rear. In the whole set-up, they'd gotten one thing right. If he were going to go out with either of them—and he wasn't— he'd go out with Kayla, even though Esme had this weird kind of power to make people feel protective of her. That might have been what Rory liked, the idea of being a protector. Rory was a funny little guy. Rory was—

fucked in a way nobody should ever—

Mike went forward, imagining the guy with the sickle, the guy's face, a couple of feet in front of him so he could punch it with a quick jab, smashing the nose in an explosion of blood, then—

What?

He put his penis where Rory's—

If you push your thumb into his eye socket, push and keep pushing—

Would his thumb know when it got past eyeball and pressed into brain?

Kill the fucker.

Crunch.

Kill the—

"HOLY FUCKING SHIT OW OW OW OW MY GOD!!!!!" At first, the pain was too blinding for Mike to do anything but scream.

Behind him, Esme screamed.

"WHAT!? WHAT!?" Kayla shouted.

Mike bent toward the pain, right foot, above the ankle, hard to see, metal, *unbelievable*, metal with teeth biting into both sides of his leg, a trap, bear trap, smaller, sized for

me

a people trap, and through the pain he tried lifting his right leg, but something rooted the trap, and the leg spilled blood all over the grey-reflecting metal to the apathetic earth.

"Got me!" Mike yelled.

"What!?" Kayla sounded frantic.

Esme crouched beside him. "Foot's caught in a trap."

Mike realized his breathing had gotten heavy, so he tried to slow down, but the effort resulted in an "AAAAAAAAAAAH" sound.

"Can you set him loose?" Kayla crouched, too, trying to see around Esme.

Head spinning, Mike looked from his clamped, bleeding foot—

The guy with the sickle killed—

to Esme and Kayla—

Help help help

Sweat dripped from his forehead, and tears slid down his cheeks, and he couldn't tell one saltwater from the other when they reached the corners of his mouth.

Esme tried to pull the trap's jaws apart.

"OOWAAAAAAAAA!" Mike screamed. The throb of his lower leg pounded against his eardrums, but he still heard the crumple of tissue paper.

Esme backed away. "It... hurts him if I try."

A fox will chew off its foot... Mike tried not to imagine Esme and Kayla chewing off his foot. He failed. He thought of the girls chewing while they contemplated in silence.

"Maybe," Esme said, at last, "I should get a look from the other side." He didn't like the look she gave Kayla. "Mike, I've got to squeeze by."

Oh. Mike filled the width of the tunnel, and he couldn't step aside because the trap held his foot in place, but Esme came to his left side before he could object, and he recoiled. Even pulling his left leg toward his right, shifting his body, made his captured right leg screech agony, but when Esme took the wide step to get over and around him, she teetered, and rather than flatten herself against the infested wall, she grabbed onto Mike for stability. One of his hands went into the wall near his right leg, and he didn't hear a *crunch*, but he thought he heard a *rip* as something not far above his ankle tore. His vision took on all colors, and he didn't know what noise he made, but eventually, he saw Esme again, crouched on the path in front of him, looking at the trap.

"Kayla, I don't know," Esme said. "You're better at figuring out mechanical stuff. You've got to come over here." Esme backed away.

No, no, no!

"I don't know if I can fit," Kayla said.

NO!

"You've got to," Esme said. Rory loved her. Rory, who got fucked—"Or we'll all be stuck here. You can take it, right, Mike?"

The guy with the sickle.

"Y..." NO! "...yeah." They didn't want to be stuck here.

Kayla came the same way Esme had, but Kayla, breasts surging from her bodice, hips broad, would do more than give

Mike a quick grab for stability. She was about to *push* him. Jaw clenched, muscles tight—which made the teeth on his right leg bite harder—he waited.

She pushed through. Their eyes met. She looked so apologetic. If they all lived, maybe he'd break up with Sheri and go out with her after all.

Riiiiiiiiip.

His stomach flipped, but his mouth stayed closed as he tasted bile and swallowed. He thought his foot would come off, but it didn't. He couldn't resist screaming. Kayla reached the other side, where Esme had made room for her. She crouched by the trap. "I don't see a mechanism. A spring... sprung... and now it's... attached. We'd have to pry it off him."

"Please," Mike said.

Kayla tried pulling the jaws apart. The moving teeth in the wounds brought fresh pain.

"We should get help," Esme said.

Kayla grunted. "I can get them apart... some."

"It won't work," Esme said. "We should go."

With a huff and a louder grunt, Kayla tried harder.

"We don't want to be here."

Mike understood. Maybe he should make the situation easier, give them his blessing, but with the tears pouring down his cheeks and the snot dangling from his chin, he didn't feel noble.

Kayla tried harder.

"Leave him," Esme said.

Kayla did her best to release the jaws slowly, but the return of the teeth to their deepest points hurt like hell.

Her eyes looked even more apologetic before she turned to follow Esme away.

Alex

His house would take care of his visitors for a while.

Giving Bruce and Aaron some personal time during the post-Rory lull would help ensure that he had uninterrupted time later when he next indulged. He returned to his Los Angeles bedroom, put on a t-shirt and shorts, and headed for the house's largely conjoined socializing spaces.

Bruce sat in the living room area, stretched on the reclining chair with a mystery novel he might or might not have been reading. A silhouette over Elvis announced Aaron's presence in his makeshift studio. Soft piano music played— Alex guessed Chopin, Bruce's favorite. Alex liked it but Aaron merely tolerated it, which meant Aaron was feeling inclined to indulge Bruce, which meant...?

Had Bruce confronted Aaron over the video? The room was *too* peaceful for Bruce to know the whole truth, but Alex's little powwow with Bruce about whether Aaron pressured him to be on camera had to mean Bruce knew *something*.

"Hey Bruce," Alex said. "How's it going?"

Bruce snapped his hardbound book shut and sat up in the recliner. "Fine." His voice was about half an octave too high. "How's it going, Aaron?"

"Fine." Aaron sounded more natural but not natural. He appeared from behind the divider seconds later. "How are you, Alex? Having a relaxing Saturday?"

"You've hardly left your room all day." Bruce stood. "Not even to use the bathroom."

He could take care of basic needs at his house. "You're not monitoring my bathroom trips," Alex said, squinting an eye at Bruce and crossing far enough into the room to stand equidistant from them both. "That would be weird. Wouldn't it?" He looked at Aaron. "Volunteering to be on camera is one thing. But a camera in the bathroom. Pretty weird."

Bruce and Aaron looked at each other. Alex could see the tension in Aaron's jaw, countered by a slackness in Bruce's. Their loss for words delighted him.

"Hey, I was thinking." Alex recaptured their eyes and drew them toward the kitchen. "Bruce picked up all those veggies at the downtown farmer's market yesterday. I want to chop some up, steam some rice, stir fry in some peanut and sesame oil... you up for some early dinner?"

"Um... sure?" Bruce said.

"You cook?" Aaron said.

"I'm full of surprises." Alex sprung into kitchen action. He started the rice boiling and gathered carrots, onions, peppers, baby broccoli, and squash from the fridge as well as water chestnuts and baby corn from the pantry. Satisfied—both with his basic ingredients and with Bruce and Aaron, who positioned themselves at the dining table with full views of the kitchen—he went into a chopping frenzy, dexterous with the chef's knife.

"You *are* full of surprises," Aaron said.

"My parents left me money for takeout on a lot of nights when they went out. I like pizza, but I could get groceries delivered, too, and I taught myself to cook because you can only eat so much pizza." Alex alternated stirring the carrots and onions in the wok with chopping the other vegetables. "Kind of like I told you about teaching myself to meditate, Bruce."

"A true *wunderkind*," Bruce said.

"Aw shucks." Alex flashed a smile but concentrated on cooking.

"Was that what you were doing most of today, Alex? Meditating?" Bruce's voice had a wonderful combination of suspicion and cluelessness.

"Reading, mostly, though you did catch me on a little... voyage out... earlier." Alex laughed and stirred vegetables.

"What are you reading?" Bruce asked. Did he want to make sure Alex actually *had* been reading? What other sort of mischief could Bruce imagine him getting up to?

"I thought I'd take a break from brain-busting European philosophy and give the Brontë sisters a try. I've almost finished *Jane Eyre*. So many great free books online." Alex had read *Jane Eyre* in the third grade. He preferred *Wuthering*

Heights.

"I think I read that when I was about your age," Aaron said.

"What do you think of it?" Bruce asked.

"I guess I liked it enough," Aaron said.

"I was asking Alex."

He was going to finish the vegetables before the rice was ready. Turning down the heat on the wok, he said, "I like it enough is a pretty good review. The early stuff is good. But once Jane learns that Rochester has been dishonest with her the whole time about already being married... I don't know."

"What do you mean?" Bruce asked.

"I mean," Alex stopped stirring long enough to look at Aaron, then Bruce, then Aaron again, "it's obvious she's destined to return to Rochester or whatever, but I don't know how you bounce back from that kind of betrayal. I'd leave him for good and never look back."

"You would?" Aaron said.

"Wouldn't you?" Alex asked.

"Sometimes love is complicated," Aaron said.

"Adult decisions aren't always clear cut," Bruce said. "It's hard to be sure you have all the facts."

"Can you ever have *all* the facts, Bruce? She's just got to get to a point where she says, 'Enough is enough!'" Alex turned the heat down to a low simmer.

"She does," Bruce said.

The strain in his voice was exquisite.

15. CLOSED CIRCUIT

Kayla

Esme walked in front of her and didn't look back, so Kayla wouldn't look back, even though the sound—Mike whimpered at medium volume—pulled like a magnet. What could they do? Cut off his foot? They still had knives. Esme's meat cleaver might work. But Esme wouldn't do it. Kayla didn't think she could do it.

Mike had a butcher knife. Let him fucking decide.

At last, the tunnel turned, which meant their necks could turn. Esme looked back at Kayla almost immediately, as if she'd been as impatient or more impatient to see the angle forbidden by the possibility of seeing Mike. The corners of her lips curved, not a smile but an offering of reassurance even though she didn't have any. Kayla's eyes watered, and she felt stupid because she wondered how bad her mascara was.

"Want to go back?" Esme said. Checking in front of her, checking the ground, and checking Kayla made Esme's advance slow.

"Back to do what?" Kayla asked.

"Exactly," Esme said. Her pace picked up. "My guess, he's not even there anymore."

Kayla felt like she understood. "What do you mean?"

"The hall... Rory... it swallowed him up. One second with us, the next...."

Kayla shook her head. "We're not that far. We'd hear Mike scream." The whimper had shut off.

"I didn't hear Rory scream when he got nailed to a wall."

Kayla liked hearing Esme say "I don't want to be here" better than what she was saying now. "I don't want to be here" was where Kayla's mind could operate right now. She could scream, *I DON'T WANT TO BE HERE*, but raising her voice so much seemed dangerous. Going back to see whether Mike had been swallowed seemed dangerous. They went forward, but that was dangerous, too.

They stayed quiet for a while. A turn. Another.

Finally, a door. The tunnel presented no other options, though it widened and brightened near the door, making an almost-room like where they'd first come into this... moist... crawling... wandering... trail. More yellow light, less greylight. The door looked like the one in the kitchen, wood with a brass knob, normal if it didn't seem so out of place.

"Want to bet he's on the other side?" Esme asked.

Kayla felt as sure demon boy would be there as she felt sure they'd go there. "No. Should I open it?"

"Be my guest." Esme took long backward strides.

Thinking she should be paralyzed, she felt energized, grabbed the knob, pushed—nothing—then pulled, stepping back, door opening. Disoriented by the brightness and amazement of where they were, Kayla stepped, dazzled, onto grey, foggy carpet bordered by a red wall on one side and a banister on the other, into *the house*, and Esme wandered out, sticking close behind her, where they were upstairs, at the top of the stairs that went up from the foyer where they'd stood near the front door, the front door so near now, and—

SLAM!

Kayla and Esme spun toward the door they'd come through, except where it had been was red wall, no trace of portal or tunnel. "Fuck," Kayla said, teeth together. Maybe it was okay. They were so close to the front door!

On the wall beside her, she saw what looked like a dead fetus from one of those anti-abortionist posters, but it was 3-D.

"Downstairs," Esme said.

"Right."

The rails slithered, but they didn't bite, so the girls went down, side-by-side, hands on scaly rails, careful but hurried, and they got halfway down before the mockery froze them.

Clap, clap, clap.

Not even fucking assholes do the slow clap anymore.

Clap, clap, clap.

Looking as if he'd showered and put on clean undies, though undies were still his only apparel, demon boy emerged from the downstairs hall, white skin without a trace of red. The obnoxious claps drew attention to his hands, empty, no weapon, but Kayla strongly suspected he still had the advantage. Nevertheless, she readied her carving knife in her right hand and gestured for Esme to stay behind her.

Esme held the cleaver at hip height.

"Congratulations, Esme and Kayla. You seized girl power and left the boys to die. Way to go!" When he laughed his stomach muscles showed.

"Fuck you," Kayla said. He moved toward the stairs, and Esme led from behind as they faced him, prepared for him to make a sprint and grab or jab through the banister's posts, while they also took great care to step up backward, higher, up one step, then another. The fight to control panicky breathing made her think for the millionth time that maybe the bodice had to go. She imagined Esme might also be rethinking the fishnets and miniskirt ensemble. Kayla imagined that, if she survived, life from now on would center much more on practicality. Maybe kung-fu.

"You know," the boy said. He was a boy, wasn't he? Not a monster, except in that way boys could be monsters, except... what he had done... like cutting an idiot's idea of a vagina into another boy and sticking your dick in it. "You know, I haven't ruled that out."

He reached the bottom of the stairs. Esme and Kayla were almost at the top.

"Ruled out what?" Kayla felt lost.

"Fucking you. Or one of you, anyway. Eeny, meeny, miny...." He laughed again and patted his stomach before setting one foot on the bottom step. "Forgive my chattiness. I just ate and feel a little... lazy."

Esme and Kayla looked at one another. Each knew what the other was thinking demon boy might have eaten.

When they were finally at the top of the stairs and at a loss for where to go, from the third step up he laughed the same jovial laugh that might have been charming. If he wasn't a fucking psycho who fell from the sky on a mission to kill them all in unspeakable ways. Oh, the ifs. Kayla chuckled.

"Come on, Kay. Don't get hysterical on me." Esme, apparently, still had reserves.

"Oh, Esme! Let Kayla have a little laugh!" He got higher and higher on the stairs. "And I did *not* eat either of your friends, if that's what you're thinking. The meal was vegetarian." Kayla and Esme backed up as far as the wall where the fetus was nailed, but the distance was narrowing. "Huh. I just realized that I know *your* names, but you don't know mine."

Kayla watched way too much TV for this one. "It's okay, you let us go, and we won't—"

"I'm Alex Packard, Alex is fine. I'm still new enough at your school to be a 'new kid,' but you and some others caught *my* eye right away. You can see I've already pictured you in the heavens." He gestured to their right, away from the stairs, toward where the hall turned and got darker. Pictures like Hollywood headshots were pinned to the wall like the fetus was, and Kayla saw what he meant right away. She saw herself beside Kayla, two pictures in a row with two other girls, one she didn't know and one that bitch Marian from the Purity Ring Force or whatever they called themselves. Rory and Mike were in a row with two other boys.

"There's that girl from that play. The one from the trees." Esme pointed to a row of pictures that mixed boys and girls. They were all boys and girls, all about their age.

Winding through, under, and around the pictures were places where the wall, or a thin layer of its red coating, rose and fell like pulsing veins. Kayla wanted to stab one of them to see if it bled, but she was afraid. Their situation might get worse if she made the house angry.

She chuckled again, and Esme scowled at her.

"So, you like the display? The superstars of yesterday, today, and tomorrow?" Alex had reached the top of the stairs. He grinned at them, close enough to lunge forward and swallow them.

Esme darted into the hall and turned right. Kayla followed. The red walls here had even stranger displays, animals, or animal parts on one side, swatches of human skin, with what was probably a human face on top, on the other side. The hallway ended with two doors, one straight ahead and one to the right. Esme started opening the door straight ahead.

Alex stood in the hall behind them. "Not that way! It would be so much worse!"

Kayla grabbed the knob on the right, pushed through the doorway, and then she and Esme stood in a bedroom mostly occupied by an unthreatening waterbed. The paintings on the walls, though... shapes, thankfully, relief from the ubiquitous red... though crimson and violet dominated, not taking her thoughts far from blood and viscera, which she'd never think of the same way again now that she'd seen what she'd seen. The shapes, jagged lines and distorted circles, looked like abstractions when she looked at them directly, but when she tried to look away, they became faces looking back at her. She couldn't see any of them, not really, but they were everywhere, watching.

Chains that ended with cuffs hung from the wall not far from where they'd entered.

Alex's voice came from the hall: "Did I say you could go in my room?"

Esme slammed the door they'd come through and turned the lock on the knob. Kayla felt disproportionate relief.

If the door *had* a lock, then maybe they were *supposed to—*

Rhythmic laughter came from the door's other side. Kayla squeaked, "Ha-HA-ha!" in response.

"Do you really think they'll let you keep me out of my own bedroom?" The door barely muffled Alex's voice.

They were everywhere, watching.

The room had one other door. It had to be a closet.

Kayla wanted to laugh and scream at the same time, but she also felt serenity.

The closet door opened in toward the bedroom, as did the door from the hall. If she and Esme wanted to attack someone coming from Alex's direction, they wanted to be on the closet side of their door options. Clearer shot. Some military strategist might tell her the opposite, that in the reverse scenario the door could be a shield or something, but she felt drawn to the closet. Away from all that watching.

Taking Esme's hand, she said, "Come on," and led toward the closet door.

"Wait, I don't know—"

Esme seemed surprised because Kayla *did* wait, stopped short, having glimpsed, by chance, if chance even worked anymore, the lock on the hallway door's knob turn, by itself, to the unlocked position. The door opened. Alex said, "I'm afraid the chase is almost over."

Kayla yanked Esme into the closet, and the smells of piss, shit, and rot assaulted them, blocking everything else. The walls were metallic. The floor was metallic. Kayla turned around and, as it shut, saw that this side of the door was metallic. Her brain placed the next sound with startling immediacy: a metal bar on the door's other side slid into position, barricade for a prison door.

Esme said, "I wonder who she was."

Confused, Kayla looked at Esme, who nodded downward toward the room's center. A corpse lay there, not rotten skeleton corpse but dried out like a vampire had been at it for days corpse. It had been a girl, unidentifiable from the bluish shriveled skin but Black from the look of her well-preserved hair. She was probably younger than any of them. Had been. It had been.

Also at the center of the room, against one of the long walls of the very large metal closet, on a shelf the perfect height for a sofa, sat a small television, its screen so tiny that even Esme would need to bend down to see it right. The room didn't have a sofa or anywhere else to sit.

"You girls should have everything you need, so enjoy the show, and don't worry. I'll come back for you." Alex's voice sounded warped coming through metal.

The TV turned on.

Esme

She expected a twist, like if they spent too long looking at the TV screen, which had the image of static accompanied by a whir, the dead girl in the middle of their cell would get up and attack. She couldn't think of why that would happen, but she couldn't think of why any of this would happen, and why else would a corpse be in their cell? It *was* a cell, like the place where Alex killed Rory was a cell. Alex. Such a normal name.

The dead girl could be there to scare them, kind of a "you're next."

She could be there *because* she was disgusting. Like the shit. Esme followed her nose to the bucket in the corner and saw it was mostly full of what looked like the dark depths of a port-a-potty. Esme didn't want to think about

trapped in here used the bucket as a toilet trapped until she withered

because this cell was not the end, not hers or Kayla's, because Alex wasn't done with them, he'd said as much, small comfort, but still the sliver of a chance.

Kayla appeared to be under the spell of a hypnotist, head moving from TV to corpse to door and back as if following a steadily swinging pendulum. Esme hitched the meat cleaver's handle back through a beltloop, awkward but workable, and looked at her fingernails. The dark nail polish didn't hide the grime. She didn't want to think about what she'd touched. What had touched her.

She didn't want to think.

She didn't want to be here.

A blip in the TV's sound and image made Kayla jump. It focused Esme's attention. Stepping close, they hunched over to see. The image was color, hi-def. Esme didn't know why she'd expected some black and white, *Blair Witch* sort of thing.

Alex's face, shoulders, and extended arms filled the tiny wide screen. He held a camera on himself; it jittered in his hands. Excitement? Nervousness seemed unlikely. Doing what he did put him a long way from fear. "Girls! Welcome to the next performance."

He turned the camera, and it got even shakier as he showed his surroundings, another cell, this one like Rory's, bars, fire beyond, concrete floor, an earthen wall, but Mike wasn't nailed to it. Mike was in a very high-backed metal chair with no arms. Starting at his feet, the clear color TV image showed how silver duct tape bound him to the burnished metal beneath and behind him: tape hugged his lower legs (right foot barely attached but cauterized), his thighs, his abdomen, his arms and chest, his neck, his lower jaw, and his forehead. The tape on his jaw was weird. It wouldn't completely stop him from talking. Or screaming.

"Okay, so I hope you're glued to your television set," Alex said. He set the camera on something, probably a tripod, that made the screen fill with Mike's profile, head mashed against chair by the tape around his forehead and jaw. His brown skin glistened. His lips quivered. Between frequent blinks, his eyes stayed very wide, white sclera, brown iris. "I wanted the first show to be a closeup affair, but it wasn't really. So, I'm experimenting with this." Alex's hand waved a pair of needle-nosed pliers between the camera and Mike's distressed profile. "And with these."

Mouth opened a fraction of an inch, Mike forced out, "I'll kill you, I'll kill you, *I'll kill you!*"

Off camera, Alex said, "No. You won't."

Mike's face contracted in strain. Cords in his neck pushed against tape, but the tape was stronger.

"Under the circumstances, I should also use this, shouldn't I?" A white hand waved a box cutter, blade out, between the camera and Mike's profile.

Kayla gasped but didn't look away. Neither of them would look away.

Seconds didn't pass before white fingers grabbed Mike's upper lip—he had full lips, not overly large but plush—and Esme saw a flash of the lip the fingers pinched popping. Instead, the pliers replaced the fingers, latching on, and they pulled the lip, stretched it and stretched it until the skin looked thin. Mike's lower jaw managed a little wiggle, like maybe he wanted to bite, like maybe any part of his body would fight if it could. He made a loud, low sound, a hollow cry lost somewhere between his chest cavity and the back of his throat.

Alex cut the thin, stretched skin with the box cutter, removing Mike's upper lip. What remained in the grasp of the pliers didn't look like a lip. Distended, dripping like the thin frown of face above the upper row of teeth and braces now exposed, it didn't look like anything. Fascination, sickness. It disappeared from the screen.

Esme and Kayla glanced at each other. They couldn't do anything to help Mike or themselves, but they had an obligation to see what would happen next. That made Mike less alone, didn't it? It was worse if he was alone.

She'd have to cut her fingernails. Soak her fingers in peroxide or something to get at the filth.

Next, no big surprise, Alex stretched Mike's lower lip and cut it off. The blood coursing over his white teeth and gathering around the braces' brackets and wires provided vivid contrast on screen. The edges of face that were all wound twitched where she imagined muscles tried to connect to lips and nerves fired for sensations like kissing. Mike looked hideous.

Alex's voice, off screen: "Now that *those* are out of the way, we can get started."

Started?

Esme and Kayla glanced at each other. Bending over so long to watch the screen was painful. Esme's back ached, but Kayla had ridiculous tits, so it had to be worse for her. It wasn't going to stop either of them, though. They'd only just started.

Alex jammed the pliers into Mike's mouth on the side they couldn't see. The eye on screen transitioned from an oblivion of pain and terror to a cloud of confused awareness, not understanding but wondering, like Esme was wondering, what Alex was doing. Then pure pain returned with a guttural "AAAAAAAA" louder than the noises Mike had managed during the clipping of either lip.

The white hand twisted the pliers nose-upward and pulled. Esme didn't understand until the metal jaws got far enough from Mike's jaw for the bloody spittle to reflect the mixture of orange firelight with greylight. That reflection brought another, dimmer detail into view, more metal coated red, wire. Alex was pulling out the wire from Mike's braces. Esme had braces in middle school. Tiny tweaks of one of those wires could hurt a lot.

"Look at that mess. Popped two brackets and almost took a tooth. I doubt the camera mic caught that little rip when the tooth started to give, but I'm pretty sure I didn't imagine it. Did you hear it, Mike? I guess you can't nod. Can you give me a yes?"

Mike spat blood.

"You're no fun." Off screen, Alex's sigh was audible. "Girls, you probably want a look at this. It'll be more difficult with the camera in the way, but I think I've got enough leverage."

They watched.

The pliers started upright this time; the white hand shoved the open jaws into the upper row of teeth and grabbed hold of the wire. Puuuuuuuullllllll. "AAAAAAAAAAA."

Alex had strong hands. The wire gave way, bent, and scraped out of the brackets. Some brackets broke from the teeth. One bracket took a lateral incisor with it, and the rip Esme heard might have been her imagination. The blood spray wasn't. Alex didn't remove the wire completely. He let it poke out of Mike's mouth, bent, a tooth attached to it.

The wire from the lower row on the camera side came next. He let it stick out too—no tooth attached to the part removed—and then bent it so the two ends of the lower wire met. With the pliers he wound them together. Clasping the connected pieces, he pulled. He groaned with exertion.

Mike's noise was a ululating, guttural scream.

Some brackets broke off, but most pulled teeth.

Alex

He'd created his own version of Aaron's handheld Sony to use in his house, and then he'd had the idea of a feed to a TV for an audience who could see one of his shows up close. It worked well, or it seemed to. It might have worked better if he'd made it two-way, with a camera in the bedroom closet cell and a TV on his side so he could watch their reactions, but he sensed *they* were pleased with the experiment, which meant he was doing something right. He kept thinking he'd have to wipe blood off the lens, which would mean finding a rag, but none ever splashed that way.

Mike glazed over, but he was conscious and reactive enough to seem like he knew what was happening to him, which made the activity more enjoyable. Pulling on the wires from the braces, Alex extracted the teeth that he could, twisting from different angles in efforts to get the more stubborn masticators. Eventually he yanked the wires and tore out the remaining teeth directly, a lengthy but rewarding process. Esme and Kayla would not lose interest. Anything but watching would require facing their actual circumstances.

All the work in Mike's mouth loosened the tape on his jaw, giving him enough mobility to talk toothlessly or, if he had faith in his gums' firmness, to try biting. The sad young man seemed adrift on a sea of pain, however, and Alex felt unconcerned. One more stroke would finish the show.

The jaws of the needle nosed pliers weren't scissor-sharp but did have sharp ridges, so when Alex held open Mike's mouth with his left hand, pushed in the pliers with his right, and clamped down on the back of Mike's tongue, he expected he broke tastebud-dotted flesh. He squeezed the tool's grips and pulled. Mike *did* try to bite, so Alex's left hand worked to keep the jaw open while the right hand squeezed and pulled. Careful not to tip the chair over, he used Mike's immobilized body for extra leverage, pulling like he never had for any of the teeth, squeezing and pulling. Greater gushes of blood poured around his hand. Mike made choking sounds. Puuuuuullllllll.

Rip!

Mike's tongue came loose, and Alex removed it from Mike's mouth without letting it drop from the pliers' grip. He held it up to his own eyes for inspection, then held it close to the camera's lens. The final word, so to speak. Now Mike could bleed to death, choke on his own blood, whatever suited him.

16. LEARNING

Esme

For what could have been hours but was probably only a couple of minutes, they watched the small screen. Alex announced his departure. Mike made the gagging sounds while blood poured from a mouth that might not have been closable. A shudder tried to pass through Mike's constricted body. Mike became silent and still.

Esme stood up straight, then bent backward, stretching, hands reaching around to sooth the muscles in her aching back. Worrying about how much her back hurt after bending over to watch Mike die seemed callous. She would be callous, then.

Kayla was standing up straight, too, and looking at her. "What?" Esme said.

"They're dead," Kayla said. "He killed them."

"Uh-huh." How gonzo had her friend gone?

"What do we do?" Kayla said.

"What do we do?" Even if Kayla had snapped, Esme didn't want to soft pedal the facts. "We die."

"DON'T SAY THAT!"

Shouting in the small metal room hurt her ears. Softly, Esme said, "What should I say?"

"Think, damn it! There's got to be a way out of here."

Esme looked down at the desiccated corpse. "She never found a way."

"We'll be smarter." Kayla's voice cracked.

Taking the meat cleaver into her hand, Esme crossed to the door. She checked around the doorframe with the blade to see if it caught against the bar holding the door, to see if the skinny metal could slip through and lift the barricade, but the knife didn't catch anything. "There's a way out," she said to Kayla, who had crept up behind her. "He said he'd be back."

"And then what?"

"We get out. We die."

"Damn it, Esme!"

"What?" Her best friend couldn't be an idiot. "You want me to pretend that those two nerd boys and the two of us weren't pulled into some kind of trap so that this... psycho... Alex... could torture and kill us? Pretend that the outcome wasn't fixed from the start?"

Kayla took her own knife in hand and pointed to Esme's. "We can still fight!"

"It won't make any difference."

"Don't be such a bitch!"

"I'm not being a bitch!" Esme *was* getting mad. "I'm being a realist."

"Realist? *Real?*" Kayla's open-mouthed smile was wide enough to suit The Joker. "What does ANY of this have to do with REAL?" Her chuckle had a maniacal edge.

"I told you not to get hysterical," Esme said. "And don't be stupid, either."

"I'M NOT THE ONE GIVING UP AND SAYING THERE'S NOTHING TO DO BUT D—"

Metal screeched against metal, interrupting Kayla. The sliding sound had to be someone—who else?—removing the bar from the cell door. Vaguely, Esme recalled a plan to rush Alex when the door opened outward, but she wouldn't do that now. Now, she would die.

Unless there was an opening.

With another screech, the door swung wide, and Alex stood before them, blood on his face and in his blond hair, blood drying all over his bare white torso. "I sense conflict," he said.

Esme stood at Kayla's side.

"Eeny, meeny...." Alex laughed. "Kayla, will you come out here and join me please?"

"NO!" Kayla screamed, her voice buzzing along the cell's metal walls.

Alex waved a hunting knife, blade about six inches, curved at the tip, and said, "Kayla, you'll come here, or I'll stab Esme in the throat."

Esme gazed into Kayla's eyes, deciding to plead. "We have to do what he says." *Prolong the inevitable.* Why, at the end, did every moment of survival become so valuable? She thought of her great-grandfather, unable to communicate, clinging to life through a respirator while her great-grandmother called every day a "gift." *Give me this gift, Kayla. Prolong the inevitable.*

As if answering Esme's plea, Kayla stepped forward. Alex lowered the knife as she left the cell. He cleared the way for her to walk in the direction of the bedroom door. The exit. But Esme doubted he was showing her out.

They both disappeared from the view afforded by the doorframe. If Esme wanted to see what came next, she would have to leave the cell—get closer.

Rattling, jingling—what the fuck?—Kayla's voice, "How —"

A human noise, *oomph,* probably Kayla because the next noise, a scream, was definitely her.

"Quiet!" Alex barked. "I'm not going to hurt you unless I have to. Have I lied to you yet?"

Kayla sniveled. Esme chopped at the air with the cleaver. She shook her head from side to side. Going against him wouldn't work. *They* wouldn't let it work. Not here. Not in *his* house. Dead people in the trees, human skin and animal parts in the hall, even the fetus, all *his.*

She'd never met anything closer to a god. Or an angel. Or a devil. Funny how quickly herd morality asserted itself. But maybe she was confused. Maybe she meant to think of him as an *Übermensch.*

"Esme," said his voice, soft and smooth. "Ehhhhhhhhzzzzzzzzzzzzmmmmmmmmeeeeeeeeeeee."

She took a deep breath and marched out of the cell.

In the bedroom by the closed door to the hall, Kayla stood bound to the wall by the chains that had been there, the cuffs around her wrists tightened like they'd been welded. She regarded Esme with abject terror. Her mascara looked awful, and the tears kept flowing through the black moraines. Her whole body trembled, making the chains rattle and her tits inside the bodice jiggle.

Alex used his hunting knife to wave Esme forward. "Come closer. I won't bite. See?" Without warning, he rushed his face to Kayla's and planted a kiss on her lips before she could pull her head away. When she did pull away, she didn't use all the distance the chains would give her. Esme understood. Fear only let defiance take her so far.

Esme knew what she had to do. She dropped the meat cleaver and moved toward Alex, loosening her hips.

"Wait!" Alex said. "Pick that back up!" Did he mean the cleaver? "You're going to need it!"

Kayla

We'll die. We'll die. We'll die.

Chains held her to a wall, and two boys were dead, and the boy who killed them stood close to her with a knife, and she didn't have a knife anymore, but Esme had a meat cleaver, and Alex, the killer with blood in his short blond hair, held Esme at arm's length.

She didn't want to piss herself.

"Esme, please, I'll turn the show over to you in a moment, but you have to indulge me in one thing." Alex beamed.

Kayla shivered, rattling chains.

Esme shrugged.

"Kayla, I said I'm not going to hurt you, and I won't unless you can't stay still, understand?"

Kayla didn't understand, but she nodded.

Alex's right hand, holding the knife, came toward her, coasting with deliberate slowness down toward her belly. The left hand was wily; she didn't know what it was doing until it was already pulling the tight bodice away from her skin. Now she could see his hands coordinating, the left lifting the bodice, the right using the curved end of the knife like a hook beneath the bottom laces holding the bodice together. "Let's test the meaning of 'bodice ripper,' okay?" Alex winked at her.

She realized what he would do an instant before he did it. As she tried to implode, pulling as much of herself away from her clothes as she could, he pulled his blade upward, cutting strings, and she felt the metal, its cool, foreign hardness—

but it didn't touch her. He flung open the split bodice like drapes, exposing her.

"Like unwrapping a Christmas present. Tits to die for, huh, Ez? May I call you Ez?"

What escaped Esme's throat was hushed: "Sure."

Kayla's mind raced. Whatever he was going to do to her, it had started. Her skin was exposed. The knife, her skin—

Why did he ask Esme to pick the meat cleaver back up?

"You can't tell me, Ez," he said, "that you're not jealous."

Oh God.

"What do you think? You want to cut them off?" Alex cupped a hand by Esme's ear but didn't lower his volume enough to keep Kayla from hearing: "I can say from experience, it's a lot of fun."

Kayla's heart pounded, and she was afraid he would see.

"No," Esme said.

Of course, no. They had been friends since they were little, and "little" was funny because Esme was older but Kayla was always bigger, which matched how they looked out for each other in different ways, each being in charge in different ways, or being brave at different times. Kayla didn't know who was supposed to be the brave one now.

"Okay, Esme! That was a warmup question! God, I feel like a gameshow host." Alex looked pleased with himself. "It's time for you to step up and play for real! Would you like to know what you're playing for?"

Esme looked from Kayla to him and put on a bad fake smile. "Sure. Tell me."

"Why, a ticket out of here! Think about how far away the idea seems right now, the idea of being back in your own home, maybe taking a shower, maybe getting into bed...." He inhaled through noticeable nostrils. "Ah! Such a relief!"

He got off on teasing them. Like he couldn't simply *kill* Rory and Mike. And like their deaths had to be so unlike each other. He was what her mom called an emotional tourist, but... the serial killer kind.

"What do you want me to do?"

Don't ask....

"Simple enough." Alex gestured to Kayla with both hands in a flourish. "Kill her!"

She wasn't going to piss herself!

Esme stepped back. "I—"

"Wait a minute," Alex said. "Don't get too excited and do it all at once. You have to follow my instructions. *Ease* into it. After all, it'll be as easy to quit later as it is now."

Battles for composure raged in Esme's knees, hands, and chin. Her grip on the meat cleaver held.

But she *wouldn't*. She had to know that they needed to show solidarity, not play his games, certainly not hurt each other—

"Okay," Esme said.

NO!

"Good. To begin, I want you to make a shallow, vertical cut—it has to bleed!—going from her bellybutton to the space between her tits. The space between the tits. There's got to be a name for that, doesn't there? Teat Valley. Draw a Red Road from Belly Crater to Teat Valley."

Kayla backed all the way to the wall. "Esme. Don't."

Esme walked... no, sauntered... toward her. "Like he said before, hold still."

Doubt about whether Esme would go through with it lingered until the cleaver's sharp corner pierced the skin between her breasts, and Esme stared at the rectangular knife as she pushed more of it in and dragged it down, bisecting Kayla's belly in red that soon welled over. By the time Esme was done with that first, long cut, Kayla's chest and stomach were a mess. She pissed herself.

It was the first cut of many.

Esme

She expected Alex to tell her to cut off more of Kayla's clothes, but he didn't. When clothing blocked access to thighs or arms or sides or back, he instructed her to cut through the offending fibers, which almost always led to deeper damage to the flesh beneath, probably his motivation. The hunting knife appeared at Kayla's throat to answer attempts to evade Esme's efforts to carry out Alex's instructions. Kayla gave up fighting quickly. She didn't help when Alex told Esme to slice across Kayla's ass so that she'd have a new crevasse to turn her backside into a plus, but she let herself be moved.

Alex challenged Esme to make cuts with little chops instead of long slices. "Trust yourself," he said. "You can control how deep you chop. It's less painful if it's quick. Isn't that right, Kayla?"

Breathing was Kayla's primary business, but she managed to say, "What are you?"

He instructed Esme to chop into muscle slightly above the collar bone.

Kayla accumulated deep cuts in so many places that Esme began to wonder whether Alex intended the proverbial death by a thousand cuts, four or five cuts on each arm, five or six on each leg, at least that many on the torso after the center split, more around the shoulders and on the back, one on the face Esme hadn't meant to split the eye socket, but it had. Kayla was in a bad way, but she was still standing.

"Hack into one of her feet," Alex said. "Cut a foot in half."

Sudden dizziness made Esme think she was about to fall in Kayla's place. The room spun, became a blur, and spun, slowed, and spun, settling, and her vision settled on Alex's bloody face. He kissed her, soft lips, soft peck. "Try it on your knees," he said. "Chop, chop."

Esme dropped to her knees. She felt drunk. Her arm raised the meat cleaver and brought it down on Kayla's shoe. Again. Again. The foot came apart. Kayla, more bawling than screaming, fell forward, but the chains caught her, and she achieved a balance with the chains and one foot that kept her from crumpling.

"Better for the feet to match, isn't it?"

Esme turned to the other foot. Chop, chop.

At Kayla's tenth's birthday party, Kayla's mom had given Esme a tiara so she wouldn't feel left out. Esme had felt too old to need it, but she had also felt like it was a really nice thing.

Kayla drooped to the floor, arms held up by the cuffs that seemed fused to her skin, the rest of her sagging.

"I know! Maybe if you cut her hands off, she can get free!" Alex pointed enthusiastically to a portion of wrist above a cuff.

Esme had doubts.

"Cut her hands off," he repeated.

"Sure," she said. Somehow, smiling was easier with the sensation of his lips still on hers.

Kayla must have been in shock because her reactions were like halved reflexes. The best Esme could do was hold one of Kayla's hands in one hand while she sawed with the cleaver in the other. The operation took patience, back and forth and up down and around. The initial spray surprised her, but she already had blood on her face running with her makeup. She probably looked as insane as Alex. Maybe by now she was. Back and forth and up down and around. She had to hack at the bone, which required not caring whether she hit her own hand, holding Kayla's so tightly even though it had long ago stopped returning her grip. Hack. Hack. Hack. She tried bending the hand back to see if the bone would snap off.

When she removed one hand, she had to do it all again with the other hand.

"She's about used up, isn't she?" Alex asked, standing near Esme, who might have chopped at him, but she didn't dare.

"She isn't dead." Esme knew because the spurting blood had a pulse.

"No, but she has become boring. I think you should go ahead and chop off her head." Alex gave her room.

"I should...."

"I recommend doing it from standing and bending a bit, holding her up by the hair."

Esme always liked Kayla's hair, even though she had to dye it to get it as black as Esme's own. She stood, took a handful of the dyed locks, and lifted the head until the neck, bloody from surrounding wounds, was exposed. Chop, chop.

The body fell away, suspended on chains, but the head swung at the end of the hair Esme held, freed.

Freed.

It was over.

She turned to Alex, who took the head from her hand and tossed it aside. He took the cleaver from her other hand and dropped it. He took her in his arms and kissed her. "You *are* amazing," he said. He kept kissing her, lips on cheeks, chin, lips, closed eyes, lips, cheeks, neck, lips.

She put her arms around him. "And after," she said, trying to sound seductive, "I get to go?"

"Oh *yes*," Alex said.

Her heart, or whatever remained in her chest, expanded. She looked into Alex's eyes, such grey eyes, such bright grey eyes. She felt the softness of his lips exploring her blood-covered chest, and the light from his eyes still penetrated her in her memory, the greylight that made this moment, not any other, all she could feel.

17. LEARNING TOO MUCH

Bruce

He didn't pretend to read. Beside him, Aaron sat up in bed with an equally silent stare at the turned-off television. Which of them would talk first? His own thoughts muddled concern with curiosity. A desire to know masqueraded as a need, or a need felt like a desire. Aaron only added more uncertainty, and talking to him only had intermittent attraction.

"You worried?" Aaron broke the spell.

"Yes," Bruce said.

"Okay." They kept looking at the blank TV screen. "About what?"

"About Alex. About you."

"Okay."

Surprised by Aaron's clipped answer, Bruce looked at his husband. "I think you're both lying to me."

Aaron met his eyes. "What am I lying about?"

"What's going on with you and Alex?"

Aaron huffed. "You still think I make kiddie porn?"

"Did you?"

"You think I'm a pedophile?"

Bruce didn't answer. The honest response—that he thought it was possible—would be too hurtful. He didn't know what to think. Whatever his suspicions, he felt protective of

Alex and Aaron both.

"What is Alex lying about?" Aaron asked. "Me?"

"No," Bruce said. "At least, that's not what worries me. Primarily."

"Okay," Aaron said. "We might have something in common, then. Alex is secretive."

"He's a loner," Bruce said. *Antisocial.* He woke up his cell phone's screen.

"He plays with people." Aaron shifted attention to Bruce's phone. "What are you doing?"

"Earlier today, I put the number for the Decatur Police on my phone." Bruce retrieved the number from Contacts.

"The Decatur... where Alex lived with his parents. Why?"

"I want an update on Letta and Dave and... Alex." Bruce's thumb hovered over the Call button.

"You think Alex lied about the murders?" Aaron acted as if Bruce had used a foreign language.

"I don't know," Bruce said. He pressed the button.

Aaron sighed. "Don't call now. It's late here. It's the middle of the night there. They'll just tell you to call back."

The phone rang three times before a young woman's voice answered. Bruce informed her that he had called for an update on the investigation into the murders of Letta and David Packard. Yes, he knew what time it was. No, he didn't want to call back. He was calling from a different time zone and preferred to get whatever information the Department could provide now, please. No, he wasn't another one of "those nutjobs." He was family, Letta Packard's closest surviving family member, other than her son, whom he'd adopted. The family needed an update. Her understanding meant a lot. Anything she could do, he'd appreciate. Nicholson. Bruce Nicholson. Letta Packard's brother.

Officer Andrews, who had a wispy Southern accent, put him on hold. After a few minutes, during which Aaron stared at him and Bruce stared at nothing, a man's voice said, "Hello?"

"Hello?" Nervousness galvanized him. "Who's this? I was talking to Officer Andrews? She—"

"This is Detective Grant." His deep, gravelly voice conjured the perfect image of an overweight and balding, hardboiled and grizzled, always-needing-a-shave detective. "Is this really Bruce Nicholson?"

The question made "Bruce Nicholson" sound like a celebrity name. "Yes, but who—"

"I'm in charge of your sister's case." He grunted. "Mostly. I always figured you'd call me, just not at one-o-fucking-clock in the goddamned morning on a Satur, er, Sunday."

"It's just past ten here." What a stupid thing to say! "Are a lot of homicide detectives at their desks at one-o-fucking-clock in the goddamned morning on a Sunday?" In addition to the voice conjuring an image of a clichéd bear of a cop, it had apparently also put that image in a desk chair with its feet on a desk.

"That's right," Detective Grant said, "you took the kid all the way to Los Angeles. With all the lawyers and social workers and *you* buzzing around him, I never got a crack at him, and now he's out of reach, isn't he? Couldn't have planned it better if he did."

Bruce faced Aaron as he said, "You're talking about Alex."

"Hey, we could have something in common," the detective said. "We can't get to sleep. You called for an update?"

"Yes." Bruce was about to get what he was after, and he didn't like it.

"No leads, and we only ever had one suspect," Detective Grant said. Did the Decatur Police Department allow smoking indoors? The rumble in the detective's voice made sense with a lifetime of cigarettes. His dramatic pauses could be drags on an... unfiltered... deathstick.

"You're going to say it was Alex." Bruce kept all emotion from his voice.

Detective Grant laughed. "That's why you called, isn't

it? You noticed something off? Did some animals in the neighborhood go missing?"

"Animals? What are you talking about?" Bruce saw his own bewilderment on Aaron's face.

Aaron whispered, "Put him on speakerphone."

Bruce shook his head *no*.

"The Packards' next-door neighbor was a cop. She was convinced Alex killed her cat for shits and giggles. Her instincts told her he at least knew *something* more about Letta and Dave." Detective Grant snorted.

Where was Herb? Not the most social cat, but he usually hopped up to be with them at bedtime. "You think Alex killed his neighbor's cat." *For shits and giggles.*

"A lot of animals went missing in that neighborhood, and a lot of people used words like 'creepy' to describe Alex Packard," the detective said.

"What are you saying, Detective?"

"Other kids were afraid of him."

"He's a loner, a different kind of kid, socially awkward," Bruce said. "People are afraid of what's different." He didn't add: *especially in the South*. His grip on the phone tightened.

"They start with animals," Detective Grant said. "They don't stop there. They work their ways up."

"Who's 'they?'"

"I was there, you know," Detective Grant said. "The morning when the crime scene was discovered. I got there before they took the boy away. I saw him look at his parents' bodies—worst mess I ever saw, made me glad I skipped breakfast—total lack of emotion. Then he caught me looking, and the blankness went away. He turned into a confused, traumatized boy."

Bruce felt tension building in his shoulders and chest. He turned away from Aaron and spun his legs so that he sat on the edge of the bed. "What are you saying about Alex, Detective?"

"What were you hoping to find out when you called?"

That rumbling, know-it-all voice.

"We're talking about a kid."

"I know."

"We're talking about my *nephew*. More or less, my son."

"I know."

"WELL I DON'T MUCH APPRECIATE WHAT YOU'RE SAYING!"

"I gathered that."

"You can't solve the goddamned case, so you want a scapegoat who can't defend himself."

"No evidence, other than him being in the same house, which isn't any kind of evidence considering he lived there, links the boy to the murders. Nobody is coming after him for this."

"Then what—the fuck—are you trying to accomplish with the shit coming out of your mouth?" At some point, Aaron had gotten out of bed. He stood near the edge where Bruce sat, eying him with befuddled shock.

"Mr. Nicholson, I apologize for having upset you. I'm only sharing information I have and, I guess, trying to tell you to keep an eye on the boy. He needs watching. A reputation isn't evidence, either, especially when a kid is involved, but it's enough to take as a warning."

"Consider me warned." Bruce hung up and slammed the phone on his nightstand, not caring if he cracked the screen.

"Yikes," Aaron said. "You look furious."

Bruce stood. "I *am* furious." Why was he so furious? "You know what that asshole detective did?"

Aaron, looking particularly narrow stripped to his boxer briefs for bedtime, sat on the bed in the spot next to where Bruce had been, encouraging Bruce to sit again. Instead, Bruce paced in front of him. "What did he do?"

"Where's Herb?" Bruce's mind raced.

"What did the cop say?"

"The cop. Fucking cop. Irresponsible hick asshole with a badge. He tried to say Alex is a psychopath."

Aaron's chin dipped toward his collarbone as if he were trying to swallow the word "psychopath." "You're kidding. Why?"

"No real reason." Bruce paced faster. "Some speculation from fellow hicks and a need for someone to blame. It makes me—eergh!" He clawed at the air as if he could throttle Detective Grant's neck.

"It's amazing there was even someone to talk to." Aaron didn't seem to understand. "Why did you call? What did you think you would find out?"

"DON'T YOU START ON ME, TOO!"

"Unless you want Alex to join the conversation, keep your voice down."

"DON'T—" But Aaron was right. Alex would hear yelling through the walls. And if the goal was to protect Alex from the asshole words of the Southern bigot detective, Alex needed to stay out of the conversation.

When had that become the goal?

Aaron

Bruce was sending out mixed signals and angry in a way Aaron didn't understand, which only multiplied Aaron's frustration, frustration about the shower video and what Bruce thought of it, frustration about whatever that detective had said on the phone, frustration about Bruce's inscrutability in a moment of high dudgeon. And what *was* Alex's game? "Psychopath" was a ridiculous label, but the boy was devilish... adorably devilish... but most devils would be adorable if they could, wouldn't they? The devil's first duty is to *persuade*.

"Where's Herb?" Bruce repeated.

"What's Herb got to do with anyth—" but during the phone conversation, Bruce had said something about Alex killing a cat—"you think Alex might have done something to Herb?"

Bruce went to the dresser and got a t-shirt and sweatpants. "Come on. Let's find the cat."

"You *really* think Alex did something to Herb?"

"Of course not." Bruce's words still sounded too angry for Aaron to discern whether they were honest. "We'll find Herb, and that Detective Grant can go fuck himself."

Herb wasn't allowed outside—too much traffic—so Aaron figured a t-shirt would be enough for what would be a brief, indoor search. Bruce put on slippers. Aaron didn't.

They searched the bedroom first, under the bed, in the closet, behind the low dresser and tall chest of drawers, all around the antique chair. Lots of cat hair, no cat. Bruce muttered and grumbled. Aaron thought too much.

Psychopath?

Aaron had spent hours talking to Alex on video, and apart from the diabolical flirtation, Alex had never given any hint of craziness. How grown up he sounded was crazy, but he didn't seem cat-killer crazy or the type to hurt anyone else. He might have seen putting Aaron's relationship with Bruce in jeopardy as a game of brinksmanship, not the nicest thing, but physical harm? Even when they were jogging together, working up a sweat side by side, the boy didn't seem entirely corporeal. Aaron couldn't imagine him throwing a punch, much less anything else.

Except for fucking.

But a police detective had entertained the possibility of violence. Bruce might still be entertaining the possibility of violence. They might not know Alex as well as Aaron did. Maybe some of Bruce's anger was really anger at himself for suspecting Alex of something so vile, like he suspected Aaron of pedophilia. Bruce was a wad of contradictions. Aaron was, too, though, so at least they were together in that.

To check for a trapped cat, they opened the hall linen closet and searched every shelf, even between towels and sheets toward the back to make sure the clever kitty hadn't nested for a long exile.

Why had Bruce called the Decatur Police? He'd said he wanted information about Letta, Dave, *and* Alex. What sort of information could they provide about Alex other than the sort of information they'd provided? Bruce must have suspected that he'd hear... but at one point, the police had expressed concern about Alex's safety, if the killer or killers decided they wanted to finish the family massacre... Bruce might have expected information about Alex's relative safety. Aaron didn't think so. But barring that, in light of Bruce's reaction, calling made no sense whatsoever.

Bruce made no sense whatsoever. Why was he so damned angry about the phone call and so damned desperate to find the cat? They got to the living room, and Bruce started looking *beneath* the sofa cushions. Like the fucking cat would have flattened itself to stay hidden *beneath*—

An image popped into his head. The cat who'd be been with them as long as they'd been married lay flattened, roadkill-style, under the last cushion Bruce lifted. Except at the very moment when Aaron saw the image in his head, and his heart hiccoughed, he knew Herb hadn't been squashed by a careless driver—

he'd been pulverized by a meat tenderizer in Alex's gleeful hand.

Right. The boy who spent his Saturday reading *Jane Eyre* and then talked about it while making vegetarian stir fry. "Herb?" Aaron called. "You want a treat?" Maybe the cat got out. If the cat wasn't here, the other explanation was... absurd.

While Bruce examined other places in the living room, Aaron looked under the dinner and at the chairs, and then while Bruce searched the few possible places in the kitchen, Aaron checked the big closet. No cat.

"Help me move the sofa," Bruce said.

"Don't you think he would have come out—"

"I want a clear look behind the sofa." Bruce's tone permitted no argument. They pulled the sofa away from the wall, letting light shine on dust bunnies, wads of cat hair, and no cat.

"We should look outside," Bruce said.

If Herb had gone outside, they wouldn't find him in the dark unless he meant to be found.

If Alex had done something to Herb, they wouldn't find him unless Alex meant for him to be found.

Found, like Bruce found the camera this morning.

But devilish didn't mean *cat killer*.

And what would cat killer mean? "Psychopath?" Not Alex.

About to agree to searching outside, Aaron stopped. He saw Elvis.

Neither of them had checked his sliver of workspace.

Propelled less by hope than by certainty, Aaron hurried to his corner and looked in the chair at his little computer desk and yes, crescent-curled, Herb snoozed on the seat, unaware of the thoughts, hidden accusations, he had inspired. "Um, Bruce?" Aaron spoke softly. "Could you come over here?"

Bruce appeared beside him and looked down at the chair. "See? Nothing to worry about," Bruce said.

"Uh, yeah. You realize I wasn't the one who urgently insisted we go on a cat search?" Aaron looked for the clouds of confusion between them to part, but they swirled.

"I just wanted to prove we had nothing to worry about," Bruce said, worry carving lines all over his face.

"By proving Herb is okay," Aaron said.

"Exactly."

"By proving Alex didn't hurt him."

"Exactly. No! I mean...." Bruce rarely seemed so flustered.

Aaron didn't know how to help. "Why would you suspect Alex of hurting Herb?" *Hurting Herb*. Sounded like a sitcom. In Hell.

"The Detective on the phone," Bruce said.

"I knew he'd said something."

"But it's...."

"What?"

Bruce walked into the main part of the living room, sat in the recliner, and clasped and unclasped his hands, a show of needing to do but not knowing what to do. Aaron sat nearby on the sofa. After a long pause, Bruce said, "I worry."

"Believe it or not, I'd figured that out." Aaron tried for caring eyes.

Bruce half-smiled and nodded but looked far away. "Some things are hereditary, you know? My sister, before Dave finally got her to a psychiatrist, as far as I know, she never did anything, but she talked about a lot of weird shit. And if what Alex has been through could trigger... I don't know. I'm a little screwed up about it, I think."

"It's okay," Aaron said. He reached for Bruce's hand and felt a ton of pressure in his chest release when their fingers touched. "There was a tragedy, and all our lives changed so fast. It's okay for us all to be a little screwed up."

"It is?"

"It is."

18. DUH—
I WAS LYING!

Bruce

At midnight in the Valley, when you couldn't sleep but had no appetite for bars or clubs or all-night diners, you could always find shelter in one place and scratch items from your to-do list in the process: Ralphs Supermarket, with most locations open to redeye shopping. After the digital clock passed twelve, Bruce concluded that he felt no closer to sleep than he had an hour ago and that he wasn't likely to get any closer in the next hour, so he got up and went to Ralphs. He put back on the sweatpants and t-shirt. No one cared how you looked at Ralphs in the middle of the night. That was one of redeye shopping's great advantages. Another was not having to look at many other people in the first place. They even had self-checkout.

Pushing his cart through aisles, grabbing items he wasn't even sure that they needed, Bruce let his mind wander. He had kind of freaked out at the detective on the phone. Then he'd freaked out about the cat. What was he really worried about? Detective Grant hadn't said it, but it was lying there beneath everything he had said. But was Bruce *really* worried that Alex had killed Letta and Dave? It seemed like the definition of preposterous. Why did the idea make him want to build a fort around Alex? Build a fort and stay with him on the inside?

Because none of this was Alex's fault.

Not that Alex had actually *done* anything.

He sensed something toxic about the way—

metal collided with metal, snapping him out of his reverie as he detected a muted yelp from the voice of a nearby woman. He'd reached the end of an aisle, and his cart had slammed into another, driven by a Black woman about his age, maybe a little later in her thirties, with long skinny braids separated into layers so that they cascaded from high on her head to her shoulders and back. Her thin, athletic body looked comfortable in a t-shirt and sweatpants not too different from his own. "You startled me," she said. "I guess I was daydreaming." She laughed and looked down at the newspaper she held in the hand that wasn't steering her cart. "Night-dreaming?" Head cocked to one side, she seemed actually to want an answer.

"Whatever it is, I think I was doing the same thing," Bruce said. "My apologies. I hope you weren't injured?"

"Nope," she said. "Hadn't even picked up the eggs yet. Everything of yours in one piece?"

"Everything copacetic."

Expecting her to smile and push away, Bruce was surprised when instead of moving she said, "It's just this news story. Tabloid trash is more like it, but it's in our backyard, so it's extra creepy."

A lot of people used words like "creepy" to describe Alex Packard.

"What's the story?" Bruce wasn't in a hurry. When he'd left, Aaron had been snoring. Light had still been on in Alex's room, but he might have fallen asleep reading. The boy didn't like being checked up on. Bruce understood that.

"You've got to have heard about it, assuming you live around here," the woman said.

"Yep, this is my neighborhood grocery store." He extended a hand in her direction and then remembered that maybe that was a bad idea post-COVID. "I'm Bruce," he said, accepting that the damage was done.

She shook his hand. "Alondra Whitcomb," she said. "Also in the neighborhood. Yeah, this story. The kids at Rose Park High."

The school Alex attends.

"No, I... what's going on?"

"Three kids have been murdered." Alondra lowered her voice. "And if you ask me, it's more accurate to say three kids have been murdered *so far.*"

"That's terrible." Bruce hoped his voice conveyed the right kind of concern. "Do they know who did it?"

"No. The leading theory is it's someone who knew them all. People are freaking the fuck out. If you'll pardon my language." Alondra fluttered lashes and smirked.

"How...." Bruce hesitated. He wanted to know if the killings were as brutal as the killings of his sister and her husband, the sort that made him feel like a sick person for wanting to look at the damage. Alondra was stirring gossip with a stranger at the supermarket in the middle of the night, so she *probably* wouldn't be offended by morbid curiosity. "How did he do it? I mean, are we talking about a psycho-killer?"

"Most definitely." Alondra lowered her voice again. "One body was partially skinned. Another was sliced like meat on a spit, with the throat cut. Another showed signs of rape, no fluids, but damage to the body was so severe that signs were inconclusive."

She got all this from newspapers? Tabloids? About underage victims? "Terrible," he said.

Her gaze lingered on him for a moment that became very uncomfortable, but then her rigid posture broke, and she shook her head. "Excuse me for prattling. Have a good night, Mr. Nicholson." She steered her cart away, dividing her attention between the lane ahead and her paper.

Bruce felt paranoid. Brutal murders. Letta, Dave. Suspicious cop. Three kids at Alex's school.

But Herb was fine! Strange thoughts. Like maybe the need to protect Alex, to protect family, was more important than condemning murder.

And he didn't remember telling Alondra Whitcomb his last name.

Esme

A case of one brutal killer kissing another. Nothing more.

Even though younger boys weren't her typical fare —why she never thought to weigh Rory's affections—her body responded with heat to the closeness of Alex's near-nakedness. The black midriff tank top she wore to show off her bellybutton ring gave him plenty of access to her chest, shoulders, and arms, which he kissed delicately, and when he finished with her lips, she took a turn kissing him, telling herself they were the same now, and everything was okay, and his salty, coppery, red and white skin was like her red and brown skin, dirty because they were dirty. She kissed his navel and flat stomach, around his pecs and his nipples, up his neck to his chin and paused at his lips like he had at hers.

"I want you to fuck me," she said, and deep in her brain a voice screamed *NO*, but what she wanted was to *survive*, and doing what he wanted seemed like the best way to make him keep his promise and let her go.

His arms dropped to his sides, and he stepped back, appraising her. "That's intriguing." He tapped his leg with his hunting knife. "Show me."

She didn't know what he meant, but she had to do something, so she peeled off the tank top, exposing her braless breasts, which she expected him to grab, but he didn't. She rubbed them, thinking about ways to turn him on, worried that the only vagina she'd seen him fuck was the one he'd carved into Rory. Whatever. This was a striptease. She moved back and forth in front of him, letting her upper and lower body trade sides in ripples, finally unzipping the side of her short skirt, which she let fall, caught with her shoe, and kicked toward a corner of the room.

"Bravo," Alex said. He might have had—she thought she saw—stiffness in his boxer shorts.

Blood had covered too much of her skin, and she didn't like the look of it, so she closed her eyes and let her hands trace her hips, her belly, her breasts, imagining she was cleaning herself, hoping she was seductive. She opened her eyes and smiled at Alex, who seemed attentive. She stepped out of her shoes.

To extricate the fibers of her fishnet stockings from the skin of her calves and thighs, she leaned against the wall not far from where the majority of Kayla's remains dangled. With the wall's support she could hold one leg up, bent, foot arched, hoping to look sexy as she pried the stocking away, substituting a smile for the wince that fought to take hold of her lips. By the time she'd removed both stockings, she felt exhausted, but Alex watched, glued with eagerness.

She turned her back to him and slid down her panties. She wiggled her ass. Alex applauded, not the slow clap this time. Naked, she faced him.

His undershorts stretched.

"Get on the bed." He motioned to the waterbed with the hunting knife.

Esme caught a slight chill and wasn't sure if Alex would see the gooseflesh. Her clothes hadn't provided much protection, but they'd still been a barrier, and now nothing separated her from him. Was she crazy?

"Lie on your back in the middle of the bed." Alex set the knife aside. "It's okay. It's a waterbed. It's like you're floating."

Getting onto the thing and maneuvering into the center was difficult, but Esme managed, and she spread from head to toe, hoping the sight of her body (thank God she'd shaved) on total display would create further arousal.

"Very nice." Alex stood at the foot of the bed, near her toes, towering over her. "Hold still."

Without sitting up, she lifted her head to follow his movement toward Kayla's corpse, and then he bent out of view. He reappeared with hands cupped and came back to her. She almost said "What," but she didn't before the lukewarm splash hit between her legs. She didn't have to see to know. Alex had drenched her pussy in Kayla's blood.

"Nice," Alex said. "Now I want you to show me how much you want me."

At first, she didn't comprehend. Her vision wobbled from the repulsive idea of Kayla's dead blood cells swarming up inside her like a rapist's sperm. This time she did say, "What?"

"You should be slippery enough." Alex chuckled. "You've got free hands. Get yourself going. Show me how turned on you are."

"What?" She thought she understood, but she couldn't comprehend.

He held up the index and middle fingers of his right hand—the hunting knife was on top of the clothes hamper by the wall opposite the exit, between the bed and the closet-cell door—and said, "You take two fingers, and you pretend they're my cock."

Kayla's blood trickled through her pubic hair.

"You pretend they're my cock, and you show me what you want my cock to do."

"W... what?"

"Make yourself come for me," Alex said.

Swallowing bile took intense effort. She reconciled herself to having him inside her, but she couldn't imagine arousal, especially with her own hands, what her hands had done. Would he know if she faked it? Her fingers moved toward the bloody swamp between her legs. How long would she have to go on to be convincing?

She had to survive.

The fingers, *Alex's cock*, slid inside. She moaned.

Greylight around her intensified. A spotlight. She pushed her fingers deeper.

Alex leaned over the bed, bringing his face close to the cleft between her spread legs. "Okay, the fingers don't *only* have to be cock. Play with your clit a little."

Esme closed her eyes and did what he said, and she felt her clitoris harden and grow. She knew how to stimulate herself, and despite herself, she was doing it. She moaned again, this time inadvertently.

"That's more like it." Alex's voice surrounded her.

She rubbed at her clit, wet with Kayla's blood, and rubbed around her labia, slippery, letting her fingers plunge inside, inside and out, inside and out. The movements got slicker, and her own fluids mixed with Kayla's, and she was grotesque—a murderer—grotesque—masturbating in the blood of her best friend—and the pleasure was a sense of how *low* she was, how *animal* she'd become and kept becoming with each touch of her fingers... that sent... warm shivers...

Working herself faster, she squeezed her eyes shut more tightly. She would come, then, come for him, scream when she came for him. "Oh God!" she yelled, not even knowing the words would escape.

"Yes!" Alex encouraged.

"Oh God!"

"Yes!"

Faster, faster. "I, I'm—"

"Yes! It's me! Say my name!"

"OH MY GOD, ALEX!"

Her whole body convulsed, creating waves that shook the waterbed. The sensation that racked her wasn't mere orgasm but rolling thunder that jostled her once, twice, again, a seizure obliterating the world and, for a merciful instant, all thought. It was the best orgasm of her life.

Alex talked to himself. "'Say my name?' Really, Alex? A little cliché, don't you think?"

Thought began to settle. Esme had come in Kayla's

blood. If she let herself scream again, she might never stop. She'd experienced the most intense pleasure she'd ever known by jilling off in the leftovers of the friend she'd killed.

"You'll let me go?" she said.

"Of course," he said.

"You promise?" she said. "I want to... go."

"I promise," he said.

"Then fuck me, and I'll like it." If she said yes, could it still be rape?

"Esme, you are a *naughty* girl." Alex laughed.

"Yes," she said, and she thought, *yes*.

Alex

He almost felt sorry for her.

Almost.

Esme wasn't a particularly stupid girl, but she had a severe case of wishful thinking. After seeing all three of the people she'd arrived with die spectacularly creative deaths, however, wishful thinking might be all she had left, naked on the bed, blood-painted and submissive. Alex didn't blame her. The whole situation had him so turned on that he didn't feel the slightest ill-will toward anyone. His good mood would only make the next part better.

He stepped out of his boxers. "See? I'm just wild about you, baby." He snickered.

Straining her neck, Esme looked from her prone position to Alex's erection and faked a smile. Her head crashed back on the bed and, not looking, she said, "I want you inside me," and her affect was flat. "Get on the bed. Get on top of me." She extended her arms.

Instead of going to her, he retrieved the Deerslayer from the top of the hamper and returned to where he'd stood while she got off. He stared until she looked up again.

"What are you doing with that? You said you wouldn't

hurt me."

"I said I'd let you go," Alex corrected. "There is a major difference." At the edge of the bed, balancing his knees on water, he straddled her ankles and waved the knife over her exposed legs.

"Please," she said. "No."

"No what?"

"No... sir?"

Alex laughed. "No, I mean, what are you saying 'no' to?"

"Don't hurt me." Her eyes focused on the knife.

"This?" He set the Deerslayer on the bed next to them. "I thought you were all about this." With his right hand, he swiped moisture from between Esme's legs and rubbed it on his cock, giving it a few strokes before he knee-walked on the waterbed's waves until he straddled Esme's chest. He leaned forward until the tip of his penis touched her cheek, then slid the tip down, tracing a line to her chin, onto her neck, over her collarbone, onto her chest, up the rise of one breast, around an areola. "You like that?"

"Yes." Esme spoke through tears. "Please... just... put it in me."

Knee-walking backward on the waterbed was even more difficult, but Alex managed, dragging his cock between Esme's perky tits, down along her stomach, into the bloody pubic hair—where he stopped. "You want me to put *this* in *there*?"

"Please," she whimpered.

He combined a laugh with a sigh. "Did you really think I would fuck you?"

Fresh alarm entered her voice. "But you said—"

"Duh!" Maybe she *was* stupid. "I was lying!"

"Will you still let me go?"

"Why would you even *consider* trusting me?"

Distracted by amusement, he didn't register the significance of her glimpse to her left, his right, but tears and whimpering became taut muscle as her body rose halfway, twisted, and launched her grasping hands at the knife, which she took with all fingers, thumbs at the hilt, pinkies toward the blade. She twisted back to him and screamed: "PLEASE DIE!"

Her strength surprised him as she jammed the knife into his torso, right beneath the sternum.

Still straddled, she fell back beneath him, the knife jutting out of him, a visual echo of his erection.

Alex looked down at the blade, stunned only for seconds, and cackled. He didn't know if he'd ever cackled before, but he was cackling now. "My house, my rules. Didn't you know the outcome was fixed from the start?"

Esme screamed and kept screaming. Alex pulled the knife out of his body—no blood—and kept it in his right hand. "Your turn." First, he used the Deerslayer's curved tip to rip out the bellybutton ring and toss it aside while the split navel squirted. Screaming went on and on. Then, he plunged the blade into Esme's stomach, changing Esme's sound but not stopping it.

Deciding to crawl up and down and side to side over her body, Alex stabbed and stabbed and stabbed, not thinking to be careful until he missed, hit the mattress, and sprung a geyser. Clean water loosened the blood caking on both of their skin. Alex's crawling became more frenetic as he stabbed at both Esme and the waterbed, enjoying jets of water and blood, Esme's screams, a percussive undercurrent, annoying but compelling.

She tried to fight back. With punctured arms and thighs, she kicked and punched at him, and he used his legs and free hand to pin and re-pin her flailing limbs while the knife hand kept stabbing. She got weaker and weaker, and so did the mattress, water spewing, the two of them thrashing in spilled gallons. At last Esme's head ended up in a place where the mattress no longer offered support. The water *almost* covered her nose and mouth. Alex shifted his body away from her, all his weight on one side, and flipped her, bleeding stomach down in puddled bloody water. He grabbed the back of her head and kept it still, face underwater.

Finding new fight, she tried to pull her head from under his hand, tried to kick while she slapped madly behind her. He stabbed her between the shoulder blades. She bled, but drowning would kill her faster than blood loss. Her fight became an instinctive battle for air as if she were submerged rather than only in a shallow face-full, but the effect was the same. Panic kept her going. Her whole body quaked in resistance until it stopped—all at once—and went limp.

Tired and soaked, Alex climbed off her and splashed onto his back at her side. "Stupid fucking bitch," he said, catching his breath. "Did you really think I would fuck *you*?"

19. SHOW ME

Alex

He resettled in his body, which had *Jane Eye* on the tablet balanced where his stiff legs met in their half-lotus fold, glanced at the string on his doorknob, which told him no one had come to look at him while he was away, and took in the hour on his digital bedside alarm clock. Almost half past midnight. Time slippage between *his* house and Bruce and Aaron's house was difficult to fathom, but he wasn't tired, and the night wasn't over.

His fingers passed through his hair, disappointed not to have to burrow through the density of drying blood. Like his skin, his hair was as clean as it had been since his morning shower. Sitting still on his bed, he hadn't broken a sweat. His only real activity had been making dinner.

Now, though, he was hopping into action. He grabbed a dark hoodie and sweatpants and turned out his light before he left his room, door closed behind him. The few places where the hallway floor creaked were easy enough to avoid, and once he got to the living room area, he figured little sounds didn't matter. Alex was most anxious to look behind the Elvis partition—Aaron's Sony wasn't sitting out in plain sight, so he hoped it was in Aaron's workspace.

Because if he didn't find the camera there, he'd have to use his phone, which didn't do as well in the dark.

Because if he didn't find the camera there, Bruce and Aaron were probably keeping it in their bedroom.

And if Bruce and Aaron were keeping it in their bedroom, they were deliberately keeping it *away* from Alex, a sign that difficulties had come early.

Next to his miniature desk, Aaron had a miniature filing cabinet with two drawers, neither of which contained files, both of which contained random technology. Alex opened the bottom drawer, and there, in its shapely, unzipped bag, was the handheld, and Alex had nothing to worry about. He took the camera out of the bag and searched both drawers without finding what he wanted. No matter. The flashlight from the kitchen would work well enough.

Hood up, Alex left the house, closed the front gate, and stopped as he looked at the street. At night, street parking close to their house was *always* impossible to find, but a spot was open a short walk away. Something was wrong.

A scan located Aaron's car a couple of houses down, but Bruce's was missing.

Bruce had gone out. Recently.

No way! Saturday or not, gay or not, Bruce was always in bed between ten and eleven. Aaron might go for a midnight drive, but not Bruce. Bruce was *disciplined*.

Alex smirked, wondering if a passerby might see his expression beneath eyes cloaked in the shadow made by streetlight and hood. Bruce had had a tough day. He might not be feeling himself. He might not be feeling *disciplined*.

Was Aaron feeling disciplined? Another question for another time. Alex was going to school.

An exhilarating nip in the night air made Alex walk faster, feeling alive. He uncapped the camera lens and recorded his journey, the street well-lit enough and the camera good enough to get a clear image of the world flying by as he raced toward his prizes. Later, he'd decide what to do with the remains at his house. Mike and Esme were probably for the trees, but he had thoughts about Kayla in the mannequin room, and Rory was too artful not to put up *somewhere*.

What he had accomplished today! They must have been

satisfied. He progressed so quickly. His games had to possess the desired *sophistication*. Very fine entertainment indeed.

The school loomed ahead, and he slowed down to inspect the area using the camera's zoom, better than his eyes for the dark areas around the building beyond the streetlights, better for revealing any lurkers, police or homeless or druggies or anyone else who might spoil his plans. He found no one.

Behind the school, Alex turned on the flashlight, not wanting to twist his ankle as the ground became more uneven on his way to the Pit. More than a guide, the flashlight was also his spotlight as he traced the ground to the depression full of rocks arguably more dangerous than a deep hole. No sign of anyone else moving—Alex hadn't even thought to bring a weapon, had never used a weapon on a person outside of *his* domain—but he didn't need to be very close for his spotlight to roam across a pair of splayed legs that connected to a bloody shirted torso connected to a head with a face—if you could call it that—mutilated lips, wires sticking out of the mouth, blood smeared on brown skin, Mike, eyes open and very white in the flashlight beam.

Confirming he had audio, Alex said, "Ladies and gentlemen, before I give you the closer look you're after, let's have an overview of the results. Then you'll get to see what the boy made and what that means the boy's made of."

With camera and spotlight, he roamed the Pit. Rory lay next to Mike. He was naked, and Alex didn't have to get close for the bloody holes in his wrists, ankles, and groin to show up red on camera. His genitals were on a rock near his feet. People would wonder what happened to his clothes. His dick and balls came back, but not his clothes. Go figure.

Esme lay across from him and was naked, too, more red than skin-colored, which the camera picked up but made very dark. Alex didn't know if she'd suffered more than the boys, but she looked worse, a pegboard of gashes. Kayla posed a problem. Her hands rested on rocks not far from her wrists, but her head

—

Where the fuck was her head?

Why would Rory's dick and balls come back but not Kayla's head?

Ollie's skin had seemed to be missing, but later Alex had figured it might've been piled up somewhere away from the body that he couldn't see. Alex *had* tossed Kayla's head aside, so it could have come back to reality... somewhere else.

He stepped out of the Pit and scanned the surrounding area with spotlight and camera.

No head.

He would proceed without it, starting with Kayla's neck stump.

Standing over her body, he pointed his tools at the stump and made it fill the viewfinder. "You'll notice many cuts on the neck, some deep, and unevenness in the stump where the head was removed. I get credit for making this, but that doesn't mean I was the only person involved. Look at those cuts! I wouldn't be so clumsy. The meat cleaver was a tool in the hands of this girl's best friend. The best friend was *my* tool."

A thrill passed through him. "I understand why Aaron wants to film *everything*. Controlling a camera is controlling a world, and you can trap people inside." He laughed. "I can relate. But more than that," and he tracked down to a severed hand, "capturing your image, what you choose to make art, makes something immortal. This dead hand is immortal. It's a godlike power here in the real world."

Alex laughed. "I guess that means I'm godlike in more ways than one." He decided Rory would be next for closeups and hoped he could make the wounds sound sexy.

Alondra

Bruce Nicholson was squirrelly. He seemed clueless, but his squirrelly tapping on his grocery cart's push bar and squirrelly, darting eyes made Alondra think he wasn't *entirely* clueless, that something about the murders of the teenagers from his nephew's school had struck a chord with him. Was she seeing what she wanted to see? Possibly. Most detectives these days relied on deductions made from forensic and other evidence, not hunches and gut feelings, but Alondra had watched a lot of cop shows growing up and thought of herself as old-fashioned and intuitive, which was probably why she was assigned to this case. The forensic evidence, copious as it was, led nowhere, but Alondra's intuition had gotten a ping from Gladys Johnson when she'd been interviewing students associated with Rose Park High's Theatre Department (they used the pretentious "re" spelling of "theater"). Theatre connected two of the victims, Warren Dell and Anna Cortez.

"There was that creepy kid who came around during rehearsals a couple of times," Gladys said.

"What creepy kid?" Alondra got ready to jot down a name.

"I don't know. His name was Luke, maybe. Warren thought he was filming us. Or them, him and Anna. Warren always thought people were checking him out, though."

"If I showed you a picture, would you recognize him?" Alondra reached for her briefcase.

She'd had a phone call with a Detective Martin Grant from Decatur, Georgia.

"I guess 'creepy' isn't very nice. At least from a distance, he seemed cute enough. A little young." Gladys lowered her voice. "Between you and me, I prefer dark meat. What about you?"

"If I showed you a picture—"

"Why don't you show me a picture and we find out?"

Gladys had been pretty sure the picture showed the creepy cute white kid. Alex Packard.

Alondra sat on her bed and looked at crime scene photos spread out in front of her. She shouldn't associate these things with the place where she slept, but she needed the surface for breadth. Oliver Pollock, dorsal and ventral, flayed limbs, flayed back. The little puncture in his lower spine that likely paralyzed him before he died. Nothing tied Oliver Pollock to Anna Cortez and Warren Dell. Nothing but being schoolmates and being killed with brutality that defied humanity. Those nothings were enough to investigate all three together, though.

Local media certainly liked the idea of a single killer. They'd been respectful of the families, though, and didn't have nearly the amount of information that Alondra had given Bruce Nicholson at the grocery store. She'd prodded him. Though evidence suggested Warren Dell was at least involved in the rape of Anna Cortez, which spawned the theory that Dell was an accomplice whose buddy turned on him, Alondra's research into Dell had ruled out that theory for her—she agreed with the media. Single killer. And today, or yesterday given the hour, Detective Martin Grant had called her a second time. He wanted to let her know that something was "up" with Alex Packard and Bruce Nicholson. She might "want to keep an eye out."

Alondra promised him nothing but ended up double-parked near Mr. Nicholson's house, watching. When Mr. Nicholson left the house after midnight, she followed. She arranged a meeting. And he was squirrelly.

Above all her crime scene photos, she had the photo of Alex Packard, which she'd surreptitiously taken herself. He was a cute kid. And very white.

Could he have gutted Anna Cortez? Sliced Warren Dell into ribbons? Skinned Oliver Pollock?

A kid on the boys' JV soccer team said he saw a "creepy kid" under the bleachers one day who looked like he was taking pictures of the team with his cell phone. He said he didn't get a good look at the guy. He didn't recognize Alex Packard's picture.

A blond, handsome, creepy kid. Detective Grant said he wished he'd had a chance to talk to Alex before he'd moved thousands of miles away. Alondra lived in the neighborhood.

Her gut told her to take the chance Grant had missed.

A knock on her bedroom door made her sweep up the crime scene photos and flip them upside down. "Mommy!"

Without waiting for a response, Nate, who was almost eight, came through the door and ran halfway to the bed. His chest rose and fell with excited breath. "Mommy!"

He went back and forth between "Mom" and "Mommy" these days, reserving "Mommy" for the needier times.

"What is it, darling boy?" She consolidated the photos with papers and folders.

"The closet! I heard!"

"You think that old closet monster is back again?"

He nodded, big head movements, no hesitation.

"Let's go look. I'll show you there's nothing to be afraid of."

Nothing to be afraid of. She felt like *such* a liar.

Alex

The sound of footsteps interrupted his closeup on the torn skin of Esme's navel, one of her less egregious wounds but one sure to make anyone foolish enough to wear a bellybutton ring wince. Alex turned around. A glare blinded him. "Don't move!" The voice was male, baritone, authoritative. Its flashlight approached and obscured the man himself.

Alex pointed his light at the other light, hoping to return the blinding effect. "Who's there?" he said.

"Police!" the man said. "Show me your hands!" He lowered his flashlight, and Alex saw uniform, hat, jacket, shiny badge, all consistent with LAPD. Did he have a gun out with the flashlight?

Alex raised his hands, camera in the right, flashlight in the left. The cop's light centered on him, which meant he could see—

"SWEET JESUS HOLY HELL!" He gagged. Alex

suppressed a smile. "Stay where you are!" *Now* the cop drew his gun. He balanced the flashlight on the ground and aimed with both hands.

"It's just a camera." Alex spoke with a high pitch, trying to sound younger. "I'm making a movie. I didn't think... any trouble..." He sniffled as if he might cry.

"You mean all that's f-fake?" The cop, athletic build, probably late twenties, was authoritative. Also scared.

Alex allowed a smile. "You mean... I've been doing FX makeup since I was a little kid... you really thought... thanks, man! I mean—please don't shoot me."

The glow of the flashlight on the ground made the relaxation of the cop's shoulders visible enough. "Even so... this area... is... off limits." He took a deep breath, not lowering the gun. The cop *wanted* to believe that what he saw was fake. He didn't, not entirely; his mouth twitched. "I should take you in for trespassing. And you need permits to film, especially...."

"But this is my school." Alex was naiveté and innocence.

"You should know better, then."

"I've been looking back here, thinking, gosh, what a great place to film a horror movie. So, I borrowed my dad's camera—"

"Even so," the cop said, "I better call this in."

Keeping the gun in his left hand, the cop moved his right toward the radio clipped to his shirt. He wasn't wearing a bodycam. Before he could speak, Alex threw the flashlight at him, turned, and ran.

"STOP!"

The cop wouldn't shoot, not a kid, a *white* kid who might be unarmed, but Alex heard hard shoes pounding on shaky rocks behind him. He was being *chased*.

Behind the school, away from the street, a few stars, a crescent moon, and light pollution were all he had to see by, so he didn't know what was more than a few feet in front of him. Going toward the street wouldn't work. More people might see him being chased, possibly more cops.

Fuck!

A tall wire fence separated this side of the school's back lot from the parking lot behind the adjacent building. After a split-second's hesitation, Alex climbed. The footfalls got closer as he clambered up, one hand gripping the camera while two fingers clasped wires. The cop's breathing got closer. "STOP!"

Twisted, hard wire-ends poked out at the top of the fence, but it lacked coiled razors or other strong defenses, so Alex vaulted over and lowered himself quickly. He took a backward step and watched the cop body slam the fence, metal clanging. "Hold it right there!" The cop climbed.

Alex turned and ran through the deserted parking lot. He made it most of the way across before he heard the fence wobble and clang and then hard shoes on asphalt before, "STOP, OR I'LL SHOOT!"

He wouldn't—

A shot rang out.

Alex froze. He put the camera on the ground and raised his empty hands. *He* was scared. This was not his house. These were not his rules. He remembered the tingling sensation of Esme stabbing him in the chest. Here, a bullet would damage.

The cop approached from behind. "Don't you move. I'm tired of chasing your ass."

"I didn't do anything wrong." Alex squeezed maximum fear into his voice.

"Why'd you run? Lace your fingers together."

Alex laced his fingers together above his head. *Help me.* In his head, he repeated: *help me.*

"You carrying any weapons I should know about?"

"I dropped the flashlight," Alex said. "The camera's on the ground. All I've got is my keys."

"Drop your keys next to the camera."

Alex did.

"I'm going to pat you down. Stay still."

Alex stayed still while the cop's hands felt him everywhere, t-shirt collar to shod feet. "Okay, put your hands behind your back."

Turn around.

Alex turned around, lowering his hands.

"I didn't tell you to face me! Back to me, hands behind your back!"

As if he hadn't heard, Alex said, "Am I in trouble?"

The cop backed away. "Turn around, hands behind your back!"

Go low.

Alex caught the cop's eyes with his, held them, and didn't let them go until he dove toward the ground. The cop saw him coming and reached for his gun. Instead of bellyflopping on asphalt, Alex caught himself with hands and arms accustomed to push-ups and half-crawled, half-lunged by the cop as the cop fired, too high.

But that was the second gunshot—there would be reports and more cops.

Be fast.

Next to the holster on the cop's belt hung his collapsible baton, and with the gun free, it was grabbable. Alex took it. Very easy to extend. His first strike landed on the backs of the cop's thighs, hamstrings, femurs. The cop's body bent back and bowed forward as Alex circled him and took aim at his noodly left arm. The forearm cracked against the blow, and the hand released the gun, which clattered on pavement. Alex, a whirlwind around the stunned policeman, circled farther, kicked the gun away, and swung the baton at the back of the cop's bowed head.

CRACK!

The cop fell to his hands and knees. His hair was black, and available light didn't show Alex whether blood stuck hairs together. Anyway, not time for another blow to the head. Alex used the baton in an upward swing in an attempted scoop at the cop's right shoulder. The hit pried his right hand from asphalt, but the dazed man wasn't going to flip. Another upward swung hit his chest and made him crash sideways on his left shoulder, his side on top of his broken arm, and he howled like dogs Alex had known. A smack on the ribs made the cop collapse on his back.

Alex had what he wanted, but he felt so out of breath. Here, he had less strength. They didn't shape the field in his favor. *But they were still here, watching.*

The baton came down on the cop's ribs, and Alex got a *crack!* and a *crack!* and a *crack!* and another and another, along with more dog sounds. The cop spat something that looked black and was probably blood. It trickled over his face.

That's when Alex decided the cop shouldn't have a face.

The first baton hit crushed the nose in a satisfying burst, but the second and third didn't make much sound. Afterward, though, Alex heard cracks and crunches. He knew that inside the cop's closed mouth teeth caved in because he felt the baton meet with less resistance, but the cheeks caved in, too, and then the forehead, and skin eventually came off in patches. The face lost its shape, lips moving in one direction, nostrils moving in another, an eye beaten out of its socket. Alex kept smashing, and the cop's dog noises became more inchoate before a big smash to the forehead cut off sound.

Alex kept hitting until the head looked like a melon mashed with a sledgehammer. It was too much fun. He stayed back, and his dark clothes mostly avoided the splash zone. When he was done, he kept the baton, gathered his keys and the camera—getting a quick shot of the dead cop, just because —and ran all the way home.

20. ALEX BECOMES A STAR

Aaron

Before one a.m., Bruce crept back into the bedroom, stripped off his bum clothes, and slipped into bed. Aaron feigned sleep and waited. Bruce didn't snore, but when his breathing became more regular, Aaron felt willing to bet he had either drifted off or wouldn't get up if Aaron did. The easiest clothes to find were at the top of the dirty pile; Aaron put on the short-sleeved, soft peach, button-up collared shirt and navy slacks he'd worn for his interviews in WeHo. Sort of professional, by SoCal standards.

The light under Alex's door was off. Good. He'd gone to bed.

Aaron fetched a glass from beside the sink and the bottle of Redbreast from the cabinet and sat in the middle of the sofa, bottle on the coffee table, drink in hand. Sleep had been coming and going at intervals, twenty minutes here, twenty minutes there, nothing restful. At first he thought he was drinking to relax, so sleep would descend and stick around for a while, but after a few generous sips he realized he was drinking for courage. He wasn't going to sleep with so many questions on his mind.

Why had Alex wanted Bruce to find the shower video?

Why had he wanted to make it in the first place?

Why had Aaron helped him?

What was the game?

The light under Alex's door was off, but Aaron *could* go tap. Open it. Whisper him awake. Sit down, have a real conversation. Off camera. Get some answers.

The second glass of whiskey was only half-poured when Aaron decided to go back to Alex's bedroom.

Tap-tap. Slow turn of the knob, careful push of the door, no creak. Whisper: "Alex?"

The hall light was off, but he'd turned on a light in the living room that pushed far enough into Alex's room to shine on the bed. Unsure of what he saw, Aaron pushed the door wider, broadening the shaft of light. The top of the bed was flat. Alex wasn't in it. Without premeditation, Aaron turned on the overhead light. Alex wasn't in his room.

A quick walk through the small house confirmed that Alex wasn't home.

Aaron returned to the sofa's center and his second glass of Redbreast. Alex had snuck out, so Aaron would be parental and wait up. Whenever Alex came home, five minutes or five hours from now, they would gain clarity. And—

And he had to make Alex convince Bruce he wasn't a pedophile.

Alex had to lie. Reassure Bruce that Aaron had nothing to do with the shower video.

Would Alex do that? Aaron thought he probably would, if doing so suited him. Aaron had to think of a way to make the lie appealing enough.

Aaron was a bad person.

If Alex could embrace that lie, what else could devilish Alex lie about?

Bruce and the police and the possibility of violence. Could Alex—

all charm, a Dorian Gray, puppeteer playboy in the body of an innocent youth—

never, but he might keep secrets he shouldn't.

Aaron downed most of his glass, and a wave of

resentment hit him as he swallowed. Bruce and his suspicions! His accusations! He and Alex both might as well be criminals!

Fucking Bruce. Alex needed to focus on keeping the secrets he *should*.

Alex

Sweat came from running or from the euphoric anxiety that made him run faster, he didn't know, but no matter how fast he ran, making home closer and closer, he couldn't outrace the thoughts and images swirling in his head. The baton, still in his pocket, coming down into a head *out here*. Not in his house. Not in safety. A gun shot at him. He could have been killed. Seen. Arrested. He might have been seen! Did the cop have a partner? Someone in a car on the street? But Alex was just a tall figure in a hoodie. Nothing distinguishable.

Real risk was a rush.

It wasn't rigged. The cop had weapons and muscle on his side, but Alex won. Alex killed him.

He smiled and felt the nippy breeze against his teeth.

The blood on his clothes didn't really show, but he'd beeline to his room and do laundry in the early morning. He was thinking about laundry when, slightly winded, he let himself in through the front door.

A light was on. Aaron sat in the middle of the sofa. The whiskey was out.

Recalculating, Alex cut an immediate angle to the dinner table and, hiding the action with his body, put the camera in the spot where it would capture most of the living room area. He switched it on, turned around, and became a distraction, unzipping his hoodie, which he wore nothing beneath. He gulped air. "That was a run," he said. "Surprised you're up."

"I could say the same thing." Aaron took a lingering drink. He'd had more than one.

"Yeah, well, I had an accidental nap earlier, so I was hoping getting up for a run might wear me out enough to get back to sleep." Alex went to the hallway linen closet and grabbed a towel.

"Sleep is a stranger in our house tonight."

Aaron sounded morose. He'd never struck Alex as a maudlin drunk, but Alex supposed that tensions had been high. He thought of making them higher as he rubbed the towel over his face and ruffled it through his hair, collecting sweat. "Something on your mind?"

"You could say that," Aaron said. "You. You're on my mind."

"You don't need to worry about me," Alex said. He took off the hoodie and dropped it on the carpet. The towel mopped off his chest and stomach, most likely getting any blood that might have soaked through to his skin. He was thorough with his hands and wrists, too, thinking of holding the baton. The towel showed signs of red, but nobody would examine the towel. "I'm doing okay. Really, I am."

Aaron looked confused and poured more whiskey. "Why," he said. "What did," he said. "What are you doing?"

"Drying off." Alex flossed his back with the towel. "I want to come sit with you, but I don't want to get sweat all over the furniture."

What else could Alex do in the real world? What could he get away with?

"Thoughtful," Aaron said. Sip, sip.

Alex kicked off his shoes, did a clumsy dance peeling off socks with his toes, lowered his sweatpants, and stepped out of them. His boxers weren't damp. He wasn't *that* sweaty. Slowly, he moved the towel along his legs.

"Shouldn't you put on some clothes?" Aaron asked.

"I'm cooling off."

"Shouldn't you do that in private?" Aaron asked.

"Am I supposed to hide from you?"

"No, but... Bruce... why did you kiss me?" Aaron looked

like he wanted to ask something else. He shifted positions as if the sofa cushions were stuffed with nettle.

Alex crossed the room, taking Aaron's gaze with him, away from the camera, and flopped on the sofa beside his uncle. Alex grinned very close to Aaron's face. "Because I felt like it. Don't you ever do things you feel like doing?"

Aaron scooted to the sofa's opposite side. "It's more complicated than that."

"Why?"

"For one thing, Bruce."

"Bruce lives for his job. Investment consulting. Wealth management. He'd get over it." Alex scooted, not to the sofa's center but halfway toward Aaron.

"For another thing, I'm twice your age."

"Which makes you twenty-eight, not all that old when you think about it."

"Old enough to know better."

Alex scooted closer and put a hand on Aaron's knee. "Better than what?"

"Why did you leave that video out for Bruce to find?" Aaron didn't move Alex's hand away.

"Because I wanted him to see me."

"Why would you want him to see *that*?"

Alex gave Aaron's thigh a short squeeze and stood. "Do you think I'm attractive, Aaron?"

"You're a cute kid, sure." Aaron barely looked at him as he answered.

"That's not what I asked," Alex said.

"Do you mean in a general way," Aaron said, "or are you asking if I find you attractive?"

"Let's answer both." Alex stood between the coffee table and sofa, close enough to lean in and touch Aaron's knees with his own. "General first."

"Generally, of course, I think the other boys and girls at school will be swooning over you once they get to know you. Give them a chance." Aaron cleared his throat.

"And second?"

"Like I said, I'm twice your age."

"You're not too old to have opinions. Pretend I'm a guy from a movie. Am I an attractive guy in a movie? Would you say, 'Hey, I found that guy in that movie attractive?'"

"Y... okay. Sure. Yes." Aaron drank.

"I'm glad you find me attractive, Aaron. I'm attracted to you, too."

"I didn't mean—"

"You know what sucks about being fourteen? This thing never gives up." Alex pulled his erection through the flap at the front of his shorts. When Aaron looked up from staring at it, Alex greeted him with a smile.

Aaron stood and turned partly away without leaving the close space between sofa and coffee table. "Get dressed," he said.

"Funny," Alex said. "I don't feel like it." He pushed down his boxers. Aaron turned back to him, and Alex, naked, stood close enough to let the older, shorter man feel Alex's moist breath on his face.

Real risk was a rush.

Aaron

Oh shit.

He stood within inches of a naked fourteen-year-old boy with an impressive erection, and he wasn't backing away. "Don't stand so close to me," Aaron murmured. Sting. He was like the old man in that book by Nabokov. Pronounced correctly. Vladimir Nabokov. "Humbert Humbert." Stanley Kubrick. Adrian Lyne.

"Light of my life, fire of my loins." Alex spoke the line softly. How could a fourteen-year-old boy even *know* that?

Tadzio. Tadzio was about fourteen, wasn't he? *Death in Venice.* Visconti's over Mann's, so much color. Then there was this contemporary guy he'd read in college, Alan Hollinghurst, very respectable, and he seemed to go on and on about fucking boys.

Alex was very mature for his age.

"Let me help you relax," the boy said. Starting at the top, he unbuttoned Aaron's peach shirt, which wasn't tucked into his navy slacks. Alex's fingertips grazed his skin as they undid buttons and sent little shocks into his chest that paralyzed him, forced him to remain still while Alex continued, reached the last button and then opened the shirt wide. "Better."

Aaron realized he hadn't been breathing. He inhaled, then risked a brush against Alex's bare side to rescue his drink before backing past the edge of the coffee table, gaining a distance from Alex of at least two or three feet. He drank, looked at Alex's body, and felt bitter.

Bruce had already accused him of doing what Alex wanted now.

In his husband's eyes, he was capable. Practically already guilty.

Alex was beautiful.

Alex was dangerous.

Alex was so very, very far from okay.

But what about him? What about what Aaron wanted? When was it okay for Aaron to be not okay?

Didn't Jodie Foster almost win an Oscar for playing an underage prostitute in *Taxi Driver*?

Alex wasn't a prostitute. His seductive surface covered... not innocence, he and Bruce had ruled out that word... but inexperience. He liked playing grown-up games and had a knack for them, but he played by intuition, not *savoir faire*. Like the smoothness of his skin, his behavior covered fragility, unknowing, a need for guidance. And something about that was sexy. Shamefully sexy.

"You might as well take the shirt the rest of the way off," Alex said. He blushed. Can a person fake a blush response?

The shirt came off. What Aaron wanted. He didn't

know. But the shirt came off.

Alex took the ground Aaron had gained, and he tipped his head downward so his droopy lips almost touched Aaron's pursed ones. "Am I not good enough for you?" he asked.

They stood close enough for Alex's erection to rest against Aaron's middle, slightly above where his own cock grew harder. Alex lay one hand on Aaron's chest and used the other to hook a finger on the waistband of his slacks. He hadn't put on a belt.

Aaron pulled his head back to absorb the sudden dejectedness on Alex's face. It confused him at first, but Alex's last question, asked before his hands had made such solid contact and changed the situation, replayed. Not good enough? "It's not about good enough or not good enough—" Aaron fumbled.

"Shhh," Alex said. "Your heart's like a rabbit's. I used to chase rabbits in the yard when I was a kid."

Animals? What are you talking about?

Alex kissed him, no tongue, lips with pressure, forcing Aaron's lips to relax, yield. More fingers joined the first hook on Aaron's waistband. Aaron kept his hands at his sides.

His lips could feel Alex's smile. "I never said I was a good boy." He kept his teeth together through a slow giggle.

"You're not, are you?" Alex's eyes were grey pools, molten steel tinged with silver.

"Who wants to be a good boy?" Almost a whisper, but he was so close that the sound filled Aaron's ears.

What Aaron wanted? "Bad," he said. He was an artist. "I wasn't meant to be good."

"If you're a rabbit, then I'm a hummingbird!" Alex laughed, nothing devious, all charm. "Feel my heartbeat." He pulled slightly away and looked down at his V-shaped torso, the perfect curves of his pecs, the flatness of his stomach. His chest stood out in presentation, awaiting Aaron's touch.

The touch from which there'd be no return. The boy's white skin would work like cocaine. He'd have a little, and he'd want more. He wanted to inhale him. In his mind he saw Alex lying face-up on a giant mirror, and Aaron held an enormous razor blade. The boy was naked and urging him on. Aaron started cutting the boy's left fingertips, fine, close cuts, making bloody lines of flesh and bones out of the fingers. He snorted them and moved onto the hand.

Aaron centered his right palm on Alex's bare chest and closed his eyes, the hand hunting the heart while the pads of the fingers stroked skin.

Thump-thump, thump-thump, thump-thump. Very fast.

The hand hooked to his pants' waistband dove inside the pants, pulled back the elastic on his boxer briefs, and gripped his throbbing penis. Aaron gasped.

"We should sync up," Alex said, unbuttoning Aaron's pants with his free hand. "Do you think you can fuck me to the rhythm of your heartbeat, make mine the same as yours?"

"W-what?"

Alex whispered in his ear. "I want to know what it feels like to have someone inside me."

He wanted to know—which meant—

Aaron knew he was going to do it before Alex tugged down his pants and underwear and stroked his cock. They were on the sofa, Alex on elbows and knees, Aaron kneeling behind him, trying to concentrate on rhythm, when Aaron first thought about whether they should use a condom. For the second time, the significance of Alex's desire to know what it feels to be fucked occurred to him. Aaron got an all-clear at last testing and hadn't screwed around, Bruce didn't screw around, and Alex was learning new things. The situation seemed acceptable. Aaron came inside the boy but kept his exultation at the outstanding orgasm quiet enough to stay outside Bruce's range of hearing.

Afterward, Alex kissed him, gathered his clothes and towel, and said he'd be out again in a few minutes to spend some time in the bathroom. Aaron would snag the bathroom first for a little cleanup in the meantime.

Aaron didn't pay much attention as Alex gathered his things, but he watched him depart, still naked and again sweaty. So much for sparing the furniture. Alex walked down the hall unconscious of the form he cut merely carrying dirty laundry. Statuesque. Michelangelo would have been pleased.

When Alex disappeared into his bedroom, Aaron turned to collect his own clothes and caught sight of the dinner table. His handheld sat on one side, aimed at the living room, and he knew he hadn't put it there. He didn't think Bruce had, either. Which meant—

that devilish boy.

OH SHIT.

The camera wasn't running. Maybe Alex had only set it here after doing something else with it. Maybe he hadn't set it up to record sex that hadn't been spontaneous at all, but staged. Maybe—

He should check the memory.

One of the memory cards was missing. The one leftover lacked anything recent. Had he left out the other one when he'd deleted the shower footage? Maybe.

Who was he kidding? Alex had it. Alex had it because he'd recorded everything that happened tonight. Alex wanted to star in kiddie porn. Now he had a video of a grown man fucking him. A hot item for sure. If—

If he decided to ruin Aaron's life. Probably Bruce's, too. An idea occurred to him that had been very, very far away while his dick had been in the boy's ass.

Alex liked power.

Aaron remembered Bruce speculating about the age of consent in California. He had a strong feeling that he'd broken the law. Statutory rape. Rape. He felt like he might vomit. Alex had complete power over him now. And Alex was fucking crazy.

What kind of person would plan this sort of shit?

You think Alex might have done something to Herb?

I used to chase rabbits in the yard.

Who wants to be a good boy?

When, exactly, had Aaron decided to let this kid destroy his life, and why, exactly, was the kid so keen on doing it?

PART 3: ESCAPE IS FOR EVERYONE

21. TROUBLE WITH THE MAN

Bruce

I work long hours because when I slow down and think too much is when I get into trouble.

Bruce was thinking so much that he phoned Eddie at the office and said that he'd be telecommuting, that all his client meetings were on Zoom anyway and nobody would miss him. Eddie expressed insincere concern, and Bruce realized he hated Eddie, Eddie and most of the people at work because they weren't good at their jobs and were therefore annoying obstructions.

He worked better in his office, though, especially since he didn't like working with Aaron nearby, not on any occasion, and today would have been worse had Aaron not announced that he was working on the voiceover script for his latest documentary and wanted someone to pour him a bottomless cup of coffee while he did it. He therefore went to the café two blocks away. That he more than likely left because the tension between the two of them hadn't thinned out since the successful search for Herb sat well enough with Bruce. Aaron could have the public view of an even busier street. Bruce needed the quiet, private time at home to think.

Alex. Aaron. The trouble they were in.

Since Saturday, Aaron had looked gaunt, like he'd seen a ghost and been wasted by the experience. Alex was the complete opposite, unusually chipper, up very early Sunday doing laundry and eager to socialize throughout the day. The trend continued through Monday, and Tuesday, as Bruce telecommuted—a little—with his laptop on the dinner table, Alex got home early, probably directly from school, head bopping to whatever his earbuds hammered against his eardrums.

When he saw Bruce, he smiled in surprise and freed his ears. "Didn't think you'd be home!"

Bruce didn't return the smile; nevertheless, the bloom in the boy's face lightened the room. "Couldn't take LA traffic today, so I'm working remotely. A perk of middle management."

"Awesome." Alex unshouldered his bookbag and looked as if he might claim the chair opposite Bruce. Bruce didn't know how he felt about the possibility. "I should probably give you your space. I've got all this review homework for this history test that's going to be a killer. World War One and Geopolitical Change. What the fuck? I mean Hell? I mean heck? Ninth graders shouldn't even use words like 'geopolitical.'"

With a flourish, Alex exited down the hall. Bruce chuckled.

He thought about Alex's charm.

Sometime later, there was a knock at the front door. Aaron wouldn't knock, so the sound meant somebody else had decided to disturb Bruce's private contemplation.

The person who appeared in the open doorway should have at least startled him, but in an instinctive way he had expected to see her again. The woman from the grocery store. Her name was... Alondra. She looked different with sunlight on her dark skin, different wearing a suit, different with a badge clipped to her belt and a bulge under her jacket that meant gun. "Hi there, Mr. Nicholson. Do you remember me from the other night?"

His mind raced. "I had a feeling you were hiding something. Were you *following* me?"

With a sly grin, she said, "I do live in the neighborhood, but it's true that I timed my shopping so that I might have the opportunity to meet you."

"Alondra…"

"Whitcomb. Alondra Whitcomb. Detective Alondra Whitcomb. Not hiding anything this time."

Bruce hid the tension that wanted him to slam the door in her face. She had information he wanted. The best outcome would be to give little while taking all he could. "What can I do for you, Detective? What have I done to earn your interest?"

Alondra laughed. "Oh, you're not in any kind of trouble. I'd just like to sit down and talk for a few minutes. Could I come inside?"

Vampires needed invitations. But what reason could he have for saying no? If the police were suspicious, his job was to allay suspicion, not let his own suspicious nature get the better of him. He had to be smart. Smarter. "Sure." He stepped out of the doorway and gestured to the sofa.

"Thank you." As she crossed to the sofa, he noticed she wore pumps. Thick heels, not terribly high, but not shoes for chasing perpetrators. If she had to, would she kick off her fancy shoes and run barefoot? Why would she wear shoes like that, anyway?

Nerves.

Bruce shifted the recliner to a better angle for facing her and sat. "Oh," he said. "Did you need anything to drink?"

"No, thank you." She looked around the room as if her eyes took snapshots. Only the Elvis partition got a reaction, a quick flash of lemon-face.

Bruce regretted not insisting they stay at the door. "What can I do for you, D—"

"I don't mean to waste your time," Detective Whitcomb said. "Four more kids have been murdered since we first met. We've kept it out of the media."

"How do you do that?" Bruce asked. "How do you keep four murdered kids out of the media?"

"You'd be amazed at what we can do when the crimes involve kids, Mr. Nicholson," she said.

Bruce thought of Aaron, and he felt like a jackass for being so unfair.

"The wasn't my point, though," the detective continued. "My point is—four more kids. And a beat cop we're treating as part of it. When the news does break, it'll go national."

"It's horrifying. All kids from Rose Park High?"

"Less than two miles away from your house," she said. "The same school your nephew goes to."

She brought Alex up.

"I wish I knew something that could help," Bruce said. "I hardly know my neighbors. It's unusual that I'd be home this time of day. I work long hours downtown. I—"

"Maybe Alex knows something?" She was trying to sound casual.

"Why would Alex know anything?" Bruce tried to look genuinely curious. "He's only been at that school a matter of weeks."

"The crimes have occurred during the last couple of weeks. I've talked to a lot of students from the school."

Bruce shook his head. "You don't understand. Alex has been through a lot. He doesn't need this murder crap shoved in his face."

"One of the girls from this recent group," Detective Whitcomb said, "the four we found this weekend, the girl had been mutilated, they'd all been mutilated, and her head was missing. We found her head this morning. Why would somebody do that? Why would somebody cut off a sixteen-year-old girl's head and leave it fifty yards away from her body while leaving her severed hands stacked neatly by her wrists?"

Bruce let a little bit of outrage creep into his expression. "That's *exactly* the kind of shit I don't want you saying to Alex."

"Because of the details of his parents' murders," the detective said. "The murders were brutal, like these have been."

"I... I don't know."

"I saw disturbing things when I worked gangs, Mr. Nicholson. But the only crime photos I've seen as bad as the ones from the recent killings in our backyard are the ones from the Packard family. If Alex knows *anything*, anything at all—"

"You don't talk to him alone," Bruce said. He wanted to hear what she would ask. He wanted to see Alex respond to her. "I'm there the whole time, and if he gets uncomfortable, I show you the door."

"Agreed," Detective Whitcomb said.

Alondra

Bruce Nicholson was, for the most part, outwardly calm, but inwardly, he still seemed squirrely as fuck. If she stopped suddenly on her way down the short hall toward the open door to Alex's room, he was so close that he would ram into her, and they would have a moment of slapstick bumbling for balance as prelude to the interview she felt certain made them both nervous. She had to keep Mr. Nicholson happy enough so that he wouldn't call the station about her visit. She wasn't following procedure—not where a child suspect was involved. A complaint could get her thrown off the case or worse.

But maybe she felt more nervous about looking into the eyes of a fourteen-year-old kid and deciding whether he could be a killer who made Dahmer look reserved.

At the door she slowed. No collision from behind. She glanced into the bedroom before tapping the door to announce her presence. The boy, more attractive than in the picture she'd been using, sat on his bed in a polo shirt and shorts with a textbook open by one bare knee and a digital tablet by the other. During her brief hesitation, he seemed too involved in his work to notice her. So studious, so well-groomed.

She tapped on the door and stepped further inside the bedroom with Bruce close behind. "Alex? Is it okay if I come in?

I'm Detective Alondra Whitcomb. You can call me Alondra."

With a look of faint astonishment, Alex tore himself from his homework and met Alondra's gaze. "Hi," he said. "Um, sure." He shifted attention to Bruce, questioning.

"It's okay." Bruce didn't sound very reassuring.

Alondra figured she'd learn how to talk to fourteen-year-olds around the time Nate turned fourteen. Right now, she'd have to fake it. "If you're up for it, I'd like to talk to you about the things that have been happening at your school."

"Things? What things?" The boy looked clueless.

Alondra moved in and sat on the corner of the bed. Bruce stayed by the door but seemed ready to pounce. "I'm sure you know... about the kids in your school... who..."

"You're talking about the murders?" Alex's voice lowered. "Everybody's talking about the murders."

"You never mentioned it," Bruce said.

Alondra gave him a glance that she hoped he knew meant he should kindly shut the fuck up.

"Yeah, the murders. Everybody's pretty upset, huh?"

"Not like you might think," Alex said. Alondra tried to fix his eyes with hers, but they darted from side to side as he spoke, and his head moved as if with an invisible tide. "People are scared, sure, but it's like... you know what people are like."

"What are people like?" She glimpsed his eyes over and over. Grey, but brilliant grey. Bruce was a good-looking man. He and Alex certainly had genes in common.

"People are, like, fascinated with the morbid stuff, you know?" Alex stilled and let their eyes settle on each other. His silver-grey, shining eyes. "People seem to care less about kids being dead and more about how they died."

"Does that bother you?" Alondra asked.

"No," the boy said. He smiled. "It's just people."

Alondra's intuition raged. "Did you know any of the kids? The victims?"

"I've seen pictures, you know, since. They look familiar, like I've seen them around, but I didn't know them."

If they'd been in an interrogation room, and he'd been an adult, she would have confronted him with crime scene photos, but as-is, she would proceed with words. "Did you ever have contact with Oliver Pollock?"

"He's the one they say got his skin ripped off?"

She swallowed and willed away gooseflesh before looking to Bruce for a cue. He gave none. "That's right, Alex."

"Don't think I knew him," Alex said.

"Some of his soccer teammates thought they saw you taking pictures of him one day during practice," she lied.

"I don't think so," Alex said. He would have passed a polygraph.

"What about Warren Dell? Ever have contact with him?"

"Actually, I'm pretty sure I did."

The answer surprised Alondra, and Bruce looked taken aback as well. "What happened?" she asked.

"I ducked into the theatre after school to sit for a sec before the walk home, and we talked. Nothing special. I didn't remember his name until people were, you know. Talking and passing newspapers around." The boy sounded entirely genuine and completely fake at the same time. He was more LA than she was, and she'd grown up here.

"And you didn't talk to Anna Cortez," Alondra said.

"Like I said, she looked familiar." Alex sighed. "But I don't remember ever talking to her."

The boy's eyes had light in them. It was grey and had no logical source. Greylight. Greylight.

"Thank you for answering my questions, Alex," Alondra said. Her stomach twisted. She felt a lump in her throat. The gooseflesh went wild.

She left knowing she'd just met a boy on his way to becoming a mass murderer.

Alex

A shady area with modern metal benches attached to modern metal tables, an area that might have been Rose Park despite being roseless, sat across the street from Rose Park Elementary, and Alex sat on top of a table, looking through his phone. He had Aaron's Sony—had planned to use it—but with no vantage on the playground that didn't leave him out in the open, being obvious with a camera was a bad idea. He had other plans for the camera anyway, and here, nobody would notice him with his phone. He could be texting. On a video chat. Playing a game. Didn't matter. A kid with a phone was background. Nobody would think he was spying on the younger kids at the elementary school. Recording them.

Detective Alondra Whitcomb had come to visit Tuesday. Today was Thursday, Alex's second day in a row skipping school, which would get him into trouble, but he'd be quitting school soon enough. One way or another, he wouldn't be staying at Bruce and Aaron's house much longer, either. Detective Whitcomb meant he couldn't pretend to be part of the normal world anymore.

He didn't know how soon things would change, but he would be fine. He'd never expected to stay. First, though, he did have time to make a lasting impression. To say a big goodbye. To take a couple of chances.

When Bruce let Detective Whitcomb into the house, Alex's bedroom door was open, and he could hear almost everything she said to Bruce. She was the enemy.

And she lived in the neighborhood.

He got a look at her car as she left, even saw part of the license plate. Wednesday, he wandered the neighborhood, looking for it. She seemed to work evenings, nights. He thought finding the car in the morning would be lucky but not impossible.

A few blocks beyond the high school, Alex entered the parking lot that joined four apartment buildings, signals that this part of town was—not cheap, nowhere nearby was cheap

—but more affordable, perhaps cop-salary-friendly.

Eureka!

The car was parked close to the ungated entrance. Alex found an unobtrusive place from which to observe. He learned about Nate, Alondra's little boy. He learned about a woman, by the look of her Alondra's older sister, who helped with Nate after he got home from school. He got a sense of their schedules.

Thursday morning, he saw Alondra walk Nate to the school bus stop. The elementary school wasn't much farther away than the high school, but Alondra probably thought Nate was too young to walk by himself. A detective would be protective. She knew the things that could happen.

Thursday afternoon, Alex took video of Nate at recess. Nate was getting too big for it, but he liked the slide. He was a cute little kid, which made sense because his mom was pretty. Alex resented the little boy's mother, though, and the resentment spread easily to her spawn. He wanted to hurt her; he wanted to hurt them both.

She knew the things that could happen.

Alex tracked Nate on another winding trip down the playground slide. The kid had thin braids, like his mother's but short, sticking out all over his head, and high cheekbones that made him model adorable. When waiting for his turn on the slide, he put his finger on his chin in a way that seemed, but probably wasn't, contemplative, which Alex framed portrait-style and shot as stills. Easy prey.

Hey, little boy.

What?

Come closer.

(Small feet, small steps.)

Closer.

What big eyes you have!

I'm going to eat you.

Looking through his phone at the little boy, he felt the role of a predator like he never had outside his house.

He was the Big Bad Wolf. He wanted to leap off the table, rip off his clothes, go down on his haunches, sprout hair in ungodly places, feel his face break and stretch as a snout and long jaws extended—full of teeth, fangs, long, sharp. He would bound across the street, clutch at the tall wire fence with pointed claws as he scaled it without effort, and vault into the playground, sending all the little ones, all but one, running, screaming in fear.

The boy with the finger on his chin stood by the ladder for the slide, frozen, looking into the wolf's big grey eyes.

What big teeth you have!

A teacher screamed and ran while another looked on and tried to summon help with her phone.

The wolf tackled Nate. His claws created red gullies bordered with wads of retreating skin. The wolf bit high into the left arm and sucked off meat as his teeth scraped against bone, moving down toward the hand. The radius and ulna were small enough to floss with.

The little boy wailed for his mommy, who wasn't coming. No one was coming fast enough. The little boy wailed, and the wolf tore out his throat, taking most of the neck with it in a smear of skin, cartilage, vocal cords, and blood. Nate died, and Detective Whitcomb hurt.

He would hurt her more.

Alex pictured it all as he looked through his phone at the boy who, again, squiggled down the slide. He wasn't a wolf. That was a fantasy. But Detective Whitcomb didn't get to play hunter. That was a fantasy, too. Alex was the predator. The world was prey.

22. TROUBLE
WITH MEN

Bruce

Around the door to Bruce's office, a glass wall separated him from the main floor. It offered a view of the maze of cubicles, irregular pathways created by printer and copy stations, scanner and fax stations. The constant chirps of phones and chattering of voices threatened his thoughts, which reduced his productivity anyway, the intrusion of images, the whispers of dread that made tasks trivial, his coworkers insects, chittering, chattering, chittering, chattering. Revulsion made him hope that at home he could have a haven from unwelcome noise and unbidden thoughts alike. He could lose himself in...

something else.

Awareness that home's new magnetism flowed from protectiveness had not eluded him. He wasn't sure whom he was protecting, or from whom he was protecting him. Obviously, he felt protective of Alex. Whatever he had or hadn't done, he needed sanctuary, and he had no one else. And Bruce had no one else. Except Aaron, but... Bruce and Alex were the end of the family line. Bruce would come no closer to having children. Theoretically, depending on how similar he and Letta had been, he and Alex could almost be as genetically similar as father and son.

He felt protective of himself. Paranoia or righteous

distrust, he wanted to be there when Alex might be home. For both of their well-being—but the feeling seemed selfish—he needed to be more aware of Alex's comings and goings. He also needed to be more aware of Alex's interactions with Aaron. Neither one of them had been courteous enough to tell Bruce the entire story of what had passed between them leading up to, or even after, the shower video. Bruce sensed it. The house was too small not to sense when people kept secrets from you.

Home. Lights were on in the kitchen and dining area, off in the living room and Aaron's work area. Thursday. Aaron had spent four days this week at the café. Seemed like a lot of fucking voiceover.

Going down the hall, Bruce noticed the light on under Alex's closed door. He went into his dark bedroom, autopiloting the removal of jacket and tie while he flipped the light switch and maneuvered toward the closet. He finished changing into a t-shirt before he noticed what was on the bed.

Déjà vu.

Bruce thought about calling for Alex.

The camera, Aaron's expensive handheld camera.

Something had happened. Something Alex wanted Bruce to see.

He picked up the camera, sat on the bed, prepared the screen, and prepared to rewind.

He considered whether he should leave the camera alone. If he waited for Aaron to get home, he could ask what he *would* see if he watched. Test whether Aaron would tell the truth.

Because he already knew what he was going to see, and he didn't want to see it.

In the mode Bruce understood, the camera showed the images through which it reversed.

A sensation the size of a billiard ball but much heavier started at the top of his head and sank, growing, bulging in his throat, expanding in his chest, curdling his stomach, knotting his intestines. Revulsion. Revulsion multiplied the gravity pulling down the core of his body.

He went back to a point in the video where at least Aaron wore clothes, and the two were talking.

"Shouldn't you put on some clothes?"

"I'm cooling off."

"Shouldn't you do that in private?"

"Am I supposed to hide from you?"

It was a transparent *pas de deux*, a seduction, and Aaron should have recognized it for what it was, and recognized his own behavior for what it was, not resistance but coyness, flirtation that didn't even count as disguised, except maybe to a teenager.

He kept watching. Alex helped Aaron get undressed, but before too long, the dynamic changed, and Aaron was all over the boy, mouth and hands like conquistadors. He fucked Alex on their sofa using spit for lube. The camera didn't capture Alex's face, and since Alex made... exuberant... sounds, Bruce couldn't be sure about his assumption. He assumed that, for Alex, the experience hurt a great deal.

Bruce watched it all. Tears blurred his vision. His heart pounded; breath quickened. The tears from sadness combined with the other physical responses to form fury, but he had another physical response, too. The image of two beautiful male bodies having sex stirred arousal, but he buried it with fury and revulsion.

The video ended. He set aside the camera. He ran to the master bathroom. He vomited.

Fury and revulsion melded into disgust and disdain. Aaron's violation of Alex, an underage boy, disgusted him and warranted his disdain, but Alex was their *responsibility*, their *family*, for God's sake, which made it opportunistic incest even if it wasn't consanguineal. Alex was an oath they'd taken together; in violating that oath, in addition to their marriage, Aaron had violated Bruce twice over. He'd thought he knew Aaron, but he was the stranger in the house, not Alex. To perform *his* responsibility, Bruce needed to stay with Alex in a high tower and keep Aaron *out*. Bruce hated his marriage right now because it seemed like a burger wrapper on a ball of shit.

"Bruce lives for his job," Alex said during the *pas de deux*.

Did Alex believe that? Better yet, did Aaron? They didn't know him at all. He *hated* his job. Telling rich assholes how to become richer assholes. He hated his job, his clients, his coworkers.

He hated everything. Disgust and disdain.

Seething with disgust and disdain, he would wait until Aaron came home, and they would figure out where the imperative for protection, where safety, demanded Aaron sleep tonight.

Aaron

When he came home, the sight of Bruce, posture erect, sitting at the dinner table, glass in hand, greeted him. Two bottles, open and unopen, claimed the table's center, both Redbreast. An empty glass sat in front of the chair across from Bruce. Bruce wore a t-shirt. Aaron felt more menace from the t-shirt than he would have from a dress shirt and tie.

Bruce rarely drank at all and never drank Aaron's whiskey. Something was wrong. Aaron closed the front door behind him but didn't advance. He wondered if going to his work area to put down his laptop case would be inappropriate.

Bruce leaned to one side, reaching for something on the carpet, and came back with Aaron's Sony handheld. He set it near the Redbreast bottles. "Won't you join me?"

Taking the laptop case with him, Aaron sat in front of the empty glass. Bruce looked cloudy, with a chance of gutted. The camera looked neutral.

Oh shit.

"If you pass me your glass," Bruce said, "I'll pour for you. Otherwise, pour for yourself. But I insist that you have a drink." He drained his glass and poured himself three fingers.

Aaron slid his empty glass toward him. He made Aaron's drink equally tall.

"Where's Alex?" Aaron didn't know why, but the question made sense.

"Alex is in Alex's room," Bruce said, "doing Alex things. Except he isn't using his earbuds. If you listen, you can hear the music in his room. He probably expects shouting."

"Shouting?"

"From the fight."

"What fight?"

"The fight he expects us to have."

Aaron didn't know whether to play dumb. He followed Bruce perfectly. Alex had left the camera for Bruce to find again, and Bruce had seen something new—and Aaron could guess what it was—and Alex expected them to fight about it. Alex *wanted* them to fight about it. Devilish?

Sadistic.

The perfect complement for this whiskey? A Xanax. Maybe two. "Are you angry?" Aaron asked.

"At the present moment, I am in crisis management mode. You have turned yourself into a problem that I must manage. You understand?" Bruce studied his drink, averting his eyes as Aaron tried to break through the cold he projected. "You understand what a problem you are?"

"I think so," Aaron said. "I made the worst mistake of my life, and I'm so sor—"

"Oh, shut the fuck up." Bruce's tone was calm, his volume controlled. "'Sorry' is for when you forget to buy milk on your way home. You fucked a child. Actually, I checked. The age of consent in California is eighteen. You *raped* a child. A child in our care. If I don't call the police right now, I become your accomplice. An accessory to rape, after the fact. Or has this been going on a while?"

"NO!"

"Don't shout. You don't have shouting privileges."

Aaron lowered his voice, which made fighting the tears

harder. "It only just happened, and I swear I feel awful and I—"

"Right now, how you feel is immaterial. You may notice I am not calling the police." Bruce channeled his anger through condescension. Aaron deserved that and more, but he also realized Bruce was seizing a position of power—just as Alex had. Aaron had been demoted to a new place of lowliness. Pedophiles were, after all, filth's filth, the people murderers spat on in prison.

Spat on and worse.

"Did you know Alex was filming?" Bruce asked.

Aaron resisted shouting. "No." He could no longer resist tears.

"I believe you. Why didn't you erase the recording?"

"He took the memory card. I haven't even seen it." Aaron wondered if he sounded disappointed not to have seen it.

Bruce got lost in some calculation, and Aaron waited. "Okay," Bruce said. "I believe you. So, do you think Alex could have made a copy? Put it online?"

"I don't know if Alex has the hardware or the know-how to transfer memory from an SD card, but he knows I do it all the time and that it's not complicated, and he's had days to get at my stuff—"

"So that's a strong maybe," Bruce said.

"Yeah."

"You realize there's a police detective investigating us right now?"

"I didn't know that at the time," Aaron said. Since he'd heard about her, Detective Alondra Whitcomb had haunted him. His imagination gave her the physique of a female bodybuilder.

"Okay. So… is there any reason *not* to delete the video on *this* memory? We should assume it's not the only copy, but on the off chance that it is, getting rid of it seems like a good idea. Unless you can think of some reason we'd need it, I don't know, because the truth might be better than a version that's gone through some creative editing. Or something."

Aaron knew it was self-pity but said it anyway: "I'm already the worst. Delete it."

Bruce picked up the camera, looked at its screen, and backed through the recording at double speed. "You don't have to do it that way," Aaron said, reaching out. "I can simply—"

"I also want to secure some images in my head." Bruce's eyelids looked heavy. His entire face looked heavy. His head had an almost imperceptible bob, as if he were in constant, subtle agreement with the backward images pulling him down.

Aaron extended a slow arm toward the camera. "Why?"

"When I'm not in crisis management, we're going to have a fight. I want to refer to specifics." No trace of anger. Bruce seemed stolid as he backed toward a deletion point in the most inefficient way possible.

"You could at least go faster. If you'll let me—" Aaron reached for the button.

Bruce slapped his hand and pressed the button himself. The reversing images moved faster. "Faster I can handle," Bruce said. "This is a refresher, not an in-depth study."

"This is ridiculous." Bravery surged. He grabbed the camera and tried to lift it from Bruce's hands.

"Let go." Bruce tugged back.

"Give me my camera, and I'll take care of it. You can watch. It'll be quick and certainly less painful." Aaron tugged.

"Fuck off." Calm. Almost cheerful. With a tug.

"Be reasonable." Aaron couldn't believe they were playing tug-of-war with a camera worth thousands of dollars. "Let go."

"*You* let go. You no longer have the right—"

"Let me take care of this, and then you can talk punishment—"

"Let go!"

"Be reasonable!"

"Goddamn it, you will not—" Bruce halted when the

other voice began.

"Controlling a camera is controlling a world, and you can trap people inside." Laughter. "I can relate. But more than that, capturing your image, what you choose to make art, makes something immortal. This dead hand is immortal. It's a godlike power here in the real world." Laughter. "I guess that means I'm godlike in more ways than one."

Aaron knew the voice was Alex's, and he knew the words weren't from their encounter. Bruce had discovered something new, likely by bumping the play button after reversing had overshot the mark, landing in some other moment Alex had borrowed Aaron's camera to capture. To immortalize.

This dead hand.

Bruce was watching. His already pale and sagging face sagged further and became paler.

You think Alex might have done something to Herb?

"What?" Aaron stood. "What are you seeing?"

"Let's go in order, shall we?" Alex's voice said through the camera's high-quality speaker. "We'll start with this little guy."

As Aaron walked around the table, Bruce said, "Crisis management has reached new proportions."

Alex's voice said, "Look at the wrists and calves first. Those wounds were practical, as I kind of, you know, had to nail him to a wall."

"Oh holy *fuck*," Aaron said. He and Bruce watched together.

Bruce

Had Alex meant for him to find this video, too?
Had Alex meant for *only* him to find this video?
You know you can talk to me about anything.
Leaving these videos for Bruce to find could be Alex's

way of taking Bruce up on his offer. Alex was talking through documentary messages—like he knew his Uncle Aaron did—and he was telling secrets. Secrets about Aaron. Secrets about himself. The things he liked to do.

"To appreciate this bit of work, you have to examine the leftovers more closely." The camera caught an image of the dead boy's pubic area, the ruined place where his genitals should have been, as well as the genitals themselves, separated, lying on a rock, before Alex finished struggling to flip the body. "You see, even though we were face to face, I had a sickle, so I was able to start cutting with his asshole." He took the lens right up to the broken hole, the flesh ring severed at the bottom, where Alex demonstrated with the fingers of his free hand that the flesh continued to split, all the way through the bridge between his spread legs. The split was jagged and blood-caked—the boy had probably bled out, but the camera wasn't showing where all the blood went—and Alex flipped the body back on its back so the camera could show the split's trajectory continue all the way through remains of scrotum skin up to the opening where a penis should have been. "With an axe I might have split him all the way up, like an upside-down log," Alex said. "That wouldn't have been as good, though." A thoughtful hum. "Probably would have been way more difficult, too."

Thanks to Aaron, the boy from this video now had the power to blackmail them.

Thanks to his sister, the boy from this video was now their son.

Letta, Letta, Letta. He could no longer deny that Alex had killed his sister. And his brother-in-law Dave, but who gave a crap about Dave? And his sister, for that matter, *had* been a psycho-bitch. Not that she seemed to have passed many marbles on to her son... but Alex was different.

Alex was *his* responsibility. Nonexistent God only knew what she'd done to poison the boy. Whatever he'd done, he deserved a chance, which he'd probably never had. He deserved a role model, which he'd definitely never had.

The mutilated bodies on screen were dead. Alex was alive.

Bruce didn't have to feel anything for the dead. Alex was family.

23. TROUBLE WITH BOYS

Aaron

Aaron didn't know the timeline, and he didn't want to think about cause and effect. He felt like the abusive uncle who made the serial killer crack. But then, Alex's parents had been murdered, and he'd found the bodies, unless he'd been the one who killed them, in which case he'd made the bodies. Not made them, but put them into their horrific state of murdered-ness. Like the kids in the video.

And the video wasn't ironclad proof that Alex had killed anybody. Sure, the voiceover was a series of confessions, but Alex had a big imagination. And what a great idea! Making a documentary about killing kids from your high school. Creepy as hell. Horror movie gold. Alex could have found the bodies and taken advantage of the situation. No stars for good behavior, but understandable given his growing affinity for expressing himself through the camera. And maybe the bodies weren't even real. Alex was a fucking wunderkind. Maybe he was experimenting with FX as a hobby now that he'd developed a taste for La-La Land.

Bullshit, bullshit, bullshit.

Alex killed those kids. The other ones, too. And his parents.

"We go talk to him. We talk to him *now*," Bruce said.

Aaron wiped his face on his short sleeve. "What on

earth do we say? Don't we... I mean, we could still delete the video of me... but we have to call the police about *that*, right?"

"Pick and choose which crimes to protect? Which family members deserve protection?"

Almost breathless, Aaron said, "Be *reasonable*." What about protecting *themselves*?

"We can't do anything until we talk to him," Bruce said. "We owe him. *You* owe him."

Bruce's authority seemed absolute. Inside Aaron a sensation spread from his throat to his stomach, from his stomach through his bowels, from his bowels into his circulatory system to every extremity. Scaliness. Snakeskin, rough and cold, coated his insides. They would talk to Alex.

Alex, who understood snakeskin.

Bruce knocked on Alex's bedroom door. A light was on inside. Music played inside.

No response.

Another knock, louder. "Alex?" Bruce called.

No response. Bruce tried the knob. The door opened a crack.

"Sorry to disturb you," Bruce said, pushing in.

Did they need to be sorry to disturb him?

No response.

They went inside and saw within seconds that Alex wasn't in the room. They confirmed seconds later that Alex wasn't home. A minute after that, they set out on a search.

Bruce

The park Alex favored was virtually empty and devoid of Alex.

The area around Alex's school had heavier street and sidewalk traffic but no sign of his nephew, even around back, the cordoned-off area where the bodies in the video had been. Bruce felt ashamed for not knowing where else Alex might go.

Did he like the library? The café? He pictured Alex perpetually in the bedroom or in the park. Bruce had so much more to learn.

Bruce and Aaron wandered the neighborhood for hours, until well past sunset, and returned home, both still nursing shock from the recent turns of events. Bruce told himself Aaron could be as self-indulgent as he liked, but Bruce needed to stay focused on crisis management. "We've got to decide on a couple of things," Bruce said. They sat on the sofa beside one another.

"Okay. Thing one."

"We're not going to turn Alex in," Bruce said. He would not be severe if he could avoid it. He would present inevitable conclusions.

"Do you understand what we saw? Those kids weren't only dead, Bruce, they were—"

"We saw the same images," Bruce said. "Dead is dead. Alex is alive and our responsibility."

"Responsibility being the key word," Aaron said.

"You can't be that stupid," Bruce said. "You can't try to take the moral high ground."

Aaron flushed red. "I'm tainted now. Unentitled to opinions."

"Let your opinions be informed by your behavior," Bruce said. He felt adrift in insight, at the threshold of revelation. "I propose that we talk to Alex, and further I do propose that we attempt to keep matters in our own hands. I would take care of both of you. Alex doesn't need to be sent to some juvenile detention center or, more likely, some junior ward for the criminally insane. And you don't need to go to prison for the rest of your life because you couldn't keep your pants on."

"Was that a threat? Are *you* blackmailing me?" Aaron scowled bitterly.

"Stating facts." Aaron's scowl almost pissed him off, but in crisis management mode, Bruce wouldn't be touched. "If

Alex gets caught, we will both likely face prison time, but you much more than I. Certainly if we don't delete the video, which I think we should do as soon as possible. God knows what Alex is up to now and what kind of attention he will attract. We *need* to talk to him."

"Okay," Aaron said.

"Okay what?"

"We're not going to turn Alex in."

"Good," Bruce said.

Aaron sighed. "Thing two?"

"As I've said, we're deleting the video, both the... bodies and the sex... and we're making a plan to confront Alex about whether there are back-ups or any other incriminating videos because from now on, we've got to think about safety, and we're all going to stay together, and be able to find happiness, we're going to be safe, doing things the way they need to be done. Okay?"

"Yeah," Aaron said. "This is all insane, but yeah."

What Aaron said felt discouraging.

Alex

The walking was a lot of back and forth, but he decided to go to school—a phone call from the principal's office stirring up Bruce and Aaron too early would spoil things—and he couldn't bring the supplies to school because he might get "randomly" searched.

When the final bell rang, he rushed home, walking not running but probably getting through the front door before the school buses even left the school parking lot. He changed into black clothes, not a hoodie because the heat would only make it conspicuous, but a polo and jeans, and replaced the books and binders in his backpack with the supplies he'd readied that morning. The handheld Sony would stay home; it had work to do. Alex would rely on his iPhone.

He tucked the Deerslayer into the back of his jeans and covered it with his shirttail.

On the way back to Detective Alondra Whitcomb's apartment, the bag felt heavy, but he didn't mind. Did he feel nervous? Certainly. His house had made him close to completely confident that when Esme shoved the knife into his chest, he'd be okay. But that was *his* house. Whitcomb's apartment was outside, in actuality. They could talk to him out here, but they couldn't change the shape of space or provide convenient gifts. He'd bought the zip ties at a hardware store.

They couldn't protect him, but he was extraordinary on his own, wasn't he?

The elementary school let out later than the high school, so Alex was perched beyond notice and waiting, alternating naked-eye views with views through his phone, when little Nate, with the sculpted face and spiky braids that made him suitable for magazine covers, arrived home. The woman Alex took for his aunt walked him back from the bus stop. Whitcomb's car was in the lot, so Alex assumed she was home. With a gun. Cops had guns. He had a quiet laugh. He was bringing a knife to a gun fight.

If all went well, the "call me Alondra" detective would never threaten him at all.

His phone let him zoom in on the second-floor apartment's big front window, which had open curtains and blinds. Through the window Alex could see an open room design similar to Bruce and Aaron's house, with a blob of space minimally subdivided into living room, dining room, and kitchen areas and a hallway branching off. From the correct angle, Alex caught site of an open door in the hall leading to a small bathroom. No sign of Alondra. The Aunt prepared something in the kitchen, and Nate sat on the living room couch, already bathing in TV glow.

Not yet.

Alex opened his backpack and got out the bag of zip ties, or "cable ties" as the bag called them. Seemed faster than duct tape and reliable enough. He shoved a bunch into each of his front pockets. After an adjustment, he practiced making quick grabs for the Deerslayer.

The aunt finished chopping cantaloupe and put it in a bowl with some berries. She poured two lemonades, one in a glass, one in a plastic cup. She brought the fruit and the plastic cup to Nate and sat with him on the couch.

Not now.

They talked, but Alex couldn't read lips and would have needed serious spy equipment to eavesdrop. Alondra was probably back in her bedroom, maybe sleeping because she worked so much at night, which was why the aunt was here to look after Nate. Perfect if he could get things done while she slept, perfect if he could keep them quiet enough—

Finally, the aunt got up again. Alex supposed she'd remembered her own lemonade, abandoned in the kitchen, but instead she went into the hall and closed the bathroom door behind her.

NOW!

Alex crammed his phone into a pocket and sprinted across the street, up the exterior staircase on tiptoes, and to the Whitcomb front door. He knocked lightly.

One, two, three, four, five, six, would Nate even—

The door opened. Alex bent his knees to meet the gorgeous child eye to eye. "Your name wouldn't be Nate, would it?"

Confusion battled on the boy's face. He wasn't supposed to talk to strangers. But Alex was just a big kid. Nate looked over toward the closed bathroom door. He looked back at Alex and nodded.

"Okay, Nate. I've got a surprise for your Mommy, but you have to be really quiet, okay?" Alex smiled, trying to share his excitement.

Nate said, "Okay." He was quiet.

Alex pushed the door open wider, walked inside. He shut and locked the door behind him, fastening the chain.

"Now Nate," Alex whispered. "Come closer, and I'll tell you about the surprise. Your Mommy will love it."

Nate hesitated.

The toilet flushed.

Alex bent down, left hand in his pocket, right hand gesturing for Nate to come closer. "Hurry!" He used his biggest, friendliest smile.

Water ran in the bathroom sink.

"Come on, Nate!"

The boy scurried closer. Alex zip-tied his own left wrist to Nate's right. The sudden capture nearly jerked the boy from his feet, and he yelled, "NAH!"

"Nate?" The aunt's voice. The bathroom door opened.

Alex drew his knife with his right hand and held it in a fist that covered Nate's mouth. He dragged the boy, who made a whiny noise but didn't try to scream, so that they'd make a fine image for the aunt when she stepped into the hall.

When she did, instinct must have made her cover her mouth. Instinct must have told her that Alex's pose meant that if she screamed, the boy died.

"Good," Alex said with conversational intensity. "Quiet or the boy dies."

The aunt lowered her hand. Her cheeks quivered. "You okay, Nate?"

Into the boy's ear, Alex said, "You can stay quiet?"

Moving with Alex's knife-holding fist against his mouth, the child nodded.

"Good." Alex lowered his hand.

"Okay Aunt Rhea."

"Aunt Rhea, take a seat at the table. The close one. Right there." Alex gestured with the knife.

The fortyish Black woman kept her hair close-cut, very unlike Alondra's, but they had the same nose, cheeks, and eyes, and they both looked like Nate, and Rhea's trembling approached seizure during her slow walk to the dining room chair. "We... we don't have any drugs," the woman said.

"I don't care." Alex watched for signs that she might jump at him. Defender instincts might run in their family.

"I have some cash in my purse," she said. When she reached the chair, she turned it to face him, which was what he wanted, but had he asked? She held up her hands as if he were pointing a gun and stood by the chair. "I could buy you booze, or weed, or you could take the money and leave."

"I don't care," Alex said. "Sit down."

Aunt Rhea sat down. She kept her hands up.

All the dining table chairs had arms. Easier. He pulled a zip tie from his pocket. "You know what this is?"

She looked at the tie that held Nate to Alex instead of the one he meant to show her. "Cable tie," she said.

"Right." Whatever. "Cable tie. I'm going to give this one to you. Take it with your left hand, and fasten your right wrist to the chair."

Aunt Rhea's hand shook so much it almost flapped as she took the tie, but she managed, and securing her wrist didn't require too much effort. Even dragging Nate, Alex was faster doing her other wrist by himself, also binding her ankles to the chair legs. From now on, he'd keep a supply of *cable* ties at his house.

The tears. Always tears. Lines down Aunt Rhea's face, sheets on the boy's. Nate looked like he might wail at any moment but kept control, brave kid. Rhea would probably be the first to scream. To lose control. Alex had to be ready for anything. Bullets could fly without warning.

Real risk was a rush.

With a closed-mouth little chuckle, Alex looked from one prisoner to the other and said, "So, which one of you is going to tell me where Mommy is?"

"Mommy!" Nate yelped.

"Ssshh. Quiet, remember? Nobody needs to get hurt."

Nate squirmed against his *cable* tie but stayed quiet.

Softly, Aunt Rhea said, "You can leave. Tie the boy to a chair like me. We won't be able to call anyone anytime soon.

You can get away. You look like every other white boy to me. I won't be able to identify you. You can get away. But you have to go. Before it's too late."

Alex set the curved end of the blade against Aunt Rhea's temple and cut a line down along the curve of her cheekbone, blood chasing after the knife's sharp tip.

"STOP!" Nate yelled.

"Hush!" Alex barked. "I asked a question. This is what happens when people don't do what they're told and answer questions like they should."

Nate's whiny crying noise was constant and louder now, but not so loud that it would wake someone in the back of the apartment. The boy still had some control. Aunt Rhea's lower lip jumped like a jackhammer. "Don't hurt us," she said.

"Where's your sister?"

"She's a cop and she's home and she's got a gun and she's on her way out here to blow your fucking head off!" Aunt Rhea did not pay regard to volume, so Alex stabbed her leg above the left knee, not penetrating too deeply, but penetrating enough to stun with a pain beyond most people's experience. "ARAHHH!"

"Ssshh," Alex said. "I can do so much worse. To you and to him. But right now, your nephew and I are going to check the back, and you're going to stay quiet, or the hurt really starts. Understand?"

She looked at the blood oozing through her pants leg. "Yes," she whispered.

Halfway down the hall, Alex bent to Nate, staying close to keep from twisting their bound arms, and said, "Can you carry a gallon of milk in one hand?"

The boy nodded.

"Good." Alex took off his backpack and handed Nate the heavy cannister. "You hold onto that. Be careful not to drop it. Bad things can happen. Understand?"

The boy nodded.

The door to what was obviously Nate's room was open.

The door to what Alex assumed was a linen closet was narrow, and folding doors marked the laundry room. That left one door, closed, to be Alondra's. Alex wasn't going to knock. He got into position behind Nate, turned the knob, and gave the door a gentle push. It opened without a creak. He hoped a bullet wouldn't hit the cannister.

Nothing.

Alex marched Nate farther into the room, until he had a clear view of the queen-sized bed and the woman on top of it, curled up in a pink *Powerpuff Girls* t-shirt that would probably drape to her knees when she stood. Detective Alondra Whitcomb was not poised with a gun to save the day; she had slept through the commotion in her home.

Noticing the warm blood on the blade, Alex tucked the Deerslayer back into his jeans and took the cannister from Nate. The boy's face broadcast that he was thinking of getting his mother's attention.

Alex took off the cannister's cap and started splashing. Liquid sloshed and smacked the sleeping woman, who stirred and mumbled. The second time the liquid hit her, she opened her eyes. Coughed after an interrupted inhale. The third time, she sat up most of the way. The fumes were strong, making visible distortions in the air that reminded Alex of *them*. He'd never used gasoline before. He'd save most of it in case it needed to be fresh to ignite.

He aimed the fourth splash at Alondra's face.

Fully alert, she scrambled not toward Alex but toward a nightstand on the bed's opposite side where, Alex guessed, she had a locked box with a gun in it. He pulled the Deerslayer, held it to Nate's throat, and shouted, "DETECTIVE!"

She turned, saw, and froze. After that, getting her tied to a chair next to her sister was easy.

"Alex," Detective Whitcomb said, "why did you come after me?"

"*Alondra,*" Alex said, "I could be clever and ask why you came after me, but the truth is that you coming after me is an excuse. I just need variety. They like it. I like it. Everyone must be entertained."

"It's hard these days, isn't it?" the cop asked. "Keeping everybody entertained? My son Nate seems to devour every cartoon that's streaming. My sister Rhea sees every romantic comedy that comes out and can't get enough. Me, on the other hand, I like—"

"I need to ask you something," Alex said.

"I like horror movies," Alondra said. "True crime, too. I guess I've got the right job?" She kept looking at Nate as if the boy might do something. Fastened to Alex's left, he didn't even seem to be crying much anymore. Alex cut the cable connecting them, then tied him to a chair to make a triangle with his aunt and mother. Pushing the table to clear the path, Alex walked a circle around the triangle. Alondra followed his circuit and asked, "Who's 'they?' You said, 'they like it.' Who's 'they?'"

Alex stopped behind Aunt Rhea and put a knife to her throat. She whimpered. Alex glared at Alondra. "Tell me, Detective Horror Movie, why shouldn't I kill Big Sis?"

A tear leaked down Alondra's cheek. "She's a beautiful person. The world would be... so much less... without her."

When Alex touched Aunt Rhea's left hand, she screamed, but she yielded when he twisted, turned her palm upward, and exposed the inside of her wrist. Before she could anticipate, he drove the knife into her, pulling it through skin, arteries, and veins, halfway to her elbow. She howled. Blood flowed.

Alondra struggled in her chair, half mumbling, half screaming variations on "Stop it, let her go, goddamn you." Nate caught Rhea's tremors. Earthquake threatened. Rhea's shock and horror at seeing her forearm opened distracted her from Alex as he moved to her other arm, twisted it, and sunk the knife in for a second helping, a new burrow from palm through forearm, releasing another gush of red.

"Aly!" Aunt Rhea yelled as her blood poured over the

arms of the chair.

Alex pondered calling Alondra "Aly." It was so close to "Alex."

Aly rocked her chair back and forth, weight on the right legs, weight on the left legs. Wood wobbled. Something CRACKED.

Alex pointed the knife at her so fast he flung her sister's blood in her face. "Stop that!"

The cop kept fighting the chair.

He moved behind Nate. "Last warning!"

She kept fighting.

He sliced off the boy's ear, accidentally taking a couple of braids with it. As the boy shrieked, Alex threw the ear at his mother, again hitting her face. He was good at this!

Out of breath, Aunt Rhea shouted, "Don't fight, don't fight!"

The wobble of wood stopped. Aly's stare tried to burn holes in him. Nate wailed as blood covered the side of his face where his ear had been. He was a little less magazine-friendly now.

"Ssshh," Alex said. "Ssshh. Aly, you've already lost one. You want to lose both?"

The hate in that woman's eyes!

Nate's crying quietened, probably as he realized no relief was coming, but he didn't entirely shut up about the pain and the fear. Aly said soft, comforting things Alex could tell she didn't believe, but if Nate believed them, Alex supposed she was successful. Aunt Rhea's eyes fluttered closed when she passed out, and they were all quiet enough to hear her continued breathing. They were quiet enough to notice when it stopped.

"You'll be tried as an adult and executed," Aly said.

"Do you think," Alex said, "the blood will leak into the apartment downstairs, and they'll call the police? Should we wait and see?"

"You don't have much time," Aly said. "Run."

Alex put the fourth and final dining table chair next to Aunt Rhea's body so he could watch mother and son. Nate checked out—blank stare, tremors settled to lethargy—good for him. Aly tried conversation, some psych tricks Alex recognized and some he probably didn't, but he didn't budge. When she wasn't trying to save herself and her little boy, Aly gawked at her sister's corpse. Alex considered cutting off Aunt Rhea's head and planting it in Aly's lap, but he liked the corpse's understatement, blood having overflowed from two gashes like candlewax and collected in a circle all around her. Candlewax. Burning.

When the sun went down, Alex carried on with his initial plan. He soaked Aly's big hair with gasoline; he drenched her long pink shirt. As the fumes filled the apartment, Aly struggled a little but not much. When he threw the lit match at her, she surprised him with a quiet calm. In a few seconds, though, her upper body became a torch, and her scream was loud and agonized enough to curdle unseasoned blood. Alex splashed other parts of the room as he watched how quickly the flames reduced Aly's hair to ash and made her face peel off in flakes. He smelled her almost immediately, sizzling flesh, cooking meat. Smoke alarms went off.

Fire ate through the cable ties. Burning away from her own skeleton, Aly somehow stood, flaming arms outstretched, one foot still attached to the burning chair, which she dragged as she stepped toward Alex and her sister's corpse, stepped, dripping blistered skin and boiling fat, stepped, joints weakening as flames destroyed cartilage and tendons faster than bone, and collapsed, the carpet around her catching fire.

Alex did not splash Nate with gasoline. Nate watched his mother burn. Who knew? Maybe he would live. The fire was spreading. Alex took quick shots with his phone before saying "goodbye" to the little boy.

The gas cannister wasn't empty when he left it behind.

Heat at his back, he ran downstairs into the evening and knew he should keep going but, in the parking lot, turned to see the window he'd spied through before. The apartment looked like a box of fire. The whole building sounded like blaring alarms.

Turning to run, he slammed into a man who grabbed him by the shoulders. "Who the hell are you? What the hell are you doing here?"

Alex yanked himself away and ran blindly in the direction opposite home. It was time to disappear. A big Hollywood exit. One thing to do first. One more monumental experiment.

From behind him, he heard a soft explosion.

24. INTO THE ESCAPE

Alex

Adrenaline pounded in his ears before he started running, and endorphins kicked in soon after, so he was high as fuck and dodging sidewalk obstacles human and otherwise and not paying attention crossing streets and car horns bitched and not paying attention to buildings or signs or anything because he was so amazingly free and transcendent and wonderful and the fire was an organism a pet that could never die the fire had done his bidding was probably still doing it wished he could see building evacuation trucks ambulance police cars firefighters reporters chaos like the world flying by around him chaos like the worlds he could create and destroy chaos like—

Where the hell was he?

He stopped. Air raked his lungs. His visual field took a few spins. The moment was still awesome. Also, disconcerting.

Streetlights stood nearby, which was good. He wasn't far from a freeway underpass. Not much light made it there except for cars' headlights. The freeway thundered. Next to him was a greenspace, a park, presumably, though it looked desolate in the dusk. Maybe the alternation of grassy patches that couldn't survive without watering in a land of perpetual drought with dry, dirty patches clashed too much with the lush greenery Alex had known growing up in the South.

Maybe the tents unnerved him. Along with the lush

greenery in the South came intense fear and hatred of homeless people, a view that Angelenos didn't seem to share as universally and that Alex hadn't taken the time to reconsider. He was himself the deadliest person he knew; he'd just taken down his *second* cop. What did he have to be afraid of? Being raped and murdered was the answer, but he had the Deerslayer, and he was competent. With all its tents and undesirability, the greenspace looked like a good place to lie low. Do what needed doing.

Did what he thought needed doing actually need to be done? He was pretty sure he needed to continue alone from here. He knew what he was and felt pretty sure he could make a good, long go of it. But what if? The question bothered him. He'd had a sense for a long time about possibilities. He needed to find out, as unlikely as it seemed, whether he could trust somebody, anybody, in actuality.

He needed a place where he could go to his house and issue some invitations people couldn't refuse. A place he wouldn't be bothered. Or noticed. Where nobody would give a shit about who he was or what he was doing.

With a soft chuckle he walked toward a nearby light blue tent with a light on inside and its front door unzipped. A white woman who had stringy brown hair with streaks of grey, probably in her fifties or sixties, appeared to be cleaning out the tent, an act that consisted of transferring garbage from the interior to the exterior close by.

"Hey." Alex approached with soft footfalls. "You think that's okay?"

"Mind your business," the woman said.

He walked up to the tent doorway, very close to her, and crouched so he was at her level. "You know there's a trash can."

"Get away from me," she said. She kept shuffling out garbage as if he weren't there.

"It's right over there." Alex pointed to the corner. The trash can.

"If you don't get away from me," she said. "I've got

friends here, you know."

"I only want to show you a better way," Alex said. He picked up a wad of paper she'd expelled from the tent. He moved in toward her, and when she opened her mouth to scream, he shoved the paper inside, pushing it down into her throat until her rotting teeth scraped his knuckles. Using his superior size and momentum, he pushed her deeper into the tent, out of sight. Plenty of garbage, wads of paper, some of it used toilet tissue, remained. He grabbed what was close, and pressing on her chin to keep her jaw open, forced garbage into her mouth, garbage with rotting food clinging to it, garbage with shit clinging to it. She tried to scream but couldn't get sound around the growing obstruction. He shoved in more and more. Her mouth overflowed. Was she choking on the trash or her own vomit? He couldn't tell. She fell away from him and clutched her throat like she might cough out the invading matter making it bulge. Her eyes swelled. Rolling around on the tent's hard, bumpy floor, she eventually came to a halt.

Her neck looked longer *and* thicker. It was funny. Something yellow dripped out of her nose, and Alex couldn't guess what it was. It was simply gross.

Thanks to his own and her recent efforts, one area of the tent's floor was now clear enough to sit on without touching raw filth: destination secured. First, he wanted to move the woman's body to the farthest area of the tent, where she had a pile of dirty blankets and a stuffed trash bag that might have served as a pillow. As he grabbed her by the armpits and dragged, the body made a fart noise, might have come with shit, and the already awful smell in the tent got much worse. Alex dragged the body a little farther, not seeing a shit trail, and slung it into the bed zone. There. The lady of the house was sleeping.

Alex hadn't been concerned about sealing the tent so far —the chances of someone peeking in during the few minutes he took to kill the resident had seemed miniscule—but now he had to face trapping himself with the odor. His senses would be gone soon enough, he supposed, and he couldn't take a longer-term risk that one of the dead lady's "friends" wouldn't pop a head in while Alex was in a trance. Too much vulnerability.

Especially if police were searching for him. That guy in the detective's parking lot had gotten a good look at him. If Alondra had records, photos of him, at the police station—

The police would be searching for him.

He couldn't worry about that now. What's next was next. He took off his jeans but kept on the polo, which could be useful, and sat half-lotus on the tent floor's clean spot. He recited his mantra and felt comfort in the gathering static.

Aaron

CNN with the volume low occupied their eyes but not their minds as they sat on the sofa, not at opposite ends but close like partners, uncertain about what more they needed to say. They'd deleted all copies of all the incriminating videos that they had access to, including Aaron's back-ups, and they'd discussed how to confront Alex. *Carefully.* You confront a kid who butchered his parents *carefully.*

Aaron knew not to suggest confronting him with handcuffs and a police escort. Bruce's argument about Alex incriminating them both was sound, and besides that, at some point Aaron had missed, a point Bruce himself might not have been conscious of, Bruce had decided to go all in for the boy. Even though Bruce had sensed what might be involved, Bruce had committed. He'd made the choice for them both, just like he'd chosen for them to be Alex's godparents. Bruce didn't mean to be imperious. It happened without his knowledge.

Aaron didn't know when he'd decided to sleep with Alex. Fuck him. He'd fucked him. When he'd decided... to turn life to shit... but it was before the night when it happened...

Sparkles? Tiny electric explosions on his retinas. Seeing

things... and they hadn't even finished the first bottle of Redbreast... Aaron longed to claim the entire second bottle for himself, curl up with a blanket of self-pity because life was indeed over, drink into oblivion, black out, wake up and find out it was all a big nightmare, find the bad parts deleted like they'd deleted the video—

Spark! A brief, white flare above the coffee table made Aaron jerk backward into the sofa cushions.

"You—you saw that?" Bruce said.

Aaron turned face to face with his husband for the first time in hours or days and saw perplexity, alarm, but not, or not yet, the feeling rising in Aaron's throat—spark! spark! spark!— as the flashes went off on both sides of them, between them, in front of them—

fear—

as a mote of light stretched into a cord, zigged and zagged and then branched, two, three, forking, electric, lightning. Lightning streaked in front of them. It struck so close to Bruce's head that Bruce shrunk toward Aaron, clutched him, melted with him.

Flash! Flash! Flash!

The room around them became hard to see. White and flashes, bluish purple, lightning veins. The white faded to red, and as it did, Aaron thought, *how did he do it?*

The thought felt unwelcome, but Aaron knew the "he" was Alex and knew with equal certainty that Alex was the cause of whatever was happening. Why? How?

fear

The electric disturbance emanating from nowhere returned to nowhere and left Aaron and Bruce standing— Aaron didn't recall getting off the sofa—standing in a place with red walls that throbbed in places like the lightning branches, like veins or arteries. Fog made his feet on the blonde slats of the hardwood floor hard to see. It seeped and eddied. Cobwebs gathered all along the high imperfect corners. They stood near a staircase with a slithery banister and dingy grey carpet, overhead a faux chandelier that shined strange, grey light that tinted the whole place with shadow. It was a house's entryway, the foyer, a house dressed up like a monster, familiar but degraded and deformed. "What?" Aaron asked.

Bruce stepped further inside—what must have been the front door was behind them—and Aaron thought he was going toward the stairway until he veered toward the hall, a broad entryway to a room, a room of sorts, on his left. "I think I know where we are."

Aaron could barely get out "What," and Bruce had moved past mysterious lightning bolts in their living room, past appearing in a new and *intentionally* frightening-looking place, and all the way to a supposition about their location. How did he manage to stay so fucking calm when—

Aaron thought he knew, too.

They'd come during one of the trips to Georgia, when they were getting everything ready and needed to go through some of Alex's things. This place was Alex's house, where he grew up. Where he killed his parents. Somebody had given it the Deluxe Halloween Treatment. It was all fairly campy. Except the pulse in the walls. That effect was solid.

Even the campy stuff scared the shit out of them. If they'd been sucked into Alex's imagination, or... something similar that could have created the carnival version of his first crime scene... they were probably at the mercy of a psychopath.

"It's Alex's old house," Bruce said. "At least partially."

Hating the quiver in his own voice, Aaron said, "We do *not* want to be here."

"No, but I think he wants us here." Annoying fucking calm!

"Aren't you at least a tiny bit scared that whatever got us here is connected to—"

"To what?"

"To what he *does* to people?" Aaron felt like he should keep his voice down, but his nerves throbbed like the walls.

Bruce walked back to Aaron. "I don't see any reason to let my fear be in charge. Crisis management. I do suspect that in all probability this place is related to Alex, and Alex brought us here with some ability he has, and that ability is related to the things he does."

"Don't you think we should get *out* of here?"

"You can try the front door," Bruce said, "but I don't think it'll work. He has something to communicate, and we won't leave until he's finished."

"Fuck that." Aaron threw himself on the front door, unfastened the chain, and twisted the bolt. Focusing every bit of strength into his hand, he twisted. It didn't yield a microfraction. He grabbed the knob and shook. The door hardly budged in its frame. Bruce appeared patient but too goddamned annoyingly knowing.

Aaron gave up, scared of this place, scared of Alex, and scared of Bruce. He was less scared of how batshit crazy his situation was and more scared of the sense he made of it, the sense that meant he was, *in all probability*, completely fucked.

Bruce

Once Aaron proved him right about the front door, he turned his attention to the doorless broad entrance to what had been a living room and still retained some of a living room's features, a sofa, a loveseat, a recliner, a rocker, a television to which all the seating had lines of sight. The hardwood floor, however, vanished into dust and grass, and trees surrounded the furniture. Opposite the entrance, instead of a wall, a line of denser trees marked the boundary of a forest. Just inside the forest, past a few trees but visible as it swayed in a breeze Bruce didn't feel until he saw it work, a body dangled from a branch. He moved toward it.

"Oh fuck," Aaron said behind him, sickness in his voice. He must have seen the body, too. She should have been rottener by now, but Bruce guessed the regular rules of decomposition, and other regular rules, didn't apply here. This place somehow came from Alex. It had to do with his astral projection but went so much further. He created this place and learned to bring others in. He was brilliant. Here, his mother's body hung from a tree, entrails falling out through the vagina he'd carved into a larger opening, and elsewhere, in the world Bruce was accustomed to, his mother's body was in a refrigerated locker being preserved as evidence.

Bruce addressed the corpse. "Letta, you fucking bitch. Even if he got the psycho from you, you could have gotten him help. These things, they're nature *and* nurture. Where was the nurture? And why did you leave him to me? Did you know what would happen?"

Aaron appeared at his side. "That's what he did to your sister. You're talking to your dead sister that Alex killed."

Another breeze brought the sound of more creaking branches. Bruce walked to Dave's body and the bodies of three kids. Probably the three kids Detective Whitcomb talked about with Alex. Skinned, gutted, mutilated.

"I'm not getting anything from you. Tell me you're not disgusted," Aaron said.

"I'm disgusted." Bruce headed back toward the living room furniture. He needed to know so much more.

The living room adjoined a dining room on the left. The big, antique table filled most of the room, elegant, polished wood. Bruce saw what sat at the head of the table before he made his slow, circumspect way toward it. Aaron walked behind him and seemed not to see until Bruce rounded the first occupied chair. "Oh Jesus fuck," Aaron said, hand over his mouth.

The girl's body, head missing, had been in the video, all the rough cuts on the neck where, according to Alex's voiceover, her best friend had imprecisely hacked through. The girl's arms were at her sides, but her severed hands were neatly stacked on the table in front of her.

Slumped in the second occupied chair was the boy who was first to appear in the video. Like the girl, he was naked, and at first, he looked like he had his hands in his lap. Closer inspection revealed the girl's missing head in his lap, face buried in his crotch, and his hands tangled up in her dyed hair.

Aaron screeched. "WHAT ARE YOU—"

Bruce lifted the severed head by the hair, not extricating the dead boy's fingers, only separating the head enough from the boy's crotch to confirm that yes, in place of his genitals he had a deep gash, a gash that, in his voiceover, Alex had claimed to fuck. He didn't know which idea was more perverse, the image of the severed head devouring the kid's crotch, or the image of the crotch having been devoured. Bruce replaced the head as he had found it.

"Originally, I was going to do something else with them."

The unexpected voice made Aaron jump: "Fuck, fuck, fuck!"

"This felt inspired, though." Alex leaned in the doorway that led to the kitchen. He slid off the frame, into the kitchen, and took lazy steps away. He intended for his uncles to follow.

Alex

Alex didn't really understand the kitchen. The rotting meat and vegetables, the shit on the walls, the putrid milk: it all contributed to an atmosphere of nastiness, which he could appreciate, but the ensemble made the area feel least *his* of all the house. It reminded him of *their* part-ownership. The reminder grated on him as Aaron and Bruce struggled to breathe in the room's astounding funk. They got through to the breakfast nook, though, seeming even to adjust somewhat before they confronted the reason why Alex couldn't be courteous and invite them to have a seat with him at the round table. Three of the four chairs were already filled.

He'd worked quickly, so he'd made no spectacular poses, but he'd known to look on the back deck for them because that's where he'd found the cop whose head he'd smashed in like a melon. Aunt Rhea wasn't burnt at all. Alex guessed that because she'd died before the fire started, her body had come to his house with only the deep gashes in her arms. Alondra, however, was a crispy critter. Probably because of uneven gas splashing, parts of her had fried more deeply than others, so her body was a combination of exposed bone and charred fleshy tissue clinging at different depths and thus with varying recognizability. Nate—who hadn't survived, which Alex had kind of figured—was more evenly baked.

"I thought only other kids at your school, after Letta and Dave, I mean," Bruce said.

Aaron's head turned slowly from the table of corpses to him.

"Right! You couldn't know." Alex pointed. "That's Detective Alondra Whitcomb, her sister Rhea, and her son, Nate."

"Jesus fucking hell," Aaron said.

"You can't," Bruce said. "You can't be doing this."

"You know what, Bruce?" Alex waved the little boy's charred hand. "I can."

"They'll come after you, for killing a police detective," Bruce said. "It's not safe. You have to think safe."

To see what would happen, Alex gave the little boy's arm a hard jerk. It broke from its socket. Alex was pleased. He threw the arm and hit Aaron's chest. Aaron yelped and would've jumped out of his skin. "Bruce, you're too much about safe. When do you feel good? When do I get to feel good? You don't know what life has been like for me."

"No," Bruce said. "I don't. But I'm here to listen."

"But guess what, Uncle Bruce?" While he talked, Alex's mind summoned static. In his house, he didn't need a trance. In a lightning flash, he could move people. "I'm not here to talk about that. And none of us is here to be safe. I'm here to feel good. For me, this place is about feeling good. For you? We'll find out, won't we? Time to get on with it. We'll finish the tour later."

Blue bolts unzipped the air, and Aaron and Bruce disappeared.

25. GAME ON

Aaron

A new room, where bright yellow mixed with the greylight and reflected off eggshell-colored walls, came into focus, and Aaron felt cramped, on his feet but not standing. His body leaned backward, head, back, and legs against hard wood. Wood hugged his shoulders and held up his feet. Wood enclosed him in every direction but forward.

Forward, a few inches of wiggle room away, was a wire mesh, beyond which he saw a small room, or a big closet, with a regular door. His guess? He was in a closet. Bigger guess? His enclosure was a coffin, leaned against the closet's back wall so he could face the closet door. Next guess?

He shouldn't touch the wire mesh.

As the thought appeared clearly in his mind, he poked a wire with his left pinky finger. "Ow!" It shocked him.

"Aaron?" Bruce's voice, very close by.

"Bruce?"

"You sound like you're right next to me."

"I think... I'm in a coffin." Aaron cringed at his own high-pitched squeakiness.

"From the look and sound of things, we're both in coffins, side by side in a big closet. These wires—"

"Don't touch!"

"They hum. I think they're electrified. We're expected to stay put."

"What do we do?"

"Do you have a button close to your right hand?"

Aaron hadn't noticed it, but near his right hand, a plastic cube was mounted at the edge of the coffin's side, and on it was a button like a large red mushroom. "Yeah." Aaron's bewilderment washed out some of his terror.

"Should one of us push the button?" Bruce asked.

"Don't touch anything." Aaron fought the sudden need to pee.

Silence. Aaron imagined that Bruce waited for the closet door to open, too.

"He's going to kill us, isn't he," Aaron said.

"I don't know."

"What do we do?"

"Wait for the next thing."

It came soon: the closet door opened, and Alex, in polo and boxers, stepped inside, rolling a narrow podium in front of him and closing the door behind him. The podium shone white light on Alex's face—or the tablet on top of the podium did.

"Alex!" Aaron yelled.

He positioned the podium directly in front of him and looked in three places, to Aaron's right, at Aaron, and to Aaron's left, the source of Bruce's voice. "Grandpa, Aaron, Bruce, sorry to keep you waiting."

Grandpa? Who the hell—

"Grandpa, you can observe, but Aaron and Bruce, I welcome you as players in the exciting game of... CONFESSION!!" Alex held up his arms as if an audience roared. The closet's ceiling was high.

"Games, Alex? Do you think that's smart?" Bruce risked taunting the kid, and Aaron wondered if *that* was smart. "Where are you right now? This is where you come when you meditate, right? But your body stays behind. You're not safe, are you?"

What... the fuck... was Bruce talking about? Maybe he was pretending to make sense out of things. Maybe Aaron should pretend, too.

"In this game, Bruce, *I* ask the questions." Alex smiled. "Question One." He looked at the glowing podium. "Be sure to hit your buzzer and wait on me to call on you for your answer. Okay. Get ready. Aaron and Bruce. Here we go."

What would happen if Aaron hit the button and got a question wrong?

"Which one of you..." and then Alex changed from speaking very slowly to rushing the words, "likes me more?"

Nobody raced to mash a button. "Ten seconds."

Aaron looked in Bruce's direction even though coffin borders blocked eye contact. He didn't know how to answer. What did Alex think the answer was? Would Alex penalize Bruce if Aaron named himself? Penalize Aaron for naming Bruce?

A buzz came from Bruce's side.

"Bruce!" Alex sounded gleeful. "Your answer, please."

"It's not simple," Bruce said. "Aaron likes you more in one way. I think I like you more in another."

"So, your answer is, it's relative," Alex said.

"Yes."

"Thaaaaaat's... bullshit! Only real answers in *CONFESSION!*, Bruce!"

Alex pushed something on the podium, Aaron heard a mechanical noise followed by buzzing, and Bruce made a bouncing, low noise wrenched with pain.

Alex laughed. "Shocking, I know." Another mechanical noise, followed by Bruce's heavy breathing. "Okay, Aaron. The question is yours to answer. Ten seconds."

Aaron still didn't know what to do.

"Five seconds."

Which would be worse? Not answering or answering the wrong way?

"Three, two, one, time! Failure to answer is the same as getting an answer wrong, I'm afraid." Alex pressed his mounted tablet, and Aaron heard the mechanical noise as the wire mesh came closer. Aaron shrunk back, flattened against the wood that held him in position, but the wires kept coming until they made contact from his forehead to his ankles. The shock was minor at first, but it built quickly, a jangling screech of pain that tore at every nerve ending. Then, mechanical noise, and the wires reversed to their original distance.

Aaron pissed himself.

"Let's hope you two find the second question a little easier. Here we go." Alex took a deep breath. "Which one of you… finds me more attractive?"

Aaron's hand crept toward the button.

"Ten seconds."

Aaron's hand hovered and prepared to plunge.

A buzz came from Bruce's coffin.

"Bruce! With six seconds left! I hope you have something more concrete for me this time." Alex looked to Bruce, to Aaron, and to Aaron's right, where Aaron now imagined a third coffin holding "Grandpa," probably a corpse.

"Aaron," Bruce said. "We all know that." He did not sound loving.

"We'll see," Alex said. "Aaron, the question is yours to answer."

An odd game. Bruce had given an answer, undoubtedly the correct one, but Aaron still had to respond. If he lied and said "Bruce," would the answers cancel each other, meaning nobody got electrocuted, or would Aaron face a harsher punishment for lying? Would they both get shocked? Aaron would pretend to see sense in it. Bruce had told the truth. So would he.

"Five, four, three, two—"

BUZZZZZZZZZZ!

"Aaron! Your answer?"

"Me. Aaron. I do."

Alex hopped on both feet behind the skinny podium, giddy. "A correct answer! Congratulations!"

Aaron sighed with relief, and he thought he heard Bruce

do the same.

"Bruce, since you answered first, you get to decide who won the question."

"What?" Bruce spoke for them both.

"Not every question has a winner, but *every* question in *CONFESSION!* has a loser, and Bruce, you get to pick. Ten seconds."

"But we both—"

"Seven, six, five—"

"I did," Bruce said. "I won."

Mechanical sound. The wires made contact. After the initial shock, Aaron became unaware of places that wires touched skin or pushed against clothes. Every part of him absorbed the stinging vibrations that became waves of sizzling pain, not fire but every cell pierced and torn by needles, and only Alex daintily plugging his ears with his fingers made him aware of his own jittery attempts to scream. Aaron had no sense of time passing until Alex pressed his glowing podium and made the agony stop.

Alex seemed to study the podium while Aaron caught his breath. Bruce didn't make a sound. Bruce, who had chosen to give Aaron pain. Bruce's tiny vengeance. They were supposed to confront Alex together. They'd agreed to act together. Bruce chose to electrocute him. It felt like betrayal.

"Third and final question of Round One," Alex said.

Aaron got ready.

"Which one of you…"

Aaron's hand almost touched the button.

"… thinks I'm scarier?"

Aaron buzzed, knew he was first, and shouted, "Yes!"

"Aaron, dark horse from behind." Alex tittered. "Your answer? Ten—"

"I do!" Aaron pronounced. His teeth chattered. Aftershocks still poked his nerves.

"Bruce, your answer?"

"I think he's right. He does," Bruce said. Aaron couldn't

tell whether Bruce was scared.

"You should have buzzed in, Bruce, but I'll let that slide." Alex turned to Aaron. "I assume you're a quick learner, Aaron. Who won the question?"

As the waves of shock left him, waves of bitterness rolled in. "I did," Aaron said. "Zap him."

Bruce

"I must say, you took that like a pro." Alex left his podium and, leaning in to match the angle of Bruce's coffin, examined him. "You hardly flinched."

He'd controlled his voice during the second electrocution, but he couldn't hide his heavy breathing afterward. The pain was too literally breathtaking. Otherwise, though, he remained still, willing his heartrate to slow. "I am a professional," Bruce said. Did that sound too corny?

Alex backed up. "We'll see if that helps during Round Two, where the *stakes* are even higher!" Bruce heard soft laughter, a group of people, possibly a large group. "Let's play... *CONFESSION!!*" Applause engulfed Alex from behind. Not expecting success, Bruce searched the closet for speakers, anything that would relay recorded sound. His expectation was correct. Why?

Because this place was staged for Alex. Why *wouldn't* he have sound effects?

Alex turned his back to the coffins and addressed the invisible audience. "In Round One we learned that, while Aaron and Bruce couldn't figure out which one of them likes me more, Aaron finds me scarier *and* more attractive."

The audience made a unified "Oooooo."

"Now we push *harder* on the attraction issue and find out more about what they like." More applause. Alex turned back to the podium, looking very satisfied. "Question One. What are your husband's views on sex with underage boys?"

"Oh, fuck that!" Aaron said.

Bruce looked at the button.

"Ten seconds."

Aaron buzzed in.

"Yes, Uncle Aaron?" Alex beamed in Aaron's direction. The greylight, that sourceless, baseless illumination in the house that seemed pervasive in different intensities, matched Alex's eyes. The light in Alex's eyes, the light *from* Alex's eyes.

"Alex, I'd say my husband Bruce views sex with underage boys negatively. He condemns it. Probably leftover morality from his religious parents. He wouldn't use this word, but deep down, he thinks it's sinful. Profane." Aaron spoke with an edge that seemed meant for Bruce.

Bruce hit his button.

"Yes, Uncle Bruce?"

"Aaron would pay lip service to disapproving of it, but he'd also justify it. He might point out that sex between men and young boys was totally normal in Ancient Greece, or that a couple of centuries ago a man in his forties might marry a thirteen-year-old girl and have society's complete approval. Concepts like 'underage' and 'consent' are matters of social perspective, not universal truth, and—isn't this right, Aaron? Some kids are ready to consent earlier than others. Like you, Alex. Aaron often comments on how mature you are for your age."

Alex clasped his hands and shook them enthusiastically. "Such great answers from both of you! At the beginning of Round Two, the audience decides who won the question."

"What audience?" Aaron sounded frustrated. "I still don't understand—"

"Quiet on stage!" Alex turned his back to the coffins and addressed the invisible audience, which was somewhere in the vicinity of the closet door. "If you like the first answer, Aaron's answer, give it applause!"

Clapping, some cheers.

"Why are you doing this?" Aaron asked.

Without turning around, Alex answered, "They like showmanship. They provide for me, and I provide for them." He raised his voice for the audience: "Okay, now cheer if you like the second answer, Bruce's answer!"

More frenzied clapping, louder cheers.

"Bruce wins the question!"

"There's no audience! You decided!" Aaron shouted.

"It wasn't my call," Alex said, returning to the podium. He pressed something.

"Then who?" Aaron demanded.

"My advice is, lean into the pain. The electricity could kill you, and you won't get away anyway."

"Wha—ow!" Wow? "Ow! Jesus Christ! Fuck! Ow! Ow! God, it's drilling—fuck! Fuck! Oh my God!" Aaron's words dissolved into incoherent screams. Bruce had no idea what was happening to him.

When the screaming slowed, Bruce saw blood spreading on the hardwood floor. "Aaron?"

"I'm... alive." Aaron struggled for coherence. "Some kind of... spike... drilled through my ass and... poked out next to my hip, but... I'm alive."

"And now it's time for the second question." Alex grinned. Bruce had never seen him so happy. "Would you ever fuck an underage boy?"

The actual answer was easy, but the question triggered suspicion. Bruce sensed a trap.

"Ten seconds."

He'd won the first question not because his answer had so squarely captured Aaron's rationalizations but because his answer had pleased the audience more. It was more entertaining. His actual answer to Question Two, NO, might not excite them, whoever they were, as much as Aaron's actual answer. NO was expected. NO was right. This place wasn't about right.

"Five seconds."

Buzz! Aaron.

"Goddamn it you know I did, and that means I would, and I probably would again, I don't know. I can't say I didn't like it." Aaron.

"What an answer!" Alex half turned to the invisible audience. "Remember, hold all those applause until the right moment." He shuffled to Bruce. "The question is yours to answer."

Bruce tried to think of a way to make NO sexy. His brain didn't cooperate.

"Ten seconds." Alex leaned in and, in a confidential tone said, "Remember the game is called *CONFESSION!* It's not a confession if it's not the truth." He backed out and announced. "Five seconds!" Bruce's brain did nothing. "Three, two—"

Buzz!

"Yes, Uncle Bruce?"

"I appreciate the beauty of youth, but... no." Bruce sounded like an idiot.

"Okay then. Audience?"

Of course, the audience chose Aaron's answer.

A poke, a prick, under his right shoulder blade. The drilling sensation began with a sickening tickle that turned into a tangle of tears and twists, blinding pain as the bit bore through skin and muscle, ligament and cartilage, making a wider and deeper hole. Bruce focused on analysis to minimize his body's outrage at the violation, at having part of it ripped away to make room for invasion, reasoning that the "spike," as Aaron had called it, must have been conical, a funnel making wider and wider circles in his flesh, clearing a path with help from raised ribbing like a screw's, and if he was lucky, it wouldn't nick his right lung or his heart. If he was lucky—

He let the air out of his lungs and sucked in fresh breath, movement that hurt but couldn't be avoided, and he hadn't even known he wasn't breathing.

The tip of the cone spike poked out of his right pectoral muscle, over his nipple, and grinded away the surrounding flesh until the hole in Bruce's front was the size of a plum. Blood saturated his shirt and found its way to the floor to mingle with Aaron's. He didn't cry out. He couldn't stop the spasms in his upper body, but the rest of his body stayed still.

"The third and final question of Round Two," Alex said. He moved the podium from the center of the closet—Aaron was in the center—to the side, Bruce's side, if that had any significance, and returned to stand in the center. "It has an interactive element."

The audience ooooooed.

"The question is a two-parter. First, do you think I can turn your husband on?"

When Bruce took a deep breath, he felt like the spike was ripping through his chest.

"Ten seconds. Nine. Eight."

Bruce hit the button.

"And once again, Bruce is quicker on the draw." Alex carried his tablet away from the podium and angled his body so he could see Bruce and the audience at the same time. "So, Bruce. Even with a fresh hole in his ass—a fresh asshole! didn't think of that—do I have what it takes to make Aaron's little soldier stand up and salute?"

"Yes." Bruce heard minimal pain in his voice and felt good about it.

"And Aaron? What do you think? Bruce is less... tested... in these matters. You think I can get a rise out of him?"

"Ha! What you don't know that I know...." The pain made Aaron sound drunk. "Over the years, we've watched every kind of porn together. Lots of twink porn. Barely Legal Boys. Teacher's Favorite Punishment. Stepdads and Stepsons. Bruce never had a problem getting off." Aaron made a grunt that turned into a dramatic throat-clearing. "So, I would say yes, Alex, you can turn him on."

Alex's voice got softer. "Part Two. No need to buzz in. I'll start with Aaron this time. Aaron, was Bruce right?"

Pause.

"Ten, nine, eight—"

"I'm pretty sure, yeah, unless the blood loss is a problem." Aaron tried to sound confident. Controlled. Sexy?

"The question is yours, Bruce. Is Aaron right about this underage boy turning you on?"

The truth? The truth was that he didn't know. All kinds of things turned him on, and he didn't always agree with his libido. If he said *yes*, and the answer was probably *yes*, despite the storm of pain in his upper body, then we would be admitting—he didn't want to admit—perhaps it was inadmissible—"No," Bruce said, betraying none of his ambivalence.

"Fucking hypocrite," Aaron said.

Alex returned his tablet to the podium. "Time for the interactive portion."

As if a band played on a part of the stage just beyond the room's negotiable boundary, music, sultry, sweet and dirty, jazz, wire brushes sweeping across drumheads, saxophone squeaking out a high note and then massaging it from underneath, trumpet with a wa-wa. Alex sauntered to the closed closet door, waved at the audience, and got some excited giggles as his hips swayed back and forth to the music's tick, tick, tick.

Hushed, Bruce asked, "What is he doing?"

With uncomfortable wryness, Aaron said, "What do you think?"

Feeling like a dunce, Bruce tried harder to visualize an actual audience instead of a door in a narrow wall in order to—

But then, Alex lifted his shirt, and Bruce caught on. Alex had something to prove.

Moving with the music, eyes more often closed than open, Alex gripped the bottom of his polo and pulled it up only to lower it again, moved it this way and that, rubbed himself with it. At fourteen Bruce had been thin as a rake, didn't have defined musculature to highlight with shirt and fingers and then obscure with a turn to the audience—for whom the shirt came off—and then, with a spin, give back to Bruce, to Aaron and Bruce, a premeditated exhibition, the climax of this portion of the game.

The boy liked games, and Bruce was not without admiration. His chest shrieked around the piercing cone as he drew deeper and deeper breaths.

Alex slow danced to his podium, grabbed his tablet, and pressed it. He galloped back to Aaron's coffin and said, "Don't try to dislodge yourself. As-is, you might bleed to death… pretty fast, they tell me." He opened Aaron's wire mesh like a screened door. One of Alex's hands disappeared into Aaron's coffin, but it pulled back Aaron's hand with it, placing the hand against his chest and guiding it around, roving fingers, helping Aaron to explore his body. Aaron didn't seem to resist.

Alex reached into the coffin again. "Yep," he said. "You were both right about that one. Now, the challenge." He hurried to his tablet, pressed it, and hopped on-beat back to Bruce. "As I told Uncle Aaron, don't try to run for it when I open the wires, or that wound of yours will slow you down faster than I would." He opened the wires and faced him, almost his height, the kind of beautiful he hadn't bothered to dream of being. "Put your hand on my chest, Uncle Bruce."

Bruce rested his fingertips on Alex's collarbone beneath his neck. What was about to happen wasn't as bad as what seemed likely to happen after that. Bruce had been paying attention. The bodies, so much of the mutilation was sexual. Alex was playing a game about sex. Sex and violence. Sex *as* violence. And he kept repeating something without explanation.

They.

They.

They.

Who?

Alex guided Bruce's fingers down his smooth chest, over his sternum and taut belly, to the elastic of his underwear. Bruce pulled his hand back. Alex stepped away, turned around, raised his hands in a gesture to the audience, then dropped his boxer shorts. He bowed and wiggled his ass for Bruce and Aaron.

He faced them with his hard cock bobbing. "I need you to touch me, Uncle Bruce."

Nausea fought with the agony in his chest and shoulder. His big brain fought with his little one. He didn't like being trapped. He didn't like losing control.

"At least two of us here are already rock-hard, Uncle Bruce. Time for you to check in." In a blink Alex's naked body pressed against Bruce, chest to chest, leaning in. Alex whispered, "My heart can feel yours beating up against it."

"You're going to prove your point, and then we're done with this, okay?" Bruce said.

Alex pressed his hands against Bruce's sides and slid them roughly downward until they dug under the rim of his pants. "Sorry, Uncle Bruce. We can't skip the third and final round. It's very exciting. Aren't you excited?" Alex's hands found their way into his underwear. One squeezed his balls, the other the shaft of his erection. "You are!"

"Fucking hypocrite," Aaron grumbled.

Alex took away his hands. "No fucking for now, gentlemen. Now…" and he turned to the audience, "Ladies *and* gentlemen, it's time for Round Three, when we finally find out who wins today's exciting game of… *CONFESSION!*"

26. ONLY ONE

Aaron

His rational mind's recoil at the almost overwhelming unreality of present circumstances had to end. It served no purpose to dwell on the mind-blowing impossibilities of invisible crowds cheering and bands playing, or of torture devices especially suited to a game in Alex's head, or of teleporting from one place to another. The situation was what it was. His job was to stay alive. To be fittest, to survive, required adaptation.

Aaron was thinking *survival at any cost* when Alex slammed the wire meshes of the coffins shut. "Stay still," Alex said. "This will hurt." He poked at his tablet.

Several long seconds passed before the meaning of "this" became clear, but when it did, Aaron was first to yell. It was a long, "Ah-HAAAAAAAAA!," but he hadn't discovered anything beyond an escalating burn coming from the spike in his ass and protruding next to his hip. It was metal, and it was heating up like a burner on an electric stove. His next scream didn't sound like anything.

Bruce screamed, which made Aaron feel better.

After long enough for the pain to replace vision with fiery red, a new sensation joined the burning, movement, burnt flesh abraded, and insight broke through the thought-disrupting hurt: the spike was reversing out of the wound. As it went, it cauterized.

Torture devices impossibly suited...

ADAPT!

He wasn't going to bleed to death. Good. "Thank you, Alex." Appreciation for the boy. Good.

"Grandpa," Alex, naked, said as he walked to the area to Aaron's right, which Aaron felt sure was occupied by a coffin that contained Alex's dead Grandpa. He presumed it was Dave's father. Aaron didn't think Bruce's father had ever been in the picture. He wouldn't be part of Alex's show. Why Dave's father, though? What was up with Grandpa? "Thanks for holding on to these. We'll be needing them now."

Naked Alex crossed back to the big closet's center and held up two tools—blades—weapons, a hook of some kind and a kitchen knife. "These have enormous sentimental value." Alex tossed them on the floor near the coffins. "I'm bringing them out for this important occasion."

"What's so important?" Bruce asked.

"Hey," Aaron said. "Don't rush him."

"I told you that *CONFESSION!* doesn't always have a winner, but it *always* has a loser." Alex really did sound like a gameshow host.

"Who made the rules, Alex?" Bruce asked. Why was he asking stupid questions?

"You know, Alex," Aaron said. "We don't have to play *this* game. There are others."

"You know, Uncle Aaron, we actually have to play *this* game." Alex tapped his tablet and opened the coffins' wire meshes. He retreated and stood in front of the closet door, naked. "In *this* game, you can both lose, or only one of you loses, like I said."

"What happens to the loser?" Aaron asked.

"The loser dies. Catch up, will you? The whole point is you have to kill each other. Starting now. And I'm not going to count backward or anything, but if you don't do it fast enough, you'll both die. Oh, and, uh, don't come after me. It won't work. You might have noticed by now that this my house, and, uh, I'm in charge." Alex smirked.

"Are you?" Bruce asked.

Aaron briefly considered stabbing Bruce in the face. Instead, he said, "Come on, Bruce, help me out here." He tried to sound sexy. He tried to sound convincing. He tried to sound as if every word weren't a struggle against the pain emanating from the burnt hole in his body. "We've both confessed that we get turned on by Alex even though he's underage. Our ugly sin is in the open."

"I don't think—"

"Help me out here."

Alex laughed.

"Okay, it's out in the open," Bruce said.

"What's to stop us from embracing it? I mean, if it makes Alex happy." Aaron concentrated on looking lascivious, not desperate. Bruce still had to think highly enough of him to know that he was bluffing. He had to.

Alex sat on the floor and folded his legs. "What are you saying?"

"You don't know what you missed, Alex," Aaron said. "We found the video, not just of you and me, but of the bodies behind your school, and we talked about it. We made up our minds to protect you, no matter what. You need us for that. To protect you. We can go on, being a family." He laughed. "With benefits."

"Benefits?" Alex asked.

"What you proved today, about turning us on. If you want, we can be a... throuple... we'd have to keep it a secret... but in the privacy of our own home, we could do whatever we wanted." Aaron flashed a grin but didn't hold it for fear of highlighting his clenched jaw.

Alex looked over his shoulder and said, "How's that for a twist?"

Everywhere, laughter.

"And Uncle Bruce, you're on board for this throuple thing? You two go to work, I go to school, and in the off hours we fuck like rabbits?"

"Like Aaron said," Bruce said.

Alex stood and showed them his ass. "Ladies and gentlemen! What do you think?"

"Thaaaaaat's... BULLSHIT!" the audience chanted.

Alex returned, nodding. "My thought exactly."

Bruce

After a deep inhalation, Bruce exhaled with a long, "Fuuuuuuuuuuuuuuuuuuuck."

"That's not entirely expected, coming from you," Alex said.

As soon as he rallied, he expected to be full of the unexpected. "Right now, I feel tired. Adrenaline crash. Blood loss. Learned helplessness."

"Don't feel up to selling the 'throuple' thing?" Alex's amusement masked... relief?

"I'll sell you anything you want," Bruce said. "What do you feel like buying?"

"I... it doesn't matter," Alex said. "I know it's bullshit."

"Yeah," Bruce said.

"*Bruce!*" Aaron objected.

Realizing he was meant to, *allowed*, Bruce stepped down from his coffin and over the weapons but otherwise left Alex at the most significant distance the closet would allow. "You're obviously in control of this situation and can make it life-or-death if you want to. We're going to say whatever we think you want to hear. If that means I say we'll live in some eternal ménage à trois, I'll say it. Why not? Except—I'm too tired to insult your intelligence or tax my own by lying to you."

"Fair enough," Alex said.

"You don't want to be surrounded by people who just say what they think you want to hear. Trust me," Bruce said.

Aaron stepped down from his coffin with a doubting, hesitant, but supportive expression.

"You do need people you can confide in, though," Bruce said. "From where I'm standing, what *you* want *us* to hear seems most important." Shit. Way too therapist-blowing-sunshine-up-your-butt.

"You don't get it," Alex said. "It's bigger than you, than us, than this. That's what I've realized."

"What is 'it' that's so big?" Bruce asked.

"It's… you wouldn't understand. I don't understand. Errrr!" Alex ruffled his hair in frustration and laughed.

"Who are 'they,' Alex?" Bruce asked.

Alex shrugged, making his hairless chest, wet with Bruce's blood, look skinnier. "What do you mean?"

"Before we get on with the business of who lives and who dies, I want you to tell me who 'they' are. You mentioned *them* several times." Bruce thought of patting the boy on the shoulder.

"I guess I did. I can talk about them, I guess." For a moment, Alex sounded a lot like a kid.

Alex

Considering that, if he turned his back to Aaron and Bruce, now that they were free, they might try to tackle him, and if they did—if they were that stupid, unworthy—he might have to kill them both—he hesitated, but he turned to face the audience anyway. He wished he saw a grander theatre, like the Fox in Atlanta or the Ahmanson here in LA, but he saw the little theatre at Rose Park High, seats full of people cartoonishly beautiful, indistinct in their perfection. He also saw the closet door and the wall. *Palimpsest*, Alex thought, not recalling where he'd picked up the word. He looked out onto a palimpsest of images, but he couldn't tell which was truly the ghost.

"Ladies and gentlemen," he said, tone grave. "We seem to have another twist on our hands. Your host, Alex Packard, will now participate in a round of *CONFESSION!*"

"Oooooo."

Alex faced Aaron and Bruce. "The truth is, I don't know who they are. Or what they are."

"They're not," Bruce said, "human."

"Some kind of... imaginary...." Aaron said.

"They come from the astral plane?" Bruce asked.

Alex was impressed. "That's my best guess. But they came to me... before I learned how...." He told them about being eight years old and *them* showing up to talk to him when he had nobody to talk to, nobody to play with. They were always mischievous, but they didn't encourage him to hurt animals until he showed an interest, until he bashed in that rabbit's little skull. They got so excited! Cheering for him afterward became cheering him on, and he liked making them happy, especially since they helped him build *his* house, his own private version of the house he lived in with his parents. He hated his parents. He hated his life. But they cared about him, which justified living.

"How did they react when you first killed a person?" Bruce asked.

To be asked such a question! To talk about *his them*, and to be... believed? Was that happening?

Aaron's eyes were wide, more astonished and childlike than skeptical, though.

"The first time wasn't... what I meant to do but... they were so happy. They made me feel good." Alex blushed.

Bruce's tone maintained a level of tenderness. "Before, the bigger the animal you killed, the happier they were, right?"

"Before and after," Alex said. "We didn't work up to another person until... Mom and Dad. Well, unless you count... never mind. Leading up to Mom and Dad, they made promises about what the house would do, and I promised I would do whatever I could to make the event... spectacular."

"Is that what you wanted?" Bruce asked. "A spectacular event?"

"What do you want me to say, Uncle Bruce?"

"Did you enjoy it?" Aaron asked.

Alex didn't feel ashamed, but he didn't want to be judged, either. The desire to stay quiet wasn't new, but shyness felt unfamiliar. He didn't want to answer.

Bruce said, "You can't play CONFESSION! without telling the truth."

Awkwardness switched to amusement, and Alex laughed. "Yes, it was what I wanted, and I loved doing it," he said. "After that, and the first one here, they... rewarded me. It gets better every time. I get better every time." A dark cloud passed through his mind. He spoke more softly: "It gets bigger and bigger."

"Bigger than you can handle?" Bruce asked.

"Come on, Bruce. I'm sure Alex can handle anything," Aaron said.

"Not yet," Alex said, ignoring Aaron. "But they have appetites. Kids. Sex. Seeing me hurt people in different ways. They don't want the same shit over and over. I don't, either, but... it gets hard. Being spectacular. I won't be a kid forever. I'm afraid of... well, it doesn't matter."

"It matters to me," Bruce said.

"Me, too," Aaron said.

"What are you afraid of, Alex?"

He wanted to shout NOTHING! and shove them into their coffins or worse, but instead he answered, "I'm afraid of being boring. What if I'm not the only one? What if they leave me?"

"I'd never leave you," Aaron said.

Bruce picked up the butcher knife. "Are they here now?

Alex nodded. "They're always here in my house when I'm here. Part of me thinks they're always with me. I see them, sometimes, like distortions in the air."

"Can I talk to them?" Bruce asked.

"I've never told anyone about them," Alex said. "I'm not sure if anybody else has ever even known they exist. Talk to them? Talk away. Will they talk back? I don't know."

For no discernible reason, Bruce looked at the ceiling, near the round fixture that pumped yellow into greylight. "Hello?" he said. "I'm addressing the entities Alex calls 'they' or 'them.' If you're able, I insist that you... no, I *dare* you to talk to me. If you can."

Aaron said, "Is that such a—"

Alex heard in his head, and from the looks on Aaron and Bruce's faces, they heard, too: *Say something delicious.*

27. GROWN-UP GAMES

Bruce

"I need a better understanding of your hunger," Bruce said. "What are you really after?"

"Hold on a minute, Bruce," Aaron said. Clutching the front of his cauterized hole, he staggered toward Alex. The taller boy didn't flinch when Aaron put an arm around his shoulders. "We already know something about their appetite, and what they're after. They prey on children. Our priority can't be understanding them. It's got to be defending against them."

Bruce could almost hear the gears turning in Aaron's head. He was still searching for the right thing to say to get them out of this situation, and since he reasoned that Alex had gotten them in, appealing to Alex might get them out. Avuncular, seductive, or both, Aaron would say anything to make Alex see him as an ally, do anything to be perceived as the most supportive, the one most clearly on Alex's side. For now, though Bruce held the butcher knife, Aaron ignored the sickle on the hardwood floor. His strategy wasn't bloody. Yet.

"Let us take care of you," Aaron said. "You know I love you."

At least Aaron said "us." The first time.

"Is it love, Uncle Aaron?" Alex asked. "Is what you do love? Is what they do love? I think they might have loved me for almost as long as I can remember. I don't know if they can love, though. Can anybody, or is love a big lie? I don't know. Bruce?"

"I guess it depends on what love is supposed to be. I can't say for sure that it's real." Bruce didn't add that he was in the process of internally renegotiating the entire concept of "real."

"Bruce was right to try luring *them* out with a dare," Aaron said. "They're chickenshits. Chickenshits that exploit children."

"You wouldn't know anything about that." Bruce's comment was an aside, but everybody heard.

"You want to save me from being exploited by them?" Alex asked.

"If I can," Aaron said.

Alex said, "Thaaaaaat's," and he gestured to the audience.

The audience cried, "BULLSHIT!"

"It might not be," Bruce said.

"What?" Alex looked confused, perhaps surprised. Good.

"Thank you, Bruce," Aaron said.

Bruce glowered at his husband. "I won't comment on Aaron and exploitation, but he's right about this 'they' being chickenshit if they won't talk to us, won't show themselves. If they hide behind a fourteen-year-old kid. No offense, Alex."

"None taken."

Aaron stammered, "Do you think it's a good—"

"Chickenshits!" Bruce yelled. "Fucking scaredy-cat little chickenshits who hide behind children and won't even give themselves names because they're afraid of being known!"

Aaron said, "Bruce—"

"SHOW YOURSELVES!"

The closet quaked. "Um, Uncle Bruce?" Alex said.

"SHOW YOURSELVES, MOTHERFUCKERS!" Bruce screamed.

The quaking quickened.

Zap! Zap! Zap! Blue bolts of static, branches of lightning, filled the air. Simultaneously, Aaron repeated "Bruce," and Alex repeated, "Uncle Bruce."

A second later, in a white flash, the closet was gone.

Bruce's vision, and his mind, came back into focus, and he became aware of Alex's form as well as Aaron's beside it. The three of them stood together on a hill, on hills rolling to a forest, and in the distance crags of rock—not rock but towering irregularities—jutted into the sky, mountainous.

The forest was not a forest, either, but it looked familiar. Not wood but bone, bone, tendons, and cartilage, made up the trees, no leaves, angular branches reaching in every direction upward from thick trunks, roots like flayed fingers rising and falling beneath the sickening surface of the ground. The branches didn't sway, but they did move, aching little bends that caused what dangled from them to swing. Like in Alex's house, bodies hung from the branches. In Alex's house, the area of forest Bruce had explored, he had counted five bodies. Even from the hills, Bruce felt confident in estimating fifty bodies in the forest below, maybe one hundred, maybe more. Blood-spattered corpses, men and women, old and young, most naked, many eviscerated, swung like a conquered army in the branches of tortured bone at the base of the hills.

The hills. The ground. Patchy, like the floor in Alex's living room had been, but the patches weren't grass and dirt. The quilt of colors blended white, pink, and peach, ranges of tan, some with olive tones and some without, ranges of brown from very light to very dark, human colors, skin colors, overlapping, not stitched but mashed together, murky like mud, and what grew on it wasn't grass but, shivering in a breeze, in different densities, at different heights, in different hues, hair. The ground was skin, hairy in places. Rolling hills of skin led to the bone forest.

Like in the walls of Alex's house, in places, the skin's surface revealed veins and arteries, pulsing.

In other places, cracks appeared in the skin, punctures, little wells that made blood puddles.

The distant crags might have been giants' bones, broken and scattered, sticking out and as white as the forest at their highest, splintered extremities. These bones, unlike the trees, had flesh. Coils of muscle, the red of meat, smooth and striated, arranged arbitrarily, wrapped around the long skeletal fragments, interrupting the visibility of white. Attached to the meat, intermittent swatches of skin hung like enormous tapestries.

The solid sky glowed with greylight that defined everything's edges.

On other hills, on a plain close to the giant-bone crags, in all directions, lay heaps of remains. Hollowed bodies, strewn viscera. Not all of them were human. Bruce noticed that the ground, too, wasn't entirely human. Some of the skin was animal. Some of the hair was fur.

Alex liked killing animals.

"What did you do?" Aaron said. He took his arm away from Alex.

Bruce realized his husband was addressing him. "I told them to show themselves," Bruce said.

"I think this is *their* house," Alex said.

"I don't see *them*," Bruce said. He gestured at their macabre surroundings. "They show us all this to scare us, but they're still scared to show themselves. Hmph."

"Bruce," Aaron said, "maybe we should—"

"I'M NOT SCARED!" Bruce yelled. "WHERE ARE YOU?"

The low, rumbling voice came from all around them: "*We're here.*"

The air around the hill where they stood, in all directions, without differentiation, shimmered, shook, and wavered. Distortion engulfed them.

Aaron

Aaron thought about giving up. Healthy incredulity had kept him afloat, kept him from turning into a ball of panic, and he'd tried to master the impossible situation in every way he could imagine, but Bruce—did Bruce even want to survive? Assuming Bruce had reached the same conclusion he had, that *they* were a powerful, unnatural force that used a mere psychopath like Alex as a plaything, then why would Bruce, a reasonably intelligent man, taunt them? Perhaps Bruce had *unhealthy* incredulity. Perhaps, standing on human skin and surrounded by distorted, animated air, air that smelled like rot, Bruce was willfully blind to what he stood against.

"Thank you for taking a meeting." Bruce nodded in several directions. *Sang-froid.* "I think we can help each other. Make things sweeter. Make things *delicious*. But I'd like to get us started by restating my original question. I need a better understanding of your hunger. What are you after?"

Aaron had never joined Bruce in one of his client meetings, but he imagined his husband's facial expression and tone of voice would be the same.

After a pause, Alex said, "You guys couldn't hear that, right?"

"Hear what?" Aaron asked.

"That means no," Bruce said.

"'Media,'" Alex said. "Well, what the fuck does that mean?" Alex appeared to listen. "Okay." Alex moved so he stood equidistant from Aaron and Bruce. "They said media are all around you. Flesh, blood, and bone are media. Violence is a medium. Sex is a medium. So is pain. So are minds. They hunger for media."

Aaron thought about Alex using his camera. "Like film?"

"I thought of that," Alex said, "but they're saying you can't make anything worthwhile out of film. They're builders. They need media to build."

"What are your goals as builders?" Bruce asked.

Alex smiled, blushed, giggled. "'Beauty,' they say. They gave me a nice compliment, and then they said they made this place to help you understand building, but if they wanted a closer impression of what pain can do, they might show you a cathedral of muscle, or deliver the essence of rape as a castle of frozen tears. Delicate." He giggled again. "'Delicious.'"

"Okay, so now I have a decent understanding of your primary goal, to optimize the acquisition of building materials, right?"

Sweet Jesus. Bruce was *handling* them. He was managing a meeting with supernatural forces. He couldn't know what the fuck he was doing, but he was pulling it off.

"It was kind of hard to make out, but I'm pretty sure they said yes," Alex said.

"Am I right that you've been using Alex to gather those materials? Why is that?" Bruce didn't sound judgmental.

"Yep, I've been the go-to guy," Alex said. "They say we have a lot in common. Similar appetites."

Aaron wanted to ask if they'd kindled Alex's appetites —if they were the cause—but he'd lost the momentum for speaking.

"Okay," Bruce said. "Let's analyze your current state of acquisition. Start with your strengths. Alex blushed at a compliment a moment ago, but you were right to bring it up. Alex is a beautiful youth, and you're invested in beauty, so having him on your team is a strength, especially given your similarities. You're obviously very powerful entities, astral, trans-dimensional, I don't know, but capable of things I wouldn't have thought possible until very recently. If you can work with Alex in the way you have, you can probably work with others—not that you'd want to replace Alex, of course— but flexibility and the possibility of expansion are strengths. You're in a good position, overall."

Alex said even *he* was afraid of boring them. Bruce was fearless!

"But," Bruce said, looking at the air at several points

around them but connecting with nothing because the same wavy distortions were everywhere, "we should think about weaknesses. Areas where you should target efforts for improvement. Something to think about immediately is, and correct me if I'm wrong, what appears to be a lack of a clear business plan. You know you want to acquire and build, but you don't have a clear plan for what specifically you want to acquire, in what quantities, at what points in time, and to build what, and you don't have a roadmap with checkpoints toward reaching your goals. I can help you with that."

There it was! Bruce's in—and the way Bruce and Aaron might get out.

"You also have a narrow supply line," Bruce continued, "a weakness we can think about now in relation to both your strengths and opportunities."

They gave no indication of whether Bruce's corporate-speak dazzled or even fazed them. The air maintained its unctuous, wavy, unresponsive distortions. Alex, on the other hand, was surprising. He didn't yawn. His eyes didn't drift elsewhere, repelled by business plans and supply lines. Bruce had the boy's full attention.

"Expansion," Bruce said. "Growth. Your *potential* for planned expansion could allow you to overcome a major weakness, and you have the *opportunity* to get started with such a plan almost immediately. Increase your supply lines. Build more. Build better."

"How?" Alex asked.

Aaron found the question reasonable. If Bruce had an answer, would he be advising these *them* on how to be better mass murderers? Bruce, whose moral outrage—

"The 'how' of it is already in process. You've got an asset with unlimited value. My nephew, Alex."

"Thanks, Uncle Bruce!"

"But," Bruce said, "before I elaborate on the new opportunity Alex has presented without you even knowing, let's consider some threats we're facing. I've already brought up the danger Alex might be in—he has left his body God knows where in order to be here. What if he's discovered? What if he's hurt?"

"I was sort of careful," Alex said.

"And if a cop were to find you right now?" Bruce asked.

"I said 'sort of.'"

"And when you killed the detective, are you certain you didn't leave forensic evidence? Fire doesn't destroy everything. You killed a cop. The investigation will be relentless." Bruce looked back and forth between Alex and the distorted air. Was he trying to scare Alex? *Them*? Aaron didn't imagine them being compatible with fear, but he didn't quite know how to imagine them, so maybe they could feel threatened by the idea of Alex, their supply line, being cut off.

"I wasn't planning on sticking around," Alex said.

"You need protection." Bruce faced the distorted audience fully, with a flourish that reminded Aaron of Alex addressing his audience during *CONFESSION!*. "You ALL need protection for your interests! Alex must be safe. Without supply there's no productivity. No building. I know you must be very, very powerful, but I think there's something more powerful. And that's fate. Fate brought Alex to you, and fate prompted Alex to bring Aaron and me here. I know you're drawn to the beauty of youth, but in terms of building, have you thought about what a full-grown man could do for you? For your productivity?"

Was Bruce bluffing? What on earth could he and Aaron do for *them*?

"Think," Bruce said in that same gameshow tone, "of how we could share a vision."

Come to think of it, had Bruce ever actually been morally outraged?

Alex

What started as a mild chuckle turned into a roaring guffaw. Aaron and Bruce both eyed him with eyebrows skewed, but he couldn't stop laughing. He bent over, hands on his bare stomach. Bruce smiled, and Aaron's eyes got wider. Alex noticed that the skin under his bare feet was Esme-colored and laughed harder.

"I'd love to hear the joke," Bruce said.

Alex tried to catch his breath. "I can't—I can't—explain. It's just sometimes they're so fucking funny." There. Laughter under control. "We need private time. Talk between the ears. I'm going for a walk."

As he started walking, the breeze that made the hairs on the ground horripilate tickled his bare skin and made him more aware of being naked. Walking down a hill of skin, his own skin exposed... maybe too much skin. The forest down there, the dangling bodies, most of them naked, exposed skin, torn, ravaged, layers of flesh and muscle exposed, organs exposed, disarranged, it all made him think of his body. The breeze here prickled his skin that matched swaths of ground, and he felt aware of his limbs, his torso, his face, his physicality *here*, but Bruce also made him think of his body in that tent with that dead lady who had smelled so bad. Alex didn't know about dead bodies in actuality. Would she start smelling worse? No—*when* would she start smelling worse? What if the smell attracted attention? The tent didn't exactly have a lock.

You need protection.

When had anybody ever protected him? Okay, so he'd always had food, clothing, shelter, entertainment—but somebody really watching over him, trying to understand him, shielding all aspects of him—he'd never taken the idea of "adoption" seriously.

Aaron and Bruce said nothing as he passed, going down hills, into the bone woods where too many bodies to count hung from branches. The chatter started in his head, the way they communicated without saying any one thing clearly.

Tuning in, he felt his left foot plop into something squishy. He looked at the ground and saw himself standing on an organ, a liver if he had to guess, now disfigured by the weight of his step. The man connected to the branch overhead didn't seem to mind. The yuck sensation between Alex's toes, though, reminded him that he'd have to concentrate on making out what they were saying and on watching the ground. Tripping over the trees' bony roots would be even less pleasant than stepping in gore.

They were chattering about Bruce. Could they trust Bruce? Could they trust Aaron? Did Alex trust Bruce and Aaron? What did Alex think of what Bruce said? Was it BULLSHIT? They wanted to make beautiful worlds. They wanted Alex to have beautiful worlds. They wanted what Alex wanted. Alex wanted what they wanted. Did Bruce want what Alex wanted? Did Aaron? Why had Bruce spoken to them the way he had? What was the value of a full-grown man?

The repetition of "increased productivity" within the chatter made Alex smile as he maneuvered through the corpses.

Expansion. Expansion. Expansion.

Alex must be safe!

Increased productivity.

He walked back up the hills of skin, his understanding growing.

Share a vision.

Aaron and Bruce watched him approach, so he started talking before he reached them. "They like your proposal. They have a counterproposal that they think you'll find satisfactory."

Alex was only a messenger. He knew the gist, but he didn't know the specifics of what Bruce was about to hear.

28. FOREVER ESCAPE

Bruce

His brain felt like a bag of drowning kittens, a bundle of thrashing and clawing parts, suffocated, overwhelmed, immersed in chaos and understanding nothing. The cacophony brought his hands to his ears so fast that he almost cut himself with the butcher knife, which until then he hadn't realized had come with him from the closet. Dizziness made him wobble on ground-skin too soft for balanced footing—

"Bruce, what's happening?" Aaron sounded far away and underwater.

"You can't hear them?!" Bruce yelled.

Alex laughed, his sound clearer than Aaron's.

"Hear what?" Aaron didn't hear them.

The sound, a noisy bar, everyone shouting to be heard over the music, not music but razors scraping against guitar strings, ear-splitting dissonance.

Bruce looked to Alex, who said, "Relax," clearly, audibly.

The dissonance retreated, and the mélange of voices thinned. Individual words and phrases popped out of the conversational whirlwind. The voices continued to overlap so much that none stood out, but Bruce began to hear patterns in the chatter. Bruce began to detect meaning.

"They're talking to you but not me," Aaron said. "Why?"

Bruce was too busy listening to respond.

"Relax, Uncle Aaron. Uncle Bruce did all the talking a minute ago. They probably think they need to repay him, you know, mind bomb for mind bomb." Alex laughed.

It was a mind bomb. The fuse was just long enough for Bruce to sense what was coming, and then—BOOM! The counterproposal. He knew what they wanted. They'd drafted the first steps of a business plan. His improvised riff on Intro to Business Planning and Consulting had moved infernal regions.

As the bomb went off, and Bruce tried to absorb the significance of its consequences, static gathered around them. The now-familiar forks of blue-purple lightning streaked and formed a triangle that grouped him with Aaron and Alex, and then blink, white, and they were back in the closet.

Aaron's coffin, Bruce's coffin, and the podium were gone. The coffin with Dave Packard's dad in it now lay flat on the floor, still open, the skeleton wearing a skin-tarp still visible.

The sickle was on the floor. So were Alex's polo and underwear.

Once everyone seemed adjusted to the new surroundings, Bruce said, "Alex, get dressed."

Alex cocked his head to one side and squinted, studying him. "Okay." He pulled on his boxers.

"What did they say?" Aaron asked.

The closet didn't leave much room for positioning. Bruce moved closer to Aaron along an arc. The sickle lay on the floor between them. "I can't explain," Bruce said. "It was more like... like a download... than talk or like... information at the speed of sight."

"Outstanding," Aaron said. His eyes shifted to Alex, who was buttoning up his polo's collar, and back to Bruce. "What are we supposed to do?"

Bruce had the butcher knife in his right hand. He dragged the blade's sharp edge against the side of his pants, savoring the sound's softness after the deafening volume of the noise in his head. "Do you mean, what can we do to get out of here alive?"

"Uh..." Aaron searched for the right answer. "Yeah.

With Alex. Can we take Alex and get out of here somehow?"

"I know what *you* need to do," Bruce said.

Aaron's expression combined disbelief with dawning comprehension. "W-what?"

"Pick up the sickle." Bruce gestured to the weapon in case Aaron didn't know what he meant.

"Why?"

"Because you need it. Pick it up." Bruce didn't give commands often enough. The feeling fit.

Aaron picked up the sickle with a shaking hand. "Can we get out of here?"

"Answer a question." Bruce felt like he should get angry.

"Your question? Their question? What's going on?" Aaron's voice had a little vibrato.

"Which do you think with more, your eyes or your dick?" Bruce's question arrived without passion.

"W-what?"

Alex said, "Ew, Uncle Bruce, way to—"

"Answer the question," Bruce said.

Aaron calculated. "Are you asking if I slept with Alex more for aesthetic reasons or sexual ones?"

"Answer," Bruce commanded.

"Eyes," Aaron said. "Dick. Hell, I don't know."

Bruce raised the knife and slashed Aaron's cheek, leaving a red line that dripped instantly. Aaron shouted "Ay!," perhaps in more surprise than pain, as he jerked back. Bruce said, "Real answer required."

"Fuck!" Aaron said. He looked at the sickle he held in his right hand and looked at Bruce. "Okay, okay. Eyes, I guess. I wish I'd looked like that at fourteen. Or ever."

Beauty.

"You know what you did," Bruce said.

"Yeah, okay, I fucked a kid. I'm a goddamned dirtbag. It's a way of life for straight guys in the South, but I do it and—"

Bruce slashed the other side of Aaron's face and drowned out his cry with, "Shut the fuck up."

"What are you—"

"You didn't simply fuck a kid. You put Alex in danger. You put all of us in danger. Alex's safety is the top priority. You get that, right?" Bruce looked at the length of Aaron, head to toe, and his anger was principled, not passionate, and he thought about Alex's question about love. *Big lie.*

One investigator did remark on the boy's "apparent lack of emotion."

Bruce *had* felt for Aaron, and he *would* feel in the moments to come. But overwhelmingly, he felt his calling—to be the one who made Alex safe. Who made them all safe.

"I guess I get that, yeah," Aaron said.

Bruce shook his head, faked a laugh, and paced on a short line perpendicular to his husband. "You make us all look bad, you know. You make these documentaries about the community, and progress, and fighting prejudice, and then you set us back fifty years by giving right-wing hatemongers good reason to claim we're all sickos and pedophiles. If anybody found out!"

"You're more worried about how it looks," Aaron said.

Bruce swung the knife, slicing into Aaron's side above the cauterized hole. Aaron grabbed the new wound with his left hand, looked at his newly bloodied palm and fingers, and took a firmer hold of the sickle in front of him. "Fucking stop it, Bruce. We have to work together. Alex, tell him—"

"Tell him what, Uncle Aaron? What it felt like to have your dick up my ass?"

Bruce slashed Aaron's right leg. Aaron shifted his weight from side to side, looking more uncomfortable with each movement. "Family, right Bruce?"

Bruce raised the knife. The pain in his pierced shoulder was not prohibitive.

Aaron pulled back the sickle, ready to swing, the move Bruce was waiting for. A quick slam of Bruce's forearm against Aaron's wrist disrupted the swing with an impact hard enough to force open Aaron's hand. The sickle clattered on the floor.

Aaron lost balance and stumbled backward, looking as if he would crash ass-first into Grandpa Packard's coffin. Bruce grabbed his flailing left hand and pulled him closer before he could fall.

Close enough to jam the butcher knife into his gut. The initial stab met resistance, so Bruce pushed, leaned weight into it until it penetrated almost up to the hilt.

"Bruce?" Aaron's face mixed awe with heartbroken disappointment. The bloody cheeks combined with the extreme emotion to make his face mask-like. He might have been a doll or a mannequin.

Without gentleness, Bruce twisted the knife until the sharp edge pointed upward. Summoning strength, he pushed against the top of the wound, which finally made Aaron scream. The screaming was inconsequential; he and Alex would be the only people to hear. Bruce began sawing, splitting through Aaron's abdomen, which his hand sometimes slipped inside. The forest in the living room, the forest of bone: they'd seen plenty of eviscerations, but this one was special, more than the piss and shit and stomach acid and bile and whatever else spilled out of him, because so much more than blood spilled out of him. It was a new beginning for Alex and for Bruce, too. Opening up Aaron meant opening up a door.

The screams became gurgles. Bruce imagined he'd cut through Aaron's diaphragm muscle, so something else was making blood spill from his mouth. The knife wasn't going to be sharp or strong enough to cut through the sternum and ribs unless Bruce started stabbing to create a path, an unnecessary measure. A few zigs and zags would spill much of Aaron on the floor.

Aaron wasn't dead yet, though, and Bruce had another idea.

When Bruce removed the knife, Aaron fell backward, hitting Grandpa's coffin but sliding off in a heap instead of joining its inhabitant. He didn't try to move, so Bruce figured he couldn't.

"You going to leave him like that, Uncle Bruce?" Alex asked.

Aaron's eyes were wide. He'd lose consciousness soon.

"No," Bruce said. "They deserve a little more entertainment, don't they?"

"Up to you how you seal the deal," Alex said.

Bruce yanked Aaron's legs so that his upper body fell flat on the floor. He unfastened his husband's pants—for the last time, he thought—and exposed his genitals. Leaving them, he crouched over Aaron's chest and looked into his eyes. "Eyes not dick, huh?"

Aaron struggled to breathe.

Bruce used the fingers of his left hand to hold open Aaron's left eyelids. Bruce, aiming with his right hand so he could use the knife's tip for scooping leverage, plucked out Aaron's left eye. Small movements animated Aaron's limbs, muscles contracting in a useless pantomime of resistance.

Bruce plucked out his husband's right eye. He set the eyes together, on the floor, near one of Aaron's twitching hands. Aaron kept breathing in quick, shallow gasps.

By the time Bruce returned to Aaron's exposed genitals, the blood flowing from his split abdomen had soaked the area that pants had previously protected. The blood would not be a problem. Bruce didn't need precision. He slid the blade beneath Aaron scrotum until he hit the base of the penis, twisted, and cut through skin, veins, arteries, ducts, and tubules. When the severed testicles were finally loose in his hand, he shoved them into Aaron's empty eye sockets.

Alex

(a week later)

The king-sized bed with the super-plush mattress barely fit in the room, but Alex thought it fit better than a waterbed in a bedroom with drawings on the walls that looked at you, drawings Alex had made with his own hands while those hands might have had other guides. When Bruce asked, "You really did all this? The building? The decorations?" Alex had to say *they helped*. Alex showed Bruce the basement with the cells and the firepits and admitted they did all of it.

"But it is *yours*," Bruce said. No hint of a question in his voice.

"Yes," Alex said. "It's mine." He lay on the new bed, close to the wall opposite the door, fully dressed minus shoes. Bruce was taking off his shoes, dressy shoes, as always.

Tube socks! Beneath his black dress shoes, Bruce wore tube socks!

Bruce had many quirks. He also had certain mannerisms that evoked Alex's mother, which Alex noticed now that he was paying a lot more attention to the man. Alex went to school—Bruce insisted—and Bruce went to work —Alex insisted—but they had evenings together, focused on getting to know each other, in and out of actuality.

In *his* house, they stretched out on opposite sides of the king-sized bed, hands tucked under heads propped up by pillows. In actuality, they had a hotel room, separate queen-sized beds, and ordered a lot of room service. Home was still a crime scene. Bruce had decided to call in the "discovery" of Aaron's body, to face the police questioning—which made quick connections to Alondra Whitcomb's concerns about Alex—instead of going on the run. Call-me-Alondra had had suspicions, not evidence, Bruce said. No forensic evidence tied them to what had happened to Aaron. They had to be careful. Very careful. They had to be ready to run. But they didn't have to run yet.

And Bruce had plans that would work better if they stayed.

A leading theory of the crime—other than the one implicating Alex and Bruce—was that the killer who had been targeting high school kids had made a connection from

Alondra to Alex and felt threatened somehow, which put the entire household in danger. Bruce and Alex's hotel room, therefore, had police "protection," which Bruce said really meant surveillance. They didn't leave the room much in the evenings, though. Bruce sat on his bed, Alex on his. Bruce sucked at doing a half-lotus position. His knees popped. "You should hope you're so limber at my age," he said.

"Do you miss him?" Alex asked as they lay a respectable distance from one another on the bed in his house.

"Who? Aaron?"

"Yeah."

"Sort of," Bruce said. "I don't like the vacancy."

"I might like to be with someone, someday," Alex said. His mind hadn't quite figured out how it would work.

"You will," Bruce said. "But stick to your own age group. At least until your twenties." They shared a contemplative pause before Bruce said, "Ready?"

Alex nodded and smiled. On their way out of the room, he picked up his Deerslayer, and Bruce picked up his own hunting knife, which had a longer, fatter blade, a serrated edge, and a curved, sharp tip. He'd paid cash for it at a discount store. He called it the Size Queen.

They'd redecorated his house's version of his parents' bedroom. Instead of the king-sized bed, the room contained, almost at center, an adjustable slab, currently jacked up to a forty-five-degree angle. The rest of the room, except for the blue veins in the walls, was, after Bruce's suggestion, white, white tiled floor, white laminate wall covering. The greylight kept the room from shining hospital fluorescent, but Alex appreciated, and they appreciated, the effect Bruce wanted. Deep red on a white background made even slight splatter appear bold.

The first drops, from accidental cuts on Tosh's scalp, had proven the point, each a stunning pool of color. Bruce and Alex had shaved Tosh's head, mowing down the beautiful black asymmetrical locks that hung down over one side of his face and hugged the back of his head. His look was glamorous, or had been, and he'd always led a pack in the hallways at school. He flirted with everyone, pansexual, non-binary, and everyone liked him. He was singular. Distinguished. Or he had been. His current appearance—stripped, regular and unimpressive male genitals exposed, head shaven and dribbling red—said "refugee," not "superstar."

Tosh, probably short for Toshio, had stopped wailing for help about ten minutes ago, but when he saw Bruce and Alex reenter the room with the Size Queen and the Deerslayer, he screamed, "No, no, please God, you've got to let me out of here!" Strong, narrow straps held his head, shoulders, wrists, waist, and knees to the slab. Some of his gorgeous tan skin was slick with sweat, fear sweat with an odor not entirely displeasing.

Bruce took a lazy swing at Tosh's arm with his blade, scraping off a strip of skin. Tosh shouted and quaked as blood welled and spilled. Bruce gave Alex an expectant look, and Alex dipped his knife shallowly into Tosh's chest and flicked off a few inches of flesh.

Tosh screamed.

Bruce skimmed off some of the right thigh. Alex skimmed off some of the left. Stomach, arm, leg, foot, hand, neck, face, skin curling, an accidental chunk here, an accidental chunk there, more like peeling a carrot than an apple because Tosh was more lines than curves, and the stretches they removed got longer and longer. Blood made their work harder to see, so they looked less at each other and more at the dwindling, screaming carrot, and when they removed the dermal layers, they peeled into muscle. Their tools weren't "optimal" for this kind of killing. Bruce called it uneven, haphazard. They would perfect their methods. Their craft. Their art. Even though Bruce's tool was clumsier, his cuts were neater. A few times, Alex let Bruce guide his hand.

Their cuts went in all directions, and so did Tosh. White floors, white walls—covered in streaks and splotches of the richest red and globs of deeper soaked shades. What they made enveloped them.

"Alex," Bruce said, face and dress shirt drenched.

"Yeah, Uncle Bruce?"

"Would you ever think of calling me 'Dad?'"

He didn't have to think. "Yeah Dad," Alex said. "Sure."

Bruce

(several weeks later)

When Alex roamed around the house, he did it with clothes on. He and Bruce were working on mutual respect, regard for one another even if empathy was impossible, and they aimed for disclosure. Alex talked about killing animals, his parents—an episode he related with humor that Bruce appreciated, especially where Letta was concerned—and the kids from school. How did he choose which people to take back to his house? "I follow my heart," Alex said. The answer was as good as any.

Bruce told Alex about his own father, the grandfather Alex would never meet, catching him in the midst of vivisecting a dog. It was the Devil's work. Being gay was the Devil's work. When he got away from his parents, he stopped believing in the Devil, but he didn't get away from anxiety about doing his work. Therapy helped him to accept being gay, but no therapy in the world would help him come to terms with his other... desires... which he fought to keep dormant by focusing on other work. They, with Alex's help, had freed him.

"Dad, did you ever notice we have the same color eyes?" Alex asked.

Bruce hadn't noticed. He wondered if it had always been true.

These things run in families. Alex seemed like a product of incest, the spawn of his and his sister's psychoses. Dave

Packard might have been completely irrelevant—except Dave's father had made an impression. Grandpa Packard had sparked the idea.

A man's house is his castle.

A castle in my head?

"Grandpa would sit at the window with a rifle, watching for others to come," Alex told him.

Perhaps *they* learned from Grandpa Packard, too. Perhaps the old man's curmudgeonly habits for mental and social isolation combined with Alex's natural inclination toward antisocial behavior to create the perfect opening for them, whatever they were—and no matter how much Bruce felt them, he knew no more about what they were, where they came from, or why their idea of beauty involved the hewing of so much human flesh. Bruce and Alex focused on disclosure. *They* did not.

Again and again, Alex brought the static, and the static brought them to Alex's house. Bruce observed. He learned. In his mind, he grew. Finally, one night after they were back in the house, after the police had stopped asking so many questions, he said to Alex, "It's my turn. I'd like to show you, and them, the value of a grown-up."

"Show me," Alex said.

The first step felt like a leap, but the static came without too much effort, without too much concentration, and in flash and a blink, Bruce and Alex arrived on the mottled, dark grassy-green tiled floor Bruce had prepared as a foothold for the show he was about to put on. Beyond the floor was greylight. It seemed substantial, thick, soupy, like a dense fog in the void immeasurable distances from the green floor, but it was energy, not matter, not palpable no matter how it seemed.

"Cue the music!" Bruce commanded. He'd chosen "Facades" by Philip Glass rather than Beethoven or Wagner or something similarly bombastic. He held his arms in line with his shoulders as the strings came up, and when the oboe began to sing, his arms rolled and slowly flapped. Waves came off them, rippling the floor.

"Nice," Alex said. "I never tried a sound system."

Bruce smiled, and as the saxophone brought the piece to its most layered presentation of sound, his arms stopped rolling and flapping, twisted so his palms faced the infinite upward grey, and rose until he stood as a Y. The ground trembled. Alex moved to stand closer to him. Bruce's smile grew.

White columns rose from the dark green floor, and, keeping his arms raised, Bruce used his hands to encourage the columns to keep rising. His neck craned backward so he could see what was coming from above, and his hands encouraged its descent. Along with the columns, bigger shafts started to rise, parallelograms covered in metallic, reflective panels, shining with greylight. They raced to catch up with the columns, growing on a collision course with the flat plane descending from above.

The descending plane, white like the columns, had pieces missing, parallelogram pieces, pathways through which the shafts, now taller than the columns, could pass. Bruce moved his arms, directing all the moving parts, like a music conductor, though the movements of the columns, shafts, and descending plane didn't correspond to the Glass piece.

As the bottoms of the shafts became more defined, developing doors, the tops of the shafts passed through the perfectly sized openings in the plane from above that lowered while the columns rose until plane and columns met, ceiling and supports. Walls, too, as white as the columns, came from the greylight distances and snapped into place around the edges of the dark green floor, finishing the larger assembly as the details of the elevators settled and the lobby, at least three stories tall, maybe taller, the lobby of a skyscraper, took form.

"Whoa," Alex said. "Is this, like, part of your house, Dad?"

"No," Bruce said, happy with the wonder he heard in Alex's voice. "Let me show you." He led the boy to the simulacrum of the elevator he rode almost every day. He pressed the up arrow, and they boarded, bound for the thirty-third floor.

"Are you taking me to your office?" Alex asked.

"My office *inside* my office," Bruce said. "It's what I learned from you." He tousled the boy's hair. "I'm going to build it in front of you."

"What about... them?"

"They'll help however they help, I guess. I'd say anybody who takes a pronoun for a name has more than an insignificant mystery fetish. I don't think they want to be solved, do you?" Bruce tilted his head ever-so-slightly downward to drill into Alex with googly eyes, and he felt glad that, for at least a little while longer, he had some height on the boy.

"No, they like being mysteries." Alex grinned, and Bruce pulled back.

The elevator doors opened on greylight. The next musical selection—excerpts from Chopin's Piano Concerti, with some bombast, but he couldn't resist—began as Bruce ushered in a floor with pleasant cornflower blue carpet, out onto which they stepped, and he spun a three-sixty to make the rest of the room, double doors on each end, more elevators, a tropical plant he could never comprehend, all fall into place. He led Alex through the set of double doors that would normally have had the name and logo of West Coast Global Integrated Wealth Solutions stenciled across them, but they were blank and would be until Bruce felt ready to brand.

First, to complete the main arena. Taking inspiration from Alex's awe, he picked up the pace and put pieces of the cubicle maze together in seconds, calling them out of many points of nowhere and connecting them with a click. Desks, chairs, tables, machines, and coat racks, too many coat racks for Los Angeles, settled into their places, and myriad personal items flew through the cubicles' common airspace as pens and pads of paper searched for homes. The outer layer, the offices with doors and windows, of which Bruce's was one, took form. Out of sight, more of the suite filled in. He built it in his mind as he led Alex toward his personal office cell.

"Dude, this is... you don't even realize," Alex said.

"What don't I realize?"

"My house... I was a kid, but still... my house... a few rooms took months... and this detail... it's like instant grits...."

Adult capacity.

Adult concentration.

Adult experience.

Adult expertise.

"Benefits of a highly disciplined mind," Bruce said.

"Mmm, you mean, benefits of being a grown-up," Alex said.

"That was only setting the stage." He pointed to the glass around the door to the main floor. "From here you should have an excellent view."

"I don't get to play?"

"You'll watch, and I'll be a catalyst and watch," Bruce said. "Don't leave this room."

Bruce left Alex in the office and closed the door behind him, but he didn't go far. He again assumed the shape of a Y, and the items he imagined, that he'd studied but never seen or touched, fell, inaccurate in construction but made to function anyway, to the floor in many strategic locations. "Cue music," he said. He needed a different sort of classic. Bombastic would be fine. He could be contemporary and aggressive. He believed *Mechanical Animals* by Marilyn Manson would do the trick. *Contemporary*, not *current*.

As the first track began, sparks brightened the room like the finale of a fireworks display. They turned into lines and forks and branches, and the arena, and the offices, and the whole suite came to life with the lightning Alex had shown him how to create. Alex had never done what Bruce was doing now, though, pulling from more than forty locations, most of management, the drones, the office staff, none of the admins, who didn't have it coming.

The mass transport didn't even require his full concentration. He walked a short distance down the path alongside the office cells like his and picked up what he felt reasonably certain was an Uzi.

Alex

Alex didn't know what *they* would think, but *he* found Bruce's performance charming. Of course, Bruce had to one-up Alex in every way, one-or-more-up, really, to prove his point about the value of a grown-up, as grown-ups didn't offer one sort of beauty Alex understood to be their *objective*. Alex didn't mind. If being a grown-up meant being more of a badass, he had something to look forward to. Bruce seemed on the brink of proving the adage, "It gets better!"

The room filled with lightning, bigger and brighter than Alex had ever summoned, and in a white flash, it filled with people. Men and women, some in their twenties, some older, a few much older, appeared scattered around the room with what Bruce called the "maze of cubicles." Some wore pajamas, some wore underwear, a few were naked, and a few were in regular clothes. Bruce had wanted to start late at night. He'd planned to catch these people, whoever they were, in bed.

Alex felt pretty sure the music playing was Marilyn Manson. He wasn't really into the heavy shit. Besides, hadn't Marilyn Manson been canceled?

Bruce moved quickly from person to person, saying things in their ears. Alex wished he could hear. Some of them looked scared when they saw Bruce coming. They were groggy, disoriented. They didn't know what to do with the image of Bruce coming toward them carrying a modestly sized machine gun (Size Queen was tucked into the back of his pants). Whatever he said to them inevitably turned their attentions somewhere else, often to someone else in a state of befuddlement.

The lights dimmed.

Small sirens descended from the ceiling. Horizontal wheels connected them in spinning clusters. They lit up red, synced to a whirling, blaring, deafening alarm, and the volume of the music tripled, allowing it to compete with the alarm sound warping around between two notes.

People held their ears and scurried in all directions, some intent on reaching an office or cubicle, some seeking an exit.

One of them, a man in tighty-whities, picked up a machine gun. Bruce hurried to him and spoke in his ear. He probably had to shout to be heard.

Two more people picked up machine guns.

A woman struggled with the double doors to the elevator room. They didn't budge.

Somebody screamed. A gun went off. Another gun went off.

Bruce worked the room.

More and more people picked up guns.

The man in the white briefs shot a woman wearing a bra and panties. His gun, bigger than Bruce's, was also an automatic, and its kick surprised him. Nevertheless, the woman was close, and he sprayed her across the midsection, planting holes from her appendix scar to her left tit. She might have been trying to dodge, because she went down like she was diving into a swimming pool, hands, arms, and then head crashing into the blue carpet. She probably broke something before she suffocated from a hole in her lung or whatever.

A woman in a skirt and a t-shirt, young enough to be up this late and not regret it too much in the morning, had a shotgun and was tracking a guy in flannel pajama pants. He ran alongside the cubicles and ducked behind a photocopier just as she fired, creating a cloud of papers but missing him. She fired the second barrel, creating a cloud of smoke and sparks in the remains of the photocopier. He raised his hands and peeked out as she reloaded. "Please don't shoot me," he shouted. "I'm sorry!"

"Okay!" she yelled. She kept reloading.

He stuck his head out further and said something.

She fired. His head broke apart.

Someone nearby, Alex couldn't see who, shredded one of the fully dressed woman's arms with a machine gun. She dropped the shotgun. Her assailant kept shredding. Bullets took apart her upper half. For a split-second, Alex thought he saw her spine. Then she was a head and legs and some tatters that dropped to the floor.

Guns fired everywhere. The peaceful wallpaper, pale yellow—even in the greylight, the place looked like a fucking nursery—got splattered, brain here, innards there, blood everywhere. Bullets hit the window where Alex was standing, but the glass repelled them. Bullet-proof. Maybe unnecessary, but Bruce had planned. Out of respect, Alex stayed put. He kept watching.

Bruce kept playing his role as *catalyst*. Alex considered what he knew about that word, and he thought, *Bruce is speeding up the reaction.* Making people want to shoot each other. Like Alex had made Warren want to rape Anna, or Esme want to kill Kayla. Was he telling them they were dreaming? Was he telling them they needed to kill to get out alive? Both? And more?

Bodies piled. Bullets, not Alex's favorite, were excellent at killing. One woman's face had its jaw blown off. A man's leg was gone. His body pumped out blood while he tried to crawl. Alex couldn't see the detached leg anywhere. Somebody was a good shot because a man in boxer shorts had a decently sized hole in the middle his chest. Pieces of his heart might have remained inside of him, but most of it had been removed by what looked like a single shot. A naked man shot in the side of the head had lost part of his eye socket and associated skull, but the eyeball hung on, so it drooped close to but out of place. A bullet had torn through his belly, too, so his guts were spilling out like the eye.

Bruce left for other parts of the office suite and came back with new people, who either shot or were shot by the people still in or around the cubicle maze. One man kicked in the doors of the offices on either side of Bruce's—where Alex was secured—but he left Bruce's alone. Why? Maybe Bruce knew, and maybe he didn't. Alex did see Bruce take a bullet, though. Several. As a woman went down, someone behind her perforating her thighs, ass, and back, her gun went wild and peppered Bruce's torso. Bruce slowed down, but not for long. So maybe he knew that, no matter what happened, he and Alex weren't in any danger. Maybe he had a knack for playing the odds.

The gunfire became more sporadic, and soon the only sounds were the blaring alarms and the loud music. "Cut sound!" Bruce yelled.

Quiet.

Papers, broken glass, bodies. So much mess and chaos. Such a show.

Bruce was to Alex's left, not far from the window. A woman appeared to Alex's right. She had streaks of grey in her long, curly brown hair, and she wore a silky pink nightgown. She carried a machine gun. "Did we get everybody, Bruce? Is the game over?"

She knew him. They all knew him. This was their office, too. They were coworkers. *Bruce had just killed off about forty or fifty of his coworkers.* Without killing any of them himself.

Bruce fired at the woman with the grey streaks, making her body dance as red dots appeared all over her silky pink nightgown. Her body collapsed. "Now it's over," Bruce said.

So, Bruce killed one. Made sense. Barring Mexican standoff, the group would have inevitably reduced to a single member, and no one was ever going to survive. The outcome was fixed from the start.

29. ESCAPE INCORPORATED

Alex

Alex had to wait more than a year, until he was almost sixteen, near the end of tenth grade, for Dad to launch his "internship" at Greylight, Inc., the business he ran out of *his* office suite, the office suite inside the office suite where his former employer—he'd quit a month after starting Greylight—had resided, but West Coast Global Integrated Wealth Solutions had shut down their Los Angeles location after the inexplicable murders of forty-seven employees, the brutality and timing enough to make them seem coordinated, the number of perpetrators necessary to pull off such a thing... unimaginable... why would such organized crime target *business consultants*, threats to no one, offensive to few... except, perhaps, the envious? It could have been an act of terrorism. Most likely domestic. Class warfare. It had been coming for a long time.

Dad made sure enough other employees, ones he called "more inoffensive," survived so that he wouldn't stick out too much, but the recentness of the shit with Aaron made Dad a person of interest, so they had to deal with tons of questions again. Dad fended off regular cops and feds while telecommuting to the San Diego office during the day. At night he did what seemed like another form of telecommuting. He didn't bother sitting in a half-lotus or repeating a mantra. He sat at the small desk in what had been Aaron's work area and simply zoned out. With frequent, stern reminders about safety and responsibility, he left Alex to his own escapes.

Dad discussed the class warfare theory at length with the authorities. He wondered if he should be back under police protection; he wondered if the police needed a stronger presence in his neighborhood.

When the legal heat dropped, Dad could quit his day job because what he did at Greylight brought in money that he attributed to "investments." His arrangement involved clients, clients and their targets. In a way, he owed the inspiration for his business to Aaron. He also owed it to his love of mystery and crime novels. Aaron had cheated on him. At the end, they'd talked about safety and appearances, but they hadn't talked about loyalty and betrayal. They hadn't talked about victimization, justice, and revenge. Betrayal and revenge were business opportunities.

Real cops didn't investigate infidelity. Private investigators did. The justice system didn't punish criminals whose victims' pain didn't qualify as a legal wrong. Hired guns did. Who better to investigate—and what better assassin —than someone who can blink in and out of a place, and someone who can kill without witnesses and without leaving a shred of personally incriminating forensic evidence?

After a few weeks in a one-man operation that raked in obscene amounts of cash, Dad started vetting employees. He borrowed people from prisons and high-security mental health facilities. With help from computers that *they* probably made work, he located some candidates who were on the lam. Among other things, Greylight would be a pool of dark secrets. It would multiply and magnify crimes and the criminals.

Until Alex began his internship, Dad controlled all the coming and going. Until that afternoon a few weeks before Alex's birthday, only Dad communicated with them. Somehow, though, when Alex took the tour of the suite, which had become less corporate and more specialized for Greylight purposes, the employees, most of them draped in grey robes, with hoods and face coverings similar to hijabs, seemed to recognize him. Some of them bowed upon introduction.

He'd imagined working at his father's side, but Dad's new office was down the hall from the cubicle maze, in the "Executive Wing," which only had two other offices but featured a private bathroom and lounge. Timbo Rust, the ethnically ambiguous and young-looking man who gave him his tour, also gave him his first assignment. He was to wait, with good posture, in the elevator room for a woman he would address as "Mrs. Beverly." She would wear a black hat with a black veil, probably a black dress, too, but Timbo couldn't be certain. Alex would be courteous and charming as he showed her to the far corner room that had been an office with windows but was now repurposed. All the offices bordering the main floorspace, including his dad's old office from which he'd watched that initial employee massacre, had been repurposed. The windows looking out on the main space had black curtains, some open, some closed, according to the clients' wishes.

The rooms were for wetworks, and not everyone was a confident exhibitionist, even though all the clients knew about the concealed closed-circuit cameras. Dad said he liked to check in on works in progress. His management style could sometimes be very hands-on.

A bell rang, and the elevator doors opened. Alex stood, hands clasped at-ease behind his nevertheless straight back, and smiled, ready to greet whoever appeared. The image surprised him: he'd imagined "Mrs. Beverly" as older, billowy and Victorian, her veil spread like an umbrella. Instead, her black dress, funereal rather than cocktail but still form-fitting and contemporary, showed fit arms beneath the elbows and firm legs beneath the knees, and her small black brimless cap's veil hung to her upper lip and darkened without hiding the big, watering eyes behind it. Mrs. Beverly was crying.

The elevator doors started closing, so she quick-stepped

out into the room, high black heels making no sound on the cornflower blue carpet. "Mrs. Beverly?" Alex put his smile in his voice, beaming at her.

"Yes. I hoped someone would come to meet me. That lobby, alone. Intimidating." Her head took her big watery eyes for a spin around the room.

Alex offered his hand for a shake. "I'm Alex Packard. I'll show you where your..." he should have asked Timbo for more of a script! "your, um, event is going to happen."

Mrs. Beverly held up her hand not to be shaken but—Alex hoped he got the signal right—to be kissed. "You're a little young?"

He took her hand, bent to it, and pecked her knuckles with his lips before he released her and gestured toward the double doors that now had "Greylight, Inc." etched on them with the logo, lightning branching out from an abstract human shape, in the background. "It's not far," he said, adding a tone of excitement, *salesmanship*. "Right this way, please." He opened a door for her.

"Thank you," she said. "You're a gentleman."

He was getting it right!

Leading her through the main floor, he thought of how the redesigned cubicle maze must look. It still had desks, chairs, and what Alex thought was an excessive number of file cabinets, photocopiers, and shredders. It also had racks, shelves, labeled drawers, piles, and displays of items not usually found in the workplace. Guns of great variety, which Alex still hadn't bothered to study, were broadly accessible. The supplies, however, reflected his own preferences, which Dad shared. Knives, made for combat, hunting, cooking, or any of the above, hung from hooks and nails and rested in blocks, ready for creative use. Larger cutting tools, swords and machetes, axes, strangely shaped blades that looked like they belonged with suits of armor, shears and other yard tools... they impressed Alex, but what did Mrs. Beverly think as they passed by? Did she look at the range of chainsaws, lined up small to what-the-fuck, and think, "Wow, what fun messes I could make!" Did the blowtorches fire her imagination?

Mrs. Beverly did not speak until they reached their destination's door.

"He's in there?"

Alex assumed she meant her target, whomever she'd hired Greylight to enact vengeance upon, but in truth he had no idea what was in the repurposed office, so he didn't know how to answer. "Um... we've done our best to make sure that everything is just like you'd want."

She nodded. He opened the door. Mrs. Beverly walked by and said, "You'll stay, won't you, young Alex? I'd like somebody to watch with me."

His job *was* to be courteous. And he *was* dying to see.

Before his brain processed the room's occupants, Alex noticed the corner's big windows without curtains covering them, big windows that might look out at the city with a thirty-third-floor view—except they only revealed, and let in, greylight. The room itself was drab, grey in grey.

At the center was a gurney with medical stirrups attached to one end. A naked man had his legs up in the stirrups and his back flat against the gurney, to which leather straps bound his ankles, waist, wrists, and neck. Duct tape sealed his mouth. On the far side of the gurney, a heavy human figure hovered over the captive. The grey robe cascading over the big body combined with the anonymizing hood and face cover to make even the sex of the figure a mystery, but what the figure held, a device with a fat handle and a round, many-toothed blade on the end, was more interesting than the figure's features anyway.

Mrs. Beverly took the lead. They came to the other side of the gurney, opposite the grey figure, who said nothing but looked at them expectantly. The man on the gurney, fit, maybe thirty, about Mrs. Beverly's age, turned his head toward Mrs. Beverly with some difficulty and tried to shout with a closed mouth. "Start with the fingers," she said. The man tried to shout louder.

Alex didn't know what kind of saw the robed figure had, but when the figure revved the device's motor, making the teeth spin into an indistinct blur, Alex got excited. The man on the gurney struggled against his bindings, but that was boring because Alex had seen enough people struggle in futility when bound to beds and chairs and slabs and so on. The entertainment here was watching the spinning blade get closer and closer to fingers that clenched and unclenched, and when the blade was close enough for the man on the gurney to feel the air rushing off the spinning teeth, the fingers formed a tight fist.

The fist didn't stop the saw from working into the index finger above the knuckle and cutting until it disconnected, blood pulsing in jets. The man screamed inside his sealed mouth, and Mrs. Beverly's lips below the veil twisted upward. The saw didn't rest. It disconnected the middle finger, the ring finger, the pinky, the thumb. Alex hadn't known that finger stubs could bleed so much. The robed figure piled the severed fingers on top of the man's immobilized middle so they could rise and fall with his convulsive breaths, bouncing and making bloody trails.

"You should be careful about what you touch," Mrs. Beverly said, likely emphasizing some poetic justice she had devised. The man on the gurney was probably her husband, a cheater, like Aaron. Aaron was in the lobby with no guts and testicles in his eye sockets.

Mrs. Beverly watched the jittery finger dance on the man's belly while the sounds behind his sealed lips faded. She was crying, as she had been when she'd come out of the elevator, soft tears, steady drips. Crocodile tears? Would he understand when he was older?

"Okay," she said. "Take the hand."

The robed figure revved the saw, then lowered it slowly until the teeth chewed the joint of hand and wrist. Bone didn't faze it. The saw moved through the man. The closed-mouth howls crescendoed.

"Open the tape," she said.

The robed figure ran the saw over the tape, splattering blood as he cut lips and surrounding skin along with the adhesive plastic. As soon as his jaw could wag, though, the man on the gurney spewed words with the blood flow: "YOU FUCKING BITCH YOU FUCKING BITCH YOU—"

"You should be careful about who you lay your hands on," Mrs. Beverly said to the screaming man. To the robed figure: "Shove the hand in his mouth." Alex detected amusement.

The robed figure shoved the severed hand into the screaming man's mouth. The man stopped screaming and tried to cough. Mrs. Beverly leaned over him, picked up his pinky and ring finger, and inserted one finger into each of his nostrils. He struggled harder for air.

"You know what to do with the arm," she said. The robed figure knew what to do, which meant she'd sent prior instructions. Dad's business would require as much. Dad liked planning. Reliability. Safety in the predictable. Mrs. Beverly had thought this out, imagined it. Fantasized about it. Dad's new, very successful business didn't merely sell revenge. It sold the sorts of twisted fantasies that Alex could get used to watching.

The robed figure tied a big green rubber band around the man's armpit and shoulder. *Tourniquet.* The man fought too hard for breath to squirm meaningfully. The saw lowered to a spot beneath the tight band and cut through skin, chewed through deltoid and triceps, broke through humerus. The robed figure, grey clothes thoroughly splashed red, undid the loose arm's wrist restraint and pulled the arm as far as it would stretch, making the final cuts easier. From bleeding wrist to shoulder, the appendage separated from the body. The tourniquet didn't stop the flow entirely.

Amazement mesmerized as Alex watched the robed figure work the saw around the wrist nub. The figure walked around to the space between the man's stirrup-suspended legs. The saw cut down from the wrist at angles, sharpening flesh and bones like a pencil, making the forearm taper to a point. Mrs. Beverly moved to get a better look between the man's suspended legs. Alex adjusted, too, with no ideas what to expect—

—when the robed figure stabbed the sharpened arm into the prone man's exposed ass.

Mrs. Beverly nodded as her target shrieked, forcing the sound around the hand clogging his mouth. The robed figure adjusted the arm and got another shriek before pushing the limb deeper. Deeper. Blood from the severed arm and shadows from the looming legs kept Alex from being able to tell whether any tearing from the wide intruder added to the mess that the robed figure stood behind, that Mrs. Beverly approached.

The robed figure pushed harder and harder. The arm inched up inside the man, up to the elbow, up the rise of the bicep.

Mrs. Beverly took the arm from the robed figure. She pulled it out several inches, then pushed it back in. Out and in. Out and in. She fucked the man with his own severed arm.

It wasn't an "internship" Alex could put on his résumé, but Alex fucking loved his new job.

Bruce

He'd taken down the Elvis partition and dismantled Aaron's workspace, so Bruce's body—in actuality, as Alex would say—lay in bed all day, but he was working the longest hours of his life. He had employees to handle the ever-expanding workload, including a Vice President and a CFO he'd poached from organized crime, people who thought they'd never get out of their organizations, but Greylight, Inc. was safe. Rumors kept Greylight safe because, according to rumors, no one was safe from Greylight. Greylight could get to you anywhere, anytime. Working with Greylight was as good as working with the Devil. You don't fuck with the Devil.

In all his years reflecting on his parents' mythology, Bruce hadn't considered the hours the Devil must have worked. Sin, corruption, and mayhem were time consuming.

And this latest order required specialty work that only Bruce could do.

When a person seeking Greylight's services had the funds and a vision spectacular enough to arouse *their* excitement, Bruce would agree to construct a set, to build an island in the grey flimsier but functional in most ways like Alex's house or his own office suite, where that person's wishes could be granted. This person, "Stu," had the funds and a vision sufficient for an island, and Bruce found it distasteful, like that burnt body of Detective Alondra Whitcomb's little boy had been distasteful back before Bruce had spent a year cultivating a broader palette—but he would build it. He would even handle the extra request, though it did make him think of Aaron and what seemed like a never-ending vacancy in the bed beside his vacant body.

Stu would not be on the island. He would be in one of the wet rooms, surrounded by computer monitors. The island, a six-lane city street intersecting with a two-lane side road without a traffic light, didn't offer a vantage close enough for Stu to see what he wanted to see. He therefore requested cameras to be placed all around the intersection, in high places like trees and rooftops but also at the edges of the island, where matter didn't exist, and the cameras could float around vehicle height. Cameras these days—so many of them were made for live streaming. At his computer monitors, Stu would be able to see the exterior of the intersection from every angle.

He also needed to see inside the bus, so Bruce would put cameras there, too. It was a bus, though Stu called it "the shuttle" because the elite private school for which it collected children, kindergarten through grade five, in Stu's neighborhood called it "the shuttle." It wasn't yellow, rather a mix of cream with port-wine ruby, and it was a hybrid, but it had a door like a bus, windows like a bus, and wheels like a bus, and it performed the function of—a bus.

The bus that picked up kids in Stu's neighborhood, when it was full of kids and on the way to the school in the morning, went through an intersection very similar to the one Bruce had created.

Bruce required clients' backstories, and *they* appreciated them even when he didn't. Stu still felt humiliated by the whole tawdry thing. A decade or so ago, his wife, along with her circle of friends that consisted of other wives from the neighborhood, stumbled upon a group of college-aged male prostitutes who masqueraded as pool boys, or pool boys who also prostituted themselves—they did clean pools—and decided they would all use their services. Then Stu's wife had a crazy idea.

Wouldn't it be funny, wouldn't it just be *a lark*, if they all ended up having the pool boys' babies and passing them off as their husbands' heirs?

For reasons Stu didn't understand, maybe their wives hated them, the women agreed. Over the next few years, the bastard generation was born. The men only found out a few months ago, when one of the kids needed a blood transfusion, and neither parent was a match, which led to testing, which led to discovery, confession, neighbors telling neighbors, more testing, more discoveries…

Not all the men knew what Stu planned. Bruce put in the hours to make it happen. Late one night, his static gathered the children from their beds. Then, he sat with Stu and watched.

The bus full of the neighborhood's youngest school-age children drifted, driverless, along the two-lane side road's slight decline, into the busy six-lane intersection where no light governed traffic. Some of the kids had the sense to scream as they rolled into paths of oncoming cars and trucks.

The bus's seats didn't have seatbelts. The first collision, an SUV slamming into the bus's tender center, killed two kids immediately, a first grader who twisted and smashed against a bus wall so hard that his skull collapsed and, as the bus tilted with the impact, spilled the boy's jostled and mashed head contents onto a window. The other instant death was an older girl hit directly by the SUV prying into bus metal and at the same time pressing that metal into flesh, crunching both, collapsing the girl's lung so that bright red bloomed at her lips as the metal finished tearing open her chest.

The rest of the children flew around the bus, battered by collisions with seat, floor, roof, walls, cries, shouts, screams, no tears, too stunned. The second collision came from the same side as the first, a smaller car but hitting at an angle that pushed the bus completely onto its side. A fuel-line broke and spilled, as was required. Inside, children's bodies hammered into the wall that had been the roof. The new roof, former wall, and the former floor were bent, crinkled by the collisions. Children tried to get their bearings. They began to perceive their broken bones; screams of surprise turned into screams of pain during what seemed like a calm.

A hint of crying—

A car crashed into what had been the bus's roof, pushing it inward, driving it and the children near it like a bulldozer sliding through dirt. Torn metal divided a boy at the waist, and then his two halves rolled as the bulldozer came on, viscera from both halves spilling. The combination of the incoming car and crumpling metal crushed a girl so thoroughly that she oozed from both sides of the compressed materials. Another car hit the bus's front, and a dislodged seat decapitated a kid.

Something sparked, and all the remaining children, maimed, bruised, and broken, burned in the explosion.

Jobs like this one made Bruce wonder how far he would go. How far he *could* go. Sometimes he felt so damned tired.

30. ALEX'S EMPIRE

Alex

(about a year later)

Alex didn't receive his first assignment until more than a year into his internship, which bugged the shit out of him, so when he finally got it, he felt insulted. Just some guy, some middle management corporate fuck-up whose wife caught him cheating and now wanted his head. Literally. Dad tasked Alex with retrieving the man and removing his head, only his head, doing no further damage to the body.

"You hear me, don't you? *No further damage to the body.* Deliver the head directly to me at my desk." Dad then looked down at said desk, at some notebook his attention to which signaled Alex's time to leave.

No further damage to the body. Where was the fun? Where was the beauty?

At his own house, Alex carried on his own activities, with respect shown to Dad's safety guidelines, so he got to be extravagant on his own, but an assignment meant killing for the family business. It was important! Bigger! And he wanted it to be special! A simple decapitation was boring.

His assignment included a handsaw for the weapon. Back and forth, back and forth. Yawn. He asked if he could at least use a hatchet, catharsis in an unpredictable number of whacks. Permission denied.

When he entered the wet room where the man, Damon

Briggs, was zip-tied (cable-tied) to a metal chair with a cloth stuffed into his mouth that muted his demanding grunts, Alex carried only the handsaw, but he had his Deerslayer in his back pocket, and he had this idea that, as long as he didn't hurt the head—as long as Mr. Briggs stayed clean from the severed neck up—Alex might be doing okay.

"Mr. Briggs," Alex said. He removed the cloth.

"GET ME THE FUCK OUT OF HERE!"

"Ew. Sorry. No can do. My name's Alex. Alex Packard. And you're—"

"Fucking dumbass punk kid GET ME OUT OF HERE!"

"As I was saying, you're Damon Briggs. May I call you Damon?"

"Where are your robes? Everybody else in this... fucking... *cult*... is wearing robes. Are you some, like, teenage messiah that you don't have to dress like everybody else?"

Alex was contemplating the "teenage messiah" possibility when he saw Damon, Mr. Briggs, as if for the first time, take note of the tool in Alex's right hand. Alex hadn't made any attempt to conceal it. "What's that for, huh?"

"Mr. Briggs—"

"Fuck, call me Damon."

"Damon, the saw is for removing your head."

"*What?* Come on! Nah!"

"I'm here to cut off your head. Terribly sorry." Alex tilted his own head and half-smiled, brow furrowed in sympathy.

"You don't have to do that!" Damon struggled in his chair.

"I'd prefer not to. But I can't say no." Alex moved toward Damon's neck with the saw.

"NO! You can! Wait a fucking minute! There's—you've got to—I can tell you don't want to!"

"I have this idea that maybe I could... but you'd have to promise you're on board, promise you'll do it my way, because if it doesn't work out...." Alex grabbed Damon's hair, pulled his head back, and pressed the saw against his Adam's apple.

"I FUCKING PROMISE!"

"You want to do this my way?" Alex asked. "Because you don't have to." He "accidentally" bumped Damon's chin with saw teeth, not breaking the skin but making Damon's body go rigid.

"YOUR WAY!"

Fucking idiot.

Bruce had removed the carpet from the wet rooms, so the saw made a satisfying clang on concrete when Alex dropped it.

"Thank you," Damon said. "Thank you."

Alex took out the Deerslayer. "You'll have to be naked," he said, "but don't worry. I can undress you without you having to get up."

"What?" Damon looked down, processing. The man might have recognized his error. "W-w-why do I have to be n-naked?"

No jacket, but Damon otherwise wore a typical business ensemble, long-sleeved blue button-up shirt with a button-down collar straddling a Windsor-knotted red tie that hung to a belted waist, which squeezed a bit on early middle age's spare tire, and pleated grey slacks that fell appropriately to brown loafers. With the curved end of his knife's tip pointing upward, Alex cut a sleeve, starting above the bound wrist.

"Cut the ties," Damon said. "I'll undress myself."

"No can do, Damon." Alex nicked Damon's upper arm as he negotiated the elbow turn. He nicked him twice near the shoulder. Splotches of blood looked great on the blue fabric, and Alex almost cut a complete U under Damon's collarbone as he navigated beneath the red tie.

Damon was bleeding all over his front and grunting and saying "Don't, don't" when Alex pulled away the first big pieces of bloody shirt. Damon looked like he wanted to scream, but he didn't. His eyes went far away as he repeated "don't" in a fugue. The man actually cooperated by leaning forward when Alex went for the fabric stuck between him and the chair, an act made more amazing by the long red line Alex sliced into

Damon's back when he decided to split the shirt's rear in two. The pants, minus the seated midsection, were easiest, but the bare legs weren't yet very exciting. The midsection took a lot of small cuts at the fabric, which made a lot of cuts into what was underneath, but Alex got the rest of the pants and the underwear off. The belt and the fabric beneath it came next to last. After a feigned hew in the direction of Damon's penis, Alex cut off the red tie, not nicking Damon's neck.

"We're on our way already!" Alex said.

"Don't—what—NO!" He exchanged his rhythmic refusal for bawling.

"My preference is to see if death by a thousand cuts really works. Now let me count." He did. "At best, that's 67 so far. Such a long way to go! I must make smaller cuts from here on out."

Alex counted and cut, making railroad tracks up and down the arms and legs, in circles on the belly, in sideways eights (infinities!) around the nipples on the sagging chest. When he got past 300, the amount of blood made finding new places to cut—to be sure of cutting without repeating existing damage—extremely challenging. He toiled on. Damon became quiet, gasping at some but not all the breaks in his skin.

The count passed 630, and Alex noticed Damon wasn't breathing. Shock? Blood loss? He really needed to learn more about causes of death. No point in continuing to 1000. Alex sawed off the man's pristine head.

With his biggest grin stretching ear to ear, Alex carried the dripping severed head to Dad's executive office. As he approached Dad's desk, Dad spread plastic on the surface to receive the trophy. Alex plopped down Damon's head in triumph. "Your delivery."

"You failed," Dad said.

"What do you mean?" Alex knew he was caught. At that moment, he knew he'd wanted to get caught. "There's the head, in perfect condition."

"Do you think you're ready to take over, Alex?"

The look in Dad's eyes gave him a sick feeling in his stomach. He took the question seriously. Finding Damon Briggs and bringing him back to Greylight hadn't been as easy as bringing someone back to his own house. Could he handle a second person, a third? Maybe with practice. Dad had come on like a goddamned Jedi master since the beginning, and Alex was nowhere near his level. Like that thing with the school bus a year ago? Or the wedding last month? Alex could barely comprehend how to get that to work. He would learn. Eventually. "No, I'm not ready."

He needed Dad's help.

"Didn't you think I'd be watching?"

He admitted, "I didn't think about it."

"The damage you did to the body is going to show up in actuality, and that is precisely what the client did NOT want. We're looking at a refund and irreparable damage to our reputation. Did you think of the client, of the business, at all when you decided not to follow my very specific directions?" Dad's words were angry, but his tone was calm. The calm didn't make the scolding any better.

"I did think of the business," Alex said. "I was thinking I needed to stand out. Be worthy. Just cutting off a guy's head, that doesn't make an impression."

"Damn it, Alex, you make an impression by doing things the right way!" Dad sighed. "I gave you that assignment as a test, and you failed."

"You gave me that assignment because you won't let me do anything important around here!" It was an outburst. He wouldn't know whether to regret it until Dad responded.

Bruce took the wastebasket from beneath his desk, set it on the surface, and dropped the severed head inside. "I'll let you do something important," he said, crossing from calm into cold, "when you stop acting like a fuck-up and start acting ready. Everything... everything important is for you." *Teenage messiah.* "But you have to fit the part."

Alex saw Bruce's vision like he'd never seen it before,

and he wanted very badly to fit the part.

Bruce

Before Alex, perhaps twice, very much in the abstract, Bruce and Aaron had talked about adoption, thinking of a baby to raise and most likely brand with some amalgam of their family names. Carrying on family traditions had been important to both sets of parents, and though Bruce officially didn't care about his parents' values, he cared about being the end of the line... not that the world lacked Nicholsons... but Aaron and Bruce had both believed, even though Aaron's parents put on a show of support, that being gay meant killing off the family. For posterity. Gay was the death of posterity. Family guilt, however, was no reason to take on the responsibility of raising a child.

And then Alex, not only a new generation but a continuation of the *bloodline*. In a world full of vacancies, of zombie-like devotion to vapid pursuits, he signified a future, something to build toward, something to build for. All that heterosexual bullshit about reproduction and saving the children wasn't total bullshit after all. Before Alex, Bruce had never felt the ambition to be CEO of anything. Now he was guiding a company toward loftier and loftier heights, or deeper and deeper depths, depending on perspective, because the place he made for himself he only held for another. He had a motherfucking *heir*. Building an inheritance, a legacy, was the best of purposes he had found.

Thus, Alex needed a sheltered period. He didn't need to know that, after the deaths of Aaron and Alondra Whitcomb, a "Detective Zee," who had been close to Detective Whitcomb, came around asking more questions about Alex. He had read Detective Whitcomb's notes. He thought Aaron was Alex's doing, and the deaths that occurred while Bruce and Alex were under protective surveillance didn't dissuade him. Somehow, he even got the idea that the deaths in Bruce's office might be connected to Alex instead of Bruce. Bruce discussed the intrusiveness of Detective Zee's questions during a time of overwhelming grief with the detective's superiors. Bruce emphasized the Detective Zee had no right to approach Alex, a minor, without his presence and without, he believed, a warrant. He would get a restraining order if he had to, or contact the media. The police department assured him that Detective Zee would leave Alex alone.

Alex promised to stop hunting at his own school, and he seemed to keep the promise, but Bruce still saw Detective Zee creeping around, and he saw others, too. He used his growing fortune to gather information and to hire help.

Alondra Whitcomb's notes on cases for the last five years, collected for transfer to Records, went missing.

Detective Martin Grant of the Decatur Police Department went missing.

Witnesses who supported any of Detective Zee's wild ideas or who connected Alex to murder victims recanted or "forgot" their testimony. Detective Zee became obsessed and had vivid dreams from which he would wake unrested, sometimes with cuts and bruises. The dreams felt real. After a while, he received psychiatric leave from the Los Angeles Police Department.

Bruce installed alarm equipment, including cameras, at the house. In addition to the security, the equipment provided records of their comings and goings, alibis, if they needed them.

Alex didn't know the real reason for the added security, and he knew nothing of Bruce's extra efforts with the police. Alex went to school, stopped skipping classes, got better grades. He worked on the yearbook, which had online video content to go with the standard print pages with pictures. He participated in his school's LGBTQ+ Alliance, even dated a couple of boys. He created a safe veneer.

Bruce did, too. He had to hide his money—millions—at

least until he could find a way to fake a windfall investment to explain Alex's enormous trust. They lived comfortably. Before too long, assuming Alex's grades continued to rise so that he graduated with honors, Alex would go to a good college and then get an MBA. Then he'd return, and Bruce would hand him the reins of Greylight. *They* never thought of Bruce as the true captain of their industry. He was the Regent; Alex was born to be King.

No, not King. Bruce was building an empire. Alex was born to be Emperor. If his son was to be Alexander the Great, Bruce supposed he had to play Aristotle, imparting wisdom. Bruce, Aristotle. What a crazy, fucked-up world.

Alex

(about a year later)

Dad wasn't trying to get rid of him. His emphasis on schools in the Northeast reflected not only trust and respect but also a sincere desire for Alex to spread his wings, expand his horizons, and all that gobbledygook. True, however far Alex went from Los Angeles, he'd still see Dad every day, or almost every day, at Greylight. Dad had demonstrated time and again that he could pull people in from thousands of miles away, and on one of Alex's last assignments before the Decision, Alex was tasked with fetching a kill from Bangor, Maine. After some initial frustration, he had a breakthrough, and the transfer was easy. He realized that, though at first he'd thought of *his* house being in Georgia where his parents' house was, he'd later started thinking of it as being with him in California, and either way, his location had never made a difference when he was bringing people over. The trick, then, was understanding that Dad's office, Alex's house, and everywhere in the greylight weren't anywhere specific with regard to actual space, so distance in actuality meant nothing. Dad and Alex could be as far apart as the planet would allow and bring themselves face to face again in a matter of seconds. Going away to college wouldn't create vacancies.

Nevertheless, Alex didn't want to leave Los Angeles. The Valley could get beastly hot, especially in late summer, but otherwise, the climate was about perfect. Blue sky, palm trees, and when you got close enough, a breeze off the ocean. People wore a lot of pastels, which was good for Alex because they matched his hair and complexion. LA was stuffed full of beautiful people, and at eighteen, Alex accepted that he belonged among them, at least superficially. Dad taught him about veneer. LA was all veneer, in the best possible way. Alex belonged here as much or more than he would anywhere else.

At Dad's insistence, he applied to schools all over, but when the Decision came, he chose a liberal arts college in LA with fewer than 1,000 students. They had programs in Business Administration and Film, the combination of which interested him and would pay off at Greylight, and of course being in striking distance of *the* Business, Hollywood's Business, opened opportunities for meeting insiders and working real internships during hours not taken by his part-time, junior executive position at Greylight. The money from Greylight paid for an apartment off campus—privacy for his trances—groceries, entertainment, and a lifestyle fit for someone with celebrity parents. Alex, of course, could not discuss the source of his money or what his father did for a living. When people asked about Dad, "consulting" was the answer, which people tended to accept without further inquiry.

Alex liked the small school setting both because he'd learned the value of mentoring and because it left the big schools—UCLA, USC, Cal State LA—for him to wander with one of the cameras he inherited from Aaron. Nobody thought anything of a college-aged kid shooting footage on any of the campuses. Alex fit in well enough to be invisible as he identified visitors to take back to his house.

His house. He still thought of his house inside his parents' house as *his house*, but, since picking up tips from Dad on building, he'd added to his real—unreal?—estate holdings. The beach house in Malibu had been tough to construct because he'd never been inside such a place, but a website with an easy-to-crack password provided a video tour of a Malibu property on sale for slightly more than ten million dollars, and Alex could use his imagination, so he ended up with a fine structure on a cliffside, with a view of the sunset over crashing waves.

The Malibu house rather than *his* house became the location of his first party. Alex didn't like parties, but after the first time he spotted frat boys playing volleyball in front of their chapter house by the UCLA campus—shirtless, shorts only—he decided he wanted to host a kegger. He took twenty of the fraternity house's prettiest residents to *his* Malibu location and welcomed them, one at a time or in small groups, at the front door as if they were expected for the big party. They were disoriented, but seeing one another and, once inside, not one but *two* kegs, one of them Guiness (hard to chug) and the other Foster's (quite chuggable) put them at ease.

Alex's superior sound system blasted insipid pop while some boys gathered around the kegs and others fanned out, most asking plaintively about where the girls were at. Alex reassured them that two sororities had rented vans and were sending a small army of hot bods. Meanwhile, the bros could do bong hits. Alex had a three-foot bong.

Alex had also spent the majority of his semester focusing on his chemistry class, learning enough of the basics to advance his education on his own. His only experience as a poisoner was the sloppy but successful effort to abort his would-be sibling, but he liked hands-off killing when it got good results, so advancing his skill in the toxic arts made sense. He figured out what he wanted to try, and they made the chemicals available in the Malibu house just as they would have in the Decatur house. Alex added the powder to the kegs and the weed. Small doses would suffice.

The frat boys saw no need to wait for the girls (who weren't coming) or to stick to small doses. They chugged regardless of chuggability, and they demonstrated magnificent lung capacities. Soon, "woo-oo!" became the byword. Finish chugging? Woo-oo! About to chug? Woo-oo! Are you watching someone chug? Woo-oo! Ditto with the bong hits.

A guy close to seven feet tall but very skinny was the first to say, "I don't feel so good."

No time passed before he puked on the floor. The puke had yellow and red streaks, the red plainly blood but the yellow more mysterious, as mysterious as the chunks, which didn't look like partially digested food.

The next guy puked. Another, then another. Yellow and red, chunky. After puking, a guy typically grasped his neck, belly, or both. Regardless of his initial skin tone, his face paled and took on a shade of green as his cheeks puffed. Another puked. Another. They could see in each other's faces that they *hurt*. Puking hurt and left pain behind. Blood and spittle dribbled from the corners of their mouths after they puked. Some seemed to attempt speech and fail. Some dropped to their knees, landing in puke.

More puke. More. A rancid odor filled the house's massive living room, but Alex tolerated it. He'd created a world of puke, and the pigs with which he'd populated it were wallowing. Yellow and red. Chunks that were, Alex guessed, their own bodies, torn apart from the inside.

When the boys puked a second time, red overpowered yellow. More chunks. More puking, more red. The tall boy, the one who puked first, wasn't merely puffing out his cheeks. His face had become big all over, rounded all over. He wasn't skinny anymore. His arms and legs had ballooned. His middle had added padding. The exposed skin—he was a white boy, so Alex would have expected an allergic reaction to make it red—looked pale green. He toppled, bringing another boy, too sick to move out of the way, with him. The tall boy didn't move. The other boy floundered in puked-up yellow, red, and chunks, trying but unable to sit up. On his back, he puked and started choking.

Soon all the boys were ballooning, collapsing, floundering, choking. They weren't all choking on puke; from the swelling, Alex concluded that some of their throats simply closed. Either way, they squirmed in their own filth until they died. They all died, and Alex never touched them.

In actuality, when the boys were all found dead in their beds, a brief investigation occurred. The verdict was a very rare form of food poisoning, as Alex had hoped.

Dad congratulated him on a job well done. *They* didn't provide feedback, not that they usually did, and Alex wondered—*had* he done the job well? He'd created a big scene with an awfully big mess, and the deaths had been horrid, but was all that puke... beautiful? He didn't understand them well enough to judge. He'd keep on making the pictures, hoping the invisible audience would be satisfied.

Most of Alex's time once he got to college was quiet, quiet study, quiet reflection. He spent a lot of time at his house, his original house, not hunting but thinking. He thought about Study Abroad options and fucking and maybe killing a hot college French boy. He thought about graduating, adulthood, whatever that meant. Dad assumed he'd go to business school, and that seemed okay. Greylight, Inc. was a multi-million-dollar company, ballooning faster than those frat boys, and its work spanned the globe. Alex wanted to be ready. He wanted to be worthy. Because he planned to be in control. And keep control. He had always felt that they worked for him as much or more than he worked for them. He had to keep it that way.

He had a sense that loomed in the greylight and pecked at his skull, paranoia, probably, but come by honestly, or so he figured when he sat by the new window, the window by the front door of his first house, his true house.

ABOUT THE AUTHOR

L. Andrew Cooper

L. Andrew Cooper specializes in the provocative, scary, and strange. Other works include novel-length stories Noir Falling, The Middle Reaches, Records of the Hightower Massacre (co-authored with Maeva Wunn), Crazy Time, Burning  the Middle Ground, and Descending Lines; short story collections Leaping at Thorns, Peritoneum, and Stains of Atrocity; poetry collection The Great Sonnet Plot of Anton Tick; non-fiction Gothic Realities and Dario Argento; co-edited fiction anthologies Imagination Reimagined and Reel Dark; and the co-edited textbook Monsters. He has also written 35 award-winning screenplays. After studying literature and film at Harvard and Princeton, he used his Ph.D. to teach about favorite topics from coast to coast in the United States. He now focuses on writing and lives with his husband in North Hollywood, California. Visit https://landrewcooper.com.

"*A man's house is his castle.*"

"*My house is full of secrets nobody should know.*"

A man's house was his castle, and he had to defend it. That's what Grandpa said. He had to defend the secrets inside it, to keep them safe. Like Dad, Grandpa had safety pecking at his skull, and he sat at the window of his own house with a rifle, keeping watch. Grandpa was a smart man. He kept watch because someday, somebody *could* come for your secrets. Dad and Grandpa cared so much about safety because they knew to expect serious danger, actual threats, someday, from someone or something.

Alex knew, too, and he sat with his rifle at the window. He kept watch and would be ready.